I0822620

Aldous Huxley's Early Writings

By

Aldous Huxley

Cover Photograph: Suzanne Nilsson

ISBN: 978-1-78139-486-1

Contents

CROME YELLOW

THE BURNING WHEEL

THE DEFEAT OF YOUTH AND OTHER POEMS

MORTAL COILS

CROME YELLOW

CHAPTER I.

Along this particular stretch of line no express had ever passed. All the trains—the few that there were—stopped at all the stations. Denis knew the names of those stations by heart. Bole, Tritton, Spavin Delawarr, Knipswich for Timpany, West Bowlby, and, finally, Camlet-on-the-Water. Camlet was where he always got out, leaving the train to creep indolently onward, goodness only knew whither, into the green heart of England.

They were snorting out of West Bowlby now. It was the next station, thank Heaven. Denis took his chattels off the rack and piled them neatly in the corner opposite his own. A futile proceeding. But one must have something to do. When he had finished, he sank back into his seat and closed his eyes. It was extremely hot.

Oh, this journey! It was two hours cut clean out of his life; two hours in which he might have done so much, so much—written the perfect poem, for example, or read the one illuminating book. Instead of which—his gorge rose at the smell of the dusty cushions against which he was leaning.

Two hours. One hundred and twenty minutes. Anything might be done in that time. Anything. Nothing. Oh, he had had hundreds of hours, and what had he done with them? Wasted them, spilt the precious minutes as though his reservoir were inexhaustible. Denis groaned in the spirit, condemned himself utterly with all his works. What right had he to sit in the sunshine, to occupy corner seats in third-class carriages, to be alive? None, none, none.

Misery and a nameless nostalgic distress possessed him. He was twenty-three, and oh! so agonizingly conscious of the fact.

The train came bumpingly to a halt. Here was Camlet at last. Denis jumped up, crammed his hat over his eyes, deranged his pile of baggage, leaned out of the window and shouted for a porter, seized a bag in either hand, and had to put them down again in order to open the door. When at last he had safely bundled himself and his baggage on to the platform, he ran up the train towards the van.

"A bicycle, a bicycle!" he said breathlessly to the guard. He felt himself a man of action. The guard paid no attention, but continued methodically to hand out, one by one, the packages labelled to Camlet. "A bicycle!" Denis repeated. "A green machine, cross-framed, name of Stone. S-T-O-N-E."

"All in good time, sir," said the guard soothingly. He was a large, stately man with a naval beard. One pictured him at home, drinking tea, surrounded by a numerous family. It was in that tone that he must have spoken to his children when they were tiresome. "All in good time, sir." Denis's man of action collapsed, punctured.

He left his luggage to be called for later, and pushed off on his bicycle. He always took his bicycle when he went into the country. It was part of the theory of exercise. One day one would get up at six o'clock and pedal away to Kenilworth, or Stratford-on-Avon—anywhere. And within a radius of twenty miles there were always Norman churches and Tudor mansions to be seen in the course of an afternoon's excursion. Somehow they never did get seen, but all the same it was nice to feel that the bicycle was there, and that one fine morning one really might get up at six.

Once at the top of the long hill which led up from Camlet station, he felt his spirits mounting. The world, he found, was good. The far-away blue hills, the harvests whitening on the slopes of the ridge along which his road led him, the treeless sky-lines that changed as he moved—yes, they were all good. He was overcome by the beauty of those deeply embayed combes, scooped in the flanks of the ridge beneath him. Curves, curves: he repeated the word slowly, trying as he did so to find some term in which to give expression to his appreciation. Curves—no, that was inadequate. He made a gesture with his hand, as though to scoop the achieved expression out of the air, and almost fell off his bicycle. What was the word to describe the curves of those little valleys? They were as fine as the lines of a human body, they were informed with the subtlety of art...

Galbe. That was a good word; but it was French. Le galbe evase de ses hanches: had one ever read a French novel in which that phrase didn't occur? Some day he would compile a dictionary for the use of novelists. Galbe, gonfle, goulu: parfum, peau, pervers, potele, pudeur: vertu, volupte.

But he really must find that word. Curves curves...Those little valleys had the lines of a cup moulded round a woman's breast; they seemed the dinted imprints of some huge divine body that had rested on these hills. Cumbrous locutions, these; but through them he seemed to be getting nearer to what he wanted. Dinted, dimpled, wimpled—his mind wandered down echoing corridors of assonance and alliteration ever further and further from the point. He was enamoured with the beauty of words.

Becoming once more aware of the outer world, he found himself on the crest of a descent. The road plunged down, steep and straight, into a considerable valley. There, on the opposite slope, a little higher up the valley, stood Crome, his destination. He put on his brakes; this view of Crome was pleasant to linger over. The facade with its three projecting towers rose precipitously from among the dark trees of the garden. The house basked in full sunlight; the old brick rosily glowed. How ripe and rich it was, how superbly mellow! And at the same time, how austere! The hill was becoming steeper and steeper; he was gaining speed in spite of his brakes. He loosed his grip of the levers, and in a moment was rushing headlong down. Five minutes later he was passing through the gate of the great courtyard. The front door stood hospitably open. He left his bicycle leaning against the wall and walked in. He would take them by surprise.

CHAPTER II.

He took nobody by surprise; there was nobody to take. All was quiet; Denis wandered from room to empty room, looking with pleasure at the familiar pictures and furniture, at all the little untidy signs of life that lay scattered here and there. He was rather glad that they were all out; it was amusing to wander through the house as though one were exploring a dead, deserted Pompeii. What sort of life would the excavator reconstruct from these remains; how would he people these empty chambers? There was the long gallery, with its rows of respectable and (though, of course, one couldn't publicly admit it) rather boring Italian primitives, its Chinese sculptures, its unobtrusive, dateless furniture. There was the panelled drawing-room, where the huge chintz-covered arm-chairs stood, oases of comfort among the austere flesh-mortifying antiques. There was the morning-room, with its pale lemon walls, its painted Venetian chairs and rococo tables, its mirrors, its modern pictures. There was the library, cool, spacious, and dark, book-lined from floor to ceiling, rich in portentous folios. There was the dining-room, solidly, portwinily English, with its great mahogany table, its eighteenth-century chairs and sideboard, its eighteenth-century pictures—family portraits, meticulous animal paintings. What could one reconstruct from such data? There was much of Henry Wimbush in the long gallery and the library, something of Anne, perhaps, in the morning-room. That was all. Among the accumulations of ten generations the living had left but few traces.

Lying on the table in the morning-room he saw his own book of poems. What tact! He picked it up and opened it. It was what the reviewers call "a slim volume." He read at hazard:

"...But silence and the topless dark
Vault in the lights of Luna Park;
And Blackpool from the nightly gloom
Hollows a bright tumultuous tomb."

He put it down again, shook his head, and sighed. "What genius I had then!" he reflected, echoing the aged Swift. It was nearly six months since the book had been published; he was glad to think he would never write anything of the same sort again. Who could have been reading it, he wondered? Anne, perhaps; he liked to think so. Perhaps, too, she had at last recognised herself in the Hamadryad of the poplar sapling; the slim Hamadryad whose movements were like the swaying of a young tree in the wind. "The Woman who was a Tree" was what he had called the poem. He had given her the book when it came out, hoping that the poem would tell her what he hadn't dared to say. She had never referred to it.

He shut his eyes and saw a vision of her in a red velvet cloak, swaying into the little restaurant where they sometimes dined together in London—three quarters of an hour late, and he at his table, haggard with anxiety, irritation, hunger. Oh, she was damnable!

It occurred to him that perhaps his hostess might be in her boudoir. It was a possibility; he would go and see. Mrs. Wimbush's boudoir was in the central tower on the garden front. A little staircase cork-screwed up to it from the hall. Denis mounted, tapped at the door. "Come in." Ah, she was there; he had rather hoped she wouldn't be. He opened the door.

Priscilla Wimbush was lying on the sofa. A blotting-pad rested on her knees and she was thoughtfully sucking the end of a silver pencil.

"Hullo," she said, looking up. "I'd forgotten you were coming."

"Well, here I am, I'm afraid," said Denis deprecatingly. "I'm awfully sorry."

Mrs. Wimbush laughed. Her voice, her laughter, were deep and masculine. Everything about her was manly. She had a large, square, middle-aged face, with a massive projecting nose and little greenish eyes, the whole surmounted by a lofty and elaborate coiffure of a curiously improbable shade of orange. Looking at her, Denis always thought of Wilkie Bard as the cantatrice.

"That's why I'm going to
Sing in op'ra, sing in op'ra,
Sing in op-pop-pop-pop-pop-popera."

Today she was wearing a purple silk dress with a high collar and a row of pearls. The costume, so richly dowagerish, so suggestive of the Royal Family, made her look more than ever like something on the Halls.

"What have you been doing all this time?" she asked.

"Well," said Denis, and he hesitated, almost voluptuously. He had a tremendously amusing account of London and its doings all ripe and ready in his mind. It would be a pleasure to give it utterance. "To begin with," he said...

But he was too late. Mrs. Wimbush's question had been what the grammarians call rhetorical; it asked for no answer. It was a little conversational flourish, a gambit in the polite game.

"You find me busy at my horoscopes," she said, without even being aware that she had interrupted him.

A little pained, Denis decided to reserve his story for more receptive ears. He contented himself, by way of revenge, with saying "Oh?" rather icily.

"Did I tell you how I won four hundred on the Grand National this year?"

"Yes," he replied, still frigid and mono-syllabic. She must have told him at least six times.

"Wonderful, isn't it? Everything is in the Stars. In the Old Days, before I had the Stars to help me, I used to lose thousands. Now"—she paused an instant—"well, look at that four hundred on the Grand National. That's the Stars."

Denis would have liked to hear more about the Old Days. But he was too discreet and, still more, too shy to ask. There had been something of a bust up; that was all he knew. Old Priscilla—not so old then, of course, and sprightlier—had lost a great deal of money, dropped it in handfuls and hatfuls on every race-course in the country. She had gambled too. The number of thousands varied in the different legends, but all put it high. Henry Wimbush was forced to sell some of his Primitives—a Taddeo da Poggibonsi, an Amico di Taddeo, and four or five nameless Sienese—to the Americans. There was a crisis. For the first time in his life Henry asserted himself, and with good effect, it seemed.

Priscilla's gay and gadding existence had come to an abrupt end. Nowadays she spent almost all her time at Crome, cultivating a rather ill-defined malady. For consolation she dallied with New Thought and the Occult. Her passion for racing still possessed her, and Henry, who was a kind-hearted fellow at bottom, allowed her forty pounds a month betting money. Most of Priscilla's days were spent in casting the horoscopes of horses, and she invested her money scientifically, as the stars dictated. She betted on football too, and had a large notebook in which she registered the horoscopes of all the players in all the teams of the League. The process of balancing the horoscopes of two elevens one against the other was a very delicate and difficult one. A match between the Spurs and the Villa entailed a conflict in the heavens so vast and so complicated that it was not to be wondered at if she sometimes made a mistake about the outcome.

"Such a pity you don't believe in these things, Denis, such a pity," said Mrs. Wimbush in her deep, distinct voice.

"I can't say I feel it so."

"Ah, that's because you don't know what it's like to have faith. You've no idea how amusing and exciting life becomes when you do believe. All that happens means something; nothing you do is ever insignificant. It makes life so jolly, you know. Here am I at Crome. Dull as ditchwater, you'd think; but no, I don't find it so. I don't regret the Old Days a bit. I have the Stars..." She picked up the sheet of paper that was lying on the blotting-pad. "Inman's horoscope," she explained. "(I thought I'd like to have a little fling on the billiards championship this autumn.) I have the Infinite to keep in tune with," she waved her hand. "And then there's the next world and all the spirits, and one's Aura, and Mrs. Eddy and saying you're not ill, and the Christian Mysteries and Mrs. Besant. It's all splendid. One's never dull for a moment. I can't think how I used to get on before—in the Old Days. Pleasure—running about, that's all it was; just running about. Lunch, tea, dinner, theatre, supper every day. It was fun, of course, while it lasted. But there wasn't much left of it afterwards. There's rather a good thing about that in Barbecue-Smith's new book. Where is it?"

She sat up and reached for a book that was lying on the little table by the head of the sofa.

CHAPTER II.

"Do you know him, by the way?" she asked.

"Who?"

"Mr. Barbecue-Smith."

Denis knew of him vaguely. Barbecue-Smith was a name in the Sunday papers. He wrote about the Conduct of Life. He might even be the author of "What a Young Girl Ought to Know".

"No, not personally," he said.

"I've invited him for next week-end." She turned over the pages of the book. "Here's the passage I was thinking of. I marked it. I always mark the things I like."

Holding the book almost at arm's length, for she was somewhat long-sighted, and making suitable gestures with her free hand, she began to read, slowly, dramatically.

"'What are thousand pound fur coats, what are quarter million incomes?'" She looked up from the page with a histrionic movement of the head; her orange coiffure nodded portentously. Denis looked at it, fascinated. Was it the Real Thing and henna, he wondered, or was it one of those Complete Transformations one sees in the advertisements?

"'What are Thrones and Sceptres?'"

The orange Transformation—yes, it must be a Transformation—bobbed up again.

"'What are the gaieties of the Rich, the splendours of the Powerful, what is the pride of the Great, what are the gaudy pleasures of High Society?'"

The voice, which had risen in tone, questioningly, from sentence to sentence, dropped suddenly and boomed reply.

"'They are nothing. Vanity, fluff, dandelion seed in the wind, thin vapours of fever. The things that matter happen in the heart. Seen things are sweet, but those unseen are a thousand times more significant. It is the unseen that counts in Life.'"

Mrs. Wimbush lowered the book. "Beautiful, isn't it?" she said.

Denis preferred not to hazard an opinion, but uttered a non-committal "H'm."

"Ah, it's a fine book this, a beautiful book," said Priscilla, as she let the pages flick back, one by one, from under her thumb. "And here's the passage about the Lotus Pool. He compares the Soul to a Lotus Pool, you know." She held up the book again and read. "'A Friend of mine has a Lotus Pool in his garden. It lies in a little dell embowered with wild roses and eglantine, among which the nightingale pours forth its amorous descant all the summer long. Within the pool the Lotuses blossom, and the birds of the air come to drink and bathe themselves in its crystal waters...' Ah, and that reminds me," Priscilla exclaimed, shutting the book with a clap and uttering her big profound laugh—"that reminds me of the things that have been going on in our bathing-pool since you were here last. We gave the village people leave to come and bathe here in the evenings. You've no idea of the things that happened."

She leaned forward, speaking in a confidential whisper; every now and then she uttered a deep gurgle of laughter. "...mixed bathing...saw them out of my window...sent for a pair of field-glasses to make sure...no doubt of it..." The laughter broke out again. Denis laughed too. Barbecue-Smith was tossed on the floor.

"It's time we went to see if tea's ready," said Priscilla. She hoisted herself up from the sofa and went swishing off across the room, striding beneath the trailing silk. Denis followed her, faintly humming to himself:

"That's why I'm going to
Sing in op'ra, sing in op'ra,
Sing in op-pop-pop-pop-pop-popera."

And then the little twiddly bit of accompaniment at the end: "ra-ra."

CHAPTER III.

The terrace in front of the house was a long narrow strip of turf, bounded along its outer edge by a graceful stone balustrade. Two little summer-houses of brick stood at either end. Below the house the ground sloped very steeply away, and the terrace was a remarkably high one; from the balusters to the sloping lawn beneath was a drop of thirty feet. Seen from below, the high unbroken terrace wall, built like the house itself of brick, had the almost menacing aspect of a fortification—a castle bastion, from whose parapet one looked out across airy depths to distances level with the eye. Below, in the foreground, hedged in by solid masses of sculptured yew trees, lay the stone-brimmed swimming-pool. Beyond it stretched the park, with its massive elms, its green expanses of grass, and, at the bottom of the valley, the gleam of the narrow river. On the farther side of the stream the land rose again in a long slope, chequered with cultivation. Looking up the valley, to the right, one saw a line of blue, far-off hills.

The tea-table had been planted in the shade of one of the little summer-houses, and the rest of the party was already assembled about it when Denis and Priscilla made their appearance. Henry Wimbush had begun to pour out the tea. He was one of those ageless, unchanging men on the farther side of fifty, who might be thirty, who might be anything. Denis had known him almost as long as he could remember. In all those years his pale, rather handsome face had never grown any older; it was like the pale grey bowler hat which he always wore, winter and summer—unageing, calm, serenely without expression.

Next him, but separated from him and from the rest of the world by the almost impenetrable barriers of her deafness, sat Jenny Mullion. She was perhaps thirty, had a tilted nose and a pink-and-white complexion, and wore her brown hair plaited and coiled in two lateral buns over her ears. In the secret tower of her deafness she sat apart, looking down at the world through sharply piercing eyes. What did she think of men and women and things? That was something that Denis had never been able to discover. In her enigmatic remoteness Jenny was a little disquieting. Even now some interior joke seemed to be amusing her, for she was smiling to herself, and her brown eyes were like very bright round marbles.

On his other side the serious, moonlike innocence of Mary Bracegirdle's face shone pink and childish. She was nearly twenty-three, but one wouldn't have guessed it. Her short hair, clipped like a page's, hung in a bell of elastic gold about her cheeks. She had large blue china eyes, whose expression was one of ingenuous and often puzzled earnestness.

Next to Mary a small gaunt man was sitting, rigid and erect in his chair. In appearance Mr. Scogan was like one of those extinct bird-lizards of the Tertiary. His nose was beaked, his dark eye had the shining quickness of a robin's. But there was nothing soft or gracious or feathery about him. The skin of his wrinkled brown face had a dry and scaly look; his hands were the hands of a crocodile. His movements were marked by the lizard's disconcertingly abrupt clockwork speed; his speech was thin, fluty, and dry. Henry Wimbush's school-fellow and exact contemporary, Mr. Scogan looked far older and, at the same time, far more youthfully alive than did that gentle aristocrat with the face like a grey bowler.

Mr. Scogan might look like an extinct saurian, but Gombauld was altogether and essentially human. In the old-fashioned natural histories of the 'thirties he might have figured in a steel engraving as a type of Homo Sapiens—an honour which at that time commonly fell to Lord Byron. Indeed, with more hair and less collar, Gombauld would have been completely Byronic—more than Byronic, even, for Gombauld was of Provencal descent, a black-haired young corsair of thirty, with flashing teeth and luminous large dark eyes. Denis looked at him enviously. He was jealous of his talent: if only he wrote verse as well as Gombauld painted pictures! Still more, at the moment, he envied Gombauld his looks, his vitality, his easy confidence of manner. Was it surprising that Anne should like him? Like him?—it might even be something worse, Denis reflected bitterly, as he walked at Priscilla's side down the long grass terrace.

Between Gombauld and Mr. Scogan a very much lowered deck-chair presented its back to the new arrivals as they advanced towards the tea-table. Gombauld was leaning over it; his face moved vivaciously; he smiled, he laughed, he made quick gestures with his hands. From the depths of the chair came up a sound of soft, lazy laughter. Denis started as he heard it. That laughter—how well he knew it! What emotions it evoked in him! He quickened his pace.

In her low deck-chair Anne was nearer to lying than to sitting. Her long, slender body reposed in an attitude of listless and indolent grace. Within its setting of light brown hair her face had a pretty regularity that was almost doll-like. And indeed there were moments when she seemed nothing more than a doll; when the oval face, with its long-lashed, pale blue eyes, expressed nothing; when it was no more than a lazy mask of wax. She was Henry Wimbush's own niece; that bowler-like countenance was one of the Wimbush heirlooms; it ran in the family, appearing in its female members as a blank doll-face. But across this dollish mask, like a gay melody dancing over an unchanging fundamental bass, passed Anne's other inheritance—quick laughter, light ironic amusement, and the changing expressions of many moods. She was smiling now as Denis looked down at her: her cat's smile, he called it, for no very good reason. The mouth was compressed, and on either side of it two tiny wrinkles had formed themselves in her cheeks. An infinity of slightly malicious amusement lurked in those little folds, in the puckers about the half-closed eyes, in the eyes themselves, bright and laughing between the narrowed lids.

The preliminary greetings spoken, Denis found an empty chair between Gombauld and Jenny and sat down.

"How are you, Jenny?" he shouted to her.

Jenny nodded and smiled in mysterious silence, as though the subject of her health were a secret that could not be publicly divulged.

"How's London been since I went away?" Anne inquired from the depth of her chair.

The moment had come; the tremendously amusing narrative was waiting for utterance. "Well," said Denis, smiling happily, "to begin with..."

"Has Priscilla told you of our great antiquarian find?" Henry Wimbush leaned forward; the most promising of buds was nipped.

"To begin with," said Denis desperately, "there was the Ballet..."

"Last week," Mr. Wimbush went on softly and implacably, "we dug up fifty yards of oaken drain-pipes; just tree trunks with a hole bored through the middle. Very interesting indeed. Whether they were laid down by the monks in the fifteenth century, or whether..."

Denis listened gloomily. "Extraordinary!" he said, when Mr. Wimbush had finished; "quite extraordinary!" He helped himself to another slice of cake. He didn't even want to tell his tale about London now; he was damped.

For some time past Mary's grave blue eyes had been fixed upon him. "What have you been writing lately?" she asked. It would be nice to have a little literary conversation.

"Oh, verse and prose," said Denis—"just verse and prose."

"Prose?" Mr. Scogan pounced alarmingly on the word. "You've been writing prose?"

"Yes."

"Not a novel?"

"Yes."

"My poor Denis!" exclaimed Mr. Scogan. "What about?"

Denis felt rather uncomfortable. "Oh, about the usual things, you know."

"Of course," Mr. Scogan groaned. "I'll describe the plot for you. Little Percy, the hero, was never good at games, but he was always clever. He passes through the usual public school and the usual university and comes to London, where he lives among the artists. He is bowed down with melancholy thought; he carries the whole weight of the universe upon his shoulders. He writes a novel of dazzling brilliance; he dabbles delicately in Amour and disappears, at the end of the book, into the luminous Future."

Denis blushed scarlet. Mr. Scogan had described the plan of his novel with an accuracy that was appalling. He made an effort to laugh. "You're entirely wrong," he said. "My novel is not in the least like that." It was a heroic lie. Luckily, he reflected, only two chapters were written. He would tear them up that very evening when he unpacked.

Mr. Scogan paid no attention to his denial, but went on: "Why will you young men continue to write about things that are so entirely uninteresting as the mentality of adolescents and artists? Professional anthropologists might find it interesting to turn sometimes from the beliefs of the Blackfellow to the philosophical preoccupations of the undergraduate. But you can't expect an ordinary adult man, like myself, to be much moved by the story of his spiritual troubles. And after all, even in England, even in Germany and Russia, there are more adults than adolescents. As for the artist, he is preoccupied with problems that are so utterly unlike those of the ordinary adult man—problems of pure aesthetics which don't so much as present themselves to people like myself—that a description of his mental processes is as boring to the ordinary reader as a piece of pure mathematics. A serious book about artists regarded as artists is unreadable; and a book about artists regarded as lovers, husbands, dipsomaniacs, heroes, and the like is really not worth writing again. Jean-Christophe is the stock artist of literature, just as Professor Radium of 'Comic Cuts' is its stock man of science."

"I'm sorry to hear I'm as uninteresting as all that," said Gombauld.

"Not at all, my dear Gombauld," Mr. Scogan hastened to explain. "As a lover or a dipsomaniac, I've no doubt of your being a most fascinating specimen. But as a combiner of forms, you must honestly admit it, you're a bore."

"I entirely disagree with you," exclaimed Mary. She was somehow always out of breath when she talked. And her speech was punctuated by little gasps. "I've known a great many artists, and I've always found their mentality very interesting. Especially in Paris. Tschuplitski, for example—I saw a great deal of Tschuplitski in Paris this spring..."

"Ah, but then you're an exception, Mary, you're an exception," said Mr. Scogan. "You are a femme superieure."

A flush of pleasure turned Mary's face into a harvest moon.

CHAPTER IV.

Denis woke up next morning to find the sun shining, the sky serene. He decided to wear white flannel trousers—white flannel trousers and a black jacket, with a silk shirt and his new peach-coloured tie. And what shoes? White was the obvious choice, but there was something rather pleasing about the notion of black patent leather. He lay in bed for several minutes considering the problem.

Before he went down—patent leather was his final choice—he looked at himself critically in the glass. His hair might have been more golden, he reflected. As it was, its yellowness had the hint of a greenish tinge in it. But his forehead was good. His forehead made up in height what his chin lacked in prominence. His nose might have been longer, but it would pass. His eyes might have been blue and not green. But his coat was very well cut and, discreetly padded, made him seem robuster than he actually was. His legs, in their white casing, were long and elegant. Satisfied, he descended the stairs. Most of the party had already finished their breakfast. He found himself alone with Jenny.

"I hope you slept well," he said.

"Yes, isn't it lovely?" Jenny replied, giving two rapid little nods. "But we had such awful thunderstorms last week."

Parallel straight lines, Denis reflected, meet only at infinity. He might talk for ever of care-charmer sleep and she of meteorology till the end of time. Did one ever establish contact with anyone? We are all parallel straight lines. Jenny was only a little more parallel than most.

"They are very alarming, these thunderstorms," he said, helping himself to porridge. "Don't you think so? Or are you above being frightened?"

"No. I always go to bed in a storm. One is so much safer lying down."

"Why?"

"Because," said Jenny, making a descriptive gesture, "because lightning goes downwards and not flat ways. When you're lying down you're out of the current."

"That's very ingenious."

"It's true."

There was a silence. Denis finished his porridge and helped himself to bacon. For lack of anything better to say, and because Mr. Scogan's absurd phrase was for some reason running in his head, he turned to Jenny and asked:

"Do you consider yourself a femme superieure?" He had to repeat the question several times before Jenny got the hang of it.

"No," she said, rather indignantly, when at last she heard what Denis was saying. "Certainly not. Has anyone been suggesting that I am?"

"No," said Denis. "Mr. Scogan told Mary she was one."

"Did he?" Jenny lowered her voice. "Shall I tell you what I think of that man? I think he's slightly sinister."

Having made this pronouncement, she entered the ivory tower of her deafness and closed the door. Denis could not induce her to say anything more, could not induce her even to listen. She just smiled at him, smiled and occasionally nodded.

Denis went out on to the terrace to smoke his after-breakfast pipe and to read his morning paper. An hour later, when Anne came down, she found him still reading. By this time he had got to the Court Circular and the Forthcoming Weddings. He got up to meet her as she approached, a Hamadryad in white muslin, across the grass.

"Why, Denis," she exclaimed, "you look perfectly sweet in your white trousers."

Denis was dreadfully taken aback. There was no possible retort. "You speak as though I were a child in a new frock," he said, with a show of irritation.

"But that's how I feel about you, Denis dear."

"Then you oughtn't to."

"But I can't help it. I'm so much older than you."

"I like that," he said. "Four years older."

"And if you do look perfectly sweet in your white trousers, why shouldn't I say so? And why did you put them on, if you didn't think you were going to look sweet in them?"

"Let's go into the garden," said Denis. He was put out; the conversation had taken such a preposterous and unexpected turn. He had planned a very different opening, in which he was to lead off with, "You look adorable this morning," or something of the kind, and she was to answer, "Do I?" and then there was to be a pregnant silence. And now she had got in first with the trousers. It was provoking; his pride was hurt.

That part of the garden that sloped down from the foot of the terrace to the pool had a beauty which did not depend on colour so much as on forms. It was as beautiful by moonlight as in the sun. The silver of water, the dark shapes of yew and ilex trees remained, at all hours and seasons, the dominant features of the scene. It was a landscape in black and white. For colour there was the flower-garden; it lay to one side of the pool, separated from it by a huge Babylonian wall of yews. You passed through a tunnel in the hedge, you opened a wicket in a wall, and you found yourself, startlingly and suddenly, in the world of colour. The July borders blazed and flared under the sun. Within its high brick walls the garden was like a great tank of warmth and perfume and colour.

CHAPTER IV.

Denis held open the little iron gate for his companion. "It's like passing from a cloister into an Oriental palace," he said, and took a deep breath of the warm, flower-scented air. "'In fragrant volleys they let fly...' How does it go?"

"'Well shot, ye firemen! Oh how sweet
And round your equal fires do meet;
Whose shrill report no ear can tell,
But echoes to the eye and smell...'"

"You have a bad habit of quoting," said Anne. "As I never know the context or author, I find it humiliating."

Denis apologized. "It's the fault of one's education. Things somehow seem more real and vivid when one can apply somebody else's ready-made phrase about them. And then there are lots of lovely names and words—Monophysite, Iamblichus, Pomponazzi; you bring them out triumphantly, and feel you've clinched the argument with the mere magical sound of them. That's what comes of the higher education."

"You may regret your education," said Anne; "I'm ashamed of my lack of it. Look at those sunflowers! Aren't they magnificent?"

"Dark faces and golden crowns—they're kings of Ethiopia. And I like the way the tits cling to the flowers and pick out the seeds, while the other loutish birds, grubbing dirtily for their food, look up in envy from the ground. Do they look up in envy? That's the literary touch, I'm afraid. Education again. It always comes back to that." He was silent.

Anne had sat down on a bench that stood in the shade of an old apple tree. "I'm listening," she said.

He did not sit down, but walked backwards and forwards in front of the bench, gesticulating a little as he talked. "Books," he said—"books. One reads so many, and one sees so few people and so little of the world. Great thick books about the universe and the mind and ethics. You've no idea how many there are. I must have read twenty or thirty tons of them in the last five years. Twenty tons of ratiocination. Weighted with that, one's pushed out into the world."

He went on walking up and down. His voice rose, fell, was silent a moment, and then talked on. He moved his hands, sometimes he waved his arms. Anne looked and listened quietly, as though she were at a lecture. He was a nice boy, and to-day he looked charming—charming!

One entered the world, Denis pursued, having ready-made ideas about everything. One had a philosophy and tried to make life fit into it. One should have lived first and then made one's philosophy to fit life...Life, facts, things were horribly complicated; ideas, even the most difficult of them, deceptively simple. In the world of ideas everything was clear; in life all was obscure, embroiled. Was it surprising that one was miserable, horribly unhappy? Denis came to a halt in front of the bench, and as he asked this last question he stretched out his arms and stood for an instant in an attitude of crucifixion, then let them fall again to his sides.

"My poor Denis!" Anne was touched. He was really too pathetic as he stood there in front of her in his white flannel trousers. "But does one suffer about these things? It seems very extraordinary."

"You're like Scogan," cried Denis bitterly. "You regard me as a specimen for an anthropologist. Well, I suppose I am."

"No, no," she protested, and drew in her skirt with a gesture that indicated that he was to sit down beside her. He sat down. "Why can't you just take things for granted and as they come?" she asked. "It's so much simpler."

"Of course it is," said Denis. "But it's a lesson to be learnt gradually. There are the twenty tons of ratiocination to be got rid of first."

"I've always taken things as they come," said Anne. "It seems so obvious. One enjoys the pleasant things, avoids the nasty ones. There's nothing more to be said."

"Nothing—for you. But, then, you were born a pagan; I am trying laboriously to make myself one. I can take nothing for granted, I can enjoy nothing as it comes along. Beauty, pleasure, art, women—I have to invent an excuse, a justification for everything that's delightful. Otherwise I can't enjoy it with an easy conscience. I make up a little story about beauty and pretend that it has something to do with truth and goodness. I have to say that art is the process by which one reconstructs the divine reality out of chaos. Pleasure is one of the mystical roads to union with the infinite—the ecstasies of drinking, dancing, love-making. As for women, I am perpetually assuring myself that they're the broad highway to divinity. And to think that I'm only just beginning to see through the silliness of the whole thing! It's incredible to me that anyone should have escaped these horrors."

"It's still more incredible to me," said Anne, "that anyone should have been a victim to them. I should like to see myself believing that men are the highway to divinity." The amused malice of her smile planted two little folds on either side of her mouth, and through their half-closed lids her eyes shone with laughter. "What you need, Denis, is a nice plump young wife, a fixed income, and a little congenial but regular work."

"What I need is you." That was what he ought to have retorted, that was what he wanted passionately to say. He could not say it. His desire fought against his shyness. "What I need is you." Mentally he shouted the words, but not a sound issued from his lips. He looked at her despairingly. Couldn't she see what was going on inside him? Couldn't she understand? "What I need is you." He would say it, he would—he would.

"I think I shall go and bathe," said Anne. "It's so hot." The opportunity had passed.

CHAPTER V.

Mr. Wimbush had taken them to see the sights of the Home Farm, and now they were standing, all six of them—Henry Wimbush, Mr. Scogan, Denis, Gombauld, Anne, and Mary—by the low wall of the piggery, looking into one of the styes.

"This is a good sow," said Henry Wimbush. "She had a litter of fourteen.

"Fourteen?" Mary echoed incredulously. She turned astonished blue eyes towards Mr. Wimbush, then let them fall onto the seething mass of elan vital that fermented in the sty.

An immense sow reposed on her side in the middle of the pen. Her round, black belly, fringed with a double line of dugs, presented itself to the assault of an army of small, brownish-black swine. With a frantic greed they tugged at their mother's flank. The old sow stirred sometimes uneasily or uttered a little grunt of pain. One small pig, the runt, the weakling of the litter, had been unable to secure a place at the banquet. Squealing shrilly, he ran backwards and forwards, trying to push in among his stronger brothers or even to climb over their tight little black backs towards the maternal reservoir.

"There ARE fourteen," said Mary. "You're quite right. I counted. It's extraordinary."

"The sow next door," Mr. Wimbush went on, "has done very badly. She only had five in her litter. I shall give her another chance. If she does no better next time, I shall fat her up and kill her. There's the boar," he pointed towards a farther sty. "Fine old beast, isn't he? But he's getting past his prime. He'll have to go too."

"How cruel!" Anne exclaimed.

"But how practical, how eminently realistic!" said Mr. Scogan. "In this farm we have a model of sound paternal government. Make them breed, make them work, and when they're past working or breeding or begetting, slaughter them."

"Farming seems to be mostly indecency and cruelty," said Anne.

With the ferrule of his walking-stick Denis began to scratch the boar's long bristly back. The animal moved a little so as to bring himself within easier range of the instrument that evoked in him such delicious sensations; then he stood stock still, softly grunting his contentment. The mud of years flaked off his sides in a grey powdery scurf.

"What a pleasure it is," said Denis, "to do somebody a kindness. I believe I enjoy scratching this pig quite as much as he enjoys being scratched. If only one could always be kind with so little expense or trouble..."

A gate slammed; there was a sound of heavy footsteps.

"Morning, Rowley!" said Henry Wimbush.

"Morning, sir," old Rowley answered. He was the most venerable of the labourers on the farm—a tall, solid man, still unbent, with grey side-whiskers and a steep, dignified profile. Grave, weighty in his manner, splendidly respectable, Rowley had the air of a great English statesman of the mid-nineteenth century. He halted on the outskirts of the group, and for a moment they all looked at the pigs in a silence that was only broken by the sound of grunting or the squelch of a sharp hoof in the mire. Rowley turned at last, slowly and ponderously and nobly, as he did everything, and addressed himself to Henry Wimbush.

"Look at them, sir," he said, with a motion of his hand towards the wallowing swine. "Rightly is they called pigs."

"Rightly indeed," Mr. Wimbush agreed.

"I am abashed by that man," said Mr. Scogan, as old Rowley plodded off slowly and with dignity. "What wisdom, what judgment, what a sense of values! 'Rightly are they called swine.' Yes. And I wish I could, with as much justice, say, 'Rightly are we called men.'"

They walked on towards the cowsheds and the stables of the cart-horses. Five white geese, taking the air this fine morning, even as they were doing, met them in the way. They hesitated, cackled; then, converting their lifted necks into rigid, horizontal snakes, they rushed off in disorder, hissing horribly as they went. Red calves paddled in the dung and mud of a spacious yard. In another enclosure stood the bull, massive as a locomotive. He was a very calm bull, and his face wore an expression of melancholy stupidity. He gazed with reddish-brown eyes at his visitors, chewed thoughtfully at the tangible memories of an earlier meal, swallowed and regurgitated, chewed again. His tail lashed savagely from side to side; it seemed to have nothing to do with his impassive bulk. Between his short horns was a triangle of red curls, short and dense.

"Splendid animal," said Henry Wimbush. "Pedigree stock. But he's getting a little old, like the boar."

"Fat him up and slaughter him," Mr. Scogan pronounced, with a delicate old-maidish precision of utterance.

"Couldn't you give the animals a little holiday from producing children?" asked Anne. "I'm so sorry for the poor things."

Mr. Wimbush shook his head. "Personally," he said, "I rather like seeing fourteen pigs grow where only one grew before. The spectacle of so much crude life is refreshing."

"I'm glad to hear you say so," Gombauld broke in warmly. "Lots of life: that's what we want. I like pullulation; everything ought to increase and multiply as hard as it can."

CHAPTER V.

Gombauld grew lyrical. Everybody ought to have children—Anne ought to have them, Mary ought to have them—dozens and dozens. He emphasised his point by thumping with his walking-stick on the bull's leather flanks. Mr. Scogan ought to pass on his intelligence to little Scogans, and Denis to little Denises. The bull turned his head to see what was happening, regarded the drumming stick for several seconds, then turned back again satisfied, it seemed, that nothing was happening. Sterility was odious, unnatural, a sin against life. Life, life, and still more life. The ribs of the placid bull resounded.

Standing with his back against the farmyard pump, a little apart, Denis examined the group. Gombauld, passionate and vivacious, was its centre. The others stood round, listening—Henry Wimbush, calm and polite beneath his grey bowler; Mary, with parted lips and eyes that shone with the indignation of a convinced birth-controller. Anne looked on through half-shut eyes, smiling; and beside her stood Mr. Scogan, bolt upright in an attitude of metallic rigidity that contrasted strangely with that fluid grace of hers which even in stillness suggested a soft movement.

Gombauld ceased talking, and Mary, flushed and outraged, opened her mouth to refute him. But she was too slow. Before she could utter a word Mr. Scogan's fluty voice had pronounced the opening phrases of a discourse. There was no hope of getting so much as a word in edgeways; Mary had perforce to resign herself.

"Even your eloquence, my dear Gombauld," he was saying—"even your eloquence must prove inadequate to reconvert the world to a belief in the delights of mere multiplication. With the gramophone, the cinema, and the automatic pistol, the goddess of Applied Science has presented the world with another gift, more precious even than these—the means of dissociating love from propagation. Eros, for those who wish it, is now an entirely free god; his deplorable associations with Lucina may be broken at will. In the course of the next few centuries, who knows? the world may see a more complete severance. I look forward to it optimistically. Where the great Erasmus Darwin and Miss Anna Seward, Swan of Lichfield, experimented—and, for all their scientific ardour, failed—our descendants will experiment and succeed. An impersonal generation will take the place of Nature's hideous system. In vast state incubators, rows upon rows of gravid bottles will supply the world with the population it requires. The family system will disappear; society, sapped at its very base, will have to find new foundations; and Eros, beautifully and irresponsibly free, will flit like a gay butterfly from flower to flower through a sunlit world."

"It sounds lovely," said Anne.

"The distant future always does."

Mary's china blue eyes, more serious and more astonished than ever, were fixed on Mr. Scogan. "Bottles?" she said. "Do you really think so? Bottles..."

CHAPTER VI.

Mr. Barbecue-Smith arrived in time for tea on Saturday afternoon. He was a short and corpulent man, with a very large head and no neck. In his earlier middle age he had been distressed by this absence of neck, but was comforted by reading in Balzac's "Louis Lambert" that all the world's great men have been marked by the same peculiarity, and for a simple and obvious reason: Greatness is nothing more nor less than the harmonious functioning of the faculties of the head and heart; the shorter the neck, the more closely these two organs approach one another; argal...It was convincing.

Mr. Barbecue-Smith belonged to the old school of journalists. He sported a leonine head with a greyish-black mane of oddly unappetising hair brushed back from a broad but low forehead. And somehow he always seemed slightly, ever so slightly, soiled. In younger days he had gaily called himself a Bohemian. He did so no longer. He was a teacher now, a kind of prophet. Some of his books of comfort and spiritual teaching were in their hundred and twentieth thousand.

Priscilla received him with every mark of esteem. He had never been to Crome before; she showed him round the house. Mr. Barbecue-Smith was full of admiration.

"So quaint, so old-world," he kept repeating. He had a rich, rather unctuous voice.

Priscilla praised his latest book. "Splendid, I thought it was," she said in her large, jolly way.

"I'm happy to think you found it a comfort," said Mr. Barbecue-Smith.

"Oh, tremendously! And the bit about the Lotus Pool—I thought that so beautiful."

"I knew you would like that. It came to me, you know, from without." He waved his hand to indicate the astral world.

They went out into the garden for tea. Mr. Barbecue-Smith was duly introduced.

"Mr. Stone is a writer too," said Priscilla, as she introduced Denis.

"Indeed!" Mr. Barbecue-Smith smiled benignly, and, looking up at Denis with an expression of Olympian condescension, "And what sort of things do you write?"

CHAPTER VI.

Denis was furious, and, to make matters worse, he felt himself blushing hotly. Had Priscilla no sense of proportion? She was putting them in the same category—Barbecue-Smith and himself. They were both writers, they both used pen and ink. To Mr. Barbecue-Smith's question he answered, "Oh, nothing much, nothing," and looked away.

"Mr. Stone is one of our younger poets." It was Anne's voice. He scowled at her, and she smiled back exasperatingly.

"Excellent, excellent," said Mr. Barbecue-Smith, and he squeezed Denis's arm encouragingly. "The Bard's is a noble calling."

As soon as tea was over Mr. Barbecue-Smith excused himself; he had to do some writing before dinner. Priscilla quite understood. The prophet retired to his chamber.

Mr. Barbecue-Smith came down to the drawing-room at ten to eight. He was in a good humour, and, as he descended the stairs, he smiled to himself and rubbed his large white hands together. In the drawing-room someone was playing softly and ramblingly on the piano. He wondered who it could be. One of the young ladies, perhaps. But no, it was only Denis, who got up hurriedly and with some embarrassment as he came into the room.

"Do go on, do go on," said Mr. Barbecue-Smith. "I am very fond of music."

"Then I couldn't possibly go on," Denis replied. "I only make noises."

There was a silence. Mr. Barbecue-Smith stood with his back to the hearth, warming himself at the memory of last winter's fires. He could not control his interior satisfaction, but still went on smiling to himself. At last he turned to Denis.

"You write," he asked, "don't you?"

"Well, yes—a little, you know."

"How many words do you find you can write in an hour?"

"I don't think I've ever counted."

"Oh, you ought to, you ought to. It's most important."

Denis exercised his memory. "When I'm in good form," he said, "I fancy I do a twelve-hundred-word review in about four hours. But sometimes it takes me much longer."

Mr. Barbecue-Smith nodded. "Yes, three hundred words an hour at your best." He walked out into the middle of the room, turned round on his heels, and confronted Denis again. "Guess how many words I wrote this evening between five and half-past seven."

"I can't imagine."

"No, but you must guess. Between five and half-past seven—that's two and a half hours."

"Twelve hundred words," Denis hazarded.

"No, no, no." Mr. Barbecue-Smith's expanded face shone with gaiety. "Try again."

"Fifteen hundred."

"No."

"I give it up," said Denis. He found he couldn't summon up much interest in Mr. Barbecue-Smith's writing.

"Well, I'll tell you. Three thousand eight hundred."

Denis opened his eyes. "You must get a lot done in a day," he said.

Mr. Barbecue-Smith suddenly became extremely confidential. He pulled up a stool to the side of Denis's arm-chair, sat down in it, and began to talk softly and rapidly.

"Listen to me," he said, laying his hand on Denis's sleeve. "You want to make your living by writing; you're young, you're inexperienced. Let me give you a little sound advice."

What was the fellow going to do? Denis wondered: give him an introduction to the editor of "John o' London's Weekly", or tell him where he could sell a light middle for seven guineas? Mr. Barbecue-Smith patted his arm several times and went on.

"The secret of writing," he said, breathing it into the young man's ear—"the secret of writing is Inspiration."

Denis looked at him in astonishment.

"Inspiration..." Mr. Barbecue-Smith repeated.

"You mean the native wood-note business?"

Mr. Barbecue-Smith nodded.

"Oh, then I entirely agree with you," said Denis. "But what if one hasn't got Inspiration?"

"That was precisely the question I was waiting for," said Mr. Barbecue-Smith. "You ask me what one should do if one hasn't got Inspiration. I answer: you have Inspiration; everyone has Inspiration. It's simply a question of getting it to function."

The clock struck eight. There was no sign of any of the other guests; everybody was always late at Crome. Mr. Barbecue-Smith went on.

"That's my secret," he said. "I give it you freely." (Denis made a suitably grateful murmur and grimace.) "I'll help you to find your Inspiration, because I don't like to see a nice, steady young man like you exhausting his vitality and wasting the best years of his life in a grinding intellectual labour that could be completely obviated by Inspiration. I did it myself, so I know what it's like. Up till the time I was thirty-eight I was a writer like you—a writer without Inspiration. All I wrote I squeezed out of myself by sheer hard work. Why, in those days I was never able to do more than six-fifty words an hour, and what's more, I often didn't sell what I wrote." He sighed. "We artists," he said parenthetically, "we intellectuals aren't much appreciated here in England." Denis wondered if there was any method, consistent, of course, with politeness, by which he could dissociate himself from Mr. Barbecue-Smith's "we." There was none; and besides, it was too late now, for Mr. Barbecue-Smith was once more pursuing the tenor of his discourse.

"At thirty-eight I was a poor, struggling, tired, overworked, unknown journalist. Now, at fifty..." He paused modestly and made a little gesture, moving his fat hands outwards, away from one another, and expanding his fingers as though in demonstration. He was exhibiting himself. Denis thought of that advertisement of Nestle's milk—the two cats on the wall, under the moon, one black and thin, the other white, sleek, and fat. Before Inspiration and after.

"Inspiration has made the difference," said Mr. Barbecue-Smith solemnly. "It came quite suddenly—like a gentle dew from heaven." He lifted his hand and let it fall back on to his knee to indicate the descent of the dew. "It was one evening. I was writing my first little book about the Conduct of Life—'Humble Heroisms'. You may have read it; it has been a comfort—at least I hope and think so—a comfort to many thousands. I was in the middle of the second chapter, and I was stuck. Fatigue, overwork—I had only written a hundred words in the last hour, and I could get no further. I sat biting the end of my pen and looking at the electric light, which hung above my table, a little above and in front of me." He indicated the position of the lamp with elaborate care. "Have you ever looked at a bright light intently for a long time?" he asked, turning to Denis. Denis didn't think he had. "You can hypnotise yourself that way," Mr. Barbecue-Smith went on.

The gong sounded in a terrific crescendo from the hall. Still no sign of the others. Denis was horribly hungry.

"That's what happened to me," said Mr. Barbecue-Smith. "I was hypnotised. I lost consciousness like that." He snapped his fingers. "When I came to, I found that it was past midnight, and I had written four thousand words. Four thousand," he repeated, opening his mouth very wide on the "ou" of thousand. "Inspiration had come to me."

"What a very extraordinary thing," said Denis.

"I was afraid of it at first. It didn't seem to me natural. I didn't feel, somehow, that it was quite right, quite fair, I might almost say, to produce a literary composition unconsciously. Besides, I was afraid I might have written nonsense."

"And had you written nonsense?" Denis asked.

"Certainly not," Mr. Barbecue-Smith replied, with a trace of annoyance. "Certainly not. It was admirable. Just a few spelling mistakes and slips, such as there generally are in automatic writing. But the style, the thought—all the essentials were admirable. After that, Inspiration came to me regularly. I wrote the whole of 'Humble Heroisms' like that. It was a great success, and so has everything been that I have written since." He leaned forward and jabbed at Denis with his finger. "That's my secret," he said, "and that's how you could write too, if you tried—without effort, fluently, well."

"But how?" asked Denis, trying not to show how deeply he had been insulted by that final "well."

"By cultivating your Inspiration, by getting into touch with your Subconscious. Have you ever read my little book, 'Pipe-Lines to the Infinite'?"

Denis had to confess that that was, precisely, one of the few, perhaps the only one, of Mr. Barbecue-Smith's works he had not read.

"Never mind, never mind," said Mr. Barbecue-Smith. "It's just a little book about the connection of the Subconscious with the Infinite. Get into touch with the Subconscious and you are in touch with the Universe. Inspiration, in fact. You follow me?"

"Perfectly, perfectly," said Denis. "But don't you find that the Universe sometimes sends you very irrelevant messages?"

"I don't allow it to," Mr. Barbecue-Smith replied. "I canalise it. I bring it down through pipes to work the turbines of my conscious mind."

"Like Niagara," Denis suggested. Some of Mr. Barbecue-Smith's remarks sounded strangely like quotations—quotations from his own works, no doubt.

"Precisely. Like Niagara. And this is how I do it." He leaned forward, and with a raised forefinger marked his points as he made them, beating time, as it were, to his discourse. "Before I go off into my trance, I concentrate on the subject I wish to be inspired about. Let us say I am writing about the humble heroisms; for ten minutes before I go into the trance I think of nothing but orphans supporting their little brothers and sisters, of dull work well and patiently done, and I focus my mind on such great philosophical truths as the purification and uplifting of the soul by suffering, and the alchemical transformation of leaden evil into golden good." (Denis again hung up his little festoon of quotation marks.) "Then I pop off. Two or three hours later I wake up again, and find that inspiration has done its work. Thousands of words, comforting, uplifting words, lie before me. I type them out neatly on my machine and they are ready for the printer."

"It all sounds wonderfully simple," said Denis.

"It is. All the great and splendid and divine things of life are wonderfully simple." (Quotation marks again.) "When I have to do my aphorisms," Mr. Barbecue-Smith continued, "I prelude my trance by turning over the pages of any Dictionary of Quotations or Shakespeare Calendar that comes to hand. That sets the key, so to speak; that ensures that the Universe shall come flowing in, not in a continuous rush, but in aphorismic drops. You see the idea?"

Denis nodded. Mr. Barbecue-Smith put his hand in his pocket and pulled out a notebook. "I did a few in the train to-day," he said, turning over the pages. "Just dropped off into a trance in the corner of my carriage. I find the train very conducive to good work. Here they are." He cleared his throat and read:

"The Mountain Road may be steep, but the air is pure up there, and it is from the Summit that one gets the view."

"The Things that Really Matter happen in the Heart."

It was curious, Denis reflected, the way the Infinite sometimes repeated itself.

"Seeing is Believing. Yes, but Believing is also Seeing. If I believe in God, I see God, even in the things that seem to be evil."

Mr. Barbecue-Smith looked up from his notebook. "That last one," he said, "is particularly subtle and beautiful, don't you think? Without Inspiration I could never have hit on that." He re-read the apophthegm with a slower and more solemn utterance. "Straight from the Infinite," he commented reflectively, then addressed himself to the next aphorism.

"The flame of a candle gives Light, but it also Burns."

CHAPTER VI.

Puzzled wrinkles appeared on Mr. Barbecue-Smith's forehead. "I don't exactly know what that means," he said. "It's very gnomic. One could apply it, of course to the Higher Education—illuminating, but provoking the Lower Classes to discontent and revolution. Yes, I suppose that's what it is. But it's gnomic, it's gnognomic." He rubbed his chin thoughtfully. The gong sounded again, clamorously, it seemed imploringly: dinner was growing cold. It roused Mr. Barbecue-Smith from meditation. He turned to Denis.

"You understand me now when I advise you to cultivate your Inspiration. Let your Subconscious work for you; turn on the Niagara of the Infinite."

There was the sound of feet on the stairs. Mr. Barbecue-Smith got up, laid his hand for an instant on Denis's shoulder, and said:

"No more now. Another time. And remember, I rely absolutely on your discretion in this matter. There are intimate, sacred things that one doesn't wish to be generally known."

"Of course," said Denis. "I quite understand."

CHAPTER VII.

At Crome all the beds were ancient hereditary pieces of furniture. Huge beds, like four-masted ships, with furled sails of shining coloured stuff. Beds carved and inlaid, beds painted and gilded. Beds of walnut and oak, of rare exotic woods. Beds of every date and fashion from the time of Sir Ferdinando, who built the house, to the time of his namesake in the late eighteenth century, the last of the family, but all of them grandiose, magnificent.

The finest of all was now Anne's bed. Sir Julius, son to Sir Ferdinando, had had it made in Venice against his wife's first lying-in. Early seicento Venice had expended all its extravagant art in the making of it. The body of the bed was like a great square sarcophagus. Clustering roses were carved in high relief on its wooden panels, and luscious putti wallowed among the roses. On the black groundwork of the panels the carved reliefs were gilded and burnished. The golden roses twined in spirals up the four pillar-like posts, and cherubs, seated at the top of each column, supported a wooden canopy fretted with the same carved flowers.

Anne was reading in bed. Two candles stood on the little table beside her, in their rich light her face, her bare arm and shoulder took on warm hues and a sort of peach-like quality of surface. Here and there in the canopy above her carved golden petals shone brightly among profound shadows, and the soft light, falling on the sculptured panel of the bed, broke restlessly among the intricate roses, lingered in a broad caress on the blown cheeks, the dimpled bellies, the tight, absurd little posteriors of the sprawling putti.

There was a discreet tap at the door. She looked up. "Come in, come in." A face, round and childish, within its sleek bell of golden hair, peered round the opening door. More childish-looking still, a suit of mauve pyjamas made its entrance.

It was Mary. "I thought I'd just look in for a moment to say good-night," she said, and sat down on the edge of the bed.

Anne closed her book. "That was very sweet of you."

"What are you reading?" She looked at the book. "Rather second-rate, isn't it?" The tone in which Mary pronounced the word "second-rate" implied an almost infinite denigration. She was accustomed in London to associate only with first-rate people who liked first-rate things, and she knew that there were very, very few first-rate things in the world, and that those were mostly French.

CHAPTER VII.

"Well, I'm afraid I like it," said Anne. There was nothing more to be said. The silence that followed was a rather uncomfortable one. Mary fiddled uneasily with the bottom button of her pyjama jacket. Leaning back on her mound of heaped-up pillows, Anne waited and wondered what was coming.

"I'm so awfully afraid of repressions," said Mary at last, bursting suddenly and surprisingly into speech. She pronounced the words on the tail-end of an expiring breath, and had to gasp for new air almost before the phrase was finished.

"What's there to be depressed about?"

"I said repressions, not depressions."

"Oh, repressions; I see," said Anne. "But repressions of what?"

Mary had to explain. "The natural instincts of sex..." she began didactically. But Anne cut her short.

"Yes, yes. Perfectly. I understand. Repressions! old maids and all the rest. But what about them?"

"That's just it," said Mary. "I'm afraid of them. It's always dangerous to repress one's instincts. I'm beginning to detect in myself symptoms like the ones you read of in the books. I constantly dream that I'm falling down wells; and sometimes I even dream that I'm climbing up ladders. It's most disquieting. The symptoms are only too clear."

"Are they?"

"One may become a nymphomaniac if one's not careful. You've no idea how serious these repressions are if you don't get rid of them in time."

"It sounds too awful," said Anne. "But I don't see that I can do anything to help you."

"I thought I'd just like to talk it over with you."

"Why, of course; I'm only too happy, Mary darling."

Mary coughed and drew a deep breath. "I presume," she began sententiously, "I presume we may take for granted that an intelligent young woman of twenty-three who has lived in civilised society in the twentieth century has no prejudices."

"Well, I confess I still have a few."

"But not about repressions."

"No, not many about repressions; that's true."

"Or, rather, about getting rid of repressions."

"Exactly."

"So much for our fundamental postulate," said Mary. Solemnity was expressed in every feature of her round young face, radiated from her large blue eyes. "We come next to the desirability of possessing experience. I hope we are agreed that knowledge is desirable and that ignorance is undesirable."

Obedient as one of those complaisant disciples from whom Socrates could get whatever answer he chose, Anne gave her assent to this proposition.

"And we are equally agreed, I hope, that marriage is what it is."

"It is."

"Good!" said Mary. "And repressions being what they are..."

"Exactly."

"There would therefore seem to be only one conclusion."

"But I knew that," Anne exclaimed, "before you began."

"Yes, but now it's been proved," said Mary. "One must do things logically. The question is now..."

"But where does the question come in? You've reached your only possible conclusion—logically, which is more than I could have done. All that remains is to impart the information to someone you like—someone you like really rather a lot, someone you're in love with, if I may express myself so baldly."

"But that's just where the question comes in," Mary exclaimed. "I'm not in love with anybody."

"Then, if I were you, I should wait till you are."

"But I can't go on dreaming night after night that I'm falling down a well. It's too dangerous."

"Well, if it really is TOO dangerous, then of course you must do something about it; you must find somebody else."

"But who?" A thoughtful frown puckered Mary's brow. "It must be somebody intelligent, somebody with intellectual interests that I can share. And it must be somebody with a proper respect for women, somebody who's prepared to talk seriously about his work and his ideas and about my work and my ideas. It isn't, as you see, at all easy to find the right person."

"Well" said Anne, "there are three unattached and intelligent men in the house at the present time. There's Mr. Scogan, to begin with; but perhaps he's rather too much of a genuine antique. And there are Gombauld and Denis. Shall we say that the choice is limited to the last two?"

Mary nodded. "I think we had better," she said, and then hesitated, with a certain air of embarrassment.

"What is it?"

"I was wondering," said Mary, with a gasp, "whether they really were unattached. I thought that perhaps you might...you might..."

"It was very nice of you to think of me, Mary darling," said Anne, smiling the tight cat's smile. "But as far as I'm concerned, they are both entirely unattached."

"I'm very glad of that," said Mary, looking relieved. "We are now confronted with the question: Which of the two?"

"I can give no advice. It's a matter for your taste."

"It's not a matter of my taste," Mary pronounced, "but of their merits. We must weigh them and consider them carefully and dispassionately."

"You must do the weighing yourself," said Anne; there was still the trace of a smile at the corners of her mouth and round the half-closed eyes. "I won't run the risk of advising you wrongly."

"Gombauld has more talent," Mary began, "but he is less civilised than Denis." Mary's pronunciation of "civilised" gave the word a special and additional significance. She uttered it meticulously, in the very front of her mouth, hissing delicately on the opening sibilant. So few people were civilised, and they, like the first-rate works of art, were mostly French. "Civilisation is most important, don't you think?"

Anne held up her hand. "I won't advise," she said. "You must make the decision."

"Gombauld's family," Mary went on reflectively, "comes from Marseilles. Rather a dangerous heredity, when one thinks of the Latin attitude towards women. But then, I sometimes wonder whether Denis is altogether serious-minded, whether he isn't rather a dilettante. It's very difficult. What do you think?"

"I'm not listening," said Anne. "I refuse to take any responsibility."

Mary sighed. "Well," she said, "I think I had better go to bed and think about it."

"Carefully and dispassionately," said Anne.

At the door Mary turned round. "Good-night," she said, and wondered as she said the words why Anne was smiling in that curious way. It was probably nothing, she reflected. Anne often smiled for no apparent reason; it was probably just a habit. "I hope I shan't dream of falling down wells again to-night," she added.

"Ladders are worse," said Anne.

Mary nodded. "Yes, ladders are much graver."

CHAPTER VIII.

Breakfast on Sunday morning was an hour later than on week-days, and Priscilla, who usually made no public appearance before luncheon, honoured it by her presence. Dressed in black silk, with a ruby cross as well as her customary string of pearls round her neck, she presided. An enormous Sunday paper concealed all but the extreme pinnacle of her coiffure from the outer world.

"I see Surrey has won," she said, with her mouth full, "by four wickets. The sun is in Leo: that would account for it!"

"Splendid game, cricket," remarked Mr. Barbecue-Smith heartily to no one in particular; "so thoroughly English."

Jenny, who was sitting next to him, woke up suddenly with a start. "What?" she said. "What?"

"So English," repeated Mr. Barbecue-Smith.

Jenny looked at him, surprised. "English? Of course I am."

He was beginning to explain, when Mrs. Wimbush vailed her Sunday paper, and appeared, a square, mauve-powdered face in the midst of orange splendours. "I see there's a new series of articles on the next world just beginning," she said to Mr. Barbecue-Smith. "This one's called 'Summer Land and Gehenna.'"

"Summer Land," echoed Mr. Barbecue-Smith, closing his eyes. "Summer Land. A beautiful name. Beautiful—beautiful."

Mary had taken the seat next to Denis's. After a night of careful consideration she had decided on Denis. He might have less talent than Gombauld, he might be a little lacking in seriousness, but somehow he was safer.

"Are you writing much poetry here in the country?" she asked, with a bright gravity.

"None," said Denis curtly. "I haven't brought my typewriter."

"But do you mean to say you can't write without a typewriter?"

Denis shook his head. He hated talking at breakfast, and, besides, he wanted to hear what Mr. Scogan was saying at the other end of the table.

"...My scheme for dealing with the Church," Mr. Scogan was saying, "is beautifully simple. At the present time the Anglican clergy wear their collars the wrong way round. I would compel them to wear, not only their collars, but all their clothes, turned back to frantic—coat, waistcoat, trousers, boots—so that every clergyman should present to the world a smooth facade, unbroken by stud, button, or lace. The enforcement of such a livery would act as a wholesome deterrent to those intending to enter the Church. At the same time it would enormously enhance, what Archbishop Laud so rightly insisted on, the 'beauty of holiness' in the few incorrigibles who could not be deterred."

"In hell, it seems," said Priscilla, reading in her Sunday paper, "the children amuse themselves by flaying lambs alive."

"Ah, but, dear lady, that's only a symbol," exclaimed Mr. Barbecue-Smith, "a material symbol of a h-piritual truth. Lambs signify..."

"Then there are military uniforms," Mr. Scogan went on. "When scarlet and pipe-clay were abandoned for khaki, there were some who trembled for the future of war. But then, finding how elegant the new tunic was, how closely it clipped the waist, how voluptuously, with the lateral bustles of the pockets, it exaggerated the hips; when they realized the brilliant potentialities of breeches and top-boots, they were reassured. Abolish these military elegances, standardise a uniform of sack-cloth and mackintosh, you will very soon find that..."

"Is anyone coming to church with me this morning?" asked Henry Wimbush. No one responded. He baited his bare invitation. "I read the lessons, you know. And there's Mr. Bodiham. His sermons are sometimes worth hearing."

"Thank you, thank you," said Mr. Barbecue-Smith. "I for one prefer to worship in the infinite church of Nature. How does our Shakespeare put it? 'Sermons in books, stones in the running brooks.'" He waved his arm in a fine gesture towards the window, and even as he did so he became vaguely, but none the less insistently, none the less uncomfortably aware that something had gone wrong with the quotation. Something—what could it be? Sermons? Stones? Books?

CHAPTER IX.

Mr. Bodiham was sitting in his study at the Rectory. The nineteenth-century Gothic windows, narrow and pointed, admitted the light grudgingly; in spite of the brilliant July weather, the room was sombre. Brown varnished bookshelves lined the walls, filled with row upon row of those thick, heavy theological works which the second-hand booksellers generally sell by weight. The mantelpiece, the over-mantel, a towering structure of spindly pillars and little shelves, were brown and varnished. The writing-desk was brown and varnished. So were the chairs, so was the door. A dark red-brown carpet with patterns covered the floor. Everything was brown in the room, and there was a curious brownish smell.

In the midst of this brown gloom Mr. Bodiham sat at his desk. He was the man in the Iron Mask. A grey metallic face with iron cheek-bones and a narrow iron brow; iron folds, hard and unchanging, ran perpendicularly down his cheeks; his nose was the iron beak of some thin, delicate bird of rapine. He had brown eyes, set in sockets rimmed with iron; round them the skin was dark, as though it had been charred. Dense wiry hair covered his skull; it had been black, it was turning grey. His ears were very small and fine. His jaws, his chin, his upper lip were dark, iron-dark, where he had shaved. His voice, when he spoke and especially when he raised it in preaching, was harsh, like the grating of iron hinges when a seldom-used door is opened.

It was nearly half-past twelve. He had just come back from church, hoarse and weary with preaching. He preached with fury, with passion, an iron man beating with a flail upon the souls of his congregation. But the souls of the faithful at Crome were made of india-rubber, solid rubber; the flail rebounded. They were used to Mr. Bodiham at Crome. The flail thumped on india-rubber, and as often as not the rubber slept.

That morning he had preached, as he had often preached before, on the nature of God. He had tried to make them understand about God, what a fearful thing it was to fall into His hands. God—they thought of something soft and merciful. They blinded themselves to facts; still more, they blinded themselves to the Bible. The passengers on the "Titanic" sang "Nearer my God to Thee" as the ship was going down. Did they realise what they were asking to be brought nearer to? A white fire of righteousness, an angry fire...

CHAPTER IX.

When Savonarola preached, men sobbed and groaned aloud. Nothing broke the polite silence with which Crome listened to Mr. Bodiham—only an occasional cough and sometimes the sound of heavy breathing. In the front pew sat Henry Wimbush, calm, well-bred, beautifully dressed. There were times when Mr. Bodiham wanted to jump down from the pulpit and shake him into life,—times when he would have liked to beat and kill his whole congregation.

He sat at his desk dejectedly. Outside the Gothic windows the earth was warm and marvellously calm. Everything was as it had always been. And yet, and yet...It was nearly four years now since he had preached that sermon on Matthew xxiv. 7: "For nation shall rise up against nation, and kingdom against kingdom: and there shall be famines, and pestilences, and earthquakes, in divers places." It was nearly four years. He had had the sermon printed; it was so terribly, so vitally important that all the world should know what he had to say. A copy of the little pamphlet lay on his desk—eight small grey pages, printed by a fount of type that had grown blunt, like an old dog's teeth, by the endless champing and champing of the press. He opened it and began to read it yet once again.

"'For nation shall rise up against nation, and kingdom against kingdom: and there shall be famines, and pestilences, and earthquakes, in divers places.'

"Nineteen centuries have elapsed since Our Lord gave utterance to those words, and not a single one of them has been without wars, plagues, famines, and earthquakes. Mighty empires have crashed in ruin to the ground, diseases have unpeopled half the globe, there have been vast natural cataclysms in which thousands have been overwhelmed by flood and fire and whirlwind. Time and again, in the course of these nineteen centuries, such things have happened, but they have not brought Christ back to earth. They were 'signs of the times' inasmuch as they were signs of God's wrath against the chronic wickedness of mankind, but they were not signs of the times in connection with the Second Coming.

"If earnest Christians have regarded the present war as a true sign of the Lord's approaching return, it is not merely because it happens to be a great war involving the lives of millions of people, not merely because famine is tightening its grip on every country in Europe, not merely because disease of every kind, from syphilis to spotted fever, is rife among the warring nations; no, it is not for these reasons that we regard this war as a true Sign of the Times, but because in its origin and its progress it is marked by certain characteristics which seem to connect it almost beyond a doubt with the predictions in Christian Prophecy relating to the Second Coming of the Lord.

"Let me enumerate the features of the present war which most clearly suggest that it is a Sign foretelling the near approach of the Second Advent. Our Lord said that 'this Gospel of the Kingdom shall be preached in all the world for a witness unto all nations; and then shall the end come.' Although it would be presumptuous for us to say what degree of evangelisation will be regarded by God as sufficient, we may at least confidently hope that a century of unflagging missionary work has brought the fulfilment of this condition at any rate near. True, the larger number of the world's inhabitants have remained deaf to the preaching of the true religion; but that does not vitiate the fact that the Gospel HAS been preached 'for a witness' to all unbelievers from the Papist to the Zulu. The responsibility for the continued prevalence of unbelief lies, not with the preachers, but with those preached to.

"Again, it has been generally recognised that 'the drying up of the waters of the great river Euphrates,' mentioned in the sixteenth chapter of Revelation, refers to the decay and extinction of Turkish power, and is a sign of the near approaching end of the world as we know it. The capture of Jerusalem and the successes in Mesopotamia are great strides forward in the destruction of the Ottoman Empire; though it must be admitted that the Gallipoli episode proved that the Turk still possesses a 'notable horn' of strength. Historically speaking, this drying up of Ottoman power has been going on for the past century; the last two years have witnessed a great acceleration of the process, and there can be no doubt that complete desiccation is within sight.

"Closely following on the words concerning the drying up of Euphrates comes the prophecy of Armageddon, that world war with which the Second Coming is to be so closely associated. Once begun, the world war can end only with the return of Christ, and His coming will be sudden and unexpected, like that of a thief in the night.

"Let us examine the facts. In history, exactly as in St. John's Gospel, the world war is immediately preceded by the drying up of Euphrates, or the decay of Turkish power. This fact alone would be enough to connect the present conflict with the Armageddon of Revelation and therefore to point to the near approach of the Second Advent. But further evidence of an even more solid and convincing nature can be adduced.

"Armageddon is brought about by the activities of three unclean spirits, as it were toads, which come out of the mouths of the Dragon, the Beast, and the False Prophet. If we can identify these three powers of evil much light will clearly be thrown on the whole question.

"The Dragon, the Beast, and the False Prophet can all be identified in history. Satan, who can only work through human agency, has used these three powers in the long war against Christ which has filled the last nineteen centuries with religious strife. The Dragon, it has been sufficiently established, is pagan Rome, and the spirit issuing from its mouth is the spirit of Infidelity. The Beast, alternatively symbolised as a Woman, is undoubtedly the Papal power, and Popery is the spirit which it spews forth. There is only one power which answers to the description of the False Prophet, the wolf in sheep's clothing, the agent of the devil working in the guise of the Lamb, and that power is the so-called 'Society of Jesus.' The spirit that issues from the mouth of the False Prophet is the spirit of False Morality.

"We may assume, then, that the three evil spirits are Infidelity, Popery, and False Morality. Have these three influences been the real cause of the present conflict? The answer is clear.

"The spirit of Infidelity is the very spirit of German criticism. The Higher Criticism, as it is mockingly called, denies the possibility of miracles, prediction, and real inspiration, and attempts to account for the Bible as a natural development. Slowly but surely, during the last eighty years, the spirit of Infidelity has been robbing the Germans of their Bible and their faith, so that Germany is to-day a nation of unbelievers. Higher Criticism has thus made the war possible; for it would be absolutely impossible for any Christian nation to wage war as Germany is waging it.

"We come next to the spirit of Popery, whose influence in causing the war was quite as great as that of Infidelity, though not, perhaps, so immediately obvious. Since the Franco-Prussian War the Papal power has steadily declined in France, while in Germany it has steadily increased. To-day France is an anti-papal state, while Germany possesses a powerful Roman Catholic minority. Two papally controlled states, Germany and Austria, are at war with six anti-papal states—England, France, Italy, Russia, Serbia, and Portugal. Belgium is, of course, a thoroughly papal state, and there can be little doubt that the presence on the Allies' side of an element so essentially hostile has done much to hamper the righteous cause and is responsible for our comparative ill-success. That the spirit of Popery is behind the war is thus seen clearly enough in the grouping of the opposed powers, while the rebellion in the Roman Catholic parts of Ireland has merely confirmed a conclusion already obvious to any unbiased mind.

"The spirit of False Morality has played as great a part in this war as the two other evil spirits. The Scrap of Paper incident is the nearest and most obvious example of Germany's adherence to this essentially unchristian or Jesuitical morality. The end is German world-power, and in the attainment of this end, any means are justifiable. It is the true principle of Jesuitry applied to international politics.

"The identification is now complete. As was predicted in Revelation, the three evil spirits have gone forth just as the decay of the Ottoman power was nearing completion, and have joined together to make the world war. The warning, 'Behold, I come as a thief,' is therefore meant for the present period—for you and me and all the world. This war will lead on inevitably to the war of Armageddon, and will only be brought to an end by the Lord's personal return.

"And when He returns, what will happen? Those who are in Christ, St. John tells us, will be called to the Supper of the Lamb. Those who are found fighting against Him will be called to the Supper of the Great God—that grim banquet where they shall not feast, but be feasted on. 'For,' as St. John says, 'I saw an angel standing in the sun; and he cried in a loud voice, saying to all the fowls that fly in the midst of heaven, Come and gather yourselves together unto the supper of the Great God; that ye may eat the flesh of kings, and the flesh of captains, and the flesh of mighty men, and the flesh of horses, and of them that sit on them, and the flesh of all men, both free and bond, both small and great.' All the enemies of Christ will be slain with the sword of him that sits upon the horse, 'and all the fowls will be filled with their flesh.' That is the Supper of the Great God.

"It may be soon or it may, as men reckon time, be long; but sooner or later, inevitably, the Lord will come and deliver the world from its present troubles. And woe unto them who are called, not to the Supper of the Lamb, but to the Supper of the Great God. They will realise then, but too late, that God is a God of Wrath as well as a God of Forgiveness. The God who sent bears to devour the mockers of Elisha, the God who smote the Egyptians for their stubborn wickedness, will assuredly smite them too, unless they make haste to repent. But perhaps it is already too late. Who knows but that to-morrow, in a moment even, Christ may be upon us unawares, like a thief? In a little while, who knows? The angel standing in the sun may be summoning the ravens and vultures from their crannies in the rocks to feed upon the putrefying flesh of the millions of unrighteous whom God's wrath has destroyed. Be ready, then; the coming of the Lord is at hand. May it be for all of you an object of hope, not a moment to look forward to with terror and trembling."

Mr. Bodiham closed the little pamphlet and leaned back in his chair. The argument was sound, absolutely compelling; and yet—it was four years since he had preached that sermon; four years, and England was at peace, the sun shone, the people of Crome were as wicked and indifferent as ever—more so, indeed, if that were possible. If only he could understand, if the heavens would but make a sign! But his questionings remained unanswered. Seated there in his brown varnished chair under the Ruskinian window, he could have screamed aloud. He gripped the arms of his chair—gripping, gripping for control. The knuckles of his hands whitened; he bit his lip. In a few seconds he was able to relax the tension; he began to rebuke himself for his rebellious impatience.

Four years, he reflected; what were four years, after all? It must inevitably take a long time for Armageddon to ripen to yeast itself up. The episode of 1914 had been a preliminary skirmish. And as for the war having come to an end—why, that, of course, was illusory. It was still going on, smouldering away in Silesia, in Ireland, in Anatolia; the discontent in Egypt and India was preparing the way, perhaps, for a great extension of the slaughter among the heathen peoples. The Chinese boycott of Japan, and the rivalries of that country and America in the Pacific, might be breeding a great new war in the East. The prospect, Mr. Bodiham tried to assure himself, was hopeful; the real, the genuine Armageddon might soon begin, and then, like a thief in the night...But, in spite of all his comfortable reasoning, he remained unhappy, dissatisfied. Four years ago he had been so confident; God's intention seemed then so plain. And now? Now, he did well to be angry. And now he suffered too.

Sudden and silent as a phantom Mrs. Bodiham appeared, gliding noiselessly across the room. Above her black dress her face was pale with an opaque whiteness, her eyes were pale as water in a glass, and her strawy hair was almost colourless. She held a large envelope in her hand.

"This came for you by the post," she said softly.

The envelope was unsealed. Mechanically Mr. Bodiham tore it open. It contained a pamphlet, larger than his own and more elegant in appearance. "The House of Sheeny, Clerical Outfitters, Birmingham." He turned over the pages. The catalogue was tastefully and ecclesiastically printed in antique characters with illuminated Gothic initials. Red marginal lines, crossed at the corners after the manner of an Oxford picture frame, enclosed each page of type, little red crosses took the place of full stops. Mr. Bodiham turned the pages.

"Soutane in best black merino. Ready to wear; in all sizes. Clerical frock coats. From nine guineas. A dressy garment, tailored by our own experienced ecclesiastical cutters."

Half-tone illustrations represented young curates, some dapper, some Rugbeian and muscular, some with ascetic faces and large ecstatic eyes, dressed in jackets, in frock-coats, in surplices, in clerical evening dress, in black Norfolk suitings.

"A large assortment of chasubles.

"Rope girdles.

"Sheeny's Special Skirt Cassocks. Tied by a string about the waist...When worn under a surplice presents an appearance indistinguishable from that of a complete cassock...Recommended for summer wear and hot climates."

With a gesture of horror and disgust Mr. Bodiham threw the catalogue into the waste-paper basket. Mrs. Bodiham looked at him; her pale, glaucous eyes reflected his action without comment.

"The village," she said in her quiet voice, "the village grows worse and worse every day."

"What has happened now?" asked Mr. Bodiham, feeling suddenly very weary.

"I'll tell you." She pulled up a brown varnished chair and sat down. In the village of Crome, it seemed, Sodom and Gomorrah had come to a second birth.

CHAPTER X.

Denis did not dance, but when ragtime came squirting out of the pianola in gushes of treacle and hot perfume, in jets of Bengal light, then things began to dance inside him. Little black nigger corpuscles jigged and drummed in his arteries. He became a cage of movement, a walking palais de danse. It was very uncomfortable, like the preliminary symptoms of a disease. He sat in one of the window-seats, glumly pretending to read.

At the pianola, Henry Wimbush, smoking a long cigar through a tunnelled pillar of amber, trod out the shattering dance music with serene patience. Locked together, Gombauld and Anne moved with a harmoniousness that made them seem a single creature, two-headed and four-legged. Mr. Scogan, solemnly buffoonish, shuffled round the room with Mary. Jenny sat in the shadow behind the piano, scribbling, so it seemed, in a big red notebook. In arm-chairs by the fireplace, Priscilla and Mr. Barbecue-Smith discussed higher things, without, apparently, being disturbed by the noise on the Lower Plane.

"Optimism," said Mr. Barbecue-Smith with a tone of finality, speaking through strains of the "Wild, Wild Women"—"optimism is the opening out of the soul towards the light; it is an expansion towards and into God, it is a h-piritual self-unification with the Infinite."

"How true!" sighed Priscilla, nodding the baleful splendours of her coiffure.

"Pessimism, on the other hand, is the contraction of the soul towards darkness; it is a focusing of the self upon a point in the Lower Plane; it is a h-piritual slavery to mere facts; to gross physical phenomena."

"They're making a wild man of me." The refrain sang itself over in Denis's mind. Yes, they were; damn them! A wild man, but not wild enough; that was the trouble. Wild inside; raging, writhing—yes, "writhing" was the word, writhing with desire. But outwardly he was hopelessly tame; outwardly—baa, baa, baa.

There they were, Anne and Gombauld, moving together as though they were a single supple creature. The beast with two backs. And he sat in a corner, pretending to read, pretending he didn't want to dance, pretending he rather despised dancing. Why? It was the baa-baa business again.

Why was he born with a different face? Why WAS he? Gombauld had a face of brass—one of those old, brazen rams that thumped against the walls of cities till they fell. He was born with a different face—a woolly face.

CHAPTER X.

The music stopped. The single harmonious creature broke in two. Flushed, a little breathless, Anne swayed across the room to the pianola, laid her hand on Mr. Wimbush's shoulder.

"A waltz this time, please, Uncle Henry," she said.

"A waltz," he repeated, and turned to the cabinet where the rolls were kept. He trod off the old roll and trod on the new, a slave at the mill, uncomplaining and beautifully well bred.

"Rum; Tum; Rum-ti-ti; Tum-ti-ti..."

The melody wallowed oozily along, like a ship moving forward over a sleek and oily swell. The four-legged creature, more graceful, more harmonious in its movements than ever, slid across the floor. Oh, why was he born with a different face?

"What are you reading?"

He looked up, startled. It was Mary. She had broken from the uncomfortable embrace of Mr. Scogan, who had now seized on Jenny for his victim.

"What are you reading?"

"I don't know," said Denis truthfully. He looked at the title page; the book was called "The Stock Breeder's Vade Mecum."

"I think you are so sensible to sit and read quietly," said Mary, fixing him with her china eyes. "I don't know why one dances. It's so boring."

Denis made no reply; she exacerbated him. From the arm-chair by the fire-place he heard Priscilla's deep voice.

"Tell me, Mr Barbecue-Smith—you know all about science, I know—" A deprecating noise came from Mr. Barbecue-Smith's chair. "This Einstein theory. It seems to upset the whole starry universe. It makes me so worried about my horoscopes. You see..."

Mary renewed her attack. "Which of the contemporary poets do you like best?" she asked. Denis was filled with fury. Why couldn't this pest of a girl leave him alone? He wanted to listen to the horrible music, to watch them dancing—oh, with what grace, as though they had been made for one another!—to savour his misery in peace. And she came and put him through this absurd catechism! She was like "Mangold's Questions": "What are the three diseases of wheat?"—"Which of the contemporary poets do you like best?"

"Blight, Mildew, and Smut," he replied, with the laconism of one who is absolutely certain of his own mind.

It was several hours before Denis managed to go to sleep that night. Vague but agonising miseries possessed his mind. It was not only Anne who made him miserable; he was wretched about himself, the future, life in general, the universe. "This adolescence business," he repeated to himself every now and then, "is horribly boring." But the fact that he knew his disease did not help him to cure it.

After kicking all the clothes off the bed, he got up and sought relief in composition. He wanted to imprison his nameless misery in words. At the end of an hour, nine more or less complete lines emerged from among the blots and scratchings.

"I do not know what I desire
When summer nights are dark and still,
When the wind's many-voiced quire
Sleeps among the muffled branches.
I long and know not what I will:
And not a sound of life or laughter stanches
Time's black and silent flow.
I do not know what I desire,
I do not know."

He read it through aloud; then threw the scribbled sheet into the waste-paper basket and got into bed again. In a very few minutes he was asleep.

CHAPTER XI.

Mr. Barbecue-Smith was gone. The motor had whirled him away to the station; a faint smell of burning oil commemorated his recent departure. A considerable detachment had come into the courtyard to speed him on his way; and now they were walking back, round the side of the house, towards the terrace and the garden. They walked in silence; nobody had yet ventured to comment on the departed guest.

"Well?" said Anne at last, turning with raised inquiring eyebrows to Denis. "Well?" It was time for someone to begin.

Denis declined the invitation; he passed it on to Mr Scogan. "Well?" he said.

Mr. Scogan did not respond; he only repeated the question, "Well?"

It was left for Henry Wimbush to make a pronouncement. "A very agreeable adjunct to the week-end," he said. His tone was obituary.

They had descended, without paying much attention where they were going, the steep yew-walk that went down, under the flank of the terrace, to the pool. The house towered above them, immensely tall, with the whole height of the built-up terrace added to its own seventy feet of brick façade. The perpendicular lines of the three towers soared up, uninterrupted, enhancing the impression of height until it became overwhelming. They paused at the edge of the pool to look back.

"The man who built this house knew his business," said Denis. "He was an architect."

"Was he?" said Henry Wimbush reflectively. "I doubt it. The builder of this house was Sir Ferdinando Lapith, who flourished during the reign of Elizabeth. He inherited the estate from his father, to whom it had been granted at the time of the dissolution of the monasteries; for Crome was originally a cloister of monks and this swimming-pool their fish-pond. Sir Ferdinando was not content merely to adapt the old monastic buildings to his own purposes; but using them as a stone quarry for his barns and byres and outhouses, he built for himself a grand new house of brick—the house you see now."

He waved his hand in the direction of the house and was silent, severe, imposing, almost menacing, Crome loomed down on them.

"The great thing about Crome," said Mr. Scogan, seizing the opportunity to speak, "is the fact that it's so unmistakably and aggressively a work of art. It makes no compromise with nature, but affronts it and rebels against it. It has no likeness to Shelley's tower, in the 'Epipsychidion,' which, if I remember rightly—"

"'Seems not now a work of human art,
But as it were titanic, in the heart
Of earth having assumed its form and grown
Out of the mountain, from the living stone,
Lifting itself in caverns light and high.'

"No, no, there isn't any nonsense of that sort about Crome. That the hovels of the peasantry should look as though they had grown out of the earth, to which their inmates are attached, is right, no doubt, and suitable. But the house of an intelligent, civilised, and sophisticated man should never seem to have sprouted from the clods. It should rather be an expression of his grand unnatural remoteness from the cloddish life. Since the days of William Morris that's a fact which we in England have been unable to comprehend. Civilised and sophisticated men have solemnly played at being peasants. Hence quaintness, arts and crafts, cottage architecture, and all the rest of it. In the suburbs of our cities you may see, reduplicated in endless rows, studiedly quaint imitations and adaptations of the village hovel. Poverty, ignorance, and a limited range of materials produced the hovel, which possesses undoubtedly, in suitable surroundings, its own 'as it were titanic' charm. We now employ our wealth, our technical knowledge, our rich variety of materials for the purpose of building millions of imitation hovels in totally unsuitable surroundings. Could imbecility go further?"

Henry Wimbush took up the thread of his interrupted discourse. "All that you say, my dear Scogan," he began, "is certainly very just, very true. But whether Sir Ferdinando shared your views about architecture or if, indeed, he had any views about architecture at all, I very much doubt. In building this house, Sir Ferdinando was, as a matter of fact, preoccupied by only one thought—the proper placing of his privies. Sanitation was the one great interest of his life. In 1573 he even published, on this subject, a little book—now extremely scarce—called, 'Certaine Priuy Counsels' by 'One of Her Maiestie's Most Honourable Priuy Counsels, F.L. Knight', in which the whole matter is treated with great learning and elegance. His guiding principle in arranging the sanitation of a house was to secure that the greatest possible distance should separate the privy from the sewage arrangements. Hence it followed inevitably that the privies were to be placed at the top of the house, being connected by vertical shafts with pits or channels in the ground. It must not be thought that Sir Ferdinando was moved only by material and merely sanitary considerations; for the placing of his privies in an exalted position he had also certain excellent spiritual reasons. For, he argues in the third chapter of his 'Priuy Counsels', the necessities of nature are so base and brutish that in obeying them we are apt to forget that we are the noblest creatures of the universe. To counteract these degrading effects he advised that the privy should be in every house the room nearest to heaven, that it should be well provided with windows commanding an extensive and noble prospect, and that the walls of the chamber should be lined with bookshelves containing all the ripest products of human wisdom, such as the Proverbs of Solomon, Boethius's 'Consolations of Philosophy', the apophthegms of Epictetus and Marcus Aurelius, the 'Enchiridion' of Erasmus, and all other works, ancient or modern, which testify to the nobility of the human soul. In Crome he was able to put his theories into practice. At the top of each of the three projecting towers he placed a privy. From these a shaft went down the whole height of the house, that is to say, more than seventy feet, through the cellars, and into a series of conduits provided with flowing water tunnelled in the ground on a level with the base of the raised terrace. These conduits emptied themselves into the stream several hundred yards below the fish-pond. The total depth of the shafts from the top of the towers to their subterranean conduits was a hundred and two feet. The eighteenth century, with its passion for modernisation, swept away these monuments of sanitary ingenuity. Were it not for tradition and the explicit account of them left by Sir Ferdinando, we should be unaware that these noble privies had ever existed. We should even suppose that Sir Ferdinando built his house after this strange and splendid model for merely aesthetic reasons."

The contemplation of the glories of the past always evoked in Henry Wimbush a certain enthusiasm. Under the grey bowler his face worked and glowed as he spoke. The thought of these vanished privies moved him profoundly. He ceased to speak; the light gradually died out of his face, and it became once more the replica of the grave, polite hat which shaded it. There was a long silence; the same gently melancholy thoughts seemed to possess the mind of each of them. Permanence, transience—Sir Ferdinando and his privies were gone, Crome still stood. How brightly the sun shone and how inevitable was death! The ways of God were strange; the ways of man were stranger still...

"It does one's heart good," exclaimed Mr. Scogan at last, "to hear of these fantastic English aristocrats. To have a theory about privies and to build an immense and splendid house in order to put it into practise—it's magnificent, beautiful! I like to think of them all: the eccentric milords rolling across Europe in ponderous carriages, bound on extraordinary errands. One is going to Venice to buy La Bianchi's larynx; he won't get it till she's dead, of course, but no matter; he's prepared to wait; he has a collection, pickled in glass bottles, of the throats of famous opera singers. And the instruments of renowned virtuosi—he goes in for them too; he will try to bribe Paganini to part with his little Guarnerio, but he has small hope of success. Paganini won't sell his fiddle; but perhaps he might sacrifice one of his guitars. Others are bound on crusades—one to die miserably among the savage Greeks, another, in his white top hat, to lead Italians against their oppressors. Others have no business at all; they are just giving their oddity a continental airing. At home they cultivate themselves at leisure and with greater elaboration. Beckford builds towers, Portland digs holes in the ground, Cavendish, the millionaire, lives in a stable, eats nothing but mutton, and amuses himself—oh, solely for his private delectation—by anticipating the electrical discoveries of half a century. Glorious eccentrics! Every age is enlivened by their presence. Some day, my dear Denis," said Mr Scogan, turning a beady bright regard in his direction—"some day you must become their biographer—'The Lives of Queer Men.' What a subject! I should like to undertake it myself."

Mr. Scogan paused, looked up once more at the towering house, then murmured the word "Eccentricity," two or three times.

"Eccentricity...It's the justification of all aristocracies. It justifies leisured classes and inherited wealth and privilege and endowments and all the other injustices of that sort. If you're to do anything reasonable in this world, you must have a class of people who are secure, safe from public opinion, safe from poverty, leisured, not compelled to waste their time in the imbecile routines that go by the name of Honest Work. You must have a class of which the members can think and, within the obvious limits, do what they please. You must have a class in which people who have eccentricities can indulge them and in which eccentricity in general will be tolerated and understood. That's the important thing about an aristocracy. Not only is it eccentric itself—often grandiosely so; it also tolerates and even encourages eccentricity in others. The eccentricities of the artist and the new-fangled thinker don't inspire it with that fear, loathing, and disgust which the burgesses instinctively feel towards them. It is a sort of Red Indian Reservation planted in the midst of a vast horde of Poor Whites—colonials at that. Within its boundaries wild men disport themselves—often, it must be admitted, a little grossly, a little too flamboyantly; and when kindred spirits are born outside the pale it offers them some sort of refuge from the hatred which the Poor Whites, en bons bourgeois, lavish on anything that is wild or out of the ordinary. After the social revolution there will be no Reservations; the Redskins will be drowned in the great sea of Poor Whites. What then? Will they suffer you to go on writing villanelles, my good Denis? Will you, unhappy Henry, be allowed to live in this house of the splendid privies, to continue your quiet delving in the mines of futile knowledge? Will Anne..."

"And you," said Anne, interrupting him, "will you be allowed to go on talking?"

"You may rest assured," Mr. Scogan replied, "that I shall not. I shall have some Honest Work to do."

CHAPTER XII.

Blight, Mildew, and Smut..." Mary was puzzled and distressed. Perhaps her ears had played her false. Perhaps what he had really said was, "Squire, Binyon, and Shanks," or "Childe, Blunden, and Earp," or even "Abercrombie, Drinkwater, and Rabindranath Tagore." Perhaps. But then her ears never did play her false. "Blight, Mildew, and Smut." The impression was distinct and ineffaceable. "Blight, Mildew..." she was forced to the conclusion, reluctantly, that Denis had indeed pronounced those improbable words. He had deliberately repelled her attempts to open a serious discussion. That was horrible. A man who would not talk seriously to a woman just because she was a woman—oh, impossible! Egeria or nothing. Perhaps Gombauld would be more satisfactory. True, his meridional heredity was a little disquieting; but at least he was a serious worker, and it was with his work that she would associate herself. And Denis? After all, what WAS Denis? A dilettante, an amateur...

Gombauld had annexed for his painting-room a little disused granary that stood by itself in a green close beyond the farm-yard. It was a square brick building with a peaked roof and little windows set high up in each of its walls. A ladder of four rungs led up to the door; for the granary was perched above the ground, and out of reach of the rats, on four massive toadstools of grey stone. Within, there lingered a faint smell of dust and cobwebs; and the narrow shaft of sunlight that came slanting in at every hour of the day through one of the little windows was always alive with silvery motes. Here Gombauld worked, with a kind of concentrated ferocity, during six or seven hours of each day. He was pursuing something new, something terrific, if only he could catch it.

During the last eight years, nearly half of which had been spent in the process of winning the war, he had worked his way industriously through cubism. Now he had come out on the other side. He had begun by painting a formalised nature; then, little by little, he had risen from nature into the world of pure form, till in the end he was painting nothing but his own thoughts, externalised in the abstract geometrical forms of the mind's devising. He found the process arduous and exhilarating. And then, quite suddenly, he grew dissatisfied; he felt himself cramped and confined within intolerably narrow limitations. He was humiliated to find how few and crude and uninteresting were the forms he could invent; the inventions of nature were without number, inconceivably subtle and elaborate. He had done with cubism. He was out on the other side. But the cubist discipline preserved him from falling into excesses of nature worship. He took from nature its rich, subtle, elaborate forms, but his aim was always to work them into a whole that should have the thrilling simplicity and formality of an idea; to combine prodigious realism with prodigious simplification. Memories of Caravaggio's portentous achievements haunted him. Forms of a breathing, living reality emerged from darkness, built themselves up into compositions as luminously simple and single as a mathematical idea. He thought of the "Call of Matthew," of "Peter Crucified," of the "Lute players," of "Magdalen." He had the secret, that astonishing ruffian, he had the secret! And now Gombauld was after it, in hot pursuit. Yes, it would be something terrific, if only he could catch it.

For a long time an idea had been stirring and spreading, yeastily, in his mind. He had made a portfolio full of studies, he had drawn a cartoon; and now the idea was taking shape on canvas. A man fallen from a horse. The huge animal, a gaunt white cart-horse, filled the upper half of the picture with its great body. Its head, lowered towards the ground, was in shadow; the immense bony body was what arrested the eye, the body and the legs, which came down on either side of the picture like the pillars of an arch. On the ground, between the legs of the towering beast, lay the foreshortened figure of a man, the head in the extreme foreground, the arms flung wide to right and left. A white, relentless light poured down from a point in the right foreground. The beast, the fallen man, were sharply illuminated; round them, beyond and behind them, was the night. They were alone in the darkness, a universe in themselves. The horse's body filled the upper part of the picture; the legs, the great hoofs, frozen to stillness in the midst of their trampling, limited it on either side. And beneath lay the man, his foreshortened face at the focal point in the centre, his arms outstretched towards the sides of the picture. Under the arch of the horse's belly, between his legs, the eye looked through into an intense darkness; below, the space was closed in by the figure of the prostrate man. A central gulf of darkness surrounded by luminous forms...

The picture was more than half finished. Gombauld had been at work all the morning on the figure of the man, and now he was taking a rest—the time to smoke a cigarette. Tilting back his chair till it touched the wall, he looked thoughtfully at his canvas. He was pleased, and at the same time he was desolated. In itself, the thing was good; he knew it. But that something he was after, that something that would be so terrific if only he could catch it—had he caught it? Would he ever catch it?

Three little taps—rat, tat, tat! Surprised, Gombauld turned his eyes towards the door. Nobody ever disturbed him while he was at work; it was one of the unwritten laws. "Come in!" he called. The door, which was ajar, swung open, revealing, from the waist upwards, the form of Mary. She had only dared to mount half-way up the ladder. If he didn't want her, retreat would be easier and more dignified than if she climbed to the top.

"May I come in?" she asked.

"Certainly."

CHAPTER XII.

She skipped up the remaining two rungs and was over the threshold in an instant. "A letter came for you by the second post," she said. "I thought it might be important, so I brought it out to you." Her eyes, her childish face were luminously candid as she handed him the letter. There had never been a flimsier pretext.

Gombauld looked at the envelope and put it in his pocket unopened. "Luckily," he said, "it isn't at all important. Thanks very much all the same."

There was a silence; Mary felt a little uncomfortable. "May I have a look at what you've been painting?" she had the courage to say at last.

Gombauld had only half smoked his cigarette; in any case he wouldn't begin work again till he had finished. He would give her the five minutes that separated him from the bitter end. "This is the best place to see it from," he said.

Mary looked at the picture for some time without saying anything. Indeed, she didn't know what to say; she was taken aback, she was at a loss. She had expected a cubist masterpiece, and here was a picture of a man and a horse, not only recognisable as such, but even aggressively in drawing. Trompe-l'oeil—there was no other word to describe the delineation of that foreshortened figure under the trampling feet of the horse. What was she to think, what was she to say? Her orientations were gone. One could admire representationalism in the Old Masters. Obviously. But in a modern...? At eighteen she might have done so. But now, after five years of schooling among the best judges, her instinctive reaction to a contemporary piece of representation was contempt—an outburst of laughing disparagement. What could Gombauld be up to? She had felt so safe in admiring his work before. But now—she didn't know what to think. It was very difficult, very difficult.

"There's rather a lot of chiaroscuro, isn't there?" she ventured at last, and inwardly congratulated herself on having found a critical formula so gentle and at the same time so penetrating.

"There is," Gombauld agreed.

Mary was pleased; he accepted her criticism; it was a serious discussion. She put her head on one side and screwed up her eyes. "I think it's awfully fine," she said. "But of course it's a little too...too...trompe-l'oeil for my taste." She looked at Gombauld, who made no response, but continued to smoke, gazing meditatively all the time at his picture. Mary went on gaspingly. "When I was in Paris this spring I saw a lot of Tschuplitski. I admire his work so tremendously. Of course, it's frightfully abstract now—frightfully abstract and frightfully intellectual. He just throws a few oblongs on to his canvas—quite flat, you know, and painted in pure primary colours. But his design is wonderful. He's getting more and more abstract every day. He'd given up the third dimension when I was there and was just thinking of giving up the second. Soon, he says, there'll be just the blank canvas. That's the logical conclusion. Complete abstraction. Painting's finished; he's finishing it. When he's reached pure abstraction he's going to take up architecture. He says it's more intellectual than painting. Do you agree?" she asked, with a final gasp.

Gombauld dropped his cigarette end and trod on it. "Tschuplitski's finished painting," he said. "I've finished my cigarette. But I'm going on painting." And, advancing towards her, he put his arm round her shoulders and turned her round, away from the picture.

Mary looked up at him; her hair swung back, a soundless bell of gold. Her eyes were serene; she smiled. So the moment had come. His arm was round her. He moved slowly, almost imperceptibly, and she moved with him. It was a peripatetic embracement. "Do you agree with him?" she repeated. The moment might have come, but she would not cease to be intellectual, serious.

"I don't know. I shall have to think about it." Gombauld loosened his embrace, his hand dropped from her shoulder. "Be careful going down the ladder," he added solicitously.

Mary looked round, startled. They were in front of the open door. She remained standing there for a moment in bewilderment. The hand that had rested on her shoulder made itself felt lower down her back; it administered three or four kindly little smacks. Replying automatically to its stimulus, she moved forward.

"Be careful going down the ladder," said Gombauld once more.

She was careful. The door closed behind her and she was alone in the little green close. She walked slowly back through the farmyard; she was pensive.

CHAPTER XIII.

Henry Wimbush brought down with him to dinner a budget of printed sheets loosely bound together in a cardboard portfolio.

"To-day," he said, exhibiting it with a certain solemnity, "to-day I have finished the printing of my 'History of Crome'. I helped to set up the type of the last page this evening."

"The famous History?" cried Anne. The writing and the printing of this Magnum Opus had been going on as long as she could remember. All her childhood long Uncle Henry's History had been a vague and fabulous thing, often heard of and never seen.

"It has taken me nearly thirty years," said Mr. Wimbush. "Twenty-five years of writing and nearly four of printing. And now it's finished—the whole chronicle, from Sir Ferdinando Lapith's birth to the death of my father William Wimbush—more than three centuries and a half: a history of Crome, written at Crome, and printed at Crome by my own press."

"Shall we be allowed to read it now it's finished?" asked Denis.

Mr. Wimbush nodded. "Certainly," he said. "And I hope you will not find it uninteresting," he added modestly. "Our muniment room is particularly rich in ancient records, and I have some genuinely new light to throw on the introduction of the three-pronged fork."

"And the people?" asked Gombauld. "Sir Ferdinando and the rest of them—were they amusing? Were there any crimes or tragedies in the family?"

"Let me see," Henry Wimbush rubbed his chin thoughtfully. "I can only think of two suicides, one violent death, four or perhaps five broken hearts, and half a dozen little blots on the scutcheon in the way of misalliances, seductions, natural children, and the like. No, on the whole, it's a placid and uneventful record."

"The Wimbushes and the Lapiths were always an unadventurous, respectable crew," said Priscilla, with a note of scorn in her voice. "If I were to write my family history now! Why, it would be one long continuous blot from beginning to end." She laughed jovially, and helped herself to another glass of wine.

"If I were to write mine," Mr. Scogan remarked, "it wouldn't exist. After the second generation we Scogans are lost in the mists of antiquity."

"After dinner," said Henry Wimbush, a little piqued by his wife's disparaging comment on the masters of Crome, "I'll read you an episode from my History that will make you admit that even the Lapiths, in their own respectable way, had their tragedies and strange adventures."

"I'm glad to hear it," said Priscilla.

"Glad to hear what?" asked Jenny, emerging suddenly from her private interior world like a cuckoo from a clock. She received an explanation, smiled, nodded, cuckooed at last "I see," and popped back, clapping shut the door behind her.

Dinner was eaten; the party had adjourned to the drawing-room.

"Now," said Henry Wimbush, pulling up a chair to the lamp. He put on his round pince-nez, rimmed with tortoise-shell, and began cautiously to turn over the pages of his loose and still fragmentary book. He found his place at last. "Shall I begin?" he asked, looking up.

"Do," said Priscilla, yawning.

In the midst of an attentive silence Mr. Wimbush gave a little preliminary cough and started to read.

"The infant who was destined to become the fourth baronet of the name of Lapith was born in the year 1740. He was a very small baby, weighing not more than three pounds at birth, but from the first he was sturdy and healthy. In honour of his maternal grandfather, Sir Hercules Occam of Bishop's Occam, he was christened Hercules. His mother, like many other mothers, kept a notebook, in which his progress from month to month was recorded. He walked at ten months, and before his second year was out he had learnt to speak a number of words. At three years he weighed but twenty-four pounds, and at six, though he could read and write perfectly and showed a remarkable aptitude for music, he was no larger and heavier than a well-grown child of two. Meanwhile, his mother had borne two other children, a boy and a girl, one of whom died of croup during infancy, while the other was carried off by smallpox before it reached the age of five. Hercules remained the only surviving child.

"On his twelfth birthday Hercules was still only three feet and two inches in height. His head, which was very handsome and nobly shaped, was too big for his body, but otherwise he was exquisitely proportioned, and, for his size, of great strength and agility. His parents, in the hope of making him grow, consulted all the most eminent physicians of the time. Their various prescriptions were followed to the letter, but in vain. One ordered a very plentiful meat diet; another exercise; a third constructed a little rack, modelled on those employed by the Holy Inquisition, on which young Hercules was stretched, with excruciating torments, for half an hour every morning and evening. In the course of the next three years Hercules gained perhaps two inches. After that his growth stopped completely, and he remained for the rest of his life a pigmy of three feet and four inches. His father, who had built the most extravagant hopes upon his son, planning for him in his imagination a military career equal to that of Marlborough, found himself a disappointed man. 'I have brought an abortion into the world,' he would say, and he took so violent a dislike to his son that the boy dared scarcely come into his presence. His temper, which had been serene, was turned by disappointment to moroseness and savagery. He avoided all company (being, as he said, ashamed to show himself, the father of a lusus naturae, among normal, healthy human beings), and took to solitary drinking, which carried him very rapidly to his grave; for the year before Hercules came of age his father was taken off by an apoplexy. His mother, whose love for him had increased with the growth of his father's unkindness, did not long survive, but little more than a year after her husband's death succumbed, after eating two dozen of oysters, to an attack of typhoid fever.

"Hercules thus found himself at the age of twenty-one alone in the world, and master of a considerable fortune, including the estate and mansion of Crome. The beauty and intelligence of his childhood had survived into his manly age, and, but for his dwarfish stature, he would have taken his place among the handsomest and most accomplished young men of his time. He was well read in the Greek and Latin authors, as well as in all the moderns of any merit who had written in English, French, or Italian. He had a good ear for music, and was no indifferent performer on the violin, which he used to play like a bass viol, seated on a chair with the instrument between his legs. To the music of the harpsichord and clavichord he was extremely partial, but the smallness of his hands made it impossible for him ever to perform upon these instruments. He had a small ivory flute made for him, on which, whenever he was melancholy, he used to play a simple country air or jig, affirming that this rustic music had more power to clear and raise the spirits than the most artificial productions of the masters. From an early age he practised the composition of poetry, but, though conscious of his great powers in this art, he would never publish any specimen of his writing. 'My stature,' he would say, 'is reflected in my verses; if the public were to read them it would not be because I am a poet, but because I am a dwarf.' Several MS. books of Sir Hercules's poems survive. A single specimen will suffice to illustrate his qualities as a poet."

"'In ancient days, while yet the world was young,
Ere Abram fed his flocks or Homer sung;
When blacksmith Tubal tamed creative fire,
And Jabal dwelt in tents and Jubal struck the lyre;
Flesh grown corrupt brought forth a monstrous birth
And obscene giants trod the shrinking earth,
Till God, impatient of their sinful brood,
Gave rein to wrath and drown'd them in the Flood.
Teeming again, repeopled Tellus bore
The lubber Hero and the Man of War;
Huge towers of Brawn, topp'd with an empty Skull,
Witlessly bold, heroically dull.
Long ages pass'd and Man grown more refin'd,
Slighter in muscle but of vaster Mind,
Smiled at his grandsire's broadsword, bow and bill,
And learn'd to wield the Pencil and the Quill.
The glowing canvas and the written page

Immortaliz'd his name from age to age,
His name emblazon'd on Fame's temple wall;
For Art grew great as Humankind grew small.
Thus man's long progress step by step we trace;
The Giant dies, the hero takes his place;
The Giant vile, the dull heroic Block:
At one we shudder and at one we mock.
Man last appears. In him the Soul's pure flame
Burns brightlier in a not inord'nate frame.
Of old when Heroes fought and Giants swarmed,
Men were huge mounds of matter scarce inform'd;
Wearied by leavening so vast a mass,
The spirit slept and all the mind was crass.
The smaller carcase of these later days
Is soon inform'd; the Soul unwearied plays
And like a Pharos darts abroad her mental rays.
But can we think that Providence will stay
Man's footsteps here upon the upward way?
Mankind in understanding and in grace
Advanc'd so far beyond the Giants' race?
Hence impious thought! Still led by GOD'S own Hand,
Mankind proceeds towards the Promised Land.
A time will come (prophetic, I descry
Remoter dawns along the gloomy sky),
When happy mortals of a Golden Age
Will backward turn the dark historic page,
And in our vaunted race of Men behold
A form as gross, a Mind as dead and cold,
As we in Giants see, in warriors of old.
A time will come, wherein the soul shall be
From all superfluous matter wholly free;
When the light body, agile as a fawn's,
Shall sport with grace along the velvet lawns.
Nature's most delicate and final birth,
Mankind perfected shall possess the earth.
But ah, not yet! For still the Giants' race,
Huge, though diminish'd, tramps the Earth's fair face;
Gross and repulsive, yet perversely proud,
Men of their imperfections boast aloud.
Vain of their bulk, of all they still retain
Of giant ugliness absurdly vain;
At all that's small they point their stupid scorn
And, monsters, think themselves divinely born.
Sad is the Fate of those, ah, sad indeed,

CHAPTER XIII.

The rare precursors of the nobler breed!
Who come man's golden glory to foretell,
But pointing Heav'nwards live themselves in Hell.'

"As soon as he came into the estate, Sir Hercules set about remodelling his household. For though by no means ashamed of his deformity—indeed, if we may judge from the poem quoted above, he regarded himself as being in many ways superior to the ordinary race of man—he found the presence of full-grown men and women embarrassing. Realising, too, that he must abandon all ambitions in the great world, he determined to retire absolutely from it and to create, as it were, at Crome a private world of his own, in which all should be proportionable to himself. Accordingly, he discharged all the old servants of the house and replaced them gradually, as he was able to find suitable successors, by others of dwarfish stature. In the course of a few years he had assembled about himself a numerous household, no member of which was above four feet high and the smallest among them scarcely two feet and six inches. His father's dogs, such as setters, mastiffs, greyhounds, and a pack of beagles, he sold or gave away as too large and too boisterous for his house, replacing them by pugs and King Charles spaniels and whatever other breeds of dog were the smallest. His father's stable was also sold. For his own use, whether riding or driving, he had six black Shetland ponies, with four very choice piebald animals of New Forest breed.

"Having thus settled his household entirely to his own satisfaction, it only remained for him to find some suitable companion with whom to share his paradise. Sir Hercules had a susceptible heart, and had more than once, between the ages of sixteen and twenty, felt what it was to love. But here his deformity had been a source of the most bitter humiliation, for, having once dared to declare himself to a young lady of his choice, he had been received with laughter. On his persisting, she had picked him up and shaken him like an importunate child, telling him to run away and plague her no more. The story soon got about—indeed, the young lady herself used to tell it as a particularly pleasant anecdote—and the taunts and mockery it occasioned were a source of the most acute distress to Hercules. From the poems written at this period we gather that he meditated taking his own life. In course of time, however, he lived down this humiliation; but never again, though he often fell in love, and that very passionately, did he dare to make any advances to those in whom he was interested. After coming to the estate and finding that he was in a position to create his own world as he desired it, he saw that, if he was to have a wife—which he very much desired, being of an affectionate and, indeed, amorous temper—he must choose her as he had chosen his servants—from among the race of dwarfs. But to find a suitable wife was, he found, a matter of some difficulty; for he would marry none who was not distinguished by beauty and gentle birth. The dwarfish daughter of Lord Bemboro he refused on the ground that besides being a pigmy she was hunchbacked; while another young lady, an orphan belonging to a very good family in Hampshire, was rejected by him because her face, like that of so many dwarfs, was wizened and repulsive. Finally, when he was almost despairing of success, he heard from a reliable source that Count Titimalo, a Venetian nobleman, possessed a daughter of exquisite beauty and great accomplishments, who was by three feet in height. Setting out at once for Venice, he went immediately on his arrival to pay his respects to the count, whom he found living with his wife and five children in a very mean apartment in one of the poorer quarters of the town. Indeed, the count was so far reduced in his circumstances that he was even then negotiating (so it was rumoured) with a travelling company of clowns and acrobats, who had had the misfortune to lose their performing dwarf, for the sale of his diminutive daughter Filomena. Sir Hercules arrived in time to save her from this untoward fate, for he was so much charmed by Filomena's grace and beauty, that at the end of three days' courtship he made her a formal offer of marriage, which was accepted by her no less joyfully than by her father, who perceived in an English son-in-law a rich and unfailing source of revenue. After an unostentatious marriage, at which the English ambassador acted as one of the witnesses, Sir Hercules and his bride returned by sea to England, where they settled down, as it proved, to a life of uneventful happiness.

"Crome and its household of dwarfs delighted Filomena, who felt herself now for the first time to be a free woman living among her equals in a friendly world. She had many tastes in common with her husband, especially that of music. She had a beautiful voice, of a power surprising in one so small, and could touch A in alt without effort. Accompanied by her husband on his fine Cremona fiddle, which he played, as we have noted before, as one plays a bass viol, she would sing all the liveliest and tenderest airs from the operas and cantatas of her native country. Seated together at the harpsichord, they found that they could with their four hands play all the music written for two hands of ordinary size, a circumstance which gave Sir Hercules unfailing pleasure.

"When they were not making music or reading together, which they often did, both in English and Italian, they spent their time in healthful outdoor exercises, sometimes rowing in a little boat on the lake, but more often riding or driving, occupations in which, because they were entirely new to her, Filomena especially delighted. When she had become a perfectly proficient rider, Filomena and her husband used often to go hunting in the park, at that time very much more extensive than it is now. They hunted not foxes nor hares, but rabbits, using a pack of about thirty black and fawn-coloured pugs, a kind of dog which, when not overfed, can course a rabbit as well as any of the smaller breeds. Four dwarf grooms, dressed in scarlet liveries and mounted on white Exmoor ponies, hunted the pack, while their master and mistress, in green habits, followed either on the black Shetlands or on the piebald New Forest ponies. A picture of the whole hunt—dogs, horses, grooms, and masters—was painted by William Stubbs, whose work Sir Hercules admired so much that he invited him, though a man of ordinary stature, to come and stay at the mansion for the purpose of executing this picture. Stubbs likewise painted a portrait of Sir Hercules and his lady driving in their green enamelled calash drawn by four black Shetlands. Sir Hercules wears a plum-coloured velvet coat and white breeches; Filomena is dressed in flowered muslin and a very large hat with pink feathers. The two figures in their gay carriage stand out sharply against a dark background of trees; but to the left of the picture the trees fall away and disappear, so that the four black ponies are seen against a pale and strangely lurid sky that has the golden-brown colour of thunder-clouds lighted up by the sun.

"In this way four years passed happily by. At the end of that time Filomena found herself great with child. Sir Hercules was overjoyed. 'If God is good,' he wrote in his day-book, 'the name of Lapith will be preserved and our rarer and more delicate race transmitted through the generations until in the fullness of time the world shall recognise the superiority of those beings whom now it uses to make mock of.' On his wife's being brought to bed of a son he wrote a poem to the same effect. The child was christened Ferdinando in memory of the builder of the house.

"With the passage of the months a certain sense of disquiet began to invade the minds of Sir Hercules and his lady. For the child was growing with an extraordinary rapidity. At a year he weighed as much as Hercules had weighed when he was three. 'Ferdinando goes crescendo,' wrote Filomena in her diary. 'It seems not natural.' At eighteen months the baby was almost as tall as their smallest jockey, who was a man of thirty-six. Could it be that Ferdinando was destined to become a man of the normal, gigantic dimensions? It was a thought to which neither of his parents dared yet give open utterance, but in the secrecy of their respective diaries they brooded over it in terror and dismay.

"On his third birthday Ferdinando was taller than his mother and not more than a couple of inches short of his father's height. 'To-day for the first time' wrote Sir Hercules, 'we discussed the situation. The hideous truth can be concealed no longer: Ferdinando is not one of us. On this, his third birthday, a day when we should have been rejoicing at the health, the strength, and beauty of our child, we wept together over the ruin of our happiness. God give us strength to bear this cross.'

"At the age of eight Ferdinando was so large and so exuberantly healthy that his parents decided, though reluctantly, to send him to school. He was packed off to Eton at the beginning of the next half. A profound peace settled upon the house. Ferdinando returned for the summer holidays larger and stronger than ever. One day he knocked down the butler and broke his arm. 'He is rough, inconsiderate, unamenable to persuasion,' wrote his father. 'The only thing that will teach him manners is corporal chastisement.' Ferdinando, who at this age was already seventeen inches taller than his father, received no corporal chastisement.

"One summer holidays about three years later Ferdinando returned to Crome accompanied by a very large mastiff dog. He had bought it from an old man at Windsor who had found the beast too expensive to feed. It was a savage, unreliable animal; hardly had it entered the house when it attacked one of Sir Hercules's favourite pugs, seizing the creature in its jaws and shaking it till it was nearly dead. Extremely put out by this occurrence, Sir Hercules ordered that the beast should be chained up in the stable-yard. Ferdinando sullenly answered that the dog was his, and he would keep it where he pleased. His father, growing angry, bade him take the animal out of the house at once, on pain of his utmost displeasure. Ferdinando refused to move. His mother at this moment coming into the room, the dog flew at her, knocked her down, and in a twinkling had very severely mauled her arm and shoulder; in another instant it must infallibly have had her by the throat, had not Sir Hercules drawn his sword and stabbed the animal to the heart. Turning on his son, he ordered him to leave the room immediately, as being unfit to remain in the same place with the mother whom he had nearly murdered. So awe-inspiring was the spectacle of Sir Hercules standing with one foot on the carcase of the gigantic dog, his sword drawn and still bloody, so commanding were his voice, his gestures, and the expression of his face that Ferdinando slunk out of the room in terror and behaved himself for all the rest of the vacation in an entirely exemplary fashion. His mother soon recovered from the bites of the mastiff, but the effect on her mind of this adventure was ineradicable; from that time forth she lived always among imaginary terrors.

"The two years which Ferdinando spent on the Continent, making the Grand Tour, were a period of happy repose for his parents. But even now the thought of the future haunted them; nor were they able to solace themselves with all the diversions of their younger days. The Lady Filomena had lost her voice and Sir Hercules was grown too rheumatical to play the violin. He, it is true, still rode after his pugs, but his wife felt herself too old and, since the episode of the mastiff, too nervous for such sports. At most, to please her husband, she would follow the hunt at a distance in a little gig drawn by the safest and oldest of the Shetlands.

"The day fixed for Ferdinando's return came round. Filomena, sick with vague dreads and presentiments, retired to her chamber and her bed. Sir Hercules received his son alone. A giant in a brown travelling-suit entered the room. 'Welcome home, my son,' said Sir Hercules in a voice that trembled a little.

"'I hope I see you well, sir.' Ferdinando bent down to shake hands, then straightened himself up again. The top of his father's head reached to the level of his hip.

"Ferdinando had not come alone. Two friends of his own age accompanied him, and each of the young men had brought a servant. Not for thirty years had Crome been desecrated by the presence of so many members of the common race of men. Sir Hercules was appalled and indignant, but the laws of hospitality had to be obeyed. He received the young gentlemen with grave politeness and sent the servants to the kitchen, with orders that they should be well cared for.

"The old family dining-table was dragged out into the light and dusted (Sir Hercules and his lady were accustomed to dine at a small table twenty inches high). Simon, the aged butler, who could only just look over the edge of the big table, was helped at supper by the three servants brought by Ferdinando and his guests.

"Sir Hercules presided, and with his usual grace supported a conversation on the pleasures of foreign travel, the beauties of art and nature to be met with abroad, the opera at Venice, the singing of the orphans in the churches of the same city, and on other topics of a similar nature. The young men were not particularly attentive to his discourses; they were occupied in watching the efforts of the butler to change the plates and replenish the glasses. They covered their laughter by violent and repeated fits of coughing or choking. Sir Hercules affected not to notice, but changed the subject of the conversation to sport. Upon this one of the young men asked whether it was true, as he had heard, that he used to hunt the rabbit with a pack of pug dogs. Sir Hercules replied that it was, and proceeded to describe the chase in some detail. The young men roared with laughter.

"When supper was over, Sir Hercules climbed down from his chair and, giving as his excuse that he must see how his lady did, bade them good-night. The sound of laughter followed him up the stairs. Filomena was not asleep; she had been lying on her bed listening to the sound of enormous laughter and the tread of strangely heavy feet on the stairs and along the corridors. Sir Hercules drew a chair to her bedside and sat there for a long time in silence, holding his wife's hand and sometimes gently squeezing it. At about ten o'clock they were startled by a violent noise. There was a breaking of glass, a stamping of feet, with an outburst of shouts and laughter. The uproar continuing for several minutes, Sir Hercules rose to his feet and, in spite of his wife's entreaties, prepared to go and see what was happening. There was no light on the staircase, and Sir Hercules groped his way down cautiously, lowering himself from stair to stair and standing for a moment on each tread before adventuring on a new step. The noise was louder here; the shouting articulated itself into recognisable words and phrases. A line of light was visible under the dining-room door. Sir Hercules tiptoed across the hall towards it. Just as he approached the door there was another terrific crash of breaking glass and jangled metal. What could they be doing? Standing on tiptoe he managed to look through the keyhole. In the middle of the ravaged table old Simon, the butler, so primed with drink that he could scarcely keep his balance, was dancing a jig. His feet crunched and tinkled among the broken glass, and his shoes were wet with spilt wine. The three young men sat round, thumping the table with their hands or with the empty wine bottles, shouting and laughing encouragement. The three servants leaning against the wall laughed too. Ferdinando suddenly threw a handful of walnuts at the dancer's head, which so dazed and surprised the little man that he staggered and fell down on his back, upsetting a decanter and several glasses. They raised him up, gave him some brandy to drink, thumped him on the back. The old man smiled and hiccoughed. 'Tomorrow,' said Ferdinando, 'we'll have a concerted ballet of the whole household.' 'With father Hercules wearing his club and lion-skin,' added one of his companions, and all three roared with laughter.

"Sir Hercules would look and listen no further. He crossed the hall once more and began to climb the stairs, lifting his knees painfully high at each degree. This was the end; there was no place for him now in the world, no place for him and Ferdinando together.

"His wife was still awake; to her questioning glance he answered, 'They are making mock of old Simon. To-morrow it will be our turn.' They were silent for a time.

"At last Filomena said, 'I do not want to see to-morrow.'

"'It is better not,' said Sir Hercules. Going into his closet he wrote in his day-book a full and particular account of all the events of the evening. While he was still engaged in this task he rang for a servant and ordered hot water and a bath to be made ready for him at eleven o'clock. When he had finished writing he went into his wife's room, and preparing a dose of opium twenty times as strong as that which she was accustomed to take when she could not sleep, he brought it to her, saying, 'Here is your sleeping-draught.'

"Filomena took the glass and lay for a little time, but did not drink immediately. The tears came into her eyes. 'Do you remember the songs we used to sing, sitting out there sulla terrazza in the summer-time?' She began singing softly in her ghost of a cracked voice a few bars from Stradella's 'Amor amor, non dormir piu.' 'And you playing on the violin, it seems such a short time ago, and yet so long, long, long. Addio, amore, a rivederti.' She drank off the draught and, lying back on the pillow, closed her eyes. Sir Hercules kissed her hand and tiptoed away, as though he were afraid of waking her. He returned to his closet, and having recorded his wife's last words to him, he poured into his bath the water that had been brought up in accordance with his orders. The water being too hot for him to get into the bath at once, he took down from the shelf his copy of Suetonius. He wished to read how Seneca had died. He opened the book at random. 'But dwarfs,' he read, 'he held in abhorrence as being lusus naturae and of evil omen.' He winced as though he had been struck. This same Augustus, he remembered, had exhibited in the amphitheatre a young man called Lucius, of good family, who was not quite two feet in height and weighed seventeen pounds, but had a stentorian voice. He turned over the pages. Tiberius, Caligula, Claudius, Nero: it was a tale of growing horror. 'Seneca his preceptor, he forced to kill himself.' And there was Petronius, who had called his friends about him at the last, bidding them talk to him, not of the consolations of philosophy, but of love and gallantry, while the life was ebbing away through his opened veins. Dipping his pen once more in the ink he wrote on the last page of his diary: 'He died a Roman death.' Then, putting the toes of one foot into the water and finding that it was not too hot, he threw off his dressing-gown and, taking a razor in his hand, sat down in the bath. With one deep cut he severed the artery in his left wrist, then lay back and composed his mind to meditation. The blood oozed out, floating through the water in dissolving wreaths and spirals. In a little while the whole bath was tinged with pink. The colour deepened; Sir Hercules felt himself mastered by an invincible drowsiness; he was sinking from vague dream to dream. Soon he was sound asleep. There was not much blood in his small body."

CHAPTER XIV.

For their after-luncheon coffee the party generally adjourned to the library. Its windows looked east, and at this hour of the day it was the coolest place in the whole house. It was a large room, fitted, during the eighteenth century, with white painted shelves of an elegant design. In the middle of one wall a door, ingeniously upholstered with rows of dummy books, gave access to a deep cupboard, where, among a pile of letter-files and old newspapers, the mummy-case of an Egyptian lady, brought back by the second Sir Ferdinando on his return from the Grand Tour, mouldered in the darkness. From ten yards away and at a first glance, one might almost have mistaken this secret door for a section of shelving filled with genuine books. Coffee-cup in hand, Mr. Scogan was standing in front of the dummy book-shelf. Between the sips he discoursed.

"The bottom shelf," he was saying, "is taken up by an Encyclopaedia in fourteen volumes. Useful, but a little dull, as is also Caprimulge's 'Dictionary of the Finnish Language'. The 'Biographical Dictionary' looks more promising. 'Biography of Men who were Born Great', 'Biography of Men who Achieved Greatness', 'Biography of Men who had Greatness Thrust upon Them', and 'Biography of Men who were Never Great at All'. Then there are ten volumes of 'Thom's Works and Wanderings', while the 'Wild Goose Chase, a Novel', by an anonymous author, fills no less than six. But what's this, what's this?" Mr. Scogan stood on tiptoe and peered up. "Seven volumes of the 'Tales of Knockespotch'. The 'Tales of Knockespotch'," he repeated. "Ah, my dear Henry," he said, turning round, "these are your best books. I would willingly give all the rest of your library for them."

The happy possessor of a multitude of first editions, Mr. Wimbush could afford to smile indulgently.

"Is it possible," Mr. Scogan went on, "that they possess nothing more than a back and a title?" He opened the cupboard door and peeped inside, as though he hoped to find the rest of the books behind it. "Phooh!" he said, and shut the door again. "It smells of dust and mildew. How symbolical! One comes to the great masterpieces of the past, expecting some miraculous illumination, and one finds, on opening them, only darkness and dust and a faint smell of decay. After all, what is reading but a vice, like drink or venery or any other form of excessive self-indulgence? One reads to tickle and amuse one's mind; one reads, above all, to prevent oneself thinking. Still—the 'Tales of Knockespotch'..."

He paused, and thoughtfully drummed with his fingers on the backs of the non-existent, unattainable books.

"But I disagree with you about reading," said Mary. "About serious reading, I mean."

"Quite right, Mary, quite right," Mr. Scogan answered. "I had forgotten there were any serious people in the room."

"I like the idea of the Biographies," said Denis. "There's room for us all within the scheme; it's comprehensive."

"Yes, the Biographies are good, the Biographies are excellent," Mr Scogan agreed. "I imagine them written in a very elegant Regency style—Brighton Pavilion in words—perhaps by the great Dr. Lempriere himself. You know his classical dictionary? Ah!" Mr. Scogan raised his hand and let it limply fall again in a gesture which implied that words failed him. "Read his biography of Helen; read how Jupiter, disguised as a swan, was 'enabled to avail himself of his situation' vis-a-vis to Leda. And to think that he may have, must have written these biographies of the Great! What a work, Henry! And, owing to the idiotic arrangement of your library, it can't be read."

"I prefer the 'Wild Goose Chase'," said Anne. "A novel in six volumes—it must be restful."

"Restful," Mr. Scogan repeated. "You've hit on the right word. A 'Wild Goose Chase' is sound, but a bit old-fashioned—pictures of clerical life in the fifties, you know; specimens of the landed gentry; peasants for pathos and comedy; and in the background, always the picturesque beauties of nature soberly described. All very good and solid, but, like certain puddings, just a little dull. Personally, I like much better the notion of 'Thom's Works and Wanderings'. The eccentric Mr. Thom of Thom's Hill. Old Tom Thom, as his intimates used to call him. He spent ten years in Thibet organising the clarified butter industry on modern European lines, and was able to retire at thirty-six with a handsome fortune. The rest of his life he devoted to travel and ratiocination; here is the result." Mr. Scogan tapped the dummy books. "And now we come to the 'Tales of Knockespotch'. What a masterpiece and what a great man! Knockespotch knew how to write fiction. Ah, Denis, if you could only read Knockespotch you wouldn't be writing a novel about the wearisome development of a young man's character, you wouldn't be describing in endless, fastidious detail, cultured life in Chelsea and Bloomsbury and Hampstead. You would be trying to write a readable book. But then, alas! owing to the peculiar arrangement of our host's library, you never will read Knockespotch."

"Nobody could regret the fact more than I do," said Denis.

"It was Knockespotch," Mr. Scogan continued, "the great Knockespotch, who delivered us from the dreary tyranny of the realistic novel. My life, Knockespotch said, is not so long that I can afford to spend precious hours writing or reading descriptions of middle-class interiors. He said again, 'I am tired of seeing the human mind bogged in a social plenum; I prefer to paint it in a vacuum, freely and sportively bombinating.'"

"I say," said Gombauld, "Knockespotch was a little obscure sometimes, wasn't he?"

"He was," Mr. Scogan replied, "and with intention. It made him seem even profounder than he actually was. But it was only in his aphorisms that he was so dark and oracular. In his Tales he was always luminous. Oh, those Tales—those Tales! How shall I describe them? Fabulous characters shoot across his pages like gaily dressed performers on the trapeze. There are extraordinary adventures and still more extraordinary speculations. Intelligences and emotions, relieved of all the imbecile preoccupations of civilised life, move in intricate and subtle dances, crossing and recrossing, advancing, retreating, impinging. An immense erudition and an immense fancy go hand in hand. All the ideas of the present and of the past, on every possible subject, bob up among the Tales, smile gravely or grimace a caricature of themselves, then disappear to make place for something new. The verbal surface of his writing is rich and fantastically diversified. The wit is incessant. The..."

"But couldn't you give us a specimen," Denis broke in—"a concrete example?"

"Alas!" Mr. Scogan replied, "Knockespotch's great book is like the sword Excalibur. It remains struck fast in this door, awaiting the coming of a writer with genius enough to draw it forth. I am not even a writer, I am not so much as qualified to attempt the task. The extraction of Knockespotch from his wooden prison I leave, my dear Denis, to you."

"Thank you," said Denis.

CHAPTER XV.

In the time of the amiable Brantome," Mr. Scogan was saying, "every debutante at the French Court was invited to dine at the King's table, where she was served with wine in a handsome silver cup of Italian workmanship. It was no ordinary cup, this goblet of the debutantes; for, inside, it had been most curiously and ingeniously engraved with a series of very lively amorous scenes. With each draught that the young lady swallowed these engravings became increasingly visible, and the Court looked on with interest, every time she put her nose in the cup, to see whether she blushed at what the ebbing wine revealed. If the debutante blushed, they laughed at her for her innocence; if she did not, she was laughed at for being too knowing."

"Do you propose," asked Anne, "that the custom should be revived at Buckingham Palace?"

"I do not," said Mr. Scogan. "I merely quoted the anecdote as an illustration of the customs, so genially frank, of the sixteenth century. I might have quoted other anecdotes to show that the customs of the seventeenth and eighteenth, of the fifteenth and fourteenth centuries, and indeed of every other century, from the time of Hammurabi onward, were equally genial and equally frank. The only century in which customs were not characterised by the same cheerful openness was the nineteenth, of blessed memory. It was the astonishing exception. And yet, with what one must suppose was a deliberate disregard of history, it looked upon its horribly pregnant silences as normal and natural and right; the frankness of the previous fifteen or twenty thousand years was considered abnormal and perverse. It was a curious phenomenon."

"I entirely agree." Mary panted with excitement in her effort to bring out what she had to say. "Havelock Ellis says..."

Mr. Scogan, like a policeman arresting the flow of traffic, held up his hand. "He does; I know. And that brings me to my next point: the nature of the reaction."

"Havelock Ellis..."

"The reaction, when it came—and we may say roughly that it set in a little before the beginning of this century—the reaction was to openness, but not to the same openness as had reigned in the earlier ages. It was to a scientific openness, not to the jovial frankness of the past, that we returned. The whole question of

Amour became a terribly serious one. Earnest young men wrote in the public prints that from this time forth it would be impossible ever again to make a joke of any sexual matter. Professors wrote thick books in which sex was sterilised and dissected. It has become customary for serious young women, like Mary, to discuss, with philosophic calm, matters of which the merest hint would have sufficed to throw the youth of the sixties into a delirium of amorous excitement. It is all very estimable, no doubt. But still"—Mr. Scogan sighed.—"I for one should like to see, mingled with this scientific ardour, a little more of the jovial spirit of Rabelais and Chaucer."

"I entirely disagree with you," said Mary. "Sex isn't a laughing matter; it's serious."

"Perhaps," answered Mr. Scogan, "perhaps I'm an obscene old man. For I must confess that I cannot always regard it as wholly serious."

"But I tell you..." began Mary furiously. Her face had flushed with excitement. Her cheeks were the cheeks of a great ripe peach.

"Indeed," Mr. Scogan continued, "it seems to me one of few permanently and everlastingly amusing subjects that exist. Amour is the one human activity of any importance in which laughter and pleasure preponderate, if ever so slightly, over misery and pain."

"I entirely disagree," said Mary. There was a silence.

Anne looked at her watch. "Nearly a quarter to eight," she said. "I wonder when Ivor will turn up." She got up from her deck-chair and, leaning her elbows on the balustrade of the terrace, looked out over the valley and towards the farther hills. Under the level evening light the architecture of the land revealed itself. The deep shadows, the bright contrasting lights gave the hills a new solidity. Irregularities of the surface, unsuspected before, were picked out with light and shade. The grass, the corn, the foliage of trees were stippled with intricate shadows. The surface of things had taken on a marvellous enrichment.

"Look!" said Anne suddenly, and pointed. On the opposite side of the valley, at the crest of the ridge, a cloud of dust flushed by the sunlight to rosy gold was moving rapidly along the sky-line. "It's Ivor. One can tell by the speed."

The dust cloud descended into the valley and was lost. A horn with the voice of a sea-lion made itself heard, approaching. A minute later Ivor came leaping round the corner of the house. His hair waved in the wind of his own speed; he laughed as he saw them.

"Anne, darling," he cried, and embraced her, embraced Mary, very nearly embraced Mr. Scogan. "Well, here I am. I've come with incredulous speed." Ivor's vocabulary was rich, but a little erratic. "I'm not late for dinner, am I?" He hoisted himself up on to the balustrade, and sat there, kicking his heels. With one arm he embraced a large stone flower-pot, leaning his head sideways against its hard and lichenous flanks in an attitude of trustful affection. He had brown, wavy hair, and his eyes were of a very brilliant, pale, improbable blue. His head was narrow, his face thin and rather long, his nose aquiline. In old age—though it was difficult to imagine Ivor old—he might grow to have an Iron Ducal grimness. But now, at twenty-six, it was not the structure of his face that impressed one; it was its expression. That was charming and vivacious, and his smile was an irradiation. He was forever moving, restlessly and rapidly, but with an engaging gracefulness. His frail and slender body seemed to be fed by a spring of inexhaustible energy.

"No, you're not late."

"You're in time to answer a question," said Mr. Scogan. "We were arguing whether Amour were a serious matter or no. What do you think? Is it serious?"

"Serious?" echoed Ivor. "Most certainly."

"I told you so," cried Mary triumphantly.

"But in what sense serious?" Mr. Scogan asked.

"I mean as an occupation. One can go on with it without ever getting bored."

"I see," said Mr. Scogan. "Perfectly."

"One can occupy oneself with it," Ivor continued, "always and everywhere. Women are always wonderfully the same. Shapes vary a little, that's all. In Spain"—with his free hand he described a series of ample curves—"one can't pass them on the stairs. In England"—he put the tip of his forefinger against the tip of his thumb and, lowering his hand, drew out this circle into an imaginary cylinder—"In England they're tubular. But their sentiments are always the same. At least, I've always found it so."

"I'm delighted to hear it," said Mr. Scogan.

CHAPTER XVI.

The ladies had left the room and the port was circulating. Mr. Scogan filled his glass, passed on the decanter, and, leaning back in his chair, looked about him for a moment in silence. The conversation rippled idly round him, but he disregarded it; he was smiling at some private joke. Gombauld noticed his smile.

"What's amusing you?" he asked.

"I was just looking at you all, sitting round this table," said Mr. Scogan.

"Are we as comic as all that?"

"Not at all," Mr. Scogan answered politely. "I was merely amused by my own speculations."

"And what were they?"

"The idlest, the most academic of speculations. I was looking at you one by one and trying to imagine which of the first six Caesars you would each resemble, if you were given the opportunity of behaving like a Caesar. The Caesars are one of my touchstones," Mr. Scogan explained. "They are characters functioning, so to speak, in the void. They are human beings developed to their logical conclusions. Hence their unequalled value as a touchstone, a standard. When I meet someone for the first time, I ask myself this question: Given the Caesarean environment, which of the Caesars would this person resemble—Julius, Augustus, Tiberius, Caligula, Claudius, Nero? I take each trait of character, each mental and emotional bias, each little oddity, and magnify them a thousand times. The resulting image gives me his Caesarean formula."

"And which of the Caesars do you resemble?" asked Gombauld.

"I am potentially all of them," Mr. Scogan replied, "all—with the possible exception of Claudius, who was much too stupid to be a development of anything in my character. The seeds of Julius's courage and compelling energy, of Augustus's prudence, of the libidinousness and cruelty of Tiberius, of Caligula's folly, of Nero's artistic genius and enormous vanity, are all within me. Given the opportunities, I might have been something fabulous. But circumstances were against me. I was born and brought up in a country rectory; I passed my youth doing a great deal of utterly senseless hard work for a very little money. The result is that now, in middle age, I am the poor thing that I am. But perhaps it is as well. Perhaps, too, it's as well that Denis hasn't been permitted to flower into a little Nero, and that Ivor remains only potentially a Caligula. Yes, it's better so, no doubt. But it would have been more amusing, as a spectacle, if they had had the chance to develop, untrammelled, the full horror of their potentialities. It would have been pleasant and interesting to watch their tics and foibles and little vices swelling and burgeoning and blossoming into enormous and fantastic flowers of cruelty and pride and lewdness and avarice. The Caesarean environment makes the Caesar, as the special food and the queenly cell make the queen bee. We differ from the bees in so far that, given the proper food, they can be sure of making a queen every time. With us there is no such certainty; out of every ten men placed in the Caesarean environment one will be temperamentally good, or intelligent, or great. The rest will blossom into Caesars; he will not. Seventy and eighty years ago simple-minded people, reading of the exploits of the Bourbons in South Italy, cried out in amazement: To think that such things should be happening in the nineteenth century! And a few years since we too were astonished to find that in our still more astonishing twentieth century, unhappy blackamoors on the Congo and the Amazon were being treated as English serfs were treated in the time of Stephen. To-day we are no longer surprised at these things. The Black and Tans harry Ireland, the Poles maltreat the Silesians, the bold Fascisti slaughter their poorer countrymen: we take it all for granted. Since the war we wonder at nothing. We have created a Caesarean environment and a host of little Caesars has sprung up. What could be more natural?"

Mr. Scogan drank off what was left of his port and refilled the glass.

"At this very moment," he went on, "the most frightful horrors are taking place in every corner of the world. People are being crushed, slashed, disembowelled, mangled; their dead bodies rot and their eyes decay with the rest. Screams of pain and fear go pulsing through the air at the rate of eleven hundred feet per second. After travelling for three seconds they are perfectly inaudible. These are distressing facts; but do we enjoy life any the less because of them? Most certainly we do not. We feel sympathy, no doubt; we represent to ourselves imaginatively the sufferings of nations and individuals and we deplore them. But, after all, what are sympathy and imagination? Precious little, unless the person for whom we feel sympathy happens to be closely involved in our affections; and even then they don't go very far. And a good thing too; for if one had an imagination vivid enough and a sympathy sufficiently sensitive really to comprehend and to feel the sufferings of other people, one would never have a moment's peace of mind. A really sympathetic race would not so much as know the meaning of happiness. But luckily, as I've already said, we aren't a sympathetic race. At the beginning of the war I used to think I really suffered, through imagination and sympathy, with those who physically suffered. But after a month or two I had to admit that, honestly, I didn't. And yet I think I have a more vivid imagination than most. One is always alone in suffering; the fact is depressing when one happens to be the sufferer, but it makes pleasure possible for the rest of the world."

There was a pause. Henry Wimbush pushed back his chair.

"I think perhaps we ought to go and join the ladies," he said.

CHAPTER XVI.

"So do I," said Ivor, jumping up with alacrity. He turned to Mr. Scogan. "Fortunately," he said, "we can share our pleasures. We are not always condemned to be happy alone."

CHAPTER XVII.

Ivor brought his hands down with a bang on to the final chord of his rhapsody. There was just a hint in that triumphant harmony that the seventh had been struck along with the octave by the thumb of the left hand; but the general effect of splendid noise emerged clearly enough. Small details matter little so long as the general effect is good. And, besides, that hint of the seventh was decidedly modern. He turned round in his seat and tossed the hair back out of his eyes.

"There," he said. "That's the best I can do for you, I'm afraid."

Murmurs of applause and gratitude were heard, and Mary, her large china eyes fixed on the performer, cried out aloud, "Wonderful!" and gasped for new breath as though she were suffocating.

Nature and fortune had vied with one another in heaping on Ivor Lombard all their choicest gifts. He had wealth and he was perfectly independent. He was good looking, possessed an irresistible charm of manner, and was the hero of more amorous successes than he could well remember. His accomplishments were extraordinary for their number and variety. He had a beautiful untrained tenor voice; he could improvise, with a startling brilliance, rapidly and loudly, on the piano. He was a good amateur medium and telepathist, and had a considerable first-hand knowledge of the next world. He could write rhymed verses with an extraordinary rapidity. For painting symbolical pictures he had a dashing style, and if the drawing was sometimes a little weak, the colour was always pyrotechnical. He excelled in amateur theatricals and, when occasion offered, he could cook with genius. He resembled Shakespeare in knowing little Latin and less Greek. For a mind like his, education seemed supererogatory. Training would only have destroyed his natural aptitudes.

"Let's go out into the garden," Ivor suggested. "It's a wonderful night."

"Thank you," said Mr. Scogan, "but I for one prefer these still more wonderful arm-chairs." His pipe had begun to bubble oozily every time he pulled at it. He was perfectly happy.

Henry Wimbush was also happy. He looked for a moment over his pince-nez in Ivor's direction and then, without saying anything, returned to the grimy little sixteenth-century account books which were now his favourite reading. He knew more about Sir Ferdinando's household expenses than about his own.

CHAPTER XVII.

The outdoor party, enrolled under Ivor's banner, consisted of Anne, Mary, Denis, and, rather unexpectedly, Jenny. Outside it was warm and dark; there was no moon. They walked up and down the terrace, and Ivor sang a Neapolitan song: "Stretti, stretti"—close, close—with something about the little Spanish girl to follow. The atmosphere began to palpitate. Ivor put his arm round Anne's waist, dropped his head sideways onto her shoulder, and in that position walked on, singing as he walked. It seemed the easiest, the most natural, thing in the world. Denis wondered why he had never done it. He hated Ivor.

"Let's go down to the pool," said Ivor. He disengaged his embrace and turned round to shepherd his little flock. They made their way along the side of the house to the entrance of the yew-tree walk that led down to the lower garden. Between the blank precipitous wall of the house and the tall yew trees the path was a chasm of impenetrable gloom. Somewhere there were steps down to the right, a gap in the yew hedge. Denis, who headed the party, groped his way cautiously; in this darkness, one had an irrational fear of yawning precipices, of horrible spiked obstructions. Suddenly from behind him he heard a shrill, startled, "Oh!" and then a sharp, dry concussion that might have been the sound of a slap. After that, Jenny's voice was heard pronouncing, "I am going back to the house." Her tone was decided, and even as she pronounced the words she was melting away into the darkness. The incident, whatever it had been, was closed. Denis resumed his forward groping. From somewhere behind Ivor began to sing again, softly:

"Phillis plus avare que tendre
Ne gagnant rien à refuser,
Un jour exigea à Silvandre
Trente moutons pour un baiser."

The melody drooped and climbed again with a kind of easy languor; the warm darkness seemed to pulse like blood about them.

"Le lendemain, nouvelle affaire:
Pour le berger le troc fut bon..."

"Here are the steps," cried Denis. He guided his companions over the danger, and in a moment they had the turf of the yew-tree walk under their feet. It was lighter here, or at least it was just perceptibly less dark; for the yew walk was wider than the path that had led them under the lea of the house. Looking up, they could see between the high black hedges a strip of sky and a few stars.

"Car il obtint de la bergere..."

Went on Ivor, and then interrupted himself to shout, "I'm going to run down," and he was off, full speed, down the invisible slope, singing unevenly as he went:

"Trente baisers pour un mouton."

The others followed. Denis shambled in the rear, vainly exhorting everyone to caution: the slope was steep, one might break one's neck. What was wrong with these people, he wondered? They had become like young kittens after a dose of cat-nip. He himself felt a certain kittenishness sporting within him; but it was, like all his emotions, rather a theoretical feeling; it did not overmasteringly seek to express itself in a practical demonstration of kittenishness.

"Be careful," he shouted once more, and hardly were the words out of his mouth when, thump! there was the sound of a heavy fall in front of him, followed by the long "F-f-f-f-f" of a breath indrawn with pain and afterwards by a very sincere, "Oo-ooh!" Denis was almost pleased; he had told them so, the idiots, and they wouldn't listen. He trotted down the slope towards the unseen sufferer.

Mary came down the hill like a runaway steam-engine. It was tremendously exciting, this blind rush through the dark; she felt she would never stop. But the ground grew level beneath her feet, her speed insensibly slackened, and suddenly she was caught by an extended arm and brought to an abrupt halt.

"Well," said Ivor as he tightened his embrace, "you're caught now, Anne."

She made an effort to release herself. "It's not Anne. It's Mary."

Ivor burst into a peal of amused laughter. "So it is!" he exclaimed. "I seem to be making nothing but floaters this evening. I've already made one with Jenny." He laughed again, and there was something so jolly about his laughter that Mary could not help laughing too. He did not remove his encircling arm, and somehow it was all so amusing and natural that Mary made no further attempt to escape from it. They walked along by the side of the pool, interlaced. Mary was too short for him to be able, with any comfort, to lay his head on her shoulder. He rubbed his cheek, caressed and caressing, against the thick, sleek mass of her hair. In a little while he began to sing again; the night trembled amorously to the sound of his voice. When he had finished he kissed her. Anne or Mary: Mary or Anne. It didn't seem to make much difference which it was. There were differences in detail, of course; but the general effect was the same; and, after all, the general effect was the important thing.

Denis made his way down the hill.

"Any damage done?" he called out.

"Is that you, Denis? I've hurt my ankle so—and my knee, and my hand. I'm all in pieces."

"My poor Anne," he said. "But then," he couldn't help adding, "it was silly to start running downhill in the dark."

"Ass!" she retorted in a tone of tearful irritation; "of course it was."

He sat down beside her on the grass, and found himself breathing the faint, delicious atmosphere of perfume that she carried always with her.

"Light a match," she commanded. "I want to look at my wounds."

He felt in his pockets for the match-box. The light spurted and then grew steady. Magically, a little universe had been created, a world of colours and forms—Anne's face, the shimmering orange of her dress, her white, bare arms, a patch of green turf—and round about a darkness that had become solid and utterly blind. Anne held out her hands; both were green and earthy with her fall, and the left exhibited two or three red abrasions.

CHAPTER XVII.

"Not so bad," she said. But Denis was terribly distressed, and his emotion was intensified when, looking up at her face, he saw that the trace of tears, involuntary tears of pain, lingered on her eyelashes. He pulled out his handkerchief and began to wipe away the dirt from the wounded hand. The match went out; it was not worth while to light another. Anne allowed herself to be attended to, meekly and gratefully. "Thank you," she said, when he had finished cleaning and bandaging her hand; and there was something in her tone that made him feel that she had lost her superiority over him, that she was younger than he, had become, suddenly, almost a child. He felt tremendously large and protective. The feeling was so strong that instinctively he put his arm about her. She drew closer, leaned against him, and so they sat in silence. Then, from below, soft but wonderfully clear through the still darkness, they heard the sound of Ivor's singing. He was going on with his half-finished song:

"Le lendemain Phillis plus tendre,
Ne voulant deplaire au berger,
Fut trop heureuse de lui rendre
Trente moutons pour un baiser."

There was a rather prolonged pause. It was as though time were being allowed for the giving and receiving of a few of those thirty kisses. Then the voice sang on:

"Le lendemain Phillis peu sage
Aurait donne moutons et chien
Pour un baiser que le volage
À Lisette donnait pour rien."

The last note died away into an uninterrupted silence.

"Are you better?" Denis whispered. "Are you comfortable like this?"

She nodded a Yes to both questions.

"Trente moutons pour un baiser." The sheep, the woolly mutton—baa, baa, baa...? Or the shepherd? Yes, decidedly, he felt himself to be the shepherd now. He was the master, the protector. A wave of courage swelled through him, warm as wine. He turned his head, and began to kiss her face, at first rather randomly, then, with more precision, on the mouth.

Anne averted her head; he kissed the ear, the smooth nape that this movement presented him. "No," she protested; "no, Denis."

"Why not?"

"It spoils our friendship, and that was so jolly."

"Bosh!" said Denis.

She tried to explain. "Can't you see," she said, "it isn't...it isn't our stunt at all." It was true. Somehow she had never thought of Denis in the light of a man who might make love; she had never so much as conceived the possibilities of an amorous relationship with him. He was so absurdly young, so...so...she couldn't find the adjective, but she knew what she meant.

"Why isn't it our stunt?" asked Denis. "And, by the way, that's a horrible and inappropriate expression."

"Because it isn't."

"But if I say it is?"

"It makes no difference. I say it isn't."

"I shall make you say it is."

"All right, Denis. But you must do it another time. I must go in and get my ankle into hot water. It's beginning to swell."

Reasons of health could not be gainsaid. Denis got up reluctantly, and helped his companion to her feet. She took a cautious step. "Ooh!" She halted and leaned heavily on his arm.

"I'll carry you," Denis offered. He had never tried to carry a woman, but on the cinema it always looked an easy piece of heroism.

"You couldn't," said Anne.

"Of course I can." He felt larger and more protective than ever. "Put your arms round my neck," he ordered. She did so and, stooping, he picked her up under the knees and lifted her from the ground. Good heavens, what a weight! He took five staggering steps up the slope, then almost lost his equilibrium, and had to deposit his burden suddenly, with something of a bump.

Anne was shaking with laughter. "I said you couldn't, my poor Denis."

"I can," said Denis, without conviction. "I'll try again."

"It's perfectly sweet of you to offer, but I'd rather walk, thanks." She laid her hand on his shoulder and, thus supported, began to limp slowly up the hill.

"My poor Denis!" she repeated, and laughed again. Humiliated, he was silent. It seemed incredible that, only two minutes ago, he should have been holding her in his embrace, kissing her. Incredible. She was helpless then, a child. Now she had regained all her superiority; she was once more the far-off being, desired and unassailable. Why had he been such a fool as to suggest that carrying stunt? He reached the house in a state of the profoundest depression.

He helped Anne upstairs, left her in the hands of a maid, and came down again to the drawing-room. He was surprised to find them all sitting just where he had left them. He had expected that, somehow, everything would be quite different—it seemed such a prodigious time since he went away. All silent and all damned, he reflected, as he looked at them. Mr. Scogan's pipe still wheezed; that was the only sound. Henry Wimbush was still deep in his account books; he had just made the discovery that Sir Ferdinando was in the habit of eating oysters the whole summer through, regardless of the absence of the justifying R. Gombauld, in horn-rimmed spectacles, was reading. Jenny was mysteriously scribbling in her red notebook. And, seated in her favourite arm-chair at the corner of the hearth, Priscilla was looking through a pile of drawings. One by one she held them out at arm's length and, throwing back her mountainous orange head, looked long and attentively through half-closed eyelids. She wore a pale sea-green dress; on the slope of her mauve-powdered decolletage diamonds twinkled. An immensely long cigarette-holder projected at an angle from her face. Diamonds were embedded in her high-piled coiffure; they glittered every time she moved. It was a batch of Ivor's drawings—sketches of Spirit Life, made in the course of tranced tours through the other world. On the back of each sheet descriptive titles were written: "Portrait of an Angel, 15th March '20;" "Astral Beings at Play, 3rd December '19;" "A Party of Souls on their Way to a Higher Sphere, 21st May '21." Before examining the drawing on the obverse of each sheet, she turned it over to read the title. Try as she could—and she tried hard—Priscilla had never seen a vision or succeeded in establishing any communication with the Spirit World. She had to be content with the reported experiences of others.

"What have you done with the rest of your party?" she asked, looking up as Denis entered the room.

He explained. Anne had gone to bed, Ivor and Mary were still in the garden. He selected a book and a comfortable chair, and tried, as far as the disturbed state of his mind would permit him, to compose himself for an evening's reading. The lamplight was utterly serene; there was no movement save the stir of Priscilla among her papers. All silent and all damned, Denis repeated to himself, all silent and all damned...

It was nearly an hour later when Ivor and Mary made their appearance.

"We waited to see the moon rise," said Ivor.

"It was gibbous, you know," Mary explained, very technical and scientific.

"It was so beautiful down in the garden! The trees, the scent of the flowers, the stars..." Ivor waved his arms. "And when the moon came up, it was really too much. It made me burst into tears." He sat down at the piano and opened the lid.

"There were a great many meteorites," said Mary to anyone who would listen. "The earth must just be coming into the summer shower of them. In July and August..."

But Ivor had already begun to strike the keys. He played the garden, the stars, the scent of flowers, the rising moon. He even put in a nightingale that was not there. Mary looked on and listened with parted lips. The others pursued their occupations, without appearing to be seriously disturbed. On this very July day, exactly three hundred and fifty years ago, Sir Ferdinando had eaten seven dozen oysters. The discovery of this fact gave Henry Wimbush a peculiar pleasure. He had a natural piety which made him delight in the celebration of memorial feasts. The three hundred and fiftieth anniversary of the seven dozen oysters...He wished he had known before dinner; he would have ordered champagne.

On her way to bed Mary paid a call. The light was out in Anne's room, but she was not yet asleep.

"Why didn't you come down to the garden with us?" Mary asked.

"I fell down and twisted my ankle. Denis helped me home."

Mary was full of sympathy. Inwardly, too, she was relieved to find Anne's non-appearance so simply accounted for. She had been vaguely suspicious, down there in the garden—suspicious of what, she hardly knew; but there had seemed to be something a little louche in the way she had suddenly found herself alone with Ivor. Not that she minded, of course; far from it. But she didn't like the idea that perhaps she was the victim of a put-up job.

"I do hope you'll be better to-morrow," she said, and she commiserated with Anne on all she had missed—the garden, the stars, the scent of flowers, the meteorites through whose summer shower the earth was now passing, the rising moon and its gibbosity. And then they had had such interesting conversation. What about? About almost everything. Nature, art, science, poetry, the stars, spiritualism, the relations of the sexes, music, religion. Ivor, she thought, had an interesting mind.

The two young ladies parted affectionately.

CHAPTER XVIII.

The nearest Roman Catholic church was upwards of twenty miles away. Ivor, who was punctilious in his devotions, came down early to breakfast and had his car at the door, ready to start, by a quarter to ten. It was a smart, expensive-looking machine, enamelled a pure lemon yellow and upholstered in emerald green leather. There were two seats—three if you squeezed tightly enough—and their occupants were protected from wind, dust, and weather by a glazed sedan that rose, an elegant eighteenth-century hump, from the midst of the body of the car.

Mary had never been to a Roman Catholic service, thought it would be an interesting experience, and, when the car moved off through the great gates of the courtyard, she was occupying the spare seat in the sedan. The sea-lion horn roared, faintlier, faintlier, and they were gone.

In the parish church of Crome Mr. Bodiham preached on 1 Kings vi. 18: "And the cedar of the house within was carved with knops"—a sermon of immediately local interest. For the past two years the problem of the War Memorial had exercised the minds of all those in Crome who had enough leisure, or mental energy, or party spirit to think of such things. Henry Wimbush was all for a library—a library of local literature, stocked with county histories, old maps of the district, monographs on the local antiquities, dialect dictionaries, handbooks of the local geology and natural history. He liked to think of the villagers, inspired by such reading, making up parties of a Sunday afternoon to look for fossils and flint arrow-heads. The villagers themselves favoured the idea of a memorial reservoir and water supply. But the busiest and most articulate party followed Mr. Bodiham in demanding something religious in character—a second lich-gate, for example, a stained-glass window, a monument of marble, or, if possible, all three. So far, however, nothing had been done, partly because the memorial committee had never been able to agree, partly for the more cogent reason that too little money had been subscribed to carry out any of the proposed schemes. Every three or four months Mr. Bodiham preached a sermon on the subject. His last had been delivered in March; it was high time that his congregation had a fresh reminder.

"And the cedar of the house within was carved with knops."

Mr. Bodiham touched lightly on Solomon's temple. From thence he passed to temples and churches in general. What were the characteristics of these buildings dedicated to God? Obviously, the fact of their, from a human point of view, complete uselessness. They were unpractical buildings "carved with knops." Solomon might have built a library—indeed, what could be more to the taste of the world's wisest man? He might have dug a reservoir—what more useful in a parched city like Jerusalem? He did neither; he built a house all carved with knops, useless and unpractical. Why? Because he was dedicating the work to God. There had been much talk in Crome about the proposed War Memorial. A War Memorial was, in its very nature, a work dedicated to God. It was a token of thankfulness that the first stage in the culminating world-war had been crowned by the triumph of righteousness; it was at the same time a visibly embodied supplication that God might not long delay the Advent which alone could bring the final peace. A library, a reservoir? Mr. Bodiham scornfully and indignantly condemned the idea. These were works dedicated to man, not to God. As a War Memorial they were totally unsuitable. A lich-gate had been suggested. This was an object which answered perfectly to the definition of a War Memorial: a useless work dedicated to God and carved with knops. One lich-gate, it was true, already existed. But nothing would be easier than to make a second entrance into the churchyard; and a second entrance would need a second gate. Other suggestions had been made. Stained-glass windows, a monument of marble. Both these were admirable, especially the latter. It was high time that the War Memorial was erected. It might soon be too late. At any moment, like a thief in the night, God might come. Meanwhile a difficulty stood in the way. Funds were inadequate. All should subscribe according to their means. Those who had lost relations in the war might reasonably be expected to subscribe a sum equal to that which they would have had to pay in funeral expenses if the relative had died while at home. Further delay was disastrous. The War Memorial must be built at once. He appealed to the patriotism and the Christian sentiments of all his hearers.

Henry Wimbush walked home thinking of the books he would present to the War Memorial Library, if ever it came into existence. He took the path through the fields; it was pleasanter than the road. At the first stile a group of village boys, loutish young fellows all dressed in the hideous ill-fitting black which makes a funeral of every English Sunday and holiday, were assembled, drearily guffawing as they smoked their cigarettes. They made way for Henry Wimbush, touching their caps as he passed. He returned their salute; his bowler and face were one in their unruffled gravity.

In Sir Ferdinando's time, he reflected, in the time of his son, Sir Julius, these young men would have had their Sunday diversions even at Crome, remote and rustic Crome. There would have been archery, skittles, dancing—social amusements in which they would have partaken as members of a conscious community. Now they had nothing, nothing except Mr. Bodiham's forbidding Boys' Club and the rare dances and concerts organised by himself. Boredom or the urban pleasures of the county metropolis were the alternatives that presented themselves to these poor youths. Country pleasures were no more; they had been stamped out by the Puritans.

CHAPTER XVIII.

In Manningham's Diary for 1600 there was a queer passage, he remembered, a very queer passage. Certain magistrates in Berkshire, Puritan magistrates, had had wind of a scandal. One moonlit summer night they had ridden out with their posse and there, among the hills, they had come upon a company of men and women, dancing, stark naked, among the sheepcotes. The magistrates and their men had ridden their horses into the crowd. How self-conscious the poor people must suddenly have felt, how helpless without their clothes against armed and booted horsemen! The dancers were arrested, whipped, gaoled, set in the stocks; the moonlight dance is never danced again. What old, earthy, Panic rite came to extinction here? he wondered. Who knows?—perhaps their ancestors had danced like this in the moonlight ages before Adam and Eve were so much as thought of. He liked to think so. And now it was no more. These weary young men, if they wanted to dance, would have to bicycle six miles to the town. The country was desolate, without life of its own, without indigenous pleasures. The pious magistrates had snuffed out for ever a little happy flame that had burned from the beginning of time.

"And as on Tullia's tomb one lamp burned clear,
Unchanged for fifteen hundred year..."

He repeated the lines to himself, and was desolated to think of all the murdered past.

CHAPTER XIX.

Henry Wimbush's long cigar burned aromatically. The "History of Crome" lay on his knee; slowly he turned over the pages.

"I can't decide what episode to read you to-night," he said thoughtfully. "Sir Ferdinando's voyages are not without interest. Then, of course, there's his son, Sir Julius. It was he who suffered from the delusion that his perspiration engendered flies; it drove him finally to suicide. Or there's Sir Cyprian." He turned the pages more rapidly. "Or Sir Henry. Or Sir George...No, I'm inclined to think I won't read about any of these."

"But you must read something," insisted Mr. Scogan, taking his pipe out of his mouth.

"I think I shall read about my grandfather," said Henry Wimbush, "and the events that led up to his marriage with the eldest daughter of the last Sir Ferdinando."

"Good," said Mr. Scogan. "We are listening."

"Before I begin reading," said Henry Wimbush, looking up from the book and taking off the pince-nez which he had just fitted to his nose—"before I begin, I must say a few preliminary words about Sir Ferdinando, the last of the Lapiths. At the death of the virtuous and unfortunate Sir Hercules, Ferdinando found himself in possession of the family fortune, not a little increased by his father's temperance and thrift; he applied himself forthwith to the task of spending it, which he did in an ample and jovial fashion. By the time he was forty he had eaten and, above all, drunk and loved away about half his capital, and would infallibly have soon got rid of the rest in the same manner, if he had not had the good fortune to become so madly enamoured of the Rector's daughter as to make a proposal of marriage. The young lady accepted him, and in less than a year had become the absolute mistress of Crome and her husband. An extraordinary reformation made itself apparent in Sir Ferdinando's character. He grew regular and economical in his habits; he even became temperate, rarely drinking more than a bottle and a half of port at a sitting. The waning fortune of the Lapiths began once more to wax, and that in despite of the hard times (for Sir Ferdinando married in 1809 in the height of the Napoleonic Wars). A prosperous and dignified old age, cheered by the spectacle of his children's growth and happiness—for Lady Lapith had already borne him three daughters, and there seemed no good reason why she should not bear many more of them, and sons as well—a patriarchal decline into the family vault, seemed now to be Sir Ferdinando's enviable destiny. But Providence willed otherwise. To Napoleon, cause already of such infinite mischief, was due, though perhaps indirectly, the untimely and violent death which put a period to this reformed existence.

"Sir Ferdinando, who was above all things a patriot, had adopted, from the earliest days of the conflict with the French, his own peculiar method of celebrating our victories. When the happy news reached London, it was his custom to purchase immediately a large store of liquor and, taking a place on whichever of the outgoing coaches he happened to light on first, to drive through the country proclaiming the good news to all he met on the road and dispensing it, along with the liquor, at every stopping-place to all who cared to listen or drink. Thus, after the Nile, he had driven as far as Edinburgh; and later, when the coaches, wreathed with laurel for triumph, with cypress for mourning, were setting out with the news of Nelson's victory and death, he sat through all a chilly October night on the box of the Norwich 'Meteor' with a nautical keg of rum on his knees and two cases of old brandy under the seat. This genial custom was one of the many habits which he abandoned on his marriage. The victories in the Peninsula, the retreat from Moscow, Leipzig, and the abdication of the tyrant all went uncelebrated. It so happened, however, that in the summer of 1815 Sir Ferdinando was staying for a few weeks in the capital. There had been a succession of anxious, doubtful days; then came the glorious news of Waterloo. It was too much for Sir Ferdinando; his joyous youth awoke again within him. He hurried to his wine merchant and bought a dozen bottles of 1760 brandy. The Bath coach was on the point of starting; he bribed his way on to the box and, seated in glory beside the driver, proclaimed aloud the downfall of the Corsican bandit and passed about the warm liquid joy. They clattered through Uxbridge, Slough, Maidenhead. Sleeping Reading was awakened by the great news. At Didcot one of the ostlers was so much overcome by patriotic emotions and the 1760 brandy that he found it impossible to do up the buckles of the harness. The night began to grow chilly, and Sir Ferdinando found that it was not enough to take a nip at every stage: to keep up his vital warmth he was compelled to drink between the stages as well. They were approaching Swindon. The coach was travelling at a dizzy speed—six miles in the last half-hour—when, without having manifested the slightest premonitory symptom of unsteadiness, Sir Ferdinando suddenly toppled sideways off his seat and fell, head foremost, into the road. An unpleasant jolt awakened the slumbering passengers. The coach was brought to a standstill; the guard ran back with a light. He found Sir Ferdinando still alive, but unconscious; blood was oozing from his mouth. The back wheels of the coach had passed over his body, breaking most of his ribs and both arms. His skull was fractured in two places. They picked him up, but he was dead before they reached the next stage. So perished Sir Ferdinando, a victim to his own patriotism. Lady Lapith did not marry again, but determined to devote the rest of her life to the well-being of her three children—Georgiana, now five years old, and Emmeline and Caroline, twins of two."

Henry Wimbush paused, and once more put on his pince-nez. "So much by way of introduction," he said. "Now I can begin to read about my grandfather."

"One moment," said Mr. Scogan, "till I've refilled my pipe."

Mr. Wimbush waited. Seated apart in a corner of the room, Ivor was showing Mary his sketches of Spirit Life. They spoke together in whispers.

Mr. Scogan had lighted his pipe again. "Fire away," he said.

Henry Wimbush fired away.

"It was in the spring of 1833 that my grandfather, George Wimbush, first made the acquaintance of the 'three lovely Lapiths,' as they were always called. He was then a young man of twenty-two, with curly yellow hair and a smooth pink face that was the mirror of his youthful and ingenuous mind. He had been educated at Harrow and Christ Church, he enjoyed hunting and all other field sports, and, though his circumstances were comfortable to the verge of affluence, his pleasures were temperate and innocent. His father, an East Indian merchant, had destined him for a political career, and had gone to considerable expense in acquiring a pleasant little Cornish borough as a twenty-first birthday gift for his son. He was justly indignant when, on the very eve of George's majority, the Reform Bill of 1832 swept the borough out of existence. The inauguration of George's political career had to be postponed. At the time he got to know the lovely Lapiths he was waiting; he was not at all impatient.

"The lovely Lapiths did not fail to impress him. Georgiana, the eldest, with her black ringlets, her flashing eyes, her noble aquiline profile, her swan-like neck, and sloping shoulders, was orientally dazzling; and the twins, with their delicately turned-up noses, their blue eyes, and chestnut hair, were an identical pair of ravishingly English charmers.

"Their conversation at this first meeting proved, however, to be so forbidding that, but for the invincible attraction exercised by their beauty, George would never have had the courage to follow up the acquaintance. The twins, looking up their noses at him with an air of languid superiority, asked him what he thought of the latest French poetry and whether he liked the 'Indiana' of George Sand. But what was almost worse was the question with which Georgiana opened her conversation with him. 'In music,' she asked, leaning forward and fixing him with her large dark eyes, 'are you a classicist or a transcendentalist?' George did not lose his presence of mind. He had enough appreciation of music to know that he hated anything classical, and so, with a promptitude which did him credit, he replied, 'I am a transcendentalist.' Georgiana smiled bewitchingly. 'I am glad,' she said; 'so am I. You went to hear Paganini last week, of course. "The prayer of Moses"—ah!' She closed her eyes. 'Do you know anything more transcendental than that?' 'No,' said George, 'I don't.' He hesitated, was about to go on speaking, and then decided that after all it would be wiser not to say—what was in fact true—that he had enjoyed above all Paganini's Farmyard Imitations. The man had made his fiddle bray like an ass, cluck like a hen, grunt, squeal, bark, neigh, quack, bellow, and growl; that last item, in George's estimation, had almost compensated for the tediousness of the rest of the concert. He smiled with pleasure at the thought of it.

CHAPTER XIX.

Yes, decidedly, he was no classicist in music; he was a thoroughgoing transcendentalist.

"George followed up this first introduction by paying a call on the young ladies and their mother, who occupied, during the season, a small but elegant house in the neighbourhood of Berkeley Square. Lady Lapith made a few discreet inquiries, and having found that George's financial position, character, and family were all passably good, she asked him to dine. She hoped and expected that her daughters would all marry into the peerage; but, being a prudent woman, she knew it was advisable to prepare for all contingencies. George Wimbush, she thought, would make an excellent second string for one of the twins.

"At this first dinner, George's partner was Emmeline. They talked of Nature. Emmeline protested that to her high mountains were a feeling and the hum of human cities torture. George agreed that the country was very agreeable, but held that London during the season also had its charms. He noticed with surprise and a certain solicitous distress that Miss Emmeline's appetite was poor, that it didn't, in fact, exist. Two spoonfuls of soup, a morsel of fish, no bird, no meat, and three grapes—that was her whole dinner. He looked from time to time at her two sisters; Georgiana and Caroline seemed to be quite as abstemious. They waved away whatever was offered them with an expression of delicate disgust, shutting their eyes and averting their faces from the proffered dish, as though the lemon sole, the duck, the loin of veal, the trifle, were objects revolting to the sight and smell. George, who thought the dinner capital, ventured to comment on the sisters' lack of appetite.

"'Pray, don't talk to me of eating,' said Emmeline, drooping like a sensitive plant. 'We find it so coarse, so unspiritual, my sisters and I. One can't think of one's soul while one is eating.'

"George agreed; one couldn't. 'But one must live,' he said.

"'Alas!' Emmeline sighed. 'One must. Death is very beautiful, don't you think?' She broke a corner off a piece of toast and began to nibble at it languidly. 'But since, as you say, one must live...' She made a little gesture of resignation. 'Luckily a very little suffices to keep one alive.' She put down her corner of toast half eaten.

"George regarded her with some surprise. She was pale, but she looked extraordinarily healthy, he thought; so did her sisters. Perhaps if you were really spiritual you needed less food. He, clearly, was not spiritual.

"After this he saw them frequently. They all liked him, from Lady Lapith downwards. True, he was not very romantic or poetical; but he was such a pleasant, unpretentious, kind-hearted young man, that one couldn't help liking him. For his part, he thought them wonderful, wonderful, especially Georgiana. He enveloped them all in a warm, protective affection. For they needed protection; they were altogether too frail, too spiritual for this world. They never ate, they were always pale, they often complained of fever, they talked much and lovingly of death, they frequently swooned. Georgiana was the most ethereal of all; of the three she ate least, swooned most often, talked most of death, and was the palest—with a pallor that was so startling as to appear positively artificial. At any moment, it seemed, she might loose her precarious hold on this material world and become all spirit. To George the thought was a continual agony. If she were to die...

"She contrived, however, to live through the season, and that in spite of the numerous balls, routs, and other parties of pleasure which, in company with the rest of the lovely trio, she never failed to attend. In the middle of July the whole household moved down to the country. George was invited to spend the month of August at Crome.

"The house-party was distinguished; in the list of visitors figured the names of two marriageable young men of title. George had hoped that country air, repose, and natural surroundings might have restored to the three sisters their appetites and the roses of their cheeks. He was mistaken. For dinner, the first evening, Georgiana ate only an olive, two or three salted almonds, and half a peach. She was as pale as ever. During the meal she spoke of love.

"'True love,' she said, 'being infinite and eternal, can only be consummated in eternity. Indiana and Sir Rodolphe celebrated the mystic wedding of their souls by jumping into Niagara. Love is incompatible with life. The wish of two people who truly love one another is not to live together but to die together.'

"'Come, come, my dear,' said Lady Lapith, stout and practical. 'What would become of the next generation, pray, if all the world acted on your principles?'

"'Mamma!...' Georgiana protested, and dropped her eyes.

"'In my young days,' Lady Lapith went on, 'I should have been laughed out of countenance if I'd said a thing like that. But then in my young days souls weren't as fashionable as they are now and we didn't think death was at all poetical. It was just unpleasant.'

"'Mamma!...' Emmeline and Caroline implored in unison.

"'In my young days—' Lady Lapith was launched into her subject; nothing, it seemed, could stop her now. 'In my young days, if you didn't eat, people told you you needed a dose of rhubarb. Nowadays...'

"There was a cry; Georgiana had swooned sideways on to Lord Timpany's shoulder. It was a desperate expedient; but it was successful. Lady Lapith was stopped.

"The days passed in an uneventful round of pleasures. Of all the gay party George alone was unhappy. Lord Timpany was paying his court to Georgiana, and it was clear that he was not unfavourably received. George looked on, and his soul was a hell of jealousy and despair. The boisterous company of the young men became intolerable to him; he shrank from them, seeking gloom and solitude. One morning, having broken away from them on some vague pretext, he returned to the house alone. The young men were bathing in the pool below; their cries and laughter floated up to him, making the quiet house seem lonelier and more silent. The lovely sisters and their mamma still kept their chambers; they did not customarily make their appearance till luncheon, so that the male guests had the morning to themselves. George sat down in the hall and abandoned himself to thought.

"At any moment she might die; at any moment she might become Lady Timpany. It was terrible, terrible. If she died, then he would die too; he would go to seek her beyond the grave. If she became Lady Timpany...ah, then! The solution of the problem would not be so simple. If she became Lady Timpany: it was a horrible thought. But then suppose she were in love with Timpany—though it seemed incredible that anyone could be in love with Timpany—suppose her life depended on Timpany, suppose she couldn't live without him? He was fumbling his way along this clueless labyrinth of suppositions when the clock struck twelve. On the last stroke, like an automaton released by the turning clockwork, a little maid, holding a large covered tray, popped out of the door that led from the kitchen regions into the hall. From his deep arm-chair George watched her (himself, it was evident, unobserved) with an idle curiosity. She pattered across the room and came to a halt in front of what seemed a blank expense of panelling. She reached out her hand and, to George's extreme astonishment, a little door swung open, revealing the foot of a winding staircase. Turning sideways in order to get her tray through the narrow opening, the little maid darted in with a rapid crab-like motion. The door closed behind her with a click. A minute later it opened again and the maid, without her tray, hurried back across the hall and disappeared in the direction of the kitchen. George tried to recompose his thoughts, but an invincible curiosity drew his mind towards the hidden door, the staircase, the little maid. It was in vain he told himself that the matter was none of his business, that to explore the secrets of that surprising door, that mysterious staircase within, would be a piece of unforgivable rudeness and indiscretion. It was in vain; for five minutes he struggled heroically with his curiosity, but at the end of that time he found himself standing in front of the innocent sheet of panelling through which the little maid had disappeared. A glance sufficed to show him the position of the secret door—secret, he perceived, only to those who looked with a careless eye. It was just an ordinary door let in flush with the panelling. No latch nor handle betrayed its position, but an unobtrusive catch sunk in the wood invited the thumb. George was astonished that he had not noticed it before; now he had seen it, it was so obvious, almost as obvious as the cupboard door in the library with its lines of imitation shelves and its dummy books. He pulled back the catch and peeped inside. The staircase, of which the degrees were made not of stone but of blocks of ancient oak, wound up and out of sight. A slit-like window admitted the daylight; he was at the foot of the central tower, and the little window looked out over the terrace; they were still shouting and splashing in the pool below.

"George closed the door and went back to his seat. But his curiosity was not satisfied. Indeed, this partial satisfaction had but whetted its appetite. Where did the staircase lead? What was the errand of the little maid? It was no business of his, he kept repeating—no business of his. He tried to read, but his attention wandered. A quarter-past twelve sounded on the harmonious clock. Suddenly determined, George rose, crossed the room, opened the hidden door, and began to ascend the stairs. He passed the first window, corkscrewed round, and came to another. He paused for a moment to look out; his heart beat uncomfortably, as though he were affronting some unknown danger. What he was doing, he told himself, was extremely ungentlemanly, horribly underbred. He tiptoed onward and upward. One turn more, then half a turn, and a door confronted him. He halted before it, listened; he could hear no sound. Putting his eye to the keyhole, he saw nothing but a stretch of white sunlit wall. Emboldened, he turned the handle and stepped across the threshold. There he halted, petrified by what he saw, mutely gaping.

"In the middle of a pleasantly sunny little room—'it is now Priscilla's boudoir,' Mr. Wimbush remarked parenthetically—stood a small circular table of mahogany. Crystal, porcelain, and silver,—all the shining apparatus of an elegant meal—were mirrored in its polished depths. The carcase of a cold chicken, a bowl of fruit, a great ham, deeply gashed to its heart of tenderest white and pink, the brown cannon ball of a cold plum-pudding, a slender Hock bottle, and a decanter of claret jostled one another for a place on this festive board. And round the table sat the three sisters, the three lovely Lapiths—eating!

"At George's sudden entrance they had all looked towards the door, and now they sat, petrified by the same astonishment which kept George fixed and staring. Georgiana, who sat immediately facing the door, gazed at him with dark, enormous eyes. Between the thumb and forefinger of her right hand she was holding a drumstick of the dismembered chicken; her little finger, elegantly crooked, stood apart from the rest of her hand. Her mouth was open, but the drumstick had never reached its destination; it remained, suspended, frozen, in mid-air. The other two sisters had turned round to look at the intruder. Caroline still grasped her knife and fork; Emmeline's fingers were round the stem of her claret glass. For what seemed a very long time, George and the three sisters stared at one another in silence. They were a group of statues. Then suddenly there was movement. Georgiana dropped her chicken bone, Caroline's knife and fork clattered on her plate. The movement propagated itself, grew more decisive; Emmeline sprang to her feet, uttering a cry. The wave of panic reached George; he turned and, mumbling something unintelligible as he went, rushed out of the room and down the winding stairs. He came to a standstill in the hall, and there, all by himself in the quiet house, he began to laugh.

"At luncheon it was noticed that the sisters ate a little more than usual. Georgiana toyed with some French beans and a spoonful of calves'-foot jelly. 'I feel a little stronger to-day,' she said to Lord Timpany, when he congratulated her on this increase of appetite; 'a little more material,' she added, with a nervous laugh. Looking up, she caught George's eye; a blush suffused her cheeks and she looked hastily away.

"In the garden that afternoon they found themselves for a moment alone.

"You won't tell anyone, George? Promise you won't tell anyone,' she implored. 'It would make us look so ridiculous. And besides, eating IS unspiritual, isn't it? Say you won't tell anyone.'

CHAPTER XIX.

"'I will,' said George brutally. 'I'll tell everyone, unless...'

"'It's blackmail.'

"'I don't care, said George. 'I'll give you twenty-four hours to decide.'

"Lady Lapith was disappointed, of course; she had hoped for better things—for Timpany and a coronet. But George, after all, wasn't so bad. They were married at the New Year.

"My poor grandfather!" Mr. Wimbush added, as he closed his book and put away his pince-nez. "Whenever I read in the papers about oppressed nationalities, I think of him." He relighted his cigar. "It was a maternal government, highly centralised, and there were no representative institutions."

Henry Wimbush ceased speaking. In the silence that ensued Ivor's whispered commentary on the spirit sketches once more became audible. Priscilla, who had been dozing, suddenly woke up.

"What?" she said in the startled tones of one newly returned to consciousness; "what?"

Jenny caught the words. She looked up, smiled, nodded reassuringly. "It's about a ham," she said.

"What's about a ham?"

"What Henry has been reading." She closed the red notebook lying on her knees and slipped a rubber band round it. "I'm going to bed," she announced, and got up.

"So am I," said Anne, yawning. But she lacked the energy to rise from her arm-chair.

The night was hot and oppressive. Round the open windows the curtains hung unmoving. Ivor, fanning himself with the portrait of an Astral Being, looked out into the darkness and drew a breath.

"The air's like wool," he declared.

"It will get cooler after midnight," said Henry Wimbush, and cautiously added, "perhaps."

"I shan't sleep, I know."

Priscilla turned her head in his direction; the monumental coiffure nodded exorbitantly at her slightest movement. "You must make an effort," she said. "When I can't sleep, I concentrate my will: I say, 'I will sleep, I am asleep!' And pop! off I go. That's the power of thought."

"But does it work on stuffy nights?" Ivor inquired. "I simply cannot sleep on a stuffy night."

"Nor can I," said Mary, "except out of doors."

"Out of doors! What a wonderful idea!" In the end they decided to sleep on the towers—Mary on the western tower, Ivor on the eastern. There was a flat expanse of leads on each of the towers, and you could get a mattress through the trap doors that opened on to them. Under the stars, under the gibbous moon, assuredly they would sleep. The mattresses were hauled up, sheets and blankets were spread, and an hour later the two insomniasts, each on his separate tower, were crying their good-nights across the dividing gulf.

On Mary the sleep-compelling charm of the open air did not work with its expected magic. Even through the mattress one could not fail to be aware that the leads were extremely hard. Then there were noises: the owls screeched tirelessly, and once, roused by some unknown terror, all the geese of the farmyard burst into a sudden frenzy of cackling. The stars and the gibbous moon demanded to be looked at, and when one meteorite had streaked across the sky, you could not help waiting, open-eyed and alert, for the next. Time passed; the moon climbed higher and higher in the sky. Mary felt less sleepy than she had when she first came out. She sat up and looked over the parapet. Had Ivor been able to sleep? she wondered. And as though in answer to her mental question, from behind the chimney-stack at the farther end of the roof a white form noiselessly emerged—a form that, in the moonlight, was recognisably Ivor's. Spreading his arms to right and left, like a tight-rope dancer, he began to walk forward along the roof-tree of the house. He swayed terrifyingly as he advanced. Mary looked on speechlessly; perhaps he was walking in his sleep! Suppose he were to wake up suddenly, now! If she spoke or moved it might mean his death. She dared look no more, but sank back on her pillows. She listened intently. For what seemed an immensely long time there was no sound. Then there was a patter of feet on the tiles, followed by a scrabbling noise and a whispered "Damn!" And suddenly Ivor's head and shoulders appeared above the parapet. One leg followed, then the other. He was on the leads. Mary pretended to wake up with a start.

"Oh!" she said. "What are you doing here?"

"I couldn't sleep," he explained, "so I came along to see if you couldn't. One gets bored by oneself on a tower. Don't you find it so?"

It was light before five. Long, narrow clouds barred the east, their edges bright with orange fire. The sky was pale and watery. With the mournful scream of a soul in pain, a monstrous peacock, flying heavily up from below, alighted on the parapet of the tower. Ivor and Mary started broad awake.

"Catch him!" cried Ivor, jumping up. "We'll have a feather." The frightened peacock ran up and down the parapet in an absurd distress, curtseying and bobbing and clucking; his long tail swung ponderously back and forth as he turned and turned again. Then with a flap and swish he launched himself upon the air and sailed magnificently earthward, with a recovered dignity. But he had left a trophy. Ivor had his feather, a long-lashed eye of purple and green, of blue and gold. He handed it to his companion.

"An angel's feather," he said.

Mary looked at it for a moment, gravely and intently. Her purple pyjamas clothed her with an ampleness that hid the lines of her body; she looked like some large, comfortable, unjointed toy, a sort of Teddy-bear—but a Teddy bear with an angel's head, pink cheeks, and hair like a bell of gold. An angel's face, the feather of an angel's wing...Somehow the whole atmosphere of this sunrise was rather angelic.

"It's extraordinary to think of sexual selection," she said at last, looking up from her contemplation of the miraculous feather.

CHAPTER XIX.

"Extraordinary!" Ivor echoed. "I select you, you select me. What luck!"

He put his arm round her shoulders and they stood looking eastward. The first sunlight had begun to warm and colour the pale light of the dawn. Mauve pyjamas and white pyjamas; they were a young and charming couple. The rising sun touched their faces. It was all extremely symbolic; but then, if you choose to think so, nothing in this world is not symbolical. Profound and beautiful truth!

"I must be getting back to my tower," said Ivor at last.

"Already?"

"I'm afraid so. The varletry will soon be up and about."

"Ivor..." There was a prolonged and silent farewell.

"And now," said Ivor, "I repeat my tight-rope stunt."

Mary threw her arms round his neck. "You mustn't, Ivor. It's dangerous. Please."

He had to yield at last to her entreaties. "All right," he said, "I'll go down through the house and up at the other end."

He vanished through the trap door into the darkness that still lurked within the shuttered house. A minute later he had reappeared on the farther tower; he waved his hand, and then sank down, out of sight, behind the parapet. From below, in the house, came the thin wasp-like buzzing of an alarum-clock. He had gone back just in time.

CHAPTER XX.

Ivor was gone. Lounging behind the wind-screen in his yellow sedan he was whirling across rural England. Social and amorous engagements of the most urgent character called him from hall to baronial hall, from castle to castle, from Elizabethan manor-house to Georgian mansion, over the whole expanse of the kingdom. To-day in Somerset, to-morrow in Warwickshire, on Saturday in the West riding, by Tuesday morning in Argyll—Ivor never rested. The whole summer through, from the beginning of July till the end of September, he devoted himself to his engagements; he was a martyr to them. In the autumn he went back to London for a holiday. Crome had been a little incident, an evanescent bubble on the stream of his life; it belonged already to the past. By tea-time he would be at Gobley, and there would be Zenobia's welcoming smile. And on Thursday morning—but that was a long, long way ahead. He would think of Thursday morning when Thursday morning arrived. Meanwhile there was Gobley, meanwhile Zenobia.

In the visitor's book at Crome Ivor had left, according to his invariable custom in these cases, a poem. He had improvised it magisterially in the ten minutes preceding his departure. Denis and Mr. Scogan strolled back together from the gates of the courtyard, whence they had bidden their last farewells; on the writing-table in the hall they found the visitor's book, open, and Ivor's composition scarcely dry. Mr. Scogan read it aloud:

"The magic of those immemorial kings,
Who webbed enchantment on the bowls of night.
Sleeps in the soul of all created things;
In the blue sea, th' Acroceraunian height,
In the eyed butterfly's auricular wings
And orgied visions of the anchorite;
In all that singing flies and flying sings,
In rain, in pain, in delicate delight.
But much more magic, much more cogent spells
Weave here their wizardries about my soul.
Crome calls me like the voice of vesperal bells,
Haunts like a ghostly-peopled necropole.

CHAPTER XX.

Fate tears me hence. Hard fate! since far from Crome
My soul must weep, remembering its Home."

"Very nice and tasteful and tactful," said Mr. Scogan, when he had finished. "I am only troubled by the butterfly's auricular wings. You have a first-hand knowledge of the workings of a poet's mind, Denis; perhaps you can explain."

"What could be simpler," said Denis. "It's a beautiful word, and Ivor wanted to say that the wings were golden."

"You make it luminously clear."

"One suffers so much," Denis went on, "from the fact that beautiful words don't always mean what they ought to mean. Recently, for example, I had a whole poem ruined, just because the word 'carminative' didn't mean what it ought to have meant. Carminative—it's admirable, isn't it?"

"Admirable," Mr. Scogan agreed. "And what does it mean?"

"It's a word I've treasured from my earliest infancy," said Denis, "treasured and loved. They used to give me cinnamon when I had a cold—quite useless, but not disagreeable. One poured it drop by drop out of narrow bottles, a golden liquor, fierce and fiery. On the label was a list of its virtues, and among other things it was described as being in the highest degree carminative. I adored the word. 'Isn't it carminative?' I used to say to myself when I'd taken my dose. It seemed so wonderfully to describe that sensation of internal warmth, that glow, that—what shall I call it?—physical self-satisfaction which followed the drinking of cinnamon. Later, when I discovered alcohol, 'carminative' described for me that similar, but nobler, more spiritual glow which wine evokes not only in the body but in the soul as well. The carminative virtues of burgundy, of rum, of old brandy, of Lacryma Christi, of Marsala, of Aleatico, of stout, of gin, of champagne, of claret, of the raw new wine of this year's Tuscan vintage—I compared them, I classified them. Marsala is rosily, downily carminative; gin pricks and refreshes while it warms. I had a whole table of carmination values. And now"—Denis spread out his hands, palms upwards, despairingly—"now I know what carminative really means."

"Well, what DOES it mean?" asked Mr. Scogan, a little impatiently.

"Carminative," said Denis, lingering lovingly over the syllables, "carminative. I imagined vaguely that it had something to do with carmen-carminis, still more vaguely with caro-carnis, and its derivations, like carnival and carnation. Carminative—there was the idea of singing and the idea of flesh, rose-coloured and warm, with a suggestion of the jollities of mi-Careme and the masked holidays of Venice. Carminative—the warmth, the glow, the interior ripeness were all in the word. Instead of which..."

"Do come to the point, my dear Denis," protested Mr. Scogan. "Do come to the point."

"Well, I wrote a poem the other day," said Denis; "I wrote a poem about the effects of love."

"Others have done the same before you," said Mr. Scogan. "There is no need to be ashamed."

"I was putting forward the notion," Denis went on, "that the effects of love were often similar to the effects of wine, that Eros could intoxicate as well as Bacchus. Love, for example, is essentially carminative. It gives one the sense of warmth, the glow.

'And passion carminative as wine...'

was what I wrote. Not only was the line elegantly sonorous; it was also, I flattered myself, very aptly compendiously expressive. Everything was in the word carminative—a detailed, exact foreground, an immense, indefinite hinterland of suggestion.

'And passion carminative as wine...'

I was not ill-pleased. And then suddenly it occurred to me that I had never actually looked up the word in a dictionary. Carminative had grown up with me from the days of the cinnamon bottle. It had always been taken for granted. Carminative: for me the word was as rich in content as some tremendous, elaborate work of art; it was a complete landscape with figures.

'And passion carminative as wine...'

It was the first time I had ever committed the word to writing, and all at once I felt I would like lexicographical authority for it. A small English-German dictionary was all I had at hand. I turned up C, ca, car, carm. There it was: 'Carminative: windtreibend.' Windtreibend!" he repeated. Mr. Scogan laughed. Denis shook his head. "Ah," he said, "for me it was no laughing matter. For me it marked the end of a chapter, the death of something young and precious. There were the years—years of childhood and innocence—when I had believed that carminative meant—well, carminative. And now, before me lies the rest of my life—a day, perhaps, ten years, half a century, when I shall know that carminative means windtreibend.

'Plus ne suis ce que j'ai ete
Et ne le saurai jamais etre.'

It is a realisation that makes one rather melancholy."

"Carminative," said Mr. Scogan thoughtfully.

"Carminative," Denis repeated, and they were silent for a time. "Words," said Denis at last, "words—I wonder if you can realise how much I love them. You are too much preoccupied with mere things and ideas and people to understand the full beauty of words. Your mind is not a literary mind. The spectacle of Mr. Gladstone finding thirty-four rhymes to the name 'Margot' seems to you rather pathetic than anything else. Mallarmé's envelopes with their versified addresses leave you cold, unless they leave you pitiful; you can't see that

'Apte à ne point te cabrer, hue!
Poste et j'ajouterai, dia!
Si tu ne fuis onze-bis Rue
Balzac, chez cet Hérédia,'

is a little miracle."

"You're right," said Mr. Scogan. "I can't."

"You don't feel it to be magical?"

"No."

"That's the test for the literary mind," said Denis; "the feeling of magic, the sense that words have power. The technical, verbal part of literature is simply a development of magic. Words are man's first and most grandiose invention. With language he created a whole new universe; what wonder if he loved words and attributed power to them! With fitted, harmonious words the magicians summoned rabbits out of empty hats and spirits from the elements. Their descendants, the literary men, still go on with the process, morticing their verbal formulas together, and, before the power of the finished spell, trembling with delight and awe. Rabbits out of empty hats? No, their spells are more subtly powerful, for they evoke emotions out of empty minds. Formulated by their art the most insipid statements become enormously significant. For example, I proffer the constatation, 'Black ladders lack bladders.' A self-evident truth, one on which it would not have been worth while to insist, had I chosen to formulate it in such words as 'Black fire-escapes have no bladders,' or, 'Les echelles noires manquent de vessie.' But since I put it as I do, 'Black ladders lack bladders,' it becomes, for all its self-evidence, significant, unforgettable, moving. The creation by word-power of something out of nothing—what is that but magic? And, I may add, what is that but literature? Half the world's greatest poetry is simply 'Les echelles noires manquent de vessie,' translated into magic significance as, 'Black ladders lack bladders.' And you can't appreciate words. I'm sorry for you."

"A mental carminative," said Mr. Scogan reflectively. "That's what you need."

CHAPTER XXI.

Perched on its four stone mushrooms, the little granary stood two or three feet above the grass of the green close. Beneath it there was a perpetual shade and a damp growth of long, luxuriant grasses. Here, in the shadow, in the green dampness, a family of white ducks had sought shelter from the afternoon sun. Some stood, preening themselves, some reposed with their long bellies pressed to the ground, as though the cool grass were water. Little social noises burst fitfully forth, and from time to time some pointed tail would execute a brilliant Lisztian tremolo. Suddenly their jovial repose was shattered. A prodigious thump shook the wooden flooring above their heads; the whole granary trembled, little fragments of dirt and crumbled wood rained down among them. With a loud, continuous quacking the ducks rushed out from beneath this nameless menace, and did not stay their flight till they were safely in the farmyard.

"Don't lose your temper," Anne was saying. "Listen! You've frightened the ducks. Poor dears! no wonder." She was sitting sideways in a low, wooden chair. Her right elbow rested on the back of the chair and she supported her cheek on her hand. Her long, slender body drooped into curves of a lazy grace. She was smiling, and she looked at Gombauld through half-closed eyes.

"Damn you!" Gombauld repeated, and stamped his foot again. He glared at her round the half-finished portrait on the easel.

"Poor ducks!" Anne repeated. The sound of their quacking was faint in the distance; it was inaudible.

"Can't you see you make me lose my time?" he asked. "I can't work with you dangling about distractingly like this."

"You'd lose less time if you stopped talking and stamping your feet and did a little painting for a change. After all, what am I dangling about for, except to be painted?"

Gombauld made a noise like a growl. "You're awful," he said, with conviction. "Why do you ask me to come and stay here? Why do you tell me you'd like me to paint your portrait?"

"For the simple reasons that I like you—at least, when you're in a good temper—and that I think you're a good painter."

"For the simple reason"—Gombauld mimicked her voice—"that you want me to make love to you and, when I do, to have the amusement of running away."

CHAPTER XXI.

Anne threw back her head and laughed. "So you think it amuses me to have to evade your advances! So like a man! If you only knew how gross and awful and boring men are when they try to make love and you don't want them to make love! If you could only see yourselves through our eyes!"

Gombauld picked up his palette and brushes and attacked his canvas with the ardour of irritation. "I suppose you'll be saying next that you didn't start the game, that it was I who made the first advances, and that you were the innocent victim who sat still and never did anything that could invite or allure me on."

"So like a man again!" said Anne. "It's always the same old story about the woman tempting the man. The woman lures, fascinates, invites; and man—noble man, innocent man—falls a victim. My poor Gombauld! Surely you're not going to sing that old song again. It's so unintelligent, and I always thought you were a man of sense."

"Thanks," said Gombauld.

"Be a little objective," Anne went on. "Can't you see that you're simply externalising your own emotions? That's what you men are always doing; it's so barbarously naive. You feel one of your loose desires for some woman, and because you desire her strongly you immediately accuse her of luring you on, of deliberately provoking and inviting the desire. You have the mentality of savages. You might just as well say that a plate of strawberries and cream deliberately lures you on to feel greedy. In ninety-nine cases out of a hundred women are as passive and innocent as the strawberries and cream."

"Well, all I can say is that this must be the hundredth case," said Gombauld, without looking up.

Anne shrugged her shoulders and gave vent to a sigh. "I'm at a loss to know whether you're more silly or more rude."

After painting for a little time in silence Gombauld began to speak again. "And then there's Denis," he said, renewing the conversation as though it had only just been broken off. "You're playing the same game with him. Why can't you leave that wretched young man in peace?"

Anne flushed with a sudden and uncontrollable anger. "It's perfectly untrue about Denis," she said indignantly. "I never dreamt of playing what you beautifully call the same game with him." Recovering her calm, she added in her ordinary cooing voice and with her exacerbating smile, "You've become very protective towards poor Denis all of a sudden."

"I have," Gombauld replied, with a gravity that was somehow a little too solemn. "I don't like to see a young man..."

"...being whirled along the road to ruin," said Anne, continuing his sentence for him. "I admire your sentiments and, believe me, I share them."

She was curiously irritated at what Gombauld had said about Denis. It happened to be so completely untrue. Gombauld might have some slight ground for his reproaches. But Denis—no, she had never flirted with Denis. Poor boy! He was very sweet. She became somewhat pensive.

Gombauld painted on with fury. The restlessness of an unsatisfied desire, which, before, had distracted his mind, making work impossible, seemed now to have converted itself into a kind of feverish energy. When it was finished, he told himself, the portrait would be diabolic. He was painting her in the pose she had naturally adopted at the first sitting. Seated sideways, her elbow on the back of the chair, her head and shoulders turned at an angle from the rest of her body, towards the front, she had fallen into an attitude of indolent abandonment. He had emphasised the lazy curves of her body; the lines sagged as they crossed the canvas, the grace of the painted figure seemed to be melting into a kind of soft decay. The hand that lay along the knee was as limp as a glove. He was at work on the face now; it had begun to emerge on the canvas, doll-like in its regularity and listlessness. It was Anne's face—but her face as it would be, utterly unillumined by the inward lights of thought and emotion. It was the lazy, expressionless mask which was sometimes her face. The portrait was terribly like; and at the same time it was the most malicious of lies. Yes, it would be diabolic when it was finished, Gombauld decided; he wondered what she would think of it.

CHAPTER XXII.

For the sake of peace and quiet Denis had retired earlier on this same afternoon to his bedroom. He wanted to work, but the hour was a drowsy one, and lunch, so recently eaten, weighed heavily on body and mind. The meridian demon was upon him; he was possessed by that bored and hopeless post-prandial melancholy which the coenobites of old knew and feared under the name of "accidie." He felt, like Ernest Dowson, "a little weary." He was in the mood to write something rather exquisite and gentle and quietist in tone; something a little droopy and at the same time—how should he put it?—a little infinite. He thought of Anne, of love hopeless and unattainable. Perhaps that was the ideal kind of love, the hopeless kind—the quiet, theoretical kind of love. In this sad mood of repletion he could well believe it. He began to write. One elegant quatrain had flowed from beneath his pen:

"A brooding love which is at most
The stealth of moonbeams when they slide,
Evoking colour's bloodless ghost,
O'er some scarce-breathing breast or side..."

when his attention was attracted by a sound from outside. He looked down from his window; there they were, Anne and Gombauld, talking, laughing together. They crossed the courtyard in front, and passed out of sight through the gate in the right-hand wall. That was the way to the green close and the granary; she was going to sit for him again. His pleasantly depressing melancholy was dissipated by a puff of violent emotion; angrily he threw his quatrain into the waste-paper basket and ran downstairs. "The stealth of moonbeams," indeed!

In the hall he saw Mr. Scogan; the man seemed to be lying in wait. Denis tried to escape, but in vain. Mr. Scogan's eye glittered like the eye of the Ancient Mariner.

"Not so fast," he said, stretching out a small saurian hand with pointed nails—"not so fast. I was just going down to the flower garden to take the sun. We'll go together."

Denis abandoned himself; Mr. Scogan put on his hat and they went out arm in arm. On the shaven turf of the terrace Henry Wimbush and Mary were playing a solemn game of bowls. They descended by the yew-tree walk. It was here, thought Denis, here that Anne had fallen, here that he had kissed her, here—and he blushed with retrospective shame at the memory—here that he had tried to carry her and failed. Life was awful!

"Sanity!" said Mr. Scogan, suddenly breaking a long silence. "Sanity—that's what's wrong with me and that's what will be wrong with you, my dear Denis, when you're old enough to be sane or insane. In a sane world I should be a great man; as things are, in this curious establishment, I am nothing at all; to all intents and purposes I don't exist. I am just Vox et praeterea nihil."

Denis made no response; he was thinking of other things. "After all," he said to himself—"after all, Gombauld is better looking than I, more entertaining, more confident; and, besides, he's already somebody and I'm still only potential..."

"Everything that ever gets done in this world is done by madmen," Mr. Scogan went on. Denis tried not to listen, but the tireless insistence of Mr. Scogan's discourse gradually compelled his attention. "Men such as I am, such as you may possibly become, have never achieved anything. We're too sane; we're merely reasonable. We lack the human touch, the compelling enthusiastic mania. People are quite ready to listen to the philosophers for a little amusement, just as they would listen to a fiddler or a mountebank. But as to acting on the advice of the men of reason—never. Wherever the choice has had to be made between the man of reason and the madman, the world has unhesitatingly followed the madman. For the madman appeals to what is fundamental, to passion and the instincts; the philosophers to what is superficial and supererogatory—reason."

They entered the garden; at the head of one of the alleys stood a green wooden bench, embayed in the midst of a fragrant continent of lavender bushes. It was here, though the place was shadeless and one breathed hot, dry perfume instead of air—it was here that Mr. Scogan elected to sit. He thrived on untempered sunlight.

"Consider, for example, the case of Luther and Erasmus." He took out his pipe and began to fill it as he talked. "There was Erasmus, a man of reason if ever there was one. People listened to him at first—a new virtuoso performing on that elegant and resourceful instrument, the intellect; they even admired and venerated him. But did he move them to behave as he wanted them to behave—reasonably, decently, or at least a little less porkishly than usual? He did not. And then Luther appears, violent, passionate, a madman insanely convinced about matters in which there can be no conviction. He shouted, and men rushed to follow him. Erasmus was no longer listened to; he was reviled for his reasonableness. Luther was serious, Luther was reality—like the Great War. Erasmus was only reason and decency; he lacked the power, being a sage, to move men to action. Europe followed Luther and embarked on a century and a half of war and bloody persecution. It's a melancholy story." Mr. Scogan lighted a match. In the intense light the flame was all but invisible. The smell of burning tobacco began to mingle with the sweetly acrid smell of the lavender.

"If you want to get men to act reasonably, you must set about persuading them in a maniacal manner. The very sane precepts of the founders of religions are only made infectious by means of enthusiasms which to a sane man must appear deplorable. It is humiliating to find how impotent unadulterated sanity is. Sanity, for example, informs us that the only way in which we can preserve civilisation is by behaving decently and intelligently. Sanity appeals and argues; our rulers persevere in their customary porkishness, while we acquiesce and obey. The only hope is a maniacal crusade; I am ready, when it comes, to beat a tambourine with the loudest, but at the same time I shall feel a little ashamed of myself. However"—Mr. Scogan shrugged his shoulders and, pipe in hand, made a gesture of resignation—"It's futile to complain that things are as they are. The fact remains that sanity unassisted is useless. What we want, then, is a sane and reasonable exploitation of the forces of insanity. We sane men will have the power yet." Mr. Scogan's eyes shone with a more than ordinary brightness, and, taking his pipe out of his mouth, he gave vent to his loud, dry, and somehow rather fiendish laugh.

"But I don't want power," said Denis. He was sitting in limp discomfort at one end of the bench, shading his eyes from the intolerable light. Mr. Scogan, bolt upright at the other end, laughed again.

"Everybody wants power," he said. "Power in some form or other. The sort of power you hanker for is literary power. Some people want power to persecute other human beings; you expend your lust for power in persecuting words, twisting them, moulding them, torturing them to obey you. But I divagate."

"Do you?" asked Denis faintly.

"Yes," Mr. Scogan continued, unheeding, "the time will come. We men of intelligence will learn to harness the insanities to the service of reason. We can't leave the world any longer to the direction of chance. We can't allow dangerous maniacs like Luther, mad about dogma, like Napoleon, mad about himself, to go on casually appearing and turning everything upside down. In the past it didn't so much matter; but our modern machine is too delicate. A few more knocks like the Great War, another Luther or two, and the whole concern will go to pieces. In future, the men of reason must see that the madness of the world's maniacs is canalised into proper channels, is made to do useful work, like a mountain torrent driving a dynamo..."

"Making electricity to light a Swiss hotel," said Denis. "You ought to complete the simile."

Mr. Scogan waved away the interruption. "There's only one thing to be done," he said. "The men of intelligence must combine, must conspire, and seize power from the imbeciles and maniacs who now direct us. They must found the Rational State."

The heat that was slowly paralysing all Denis's mental and bodily faculties, seemed to bring to Mr. Scogan additional vitality. He talked with an ever-increasing energy, his hands moved in sharp, quick, precise gestures, his eyes shone. Hard, dry, and continuous, his voice went on sounding and sounding in Denis's ears with the insistence of a mechanical noise.

"In the Rational State," he heard Mr. Scogan saying, "human beings will be separated out into distinct species, not according to the colour of their eyes or the shape of their skulls, but according to the qualities of their mind and temperament. Examining psychologists, trained to what would now seem an almost superhuman clairvoyance, will test each child that is born and assign it to its proper species. Duly labelled and docketed, the child will be given the education suitable to members of its species, and will be set, in adult life, to perform those functions which human beings of his variety are capable of performing."

"How many species will there be?" asked Denis.

"A great many, no doubt," Mr. Scogan answered; "the classification will be subtle and elaborate. But it is not in the power of a prophet to go into details, nor is it his business. I will do more than indicate the three main species into which the subjects of the Rational State will be divided."

He paused, cleared his throat, and coughed once or twice, evoking in Denis's mind the vision of a table with a glass and water-bottle, and, lying across one corner, a long white pointer for the lantern pictures.

"The three main species," Mr. Scogan went on, "will be these: the Directing Intelligences, the Men of Faith, and the Herd. Among the Intelligences will be found all those capable of thought, those who know how to attain a certain degree of freedom—and, alas, how limited, even among the most intelligent, that freedom is!—from the mental bondage of their time. A select body of Intelligences, drawn from among those who have turned their attention to the problems of practical life, will be the governors of the Rational State. They will employ as their instruments of power the second great species of humanity—the men of Faith, the Madmen, as I have been calling them, who believe in things unreasonably, with passion, and are ready to die for their beliefs and their desires. These wild men, with their fearful potentialities for good or for mischief, will no longer be allowed to react casually to a casual environment. There will be no more Caesar Borgias, no more Luthers and Mohammeds, no more Joanna Southcotts, no more Comstocks. The old-fashioned Man of Faith and Desire, that haphazard creature of brute circumstance, who might drive men to tears and repentance, or who might equally well set them on to cutting one another's throats, will be replaced by a new sort of madman, still externally the same, still bubbling with a seemingly spontaneous enthusiasm, but, ah, how very different from the madman of the past! For the new Man of Faith will be expending his passion, his desire, and his enthusiasm in the propagation of some reasonable idea. He will be, all unawares, the tool of some superior intelligence."

Mr. Scogan chuckled maliciously; it was as though he were taking a revenge, in the name of reason, on enthusiasts. "From their earliest years, as soon, that is, as the examining psychologists have assigned them their place in the classified scheme, the Men of Faith will have had their special education under the eye of the Intelligences. Moulded by a long process of suggestion, they will go out into the world, preaching and practising with a generous mania the coldly reasonable projects of the Directors from above. When these projects are accomplished, or when the ideas that were useful a decade ago have ceased to be useful, the Intelligences will inspire a new generation of madmen with a new eternal truth. The principal function of the Men of Faith will be to move and direct the Multitude, that third great species consisting of those countless millions who lack intelligence and are without valuable enthusiasm. When any particular effort is required of the Herd, when it is thought necessary, for the sake of solidarity, that humanity shall be kindled and united by some single enthusiastic desire or idea, the Men of Faith, primed with some simple and satisfying creed, will be sent out on a mission of evangelisation. At ordinary times, when the high spiritual temperature of a Crusade would be unhealthy, the Men of Faith will be quietly and earnestly busy with the great work of education. In the upbringing of the Herd, humanity's almost boundless suggestibility will be scientifically exploited. Systematically, from earliest infancy, its members will be assured that there is no happiness to be found except in work and obedience; they will be made to believe that they are happy, that they are tremendously important beings, and that everything they do is noble and significant. For the lower species the earth will be restored to the centre of the universe and man to pre-eminence on the earth. Oh, I envy the lot of the commonality in the Rational State! Working their eight hours a day, obeying their betters, convinced of their own grandeur and significance and immortality, they will be marvellously happy, happier than any race of men has ever been. They will go through life in a rosy state of intoxication, from which they will never awake. The Men of Faith will play the cup-bearers at this lifelong bacchanal, filling and ever filling again with the warm liquor that the Intelligences, in sad and sober privacy behind the scenes, will brew for the intoxication of their subjects."

"And what will be my place in the Rational State?" Denis drowsily inquired from under his shading hand.

Mr. Scogan looked at him for a moment in silence. "It's difficult to see where you would fit in," he said at last. "You couldn't do manual work; you're too independent and unsuggestible to belong to the larger Herd; you have none of the characteristics required in a Man of Faith. As for the Directing Intelligences, they will have to be marvellously clear and merciless and penetrating." He paused and shook his head. "No, I can see no place for you; only the lethal chamber."

Deeply hurt, Denis emitted the imitation of a loud Homeric laugh. "I'm getting sunstroke here," he said, and got up.

Mr. Scogan followed his example, and they walked slowly away down the narrow path, brushing the blue lavender flowers in their passage. Denis pulled a sprig of lavender and sniffed at it; then some dark leaves of rosemary that smelt like incense in a cavernous church. They passed a bed of opium poppies, dispetaled now; the round, ripe seedheads were brown and dry—like Polynesian trophies, Denis thought; severed heads stuck on poles. He liked the fancy enough to impart it to Mr. Scogan.

"Like Polynesian trophies..." Uttered aloud, the fancy seemed less charming and significant than it did when it first occurred to him.

There was a silence, and in a growing wave of sound the whir of the reaping machines swelled up from the fields beyond the garden and then receded into a remoter hum.

"It is satisfactory to think," said Mr. Scogan, as they strolled slowly onward, "that a multitude of people are toiling in the harvest fields in order that we may talk of Polynesia. Like every other good thing in this world, leisure and culture have to be paid for. Fortunately, however, it is not the leisured and the cultured who have to pay. Let us be duly thankful for that, my dear Denis—duly thankful," he repeated, and knocked the ashes out of his pipe.

Denis was not listening. He had suddenly remembered Anne. She was with Gombauld—alone with him in his studio. It was an intolerable thought.

"Shall we go and pay a call on Gombauld?" he suggested carelessly. "It would be amusing to see what he's doing now."

He laughed inwardly to think how furious Gombauld would be when he saw them arriving.

CHAPTER XXIII.

Gombauld was by no means so furious at their apparition as Denis had hoped and expected he would be. Indeed, he was rather pleased than annoyed when the two faces, one brown and pointed, the other round and pale, appeared in the frame of the open door. The energy born of his restless irritation was dying within him, returning to its emotional elements. A moment more and he would have been losing his temper again—and Anne would be keeping hers, infuriatingly. Yes, he was positively glad to see them.

"Come in, come in," he called out hospitably.

Followed by Mr. Scogan, Denis climbed the little ladder and stepped over the threshold. He looked suspiciously from Gombauld to his sitter, and could learn nothing from the expression of their faces except that they both seemed pleased to see the visitors. Were they really glad, or were they cunningly simulating gladness? He wondered.

Mr. Scogan, meanwhile, was looking at the portrait.

"Excellent," he said approvingly, "excellent. Almost too true to character, if that is possible; yes, positively too true. But I'm surprised to find you putting in all this psychology business." He pointed to the face, and with his extended finger followed the slack curves of the painted figure. "I thought you were one of the fellows who went in exclusively for balanced masses and impinging planes."

Gombauld laughed. "This is a little infidelity," he said.

"I'm sorry," said Mr. Scogan. "I for one, without ever having had the slightest appreciation of painting, have always taken particular pleasure in Cubismus. I like to see pictures from which nature has been completely banished, pictures which are exclusively the product of the human mind. They give me the same pleasure as I derive from a good piece of reasoning or a mathematical problem or an achievement of engineering. Nature, or anything that reminds me of nature, disturbs me; it is too large, too complicated, above all too utterly pointless and incomprehensible. I am at home with the works of man; if I choose to set my mind to it, I can understand anything that any man has made or thought. That is why I always travel by Tube, never by bus if I can possibly help it. For, travelling by bus, one can't avoid seeing, even in London, a few stray works of God—the sky, for example, an occasional tree, the flowers in the window-boxes. But travel by Tube and you see nothing but the works of man—iron riveted into geometrical forms, straight lines of concrete, patterned expanses of tiles. All is human and the product of friendly and comprehensible minds. All philosophies and all religions—what are they but spiritual Tubes bored through the universe! Through these narrow tunnels, where all is recognisably human, one travels comfortable and secure, contriving to forget that all round and below and above them stretches the blind mass of earth, endless and unexplored. Yes, give me the Tube and Cubismus every time; give me ideas, so snug and neat and simple and well made. And preserve me from nature, preserve me from all that's inhumanly large and complicated and obscure. I haven't the courage, and, above all, I haven't the time to start wandering in that labyrinth."

While Mr. Scogan was discoursing, Denis had crossed over to the farther side of the little square chamber, where Anne was sitting, still in her graceful, lazy pose, on the low chair.

"Well?" he demanded, looking at her almost fiercely. What was he asking of her? He hardly knew himself.

Anne looked up at him, and for answer echoed his "Well?" in another, a laughing key.

Denis had nothing more, at the moment, to say. Two or three canvases stood in the corner behind Anne's chair, their faces turned to the wall. He pulled them out and began to look at the paintings.

"May I see too?" Anne requested.

He stood them in a row against the wall. Anne had to turn round in her chair to look at them. There was the big canvas of the man fallen from the horse, there was a painting of flowers, there was a small landscape. His hands on the back of the chair, Denis leaned over her. From behind the easel at the other side of the room Mr. Scogan was talking away. For a long time they looked at the pictures, saying nothing; or, rather, Anne looked at the pictures, while Denis, for the most part, looked at Anne.

"I like the man and the horse; don't you?" she said at last, looking up with an inquiring smile.

Denis nodded, and then in a queer, strangled voice, as though it had cost him a great effort to utter the words, he said, "I love you."

It was a remark which Anne had heard a good many times before and mostly heard with equanimity. But on this occasion—perhaps because they had come so unexpectedly, perhaps for some other reason—the words provoked in her a certain surprised commotion.

"My poor Denis," she managed to say, with a laugh; but she was blushing as she spoke.

CHAPTER XXIV.

It was noon. Denis, descending from his chamber, where he had been making an unsuccessful effort to write something about nothing in particular, found the drawing-room deserted. He was about to go out into the garden when his eye fell on a familiar but mysterious object—the large red notebook in which he had so often seen Jenny quietly and busily scribbling. She had left it lying on the window-seat. The temptation was great. He picked up the book and slipped off the elastic band that kept it discreetly closed.

"Private. Not to be opened," was written in capital letters on the cover. He raised his eyebrows. It was the sort of thing one wrote in one's Latin Grammar while one was still at one's preparatory school.

"Black is the raven, black is the rook,
But blacker the thief who steals this book!"

It was curiously childish, he thought, and he smiled to himself. He opened the book. What he saw made him wince as though he had been struck.

Denis was his own severest critic; so, at least, he had always believed. He liked to think of himself as a merciless vivisector probing into the palpitating entrails of his own soul; he was Brown Dog to himself. His weaknesses, his absurdities—no one knew them better than he did. Indeed, in a vague way he imagined that nobody beside himself was aware of them at all. It seemed, somehow, inconceivable that he should appear to other people as they appeared to him; inconceivable that they ever spoke of him among themselves in that same freely critical and, to be quite honest, mildly malicious tone in which he was accustomed to talk of them. In his own eyes he had defects, but to see them was a privilege reserved to him alone. For the rest of the world he was surely an image of flawless crystal. It was almost axiomatic.

On opening the red notebook that crystal image of himself crashed to the ground, and was irreparably shattered. He was not his own severest critic after all. The discovery was a painful one.

The fruit of Jenny's unobtrusive scribbling lay before him. A caricature of himself, reading (the book was upside-down). In the background a dancing couple, recognisable as Gombauld and Anne. Beneath, the legend: "Fable of the Wallflower and the Sour Grapes." Fascinated and horrified, Denis pored over the drawing. It was masterful. A mute, inglorious Rouveyre appeared in every one of those cruelly clear lines. The expression of the face, an assumed aloofness and superiority tempered by a feeble envy; the attitude of the body and limbs, an attitude of studious and scholarly dignity, given away by the fidgety pose of the turned-in feet—these things were terrible. And, more terrible still, was the likeness, was the magisterial certainty with which his physical peculiarities were all recorded and subtly exaggerated.

Denis looked deeper into the book. There were caricatures of other people: of Priscilla and Mr. Barbecue-Smith; of Henry Wimbush, of Anne and Gombauld; of Mr. Scogan, whom Jenny had represented in a light that was more than slightly sinister, that was, indeed, diabolic; of Mary and Ivor. He scarcely glanced at them. A fearful desire to know the worst about himself possessed him. He turned over the leaves, lingering at nothing that was not his own image. Seven full pages were devoted to him.

"Private. Not to be opened." He had disobeyed the injunction; he had only got what he deserved. Thoughtfully he closed the book, and slid the rubber band once more into its place. Sadder and wiser, he went out on to the terrace. And so this, he reflected, this was how Jenny employed the leisure hours in her ivory tower apart. And he had thought her a simple-minded, uncritical creature! It was he, it seemed, who was the fool. He felt no resentment towards Jenny. No, the distressing thing wasn't Jenny herself; it was what she and the phenomenon of her red book represented, what they stood for and concretely symbolised. They represented all the vast conscious world of men outside himself; they symbolised something that in his studious solitariness he was apt not to believe in. He could stand at Piccadilly Circus, could watch the crowds shuffle past, and still imagine himself the one fully conscious, intelligent, individual being among all those thousands. It seemed, somehow, impossible that other people should be in their way as elaborate and complete as he in his. Impossible; and yet, periodically he would make some painful discovery about the external world and the horrible reality of its consciousness and its intelligence. The red notebook was one of these discoveries, a footprint in the sand. It put beyond a doubt the fact that the outer world really existed.

Sitting on the balustrade of the terrace, he ruminated this unpleasant truth for some time. Still chewing on it, he strolled pensively down towards the swimming-pool. A peacock and his hen trailed their shabby finery across the turf of the lower lawn. Odious birds! Their necks, thick and greedily fleshy at the roots, tapered up to the cruel inanity of their brainless heads, their flat eyes and piercing beaks. The fabulists were right, he reflected, when they took beasts to illustrate their tractates of human morality. Animals resemble men with all the truthfulness of a caricature. (Oh, the red notebook!) He threw a piece of stick at the slowly pacing birds. They rushed towards it, thinking it was something to eat.

He walked on. The profound shade of a giant ilex tree engulfed him. Like a great wooden octopus, it spread its long arms abroad.

"Under the spreading ilex tree..."

CHAPTER XXIV.

He tried to remember who the poem was by, but couldn't.

"The smith, a brawny man is he,
With arms like rubber bands."

Just like his; he would have to try and do his Muller exercises more regularly.

He emerged once more into the sunshine. The pool lay before him, reflecting in its bronze mirror the blue and various green of the summer day. Looking at it, he thought of Anne's bare arms and seal-sleek bathing-dress, her moving knees and feet.

"And little Luce with the white legs,
And bouncing Barbary..."

Oh, these rags and tags of other people's making! Would he ever be able to call his brain his own? Was there, indeed, anything in it that was truly his own, or was it simply an education?

He walked slowly round the water's edge. In an embayed recess among the surrounding yew trees, leaning her back against the pedestal of a pleasantly comic version of the Medici Venus, executed by some nameless mason of the seicento, he saw Mary pensively sitting.

"Hullo!" he said, for he was passing so close to her that he had to say something.

Mary looked up. "Hullo!" she answered in a melancholy, uninterested tone.

In this alcove hewed out of the dark trees, the atmosphere seemed to Denis agreeably elegiac. He sat down beside her under the shadow of the pudic goddess. There was a prolonged silence.

At breakfast that morning Mary had found on her plate a picture postcard of Gobley Great Park. A stately Georgian pile, with a facade sixteen windows wide; parterres in the foreground; huge, smooth lawns receding out of the picture to right and left. Ten years more of the hard times and Gobley, with all its peers, will be deserted and decaying. Fifty years, and the countryside will know the old landmarks no more. They will have vanished as the monasteries vanished before them. At the moment, however, Mary's mind was not moved by these considerations.

On the back of the postcard, next to the address, was written, in Ivor's bold, large hand, a single quatrain.

"Hail, maid of moonlight! Bride of the sun, farewell!
Like bright plumes moulted in an angel's flight,
There sleep within my heart's most mystic cell
Memories of morning, memories of the night."

There followed a postscript of three lines: "Would you mind asking one of the housemaids to forward the packet of safety-razor blades I left in the drawer of my washstand. Thanks.—Ivor."

Seated under the Venus's immemorial gesture, Mary considered life and love. The abolition of her repressions, so far from bringing the expected peace of mind, had brought nothing but disquiet, a new and hitherto unexperienced misery. Ivor, Ivor...She couldn't do without him now. It was evident, on the other hand, from the poem on the back of the picture postcard, that Ivor could very well do without her. He was at Gobley now, so was Zenobia. Mary knew Zenobia. She thought of the last verse of the song he had sung that night in the garden.

"Le lendemain, Phillis peu sage
Aurait donne moutons et chien
Pour un baiser que le volage
A Lisette donnait pour rien."

Mary shed tears at the memory; she had never been so unhappy in all her life before.

It was Denis who first broke the silence. "The individual," he began in a soft and sadly philosophical tone, "is not a self-supporting universe. There are times when he comes into contact with other individuals, when he is forced to take cognisance of the existence of other universes besides himself."

He had contrived this highly abstract generalisation as a preliminary to a personal confidence. It was the first gambit in a conversation that was to lead up to Jenny's caricatures.

"True," said Mary; and, generalising for herself, she added, "When one individual comes into intimate contact with another, she—or he, of course, as the case may be—must almost inevitably receive or inflict suffering."

"One is apt," Denis went on, "to be so spellbound by the spectacle of one's own personality that one forgets that the spectacle presents itself to other people as well as to oneself."

Mary was not listening. "The difficulty," she said, "makes itself acutely felt in matters of sex. If one individual seeks intimate contact with another individual in the natural way, she is certain to receive or inflict suffering. If on the other hand, she avoids contacts, she risks the equally grave sufferings that follow on unnatural repressions. As you see, it's a dilemma."

"When I think of my own case," said Denis, making a more decided move in the desired direction, "I am amazed how ignorant I am of other people's mentality in general, and above all and in particular, of their opinions about myself. Our minds are sealed books only occasionally opened to the outside world." He made a gesture that was faintly suggestive of the drawing off of a rubber band.

"It's an awful problem," said Mary thoughtfully. "One has to have had personal experience to realise quite how awful it is."

"Exactly." Denis nodded. "One has to have had first-hand experience." He leaned towards her and slightly lowered his voice. "This very morning, for example..." he began, but his confidences were cut short. The deep voice of the gong, tempered by distance to a pleasant booming, floated down from the house. It was lunch-time. Mechanically Mary rose to her feet, and Denis, a little hurt that she should exhibit such a desperate anxiety for her food and so slight an interest in his spiritual experiences, followed her. They made their way up to the house without speaking.

CHAPTER XXV.

I hope you all realise," said Henry Wimbush during dinner, "that next Monday is Bank Holiday, and that you will all be expected to help in the Fair."

"Heavens!" cried Anne. "The Fair—I had forgotten all about it. What a nightmare! Couldn't you put a stop to it, Uncle Henry?"

Mr. Wimbush sighed and shook his head. "Alas," he said, "I fear I cannot. I should have liked to put an end to it years ago; but the claims of Charity are strong."

"It's not charity we want," Anne murmured rebelliously; "it's justice."

"Besides," Mr. Wimbush went on, "the Fair has become an institution. Let me see, it must be twenty-two years since we started it. It was a modest affair then. Now..." he made a sweeping movement with his hand and was silent.

It spoke highly for Mr. Wimbush's public spirit that he still continued to tolerate the Fair. Beginning as a sort of glorified church bazaar, Crome's yearly Charity Fair had grown into a noisy thing of merry-go-rounds, cocoanut shies, and miscellaneous side shows—a real genuine fair on the grand scale. It was the local St. Bartholomew, and the people of all the neighbouring villages, with even a contingent from the county town, flocked into the park for their Bank Holiday amusement. The local hospital profited handsomely, and it was this fact alone which prevented Mr. Wimbush, to whom the Fair was a cause of recurrent and never-diminishing agony, from putting a stop to the nuisance which yearly desecrated his park and garden.

"I've made all the arrangements already," Henry Wimbush went on. "Some of the larger marquees will be put up to-morrow. The swings and the merry-go-round arrive on Sunday."

"So there's no escape," said Anne, turning to the rest of the party. "You'll all have to do something. As a special favour you're allowed to choose your slavery. My job is the tea tent, as usual, Aunt Priscilla..."

"My dear," said Mrs. Wimbush, interrupting her, "I have more important things to think about than the Fair. But you need have no doubt that I shall do my best when Monday comes to encourage the villagers."

"That's splendid," said Anne. "Aunt Priscilla will encourage the villagers. What will you do, Mary?"

"I won't do anything where I have to stand by and watch other people eat."

"Then you'll look after the children's sports."

"All right," Mary agreed. "I'll look after the children's sports."

"And Mr. Scogan?"

Mr. Scogan reflected. "May I be allowed to tell fortunes?" he asked at last. "I think I should be good at telling fortunes."

"But you can't tell fortunes in that costume!"

"Can't I?" Mr. Scogan surveyed himself.

"You'll have to be dressed up. Do you still persist?"

"I'm ready to suffer all indignities."

"Good!" said Anne; and turning to Gombauld, "You must be our lightning artist," she said. "'Your portrait for a shilling in five minutes.'"

"It's a pity I'm not Ivor," said Gombauld, with a laugh. "I could throw in a picture of their Auras for an extra sixpence."

Mary flushed. "Nothing is to be gained," she said severely, "by speaking with levity of serious subjects. And, after all, whatever your personal views may be, psychical research is a perfectly serious subject."

"And what about Denis?"

Denis made a deprecating gesture. "I have no accomplishments," he said, "I'll just be one of those men who wear a thing in their buttonholes and go about telling people which is the way to tea and not to walk on the grass."

"No, no," said Anne. "That won't do. You must do something more than that."

"But what? All the good jobs are taken, and I can do nothing but lisp in numbers."

"Well, then, you must lisp," concluded Anne. "You must write a poem for the occasion—an 'Ode on Bank Holiday.' We'll print it on Uncle Henry's press and sell it at twopence a copy."

"Sixpence," Denis protested. "It'll be worth sixpence."

Anne shook her head. "Twopence," she repeated firmly. "Nobody will pay more than twopence."

"And now there's Jenny," said Mr Wimbush. "Jenny," he said, raising his voice, "what will you do?"

Denis thought of suggesting that she might draw caricatures at sixpence an execution, but decided it would be wiser to go on feigning ignorance of her talent. His mind reverted to the red notebook. Could it really be true that he looked like that?

"What will I do," Jenny echoed, "what will I do?" She frowned thoughtfully for a moment; then her face brightened and she smiled. "When I was young," she said, "I learnt to play the drums."

"The drums?"

Jenny nodded, and, in proof of her assertion, agitated her knife and fork, like a pair of drumsticks, over her plate. "If there's any opportunity of playing the drums..." she began.

"But of course," said Anne, "there's any amount of opportunity. We'll put you down definitely for the drums. That's the lot," she added.

CHAPTER XXV.

"And a very good lot too," said Gombauld. "I look forward to my Bank Holiday. It ought to be gay."

"It ought indeed," Mr Scogan assented. "But you may rest assured that it won't be. No holiday is ever anything but a disappointment."

"Come, come," protested Gombauld. "My holiday at Crome isn't being a disappointment."

"Isn't it?" Anne turned an ingenuous mask towards him.

"No, it isn't," he answered.

"I'm delighted to hear it."

"It's in the very nature of things," Mr. Scogan went on; "our holidays can't help being disappointments. Reflect for a moment. What is a holiday? The ideal, the Platonic Holiday of Holidays is surely a complete and absolute change. You agree with me in my definition?" Mr. Scogan glanced from face to face round the table; his sharp nose moved in a series of rapid jerks through all the points of the compass. There was no sign of dissent; he continued: "A complete and absolute change; very well. But isn't a complete and absolute change precisely the thing we can never have—never, in the very nature of things?" Mr. Scogan once more looked rapidly about him. "Of course it is. As ourselves, as specimens of Homo Sapiens, as members of a society, how can we hope to have anything like an absolute change? We are tied down by the frightful limitation of our human faculties, by the notions which society imposes on us through our fatal suggestibility, by our own personalities. For us, a complete holiday is out of the question. Some of us struggle manfully to take one, but we never succeed, if I may be allowed to express myself metaphorically, we never succeed in getting farther than Southend."

"You're depressing," said Anne.

"I mean to be," Mr. Scogan replied, and, expanding the fingers of his right hand, he went on: "Look at me, for example. What sort of a holiday can I take? In endowing me with passions and faculties Nature has been horribly niggardly. The full range of human potentialities is in any case distressingly limited; my range is a limitation within a limitation. Out of the ten octaves that make up the human instrument, I can compass perhaps two. Thus, while I may have a certain amount of intelligence, I have no aesthetic sense; while I possess the mathematical faculty, I am wholly without the religious emotions; while I am naturally addicted to venery, I have little ambition and am not at all avaricious. Education has further limited my scope. Having been brought up in society, I am impregnated with its laws; not only should I be afraid of taking a holiday from them, I should also feel it painful to try to do so. In a word, I have a conscience as well as a fear of gaol. Yes, I know it by experience. How often have I tried to take holidays, to get away from myself, my own boring nature, my insufferable mental surroundings!" Mr. Scogan sighed. "But always without success," he added, "always without success. In my youth I was always striving—how hard!—to feel religiously and aesthetically. Here, said I to myself, are two tremendously important and exciting emotions. Life would be richer, warmer, brighter, altogether more amusing, if I could feel them. I try to feel them. I read the works of the mystics. They seemed to me nothing but the most deplorable claptrap—as indeed they always must to anyone who does not feel the same emotion as the authors felt when they were writing. For it is the emotion that matters. The written work is simply an attempt to express emotion, which is in itself inexpressible, in terms of intellect and logic. The mystic objectifies a rich feeling in the pit of the stomach into a cosmology. For other mystics that cosmology is a symbol of the rich feeling. For the unreligious it is a symbol of nothing, and so appears merely grotesque. A melancholy fact! But I divagate." Mr. Scogan checked himself. "So much for the religious emotion. As for the aesthetic—I was at even greater pains to cultivate that. I have looked at all the right works of art in every part of Europe. There was a time when, I venture to believe, I knew more about Taddeo da Poggibonsi, more about the cryptic Amico di Taddeo, even than Henry does. To-day, I am happy to say, I have forgotten most of the knowledge I then so laboriously acquired; but without vanity I can assert that it was prodigious. I don't pretend, of course, to know anything about nigger sculpture or the later seventeenth century in Italy; but about all the periods that were fashionable before 1900 I am, or was, omniscient. Yes, I repeat it, omniscient. But did that fact make me any more appreciative of art in general? It did not. Confronted by a picture, of which I could tell you all the known and presumed history—the date when it was painted, the character of the painter, the influences that had gone to make it what it was—I felt none of that strange excitement and exaltation which is, as I am informed by those who do feel it, the true aesthetic emotion. I felt nothing but a certain interest in the subject of the picture; or more often, when the subject was hackneyed and religious, I felt nothing but a great weariness of spirit. Nevertheless, I must have gone on looking at pictures for ten years before I would honestly admit to myself that they merely bored me. Since then I have given up all attempts to take a holiday. I go on cultivating my old stale daily self in the resigned spirit with which a bank clerk performs from ten till six his daily task. A holiday, indeed! I'm sorry for you, Gombauld, if you still look forward to having a holiday."

Gombauld shrugged his shoulders. "Perhaps," he said, "my standards aren't as elevated as yours. But personally I found the war quite as thorough a holiday from all the ordinary decencies and sanities, all the common emotions and preoccupations, as I ever want to have."

"Yes," Mr. Scogan thoughtfully agreed. "Yes, the war was certainly something of a holiday. It was a step beyond Southend; it was Weston-super-Mare; it was almost Ilfracombe."

CHAPTER XXVI.

A little canvas village of tents and booths had sprung up, just beyond the boundaries of the garden, in the green expanse of the park. A crowd thronged its streets, the men dressed mostly in black—holiday best, funeral best—the women in pale muslins. Here and there tricolour bunting hung inert. In the midst of the canvas town, scarlet and gold and crystal, the merry-go-round glittered in the sun. The balloon-man walked among the crowd, and above his head, like a huge, inverted bunch of many-coloured grapes, the balloons strained upwards. With a scythe-like motion the boat-swings reaped the air, and from the funnel of the engine which worked the roundabout rose a thin, scarcely wavering column of black smoke.

Denis had climbed to the top of one of Sir Ferdinando's towers, and there, standing on the sun-baked leads, his elbows resting on the parapet, he surveyed the scene. The steam-organ sent up prodigious music. The clashing of automatic cymbals beat out with inexorable precision the rhythm of piercingly sounded melodies. The harmonies were like a musical shattering of glass and brass. Far down in the bass the Last Trump was hugely blowing, and with such persistence, such resonance, that its alternate tonic and dominant detached themselves from the rest of the music and made a tune of their own, a loud, monotonous see-saw.

Denis leaned over the gulf of swirling noise. If he threw himself over the parapet, the noise would surely buoy him up, keep him suspended, bobbing, as a fountain balances a ball on its breaking crest. Another fancy came to him, this time in metrical form.

"My soul is a thin white sheet of parchment stretched
Over a bubbling cauldron."

Bad, bad. But he liked the idea of something thin and distended being blown up from underneath.

"My soul is a thin tent of gut..."

or better—

"My soul is a pale, tenuous membrane..."

That was pleasing: a thin, tenuous membrane. It had the right anatomical quality. Tight blown, quivering in the blast of noisy life. It was time for him to descend from the serene empyrean of words into the actual vortex. He went down slowly. "My soul is a thin, tenuous membrane..."

On the terrace stood a knot of distinguished visitors. There was old Lord Moleyn, like a caricature of an English milord in a French comic paper: a long man, with a long nose and long, drooping moustaches and long teeth of old ivory, and lower down, absurdly, a short covert coat, and below that long, long legs cased in pearl-grey trousers—legs that bent unsteadily at the knee and gave a kind of sideways wobble as he walked. Beside him, short and thick-set, stood Mr. Callamay, the venerable conservative statesman, with a face like a Roman bust, and short white hair. Young girls didn't much like going for motor drives alone with Mr. Callamay; and of old Lord Moleyn one wondered why he wasn't living in gilded exile on the island of Capri among the other distinguished persons who, for one reason or another, find it impossible to live in England. They were talking to Anne, laughing, the one profoundly, the other hootingly.

A black silk balloon towing a black-and-white striped parachute proved to be old Mrs. Budge from the big house on the other side of the valley. She stood low on the ground, and the spikes of her black-and-white sunshade menaced the eyes of Priscilla Wimbush, who towered over her—a massive figure dressed in purple and topped with a queenly toque on which the nodding black plumes recalled the splendours of a first-class Parisian funeral.

Denis peeped at them discreetly from the window of the morning-room. His eyes were suddenly become innocent, childlike, unprejudiced. They seemed, these people, inconceivably fantastic. And yet they really existed, they functioned by themselves, they were conscious, they had minds. Moreover, he was like them. Could one believe it? But the evidence of the red notebook was conclusive.

It would have been polite to go and say, "How d'you do?" But at the moment Denis did not want to talk, could not have talked. His soul was a tenuous, tremulous, pale membrane. He would keep its sensibility intact and virgin as long as he could. Cautiously he crept out by a side door and made his way down towards the park. His soul fluttered as he approached the noise and movement of the fair. He paused for a moment on the brink, then stepped in and was engulfed.

Hundreds of people, each with his own private face and all of them real, separate, alive: the thought was disquieting. He paid twopence and saw the Tatooed Woman; twopence more, the Largest Rat in the World. From the home of the Rat he emerged just in time to see a hydrogen-filled balloon break loose for home. A child howled up after it; but calmly, a perfect sphere of flushed opal, it mounted, mounted. Denis followed it with his eyes until it became lost in the blinding sunlight. If he could but send his soul to follow it!...

He sighed, stuck his steward's rosette in his buttonhole, and started to push his way, aimlessly but officially, through the crowd.

CHAPTER XXVII.

Mr. Scogan had been accommodated in a little canvas hut. Dressed in a black skirt and a red bodice, with a yellow-and-red bandana handkerchief tied round his black wig, he looked—sharp-nosed, brown, and wrinkled—like the Bohemian Hag of Frith's Derby Day. A placard pinned to the curtain of the doorway announced the presence within the tent of "Sesostris, the Sorceress of Ecbatana." Seated at a table, Mr. Scogan received his clients in mysterious silence, indicating with a movement of the finger that they were to sit down opposite him and to extend their hands for his inspection. He then examined the palm that was presented him, using a magnifying glass and a pair of horn spectacles. He had a terrifying way of shaking his head, frowning and clicking with his tongue as he looked at the lines. Sometimes he would whisper, as though to himself, "Terrible, terrible!" or "God preserve us!" sketching out the sign of the cross as he uttered the words. The clients who came in laughing grew suddenly grave; they began to take the witch seriously. She was a formidable-looking woman; could it be, was it possible, that there was something in this sort of thing after all? After all, they thought, as the hag shook her head over their hands, after all...And they waited, with an uncomfortably beating heart, for the oracle to speak. After a long and silent inspection, Mr. Scogan would suddenly look up and ask, in a hoarse whisper, some horrifying question, such as, "Have you ever been hit on the head with a hammer by a young man with red hair?" When the answer was in the negative, which it could hardly fail to be, Mr. Scogan would nod several times, saying, "I was afraid so. Everything is still to come, still to come, though it can't be very far off now." Sometimes, after a long examination, he would just whisper, "Where ignorance is bliss, 'tis folly to be wise," and refuse to divulge any details of a future too appalling to be envisaged without despair. Sesostris had a success of horror. People stood in a queue outside the witch's booth waiting for the privilege of hearing sentence pronounced upon them.

Denis, in the course of his round, looked with curiosity at this crowd of suppliants before the shrine of the oracle. He had a great desire to see how Mr. Scogan played his part. The canvas booth was a rickety, ill-made structure. Between its walls and its sagging roof were long gaping chinks and crannies. Denis went to the tea-tent and borrowed a wooden bench and a small Union Jack. With these he hurried back to the booth of Sesostris. Setting down the bench at the back of the booth, he climbed up, and with a great air of busy efficiency began to tie the Union Jack to the top of one of the tent-poles. Through the crannies in the canvas he could see almost the whole of the interior of the tent. Mr. Scogan's bandana-covered head was just below him; his terrifying whispers came clearly up. Denis looked and listened while the witch prophesied financial losses, death by apoplexy, destruction by air-raids in the next war.

"Is there going to be another war?" asked the old lady to whom he had predicted this end.

"Very soon," said Mr. Scogan, with an air of quiet confidence.

The old lady was succeeded by a girl dressed in white muslin, garnished with pink ribbons. She was wearing a broad hat, so that Denis could not see her face; but from her figure and the roundness of her bare arms he judged her young and pleasing. Mr. Scogan looked at her hand, then whispered, "You are still virtuous."

The young lady giggled and exclaimed, "Oh, lor'!"

"But you will not remain so for long," added Mr. Scogan sepulchrally. The young lady giggled again. "Destiny, which interests itself in small things no less than in great, has announced the fact upon your hand." Mr. Scogan took up the magnifying-glass and began once more to examine the white palm. "Very interesting," he said, as though to himself—"very interesting. It's as clear as day." He was silent.

"What's clear?" asked the girl.

"I don't think I ought to tell you." Mr. Scogan shook his head; the pendulous brass ear-rings which he had screwed on to his ears tinkled.

"Please, please!" she implored.

The witch seemed to ignore her remark. "Afterwards, it's not at all clear. The fates don't say whether you will settle down to married life and have four children or whether you will try to go on the cinema and have none. They are only specific about this one rather crucial incident."

"What is it? What is it? Oh, do tell me!"

The white muslin figure leant eagerly forward.

Mr. Scogan sighed. "Very well," he said, "if you must know, you must know. But if anything untoward happens you must blame your own curiosity. Listen. Listen." He lifted up a sharp, claw-nailed forefinger. "This is what the fates have written. Next Sunday afternoon at six o'clock you will be sitting on the second stile on the footpath that leads from the church to the lower road. At that moment a man will appear walking along the footpath." Mr. Scogan looked at her hand again as though to refresh his memory of the details of the scene. "A man," he repeated—"a small man with a sharp nose, not exactly good looking nor precisely young, but fascinating." He lingered hissingly over the word. "He will ask you, 'Can you tell me the way to Paradise?' and you will answer, 'Yes, I'll show you,' and walk with him down towards the little hazel copse. I cannot read what will happen after that." There was a silence.

"Is it really true?" asked white muslin.

CHAPTER XXVII.

The witch gave a shrug of the shoulders. "I merely tell you what I read in your hand. Good afternoon. That will be sixpence. Yes, I have change. Thank you. Good afternoon."

Denis stepped down from the bench; tied insecurely and crookedly to the tent-pole, the Union Jack hung limp on the windless air. "If only I could do things like that!" he thought, as he carried the bench back to the tea-tent.

Anne was sitting behind a long table filling thick white cups from an urn. A neat pile of printed sheets lay before her on the table. Denis took one of them and looked at it affectionately. It was his poem. They had printed five hundred copies, and very nice the quarto broadsheets looked.

"Have you sold many?" he asked in a casual tone.

Anne put her head on one side deprecatingly. "Only three so far, I'm afraid. But I'm giving a free copy to everyone who spends more than a shilling on his tea. So in any case it's having a circulation."

Denis made no reply, but walked slowly away. He looked at the broadsheet in his hand and read the lines to himself relishingly as he walked along:

"This day of roundabouts and swings,
Struck weights, shied cocoa-nuts, tossed rings,
Switchbacks, Aunt Sallies, and all such small
High jinks—you call it ferial?
A holiday? But paper noses
Sniffed the artificial roses
Of round Venetian cheeks through half
Each carnival year, and masks might laugh
At things the naked face for shame
Would blush at—laugh and think no blame.
A holiday? But Galba showed
Elephants on an airy road;
Jumbo trod the tightrope then,
And in the circus armed men
Stabbed home for sport and died to break
Those dull imperatives that make
A prison of every working day,
Where all must drudge and all obey.
Sing Holiday! You do not know
How to be free. The Russian snow
Flowered with bright blood whose roses spread
Petals of fading, fading red
That died into the snow again,
Into the virgin snow; and men
From all ancient bonds were freed.
Old law, old custom, and old creed,
Old right and wrong there bled to death;
The frozen air received their breath,

A little smoke that died away;
And round about them where they lay
The snow bloomed roses. Blood was there
A red gay flower and only fair.
Sing Holiday! Beneath the Tree
Of Innocence and Liberty,
Paper Nose and Red Cockade
Dance within the magic shade
That makes them drunken, merry, and strong
To laugh and sing their ferial song:
'Free, free...!'
But Echo answers
Faintly to the laughing dancers,
'Free'—and faintly laughs, and still,
Within the hollows of the hill,
Faintlier laughs and whispers, 'Free,'
Fadingly, diminishingly:
'Free,' and laughter faints away...
Sing Holiday! Sing Holiday!"

He folded the sheet carefully and put it in his pocket. The thing had its merits. Oh, decidedly, decidedly! But how unpleasant the crowd smelt! He lit a cigarette. The smell of cows was preferable. He passed through the gate in the park wall into the garden. The swimming-pool was a centre of noise and activity.

"Second Heat in the Young Ladies' Championship." It was the polite voice of Henry Wimbush. A crowd of sleek, seal-like figures in black bathing-dresses surrounded him. His grey bowler hat, smooth, round, and motionless in the midst of a moving sea, was an island of aristocratic calm.

Holding his tortoise-shell-rimmed pince-nez an inch or two in front of his eyes, he read out names from a list.

"Miss Dolly Miles, Miss Rebecca Balister, Miss Doris Gabell..."

Five young persons ranged themselves on the brink. From their seats of honour at the other end of the pool, old Lord Moleyn and Mr. Callamay looked on with eager interest.

Henry Wimbush raised his hand. There was an expectant silence. "When I say 'Go,' go. Go!" he said. There was an almost simultaneous splash.

Denis pushed his way through the spectators. Somebody plucked him by the sleeve; he looked down. It was old Mrs. Budge.

"Delighted to see you again, Mr. Stone," she said in her rich, husky voice. She panted a little as she spoke, like a short-winded lap-dog. It was Mrs. Budge who, having read in the "Daily Mirror" that the Government needed peach stones—what they needed them for she never knew—had made the collection of peach stones her peculiar "bit" of war work. She had thirty-six peach trees in her walled garden, as well as four hot-houses in which trees could be forced, so that she was able to eat peaches practically the whole year round. In 1916 she ate 4200 peaches, and sent the stones to the Government. In 1917 the military authorities called up three of her gardeners, and what with this and the fact that it was a bad year for wall fruit, she only managed to eat 2900 peaches during that crucial period of the national destinies. In 1918 she did rather better, for between January 1st and the date of the Armistice she ate 3300 peaches. Since the Armistice she had relaxed her efforts; now she did not eat more than two or three peaches a day. Her constitution, she complained, had suffered; but it had suffered for a good cause.

Denis answered her greeting by a vague and polite noise.

"So nice to see the young people enjoying themselves," Mrs. Budge went on. "And the old people too, for that matter. Look at old Lord Moleyn and dear Mr. Callamay. Isn't it delightful to see the way they enjoy themselves?"

Denis looked. He wasn't sure whether it was so very delightful after all. Why didn't they go and watch the sack races? The two old gentlemen were engaged at the moment in congratulating the winner of the race; it seemed an act of supererogatory graciousness; for, after all, she had only won a heat.

"Pretty little thing, isn't she?" said Mrs. Budge huskily, and panted two or three times.

"Yes," Denis nodded agreement. Sixteen, slender, but nubile, he said to himself, and laid up the phrase in his memory as a happy one. Old Mr. Callamay had put on his spectacles to congratulate the victor, and Lord Moleyn, leaning forward over his walking-stick, showed his long ivory teeth, hungrily smiling.

"Capital performance, capital," Mr. Callamay was saying in his deep voice.

The victor wriggled with embarrassment. She stood with her hands behind her back, rubbing one foot nervously on the other. Her wet bathing-dress shone, a torso of black polished marble.

"Very good indeed," said Lord Moleyn. His voice seemed to come from just behind his teeth, a toothy voice. It was as though a dog should suddenly begin to speak. He smiled again, Mr. Callamay readjusted his spectacles.

"When I say 'Go,' go. Go!"

Splash! The third heat had started.

"Do you know, I never could learn to swim," said Mrs. Budge.

"Really?"

"But I used to be able to float."

Denis imagined her floating—up and down, up and down on a great green swell. A blown black bladder; no, that wasn't good, that wasn't good at all. A new winner was being congratulated. She was atrociously stubby and fat. The last one, long and harmoniously, continuously curved from knee to breast, had been an Eve by Cranach; but this, this one was a bad Rubens.

"...go—go—go!" Henry Wimbush's polite level voice once more pronounced the formula. Another batch of young ladies dived in.

Grown a little weary of sustaining a conversation with Mrs. Budge, Denis conveniently remembered that his duties as a steward called him elsewhere. He pushed out through the lines of spectators and made his way along the path left clear behind them. He was thinking again that his soul was a pale, tenuous membrane, when he was startled by hearing a thin, sibilant voice, speaking apparently from just above his head, pronounce the single word "Disgusting!"

He looked up sharply. The path along which he was walking passed under the lee of a wall of clipped yew. Behind the hedge the ground sloped steeply up towards the foot of the terrace and the house; for one standing on the higher ground it was easy to look over the dark barrier. Looking up, Denis saw two heads overtopping the hedge immediately above him. He recognised the iron mask of Mr. Bodiham and the pale, colourless face of his wife. They were looking over his head, over the heads of the spectators, at the swimmers in the pond.

"Disgusting!" Mrs. Bodiham repeated, hissing softly.

The rector turned up his iron mask towards the solid cobalt of the sky. "How long?" he said, as though to himself; "how long?" He lowered his eyes again, and they fell on Denis's upturned curious face. There was an abrupt movement, and Mr. and Mrs. Bodiham popped out of sight behind the hedge.

Denis continued his promenade. He wandered past the merry-go-round, through the thronged streets of the canvas village; the membrane of his soul flapped tumultuously in the noise and laughter. In a roped-off space beyond, Mary was directing the children's sports. Little creatures seethed round about her, making a shrill, tinny clamour; others clustered about the skirts and trousers of their parents. Mary's face was shining in the heat; with an immense output of energy she started a three-legged race. Denis looked on in admiration.

"You're wonderful," he said, coming up behind her and touching her on the arm. "I've never seen such energy."

She turned towards him a face, round, red, and honest as the setting sun; the golden bell of her hair swung silently as she moved her head and quivered to rest.

"Do you know, Denis," she said, in a low, serious voice, gasping a little as she spoke—"do you know that there's a woman here who has had three children in thirty-one months?"

"Really," said Denis, making rapid mental calculations.

"It's appalling. I've been telling her about the Malthusian League. One really ought..."

But a sudden violent renewal of the metallic yelling announced the fact that somebody had won the race. Mary became once more the centre of a dangerous vortex. It was time, Denis thought, to move on; he might be asked to do something if he stayed too long.

He turned back towards the canvas village. The thought of tea was making itself insistent in his mind. Tea, tea, tea. But the tea-tent was horribly thronged. Anne, with an unusual expression of grimness on her flushed face, was furiously working the handle of the urn; the brown liquid spurted incessantly into the proffered cups. Portentous, in the farther corner of the tent, Priscilla, in her royal toque, was encouraging the villagers. In a momentary lull Denis could hear her deep, jovial laughter and her manly voice. Clearly, he told himself, this was no place for one who wanted tea. He stood irresolute at the entrance to the tent. A beautiful thought suddenly came to him; if he went back to the house, went unobtrusively, without being observed, if he tiptoed into the dining-room and noiselessly opened the little doors of the sideboard—ah, then! In the cool recess within he would find bottles and a siphon; a bottle of crystal gin and a quart of soda water, and then for the cups that inebriate as well as cheer...

A minute later he was walking briskly up the shady yew-tree walk. Within the house it was deliciously quiet and cool. Carrying his well-filled tumbler with care, he went into the library. There, the glass on the corner of the table beside him, he settled into a chair with a volume of Sainte-Beuve. There was nothing, he found, like a Causerie du Lundi for settling and soothing the troubled spirits. That tenuous membrane of his had been too rudely buffeted by the afternoon's emotions; it required a rest.

CHAPTER XXVIII.

Towards sunset the fair itself became quiescent. It was the hour for the dancing to begin. At one side of the village of tents a space had been roped off. Acetylene lamps, hung round it on posts, cast a piercing white light. In one corner sat the band, and, obedient to its scraping and blowing, two or three hundred dancers trampled across the dry ground, wearing away the grass with their booted feet. Round this patch of all but daylight, alive with motion and noise, the night seemed preternaturally dark. Bars of light reached out into it, and every now and then a lonely figure or a couple of lovers, interlaced, would cross the bright shaft, flashing for a moment into visible existence, to disappear again as quickly and surprisingly as they had come.

Denis stood by the entrance of the enclosure, watching the swaying, shuffling crowd. The slow vortex brought the couples round and round again before him, as though he were passing them in review. There was Priscilla, still wearing her queenly toque, still encouraging the villagers—this time by dancing with one of the tenant farmers. There was Lord Moleyn, who had stayed on to the disorganised, passoverish meal that took the place of dinner on this festal day; he one-stepped shamblingly, his bent knees more precariously wobbly than ever, with a terrified village beauty. Mr. Scogan trotted round with another. Mary was in the embrace of a young farmer of heroic proportions; she was looking up at him, talking, as Denis could see, very seriously. What about? he wondered. The Malthusian League, perhaps. Seated in the corner among the band, Jenny was performing wonders of virtuosity upon the drums. Her eyes shone, she smiled to herself. A whole subterranean life seemed to be expressing itself in those loud rat-tats, those long rolls and flourishes of drumming. Looking at her, Denis ruefully remembered the red notebook; he wondered what sort of a figure he was cutting now. But the sight of Anne and Gombauld swimming past—Anne with her eyes almost shut and sleeping, as it were, on the sustaining wings of movement and music—dissipated these preoccupations. Male and female created He them...There they were, Anne and Gombauld, and a hundred couples more—all stepping harmoniously together to the old tune of Male and Female created He them. But Denis sat apart; he alone lacked his complementary opposite. They were all coupled but he; all but he...

CHAPTER XXVIII.

Somebody touched him on the shoulder and he looked up. It was Henry Wimbush.

"I never showed you our oaken drainpipes," he said. "Some of the ones we dug up are lying quite close to here. Would you like to come and see them?"

Denis got up, and they walked off together into the darkness. The music grew fainter behind them. Some of the higher notes faded out altogether. Jenny's drumming and the steady sawing of the bass throbbed on, tuneless and meaningless in their ears. Henry Wimbush halted.

"Here we are," he said, and, taking an electric torch out of his pocket, he cast a dim beam over two or three blackened sections of tree trunk, scooped out into the semblance of pipes, which were lying forlornly in a little depression in the ground.

"Very interesting," said Denis, with a rather tepid enthusiasm.

They sat down on the grass. A faint white glare, rising from behind a belt of trees, indicated the position of the dancing-floor. The music was nothing but a muffled rhythmic pulse.

"I shall be glad," said Henry Wimbush, "when this function comes at last to an end."

"I can believe it."

"I do not know how it is," Mr. Wimbush continued, "but the spectacle of numbers of my fellow-creatures in a state of agitation moves in me a certain weariness, rather than any gaiety or excitement. The fact is, they don't very much interest me. They're aren't in my line. You follow me? I could never take much interest, for example, in a collection of postage stamps. Primitives or seventeenth-century books—yes. They are my line. But stamps, no. I don't know anything about them; they're not my line. They don't interest me, they give me no emotion. It's rather the same with people, I'm afraid. I'm more at home with these pipes." He jerked his head sideways towards the hollowed logs. "The trouble with the people and events of the present is that you never know anything about them. What do I know of contemporary politics? Nothing. What do I know of the people I see round about me? Nothing. What they think of me or of anything else in the world, what they will do in five minutes' time, are things I can't guess at. For all I know, you may suddenly jump up and try to murder me in a moment's time."

"Come, come," said Denis.

"True," Mr. Wimbush continued, "the little I know about your past is certainly reassuring. But I know nothing of your present, and neither you nor I know anything of your future. It's appalling; in living people, one is dealing with unknown and unknowable quantities. One can only hope to find out anything about them by a long series of the most disagreeable and boring human contacts, involving a terrible expense of time. It's the same with current events; how can I find out anything about them except by devoting years to the most exhausting first-hand study, involving once more an endless number of the most unpleasant contacts? No, give me the past. It doesn't change; it's all there in black and white, and you can get to know about it comfortably and decorously and, above all, privately—

by reading. By reading I know a great deal of Caesar Borgia, of St. Francis, of Dr. Johnson; a few weeks have made me thoroughly acquainted with these interesting characters, and I have been spared the tedious and revolting process of getting to know them by personal contact, which I should have to do if they were living now. How gay and delightful life would be if one could get rid of all the human contacts! Perhaps, in the future, when machines have attained to a state of perfection—for I confess that I am, like Godwin and Shelley, a believer in perfectibility, the perfectibility of machinery—then, perhaps, it will be possible for those who, like myself, desire it, to live in a dignified seclusion, surrounded by the delicate attentions of silent and graceful machines, and entirely secure from any human intrusion. It is a beautiful thought."

"Beautiful," Denis agreed. "But what about the desirable human contacts, like love and friendship?"

The black silhouette against the darkness shook its head. "The pleasures even of these contacts are much exaggerated," said the polite level voice. "It seems to me doubtful whether they are equal to the pleasures of private reading and contemplation. Human contacts have been so highly valued in the past only because reading was not a common accomplishment and because books were scarce and difficult to reproduce. The world, you must remember, is only just becoming literate. As reading becomes more and more habitual and widespread, an ever-increasing number of people will discover that books will give them all the pleasures of social life and none of its intolerable tedium. At present people in search of pleasure naturally tend to congregate in large herds and to make a noise; in future their natural tendency will be to seek solitude and quiet. The proper study of mankind is books."

"I sometimes think that it may be," said Denis; he was wondering if Anne and Gombauld were still dancing together.

"Instead of which," said Mr. Wimbush, with a sigh, "I must go and see if all is well on the dancing-floor." They got up and began to walk slowly towards the white glare. "If all these people were dead," Henry Wimbush went on, "this festivity would be extremely agreeable. Nothing would be pleasanter than to read in a well-written book of an open-air ball that took place a century ago. How charming! one would say; how pretty and how amusing! But when the ball takes place to-day, when one finds oneself involved in it, then one sees the thing in its true light. It turns out to be merely this." He waved his hand in the direction of the acetylene flares. "In my youth," he went on after a pause, "I found myself, quite fortuitously, involved in a series of the most phantasmagorical amorous intrigues. A novelist could have made his fortune out of them, and even if I were to tell you, in my bald style, the details of these adventures, you would be amazed at the romantic tale. But I assure you, while they were happening—these romantic adventures—they seemed to me no more and no less exciting than any other incident of actual life. To climb by night up a rope-ladder to a second-floor window in an old house in Toledo seemed to me, while I was actually performing this rather dangerous feat, an action as obvious, as much to be taken for granted, as—

how shall I put it?—as quotidian as catching the 8.52 from Surbiton to go to business on a Monday morning. Adventures and romance only take on their adventurous and romantic qualities at second-hand. Live them, and they are just a slice of life like the rest. In literature they become as charming as this dismal ball would be if we were celebrating its tercentenary." They had come to the entrance of the enclosure and stood there, blinking in the dazzling light. "Ah, if only we were!" Henry Wimbush added.

Anne and Gombauld were still dancing together.

CHAPTER XXIX.

It was after ten o'clock. The dancers had already dispersed and the last lights were being put out. To-morrow the tents would be struck, the dismantled merry-go-round would be packed into waggons and carted away. An expanse of worn grass, a shabby brown patch in the wide green of the park, would be all that remained. Crome Fair was over.

By the edge of the pool two figures lingered.

"No, no, no," Anne was saying in a breathless whisper, leaning backwards, turning her head from side to side in an effort to escape Gombauld's kisses. "No, please. No." Her raised voice had become imperative.

Gombauld relaxed his embrace a little. "Why not?" he said. "I will."

With a sudden effort Anne freed herself. "You won't," she retorted. "You've tried to take the most unfair advantage of me."

"Unfair advantage?" echoed Gombauld in genuine surprise.

"Yes, unfair advantage. You attack me after I've been dancing for two hours, while I'm still reeling drunk with the movement, when I've lost my head, when I've got no mind left but only a rhythmical body! It's as bad as making love to someone you've drugged or intoxicated."

Gombauld laughed angrily. "Call me a White Slaver and have done with it."

"Luckily," said Anne, "I am now completely sobered, and if you try and kiss me again I shall box your ears. Shall we take a few turns round the pool?" she added. "The night is delicious."

For answer Gombauld made an irritated noise. They paced off slowly, side by side.

"What I like about the painting of Degas..." Anne began in her most detached and conversational tone.

"Oh, damn Degas!" Gombauld was almost shouting.

From where he stood, leaning in an attitude of despair against the parapet of the terrace, Denis had seen them, the two pale figures in a patch of moonlight, far down by the pool's edge. He had seen the beginning of what promised to be an endless passionate embracement, and at the sight he had fled. It was too much; he couldn't stand it. In another moment, he felt, he would have burst into irrepressible tears.

CHAPTER XXIX.

Dashing blindly into the house, he almost ran into Mr. Scogan, who was walking up and down the hall smoking a final pipe.

"Hullo!" said Mr. Scogan, catching him by the arm; dazed and hardly conscious of what he was doing or where he was, Denis stood there for a moment like a somnambulist. "What's the matter?" Mr. Scogan went on. "you look disturbed, distressed, depressed."

Denis shook his head without replying.

"Worried about the cosmos, eh?" Mr. Scogan patted him on the arm. "I know the feeling," he said. "It's a most distressing symptom. 'What's the point of it all? All is vanity. What's the good of continuing to function if one's doomed to be snuffed out at last along with everything else?' Yes, yes. I know exactly how you feel. It's most distressing if one allows oneself to be distressed. But then why allow oneself to be distressed? After all, we all know that there's no ultimate point. But what difference does that make?"

At this point the somnambulist suddenly woke up. "What?" he said, blinking and frowning at his interlocutor. "What?" Then breaking away he dashed up the stairs, two steps at a time.

Mr. Scogan ran to the foot of the stairs and called up after him. "It makes no difference, none whatever. Life is gay all the same, always, under whatever circumstances—under whatever circumstances," he added, raising his voice to a shout. But Denis was already far out of hearing, and even if he had not been, his mind to-night was proof against all the consolations of philosophy. Mr. Scogan replaced his pipe between his teeth and resumed his meditative pacing. "Under any circumstances," he repeated to himself. It was ungrammatical to begin with; was it true? And is life really its own reward? He wondered. When his pipe had burned itself to its stinking conclusion he took a drink of gin and went to bed. In ten minutes he was deeply, innocently asleep.

Denis had mechanically undressed and, clad in those flowered silk pyjamas of which he was so justly proud, was lying face downwards on his bed. Time passed. When at last he looked up, the candle which he had left alight at his bedside had burned down almost to the socket. He looked at his watch; it was nearly half-past one. His head ached, his dry, sleepless eyes felt as though they had been bruised from behind, and the blood was beating within his ears a loud arterial drum. He got up, opened the door, tiptoed noiselessly along the passage, and began to mount the stairs towards the higher floors. Arrived at the servants' quarters under the roof, he hesitated, then turning to the right he opened a little door at the end of the corridor. Within was a pitch-dark cupboard-like boxroom, hot, stuffy, and smelling of dust and old leather. He advanced cautiously into the blackness, groping with his hands. It was from this den that the ladder went up to the leads of the western tower. He found the ladder, and set his feet on the rungs; noiselessly, he lifted the trap-door above his head; the moonlit sky was over him, he breathed the fresh, cool air of the night. In a moment he was standing on the leads, gazing out over the dim, colourless landscape, looking perpendicularly down at the terrace seventy feet below.

Why had he climbed up to this high, desolate place? Was it to look at the moon? Was it to commit suicide? As yet he hardly knew. Death—the tears came into his eyes when he thought of it. His misery assumed a certain solemnity; he was lifted up on the wings of a kind of exaltation. It was a mood in which he might have done almost anything, however foolish. He advanced towards the farther parapet; the drop was sheer there and uninterrupted. A good leap, and perhaps one might clear the narrow terrace and so crash down yet another thirty feet to the sun-baked ground below. He paused at the corner of the tower, looking now down into the shadowy gulf below, now up towards the rare stars and the waning moon. He made a gesture with his hand, muttered something, he could not afterwards remember what; but the fact that he had said it aloud gave the utterance a peculiarly terrible significance. Then he looked down once more into the depths.

"What ARE you doing, Denis?" questioned a voice from somewhere very close behind him.

Denis uttered a cry of frightened surprise, and very nearly went over the parapet in good earnest. His heart was beating terribly, and he was pale when, recovering himself, he turned round in the direction from which the voice had come.

"Are you ill?"

In the profound shadow that slept under the eastern parapet of the tower, he saw something he had not previously noticed—an oblong shape. It was a mattress, and someone was lying on it. Since that first memorable night on the tower, Mary had slept out every evening; it was a sort of manifestation of fidelity.

"It gave me a fright," she went on, "to wake up and see you waving your arms and gibbering there. What on earth were you doing?"

Denis laughed melodramatically. "What, indeed!" he said. If she hadn't woken up as she did, he would be lying in pieces at the bottom of the tower; he was certain of that, now.

"You hadn't got designs on me, I hope?" Mary inquired, jumping too rapidly to conclusions.

"I didn't know you were here," said Denis, laughing more bitterly and artificially than before.

"What IS the matter, Denis?"

He sat down on the edge of the mattress, and for all reply went on laughing in the same frightful and improbable tone.

An hour later he was reposing with his head on Mary's knees, and she, with an affectionate solicitude that was wholly maternal, was running her fingers through his tangled hair. He had told her everything, everything: his hopeless love, his jealousy, his despair, his suicide—as it were providentially averted by her interposition. He had solemnly promised never to think of self-destruction again. And now his soul was floating in a sad serenity. It was embalmed in the sympathy that Mary so generously poured. And it was not only in receiving sympathy that Denis found serenity and even a kind of happiness; it was also in giving it. For if he had told Mary everything about his miseries, Mary, reacting to these confidences, had told him in return everything, or very nearly everything, about her own.

"Poor Mary!" He was very sorry for her. Still, she might have guessed that Ivor wasn't precisely a monument of constancy.

"Well," she concluded, "one must put a good face on it." She wanted to cry, but she wouldn't allow herself to be weak. There was a silence.

"Do you think," asked Denis hesitatingly—"do you really think that she...that Gombauld..."

"I'm sure of it," Mary answered decisively. There was another long pause.

"I don't know what to do about it," he said at last, utterly dejected.

"You'd better go away," advised Mary. "It's the safest thing, and the most sensible."

"But I've arranged to stay here three weeks more."

"You must concoct an excuse."

"I suppose you're right."

"I know I am," said Mary, who was recovering all her firm self-possession. "You can't go on like this, can you?"

"No, I can't go on like this," he echoed.

Immensely practical, Mary invented a plan of action. Startlingly, in the darkness, the church clock struck three.

"You must go to bed at once," she said. "I'd no idea it was so late."

Denis clambered down the ladder, cautiously descended the creaking stairs. His room was dark; the candle had long ago guttered to extinction. He got into bed and fell asleep almost at once.

CHAPTER XXX.

Denis had been called, but in spite of the parted curtains he had dropped off again into that drowsy, dozy state when sleep becomes a sensual pleasure almost consciously savoured. In this condition he might have remained for another hour if he had not been disturbed by a violent rapping at the door.

"Come in," he mumbled, without opening his eyes. The latch clicked, a hand seized him by the shoulder and he was rudely shaken.

"Get up, get up!"

His eyelids blinked painfully apart, and he saw Mary standing over him, bright-faced and earnest.

"Get up!" she repeated. "You must go and send the telegram. Don't you remember?"

"O Lord!" He threw off the bed-clothes; his tormentor retired.

Denis dressed as quickly as he could and ran up the road to the village post office. Satisfaction glowed within him as he returned. He had sent a long telegram, which would in a few hours evoke an answer ordering him back to town at once—on urgent business. It was an act performed, a decisive step taken—and he so rarely took decisive steps; he felt pleased with himself. It was with a whetted appetite that he came in to breakfast.

"Good-morning," said Mr. Scogan. "I hope you're better."

"Better?"

"You were rather worried about the cosmos last night."

Denis tried to laugh away the impeachment. "Was I?" he lightly asked.

"I wish," said Mr. Scogan, "that I had nothing worse to prey on my mind. I should be a happy man."

"One is only happy in action," Denis enunciated, thinking of the telegram.

He looked out of the window. Great florid baroque clouds floated high in the blue heaven. A wind stirred among the trees, and their shaken foliage twinkled and glittered like metal in the sun. Everything seemed marvellously beautiful. At the thought that he would soon be leaving all this beauty he felt a momentary pang; but he comforted himself by recollecting how decisively he was acting.

"Action," he repeated aloud, and going over to the sideboard he helped himself to an agreeable mixture of bacon and fish.

CHAPTER XXX.

Breakfast over, Denis repaired to the terrace, and, sitting there, raised the enormous bulwark of the "Times" against the possible assaults of Mr. Scogan, who showed an unappeased desire to go on talking about the Universe. Secure behind the crackling pages, he meditated. In the light of this brilliant morning the emotions of last night seemed somehow rather remote. And what if he had seen them embracing in the moonlight? Perhaps it didn't mean much after all. And even if it did, why shouldn't he stay? He felt strong enough to stay, strong enough to be aloof, disinterested, a mere friendly acquaintance. And even if he weren't strong enough...

"What time do you think the telegram will arrive?" asked Mary suddenly, thrusting in upon him over the top of the paper.

Denis started guiltily. "I don't know at all," he said.

"I was only wondering," said Mary, "because there's a very good train at 3.27, and it would be nice if you could catch it, wouldn't it?"

"Awfully nice," he agreed weakly. He felt as though he were making arrangements for his own funeral. Train leaves Waterloo 3.27. No flowers...Mary was gone. No, he was blowed if he'd let himself be hurried down to the Necropolis like this. He was blowed. The sight of Mr. Scogan looking out, with a hungry expression, from the drawing-room window made him precipitately hoist the "Times" once more. For a long while he kept it hoisted. Lowering it at last to take another cautious peep at his surroundings, he found himself, with what astonishment! confronted by Anne's faint, amused, malicious smile. She was standing before him,—the woman who was a tree,—the swaying grace of her movement arrested in a pose that seemed itself a movement.

"How long have you been standing there?" he asked, when he had done gaping at her.

"Oh, about half an hour, I suppose," she said airily. "You were so very deep in your paper—head over ears—I didn't like to disturb you."

"You look lovely this morning," Denis exclaimed. It was the first time he had ever had the courage to utter a personal remark of the kind.

Anne held up her hand as though to ward off a blow. "Don't bludgeon me, please." She sat down on the bench beside him. He was a nice boy, she thought, quite charming; and Gombauld's violent insistences were really becoming rather tiresome. "Why don't you wear white trousers?" she asked. "I like you so much in white trousers."

"They're at the wash," Denis replied rather curtly. This white-trouser business was all in the wrong spirit. He was just preparing a scheme to manoeuvre the conversation back to the proper path, when Mr. Scogan suddenly darted out of the house, crossed the terrace with clockwork rapidity, and came to a halt in front of the bench on which they were seated.

"To go on with our interesting conversation about the cosmos," he began, "I become more and more convinced that the various parts of the concern are fundamentally discrete...But would you mind, Denis, moving a shade to your right?" He wedged himself between them on the bench. "And if you would shift a few inches to the left, my dear Anne...Thank you. Discrete, I think, was what I was saying."

"You were," said Anne. Denis was speechless.

They were taking their after luncheon coffee in the library when the telegram arrived. Denis blushed guiltily as he took the orange envelope from the salver and tore it open. "Return at once. Urgent family business." It was too ridiculous. As if he had any family business! Wouldn't it be best just to crumple the thing up and put it in his pocket without saying anything about it? He looked up; Mary's large blue china eyes were fixed upon him, seriously, penetratingly. He blushed more deeply than ever, hesitated in a horrible uncertainty.

"What's your telegram about?" Mary asked significantly.

He lost his head, "I'm afraid," he mumbled, "I'm afraid this means I shall have to go back to town at once." He frowned at the telegram ferociously.

"But that's absurd, impossible," cried Anne. She had been standing by the window talking to Gombauld; but at Denis's words she came swaying across the room towards him.

"It's urgent," he repeated desperately.

"But you've only been here such a short time," Anne protested.

"I know," he said, utterly miserable. Oh, if only she could understand! Women were supposed to have intuition.

"If he must go, he must," put in Mary firmly.

"Yes, I must." He looked at the telegram again for inspiration. "You see, it's urgent family business," he explained.

Priscilla got up from her chair in some excitement. "I had a distinct presentiment of this last night," she said. "A distinct presentiment."

"A mere coincidence, no doubt," said Mary, brushing Mrs. Wimbush out of the conversation. "There's a very good train at 3.27." She looked at the clock on the mantelpiece. "You'll have nice time to pack."

"I'll order the motor at once." Henry Wimbush rang the bell. The funeral was well under way. It was awful, awful.

"I am wretched you should be going," said Anne.

Denis turned towards her; she really did look wretched. He abandoned himself hopelessly, fatalistically to his destiny. This was what came of action, of doing something decisive. If only he'd just let things drift! If only...

"I shall miss your conversation," said Mr. Scogan.

Mary looked at the clock again. "I think perhaps you ought to go and pack," she said.

Obediently Denis left the room. Never again, he said to himself, never again would he do anything decisive. Camlet, West Bowlby, Knipswich for Timpany, Spavin Delawarr; and then all the other stations; and then, finally, London. The thought of the journey appalled him. And what on earth was he going to do in London when he got there? He climbed wearily up the stairs. It was time for him to lay himself in his coffin.

CHAPTER XXX.

The car was at the door—the hearse. The whole party had assembled to see him go. Good-bye, good-bye. Mechanically he tapped the barometer that hung in the porch; the needle stirred perceptibly to the left. A sudden smile lighted up his lugubrious face.

"'It sinks and I am ready to depart,'" he said, quoting Landor with an exquisite aptness. He looked quickly round from face to face. Nobody had noticed. He climbed into the hearse.

THE BURNING WHEEL

My thanks are due to the Editor of the Nation for permission to reprint "The Mirror," "Variations on a theme of Laforgue" and "Philosophy."

THE BURNING WHEEL.

Wearied of its own turning,
Distressed with its own busy restlessness,
Yearning to draw the circumferent pain—
The rim that is dizzy with speed—
To the motionless centre, there to rest,
The wheel must strain through agony
On agony contracting, returning
Into the core of steel.
And at last the wheel has rest, is still,
Shrunk to an adamant core:
Fulfilling its will in fixity.
But the yearning atoms, as they grind
Closer and closer, more and more
Fiercely together, beget
A flaming fire upward leaping,
Billowing out in a burning,
Passionate, fierce desire to find
The infinite calm of the mother's breast.
And there the flame is a Christ-child sleeping,
Bright, tenderly radiant;
All bitterness lost in the infinite
Peace of the mother's bosom.
But death comes creeping in a tide
Of slow oblivion, till the flame in fear
Wakes from the sleep of its quiet brightness
And burns with a darkening passion and pain,
Lest, all forgetting in quiet, it perish.
And as it burns and anguishes it quickens,
Begetting once again the wheel that yearns—
Sick with its speed—for the terrible stillness
Of the adamant core and the steel-hard chain.
And so once more
Shall the wheel revolve till its anguish cease

In the iron anguish of fixity;
Till once again
Flame billows out to infinity,
Sinking to a sleep of brightness
In that vast oblivious peace.

DOORS OF THE TEMPLE.

Many are the doors of the spirit that lead
  Into the inmost shrine:
And I count the gates of the temple divine,
  Since the god of the place is God indeed.
  And these are the gates that God decreed
Should lead to his house:—kisses and wine,
Cool depths of thought, youth without rest,
  And calm old age, prayer and desire,
The lover's and mother's breast,
  The fire of sense and the poet's fire.

But he that worships the gates alone,
  Forgetting the shrine beyond, shall see
  The great valves open suddenly,
Revealing, not God's radiant throne,
  But the fires of wrath and agony.

VILLIERS DE L'ISLE-ADAM.

Up from the darkness on the laughing stage
A sudden trap-door shot you unawares,
Incarnate Tragedy, with your strange airs
Of courteous sadness. Nothing could assuage
The secular grief that was your heritage,
Passed down the long line to the last that bears
The name, a gift of yearnings and despairs
Too greatly noble for this iron age.

Time moved for you not in quotidian beats,
But in the long slow rhythm the ages keep
In their immortal symphony. You taught
That not in the harsh turmoil of the streets
Does life consist; you bade the soul drink deep
Of infinite things, saying: "The rest is naught."

DARKNESS.

My close-walled soul has never known
That innermost darkness, dazzling sight,
Like the blind point, whence the visions spring
In the core of the gazer's chrysolite ...
The mystic darkness that laps God's throne
In a splendour beyond imagining,
  So passing bright.

But the many twisted darknesses
That range the city to and fro,
In aimless subtlety pass and part
And ebb and glutinously flow;
Darkness of lust and avarice,
Of the crippled body and the crooked heart ...
  These darknesses I know.

MOLE.

Tunnelled in solid blackness creeps
The old mole-soul, and wakes or sleeps,
He knows not which, but tunnels on
Through ages of oblivion;
Until at last the long constraint
Of each-hand wall is lost, and faint
Comes daylight creeping from afar,
And mole-work grows crepuscular.
Tunnel meets air and bursts; mole sees
Men hugely walking ... or are they trees?
And far horizons smoking blue,
And chasing clouds for ever new?
Green hills, like lighted lamps aglow
Or quenching 'neath the cloud-shadow;
Quenching and blazing turn by turn,
Spring's great green signals fitfully burn.
Mole travels on, but finds the steering
A harder task of pioneering
Than when he thridded through the strait
Blind catacombs that ancient fate
Had carved for him. Stupid and dumb
And blind and touchless he had come
A way without a turn; but here,
Under the sky, the passenger
Chooses his own best way; and mole
Distracted wanders, yet his hole
Regrets not much wherein he crept,
But runs, a joyous nympholept,
This way and that, by all made mad—
River nymph and oread,
Ocean's daughters and Lorelei,
Combing the silken mystery,
The glaucous gold of her rivery tresses—

Each haunts the traveller, each possesses
The drunken wavering soul awhile;
Then with a phantom's cock-crow smile
Mocks craving with sheer vanishment.

Mole-eyes grow hawk's: knowledge is lent
In grudging driblets that pay high
Unconscionable usury
To unrelenting life. Mole learns
To travel more secure; the turns
Of his long way less puzzling seem,
And all those magic forms that gleam
In airy invitation cheat
Less often than they did of old.

The earth slopes upward, fold by fold
Of quiet hills that meet the gold
Serenity of western skies.
Over the world's edge with clear eyes
Our mole transcendent sees his way
Tunnelled in light: he must obey
Necessity again and thrid
Close catacombs as erst he did,
Fate's tunnellings, himself must bore
Through the sunset's inmost core.
The guiding walls to each-hand shine
Luminous and crystalline;
And mole shall tunnel on and on,
Till night let fall oblivion.

THE TWO SEASONS.

Summer, on himself intent,
  Passed without, for nothing caring
    Save his own high festival.
  My windows, blind and winkless staring,
Wondered what the pageant meant,
    Nor ever understood at all.
And oh, the pains of sentiment!
  The loneliness beyond all bearing ...
    Mucus and spleen and gall!

But now that grey November peers
  In at my fire-bright window pane?
    And all its misty spires and trees
  Loom in upon me through the rain
And question of the light that cheers
    The room within—now my soul sees
Life, where of old were sepulchres;
    And in these new-found sympathies
Sinks petty hopes and loves and fears,
  And knows that life is not in vain.

TWO REALITIES.

A waggon passed with scarlet wheels
  And a yellow body, shining new.
"Splendid!" said I. "How fine it feels
To be alive, when beauty peels
  The grimy husk from life." And you

Said, "Splendid!" and I thought you'd seen
  That waggon blazing down the street;
But I looked and saw that your gaze had been
On a child that was kicking an obscene
  Brown ordure with his feet.

Our souls are elephants, thought I,
  Remote behind a prisoning grill,
With trunks thrust out to peer and pry
And pounce upon reality;
  And each at his own sweet will

Seizes the bun that he likes best
And passes over all the rest.

QUOTIDIAN VISION.

There is a sadness in the street,
And sullenly the folk I meet
Droop their heads as they walk along,
Without a smile, without a song.
A mist of cold and muffling grey
Falls, fold by fold, on another day
That dies unwept. But suddenly,
Under a tunnelled arch I see
On flank and haunch the chestnut gleam
Of horses in a lamplit steam;
And the dead world moves for me once more
With beauty for its living core.

VISION.

I had been sitting alone with books,
  Till doubt was a black disease,
When I heard the cheerful shout of rooks
  In the bare, prophetic trees.

Bare trees, prophetic of new birth,
  You lift your branches clean and free
To be a beacon to the earth,
  A flame of wrath for all to see.

And the rooks in the branches laugh and shout
  To those that can hear and understand;
"Walk through the gloomy ways of doubt
  With the torch of vision in your hand."

THE MIRROR.

Slow-moving moonlight once did pass
Across the dreaming looking-glass,
Where, sunk inviolably deep,
Old secrets unforgotten sleep
Of beauties unforgettable.

But dusty cobwebs are woven now
Across that mirror, which of old
Saw fingers drawing back the gold
From an untroubled brow;
And the depths are blinded to the moon,
And their secrets forgotten, for ever untold.

VARIATIONS ON A THEME OF LAFORGUE.

Youth as it opens out discloses
The sinister metempsychosis
Of lilies dead and turned to roses
Red as an angry dawn.
But lilies, remember, are grave-side flowers,
  While slow bright rose-leaves sail
Adrift on the music of happiest hours;
  And those lilies, cold and pale,
Hide fiery roses beneath the lawn
  Of the young bride's parting veil.

PHILOSOPHY.

"God needs no christening,"
  Pantheist mutters,
  "Love opens shutters
On heaven's glistening.
Flesh, key-hole listening,
  Hears what God utters" ...
  Yes, but God stutters.

PHILOCLEA IN THE FOREST.

I.

'TWas I that leaned to Amoret
With: "What if the briars have tangled Time,
Till, lost in the wood-ways, he quite forget
How plaintive in cities at midnight sounds the chime
Of bells slow-dying from discord to the hush whence
they rose and met.

"And in the forest we shall live free,
Free from the bondage that Time has made
To hedge our soul from its liberty?
We shall not fear what is mighty, and unafraid
Shall look wide-eyed at beauty, nor shrink from its majesty."

But Amoret answered me again:
"We are lost in the forest, you and I;
Lost, lost, not free, though no bonds restrain;
For no spire rises for comfort, no landmark in the sky,
And the long glades as they curve from sight are dark
with a nameless pain.

And Time creates what he devours,—
Music that sweetly dreams itself away,
Frail-swung leaves of autumn and the scent of flowers,
And the beauty of that poised moment, when the day
Hangs 'twixt the quiet of darkness and the mirth of the
sunlit hours."

II.

Mottled and grey and brown they pass,
The wood-moths, wheeling, fluttering;
And we chase and they vanish; and in the grass
Are starry flowers, and the birds sing
Faint broken songs of the dying spring.
  And on the beech-bole, smooth and grey,
  Some lover of an older day
Has carved in time-blurred lettering
One word only—"Alas."

III.

Lutes, I forbid you! You must never play,
  When shimmeringly, glimpse by glimpse
Seen through the leaves, the silken figures sway
In measured dance. Never at shut of day,
When Time perversely loitering limps
  Through endless twilights, should your strings
  Whisper of light remembered things
  That happened long ago and far away:
Lutes, I forbid you! You must never play...

And you, pale marble statues, far descried
  Where vistas open suddenly,
I bid you shew yourselves no more, but hide
Your loveliness, lest too much glorified
  By western radiance slantingly
  Shot down the glade, you turn from stone
  To living gods, immortal grown,
And, ageless, mock my beauty's fleeting pride,
You pale, relentless statues, far descried...

BOOKS AND THOUGHTS.

Old ghosts that death forgot to ferry
Across the Lethe of the years-
These are my friends, and at their tears
I weep and with their mirth am merry.
On a high tower, whose battlements
Give me all heaven at a glance,
I lie long summer nights in trance,
Drowsed by the murmurs and the scents
That rise from earth, while the sky above me
Merges its peace with my soul's peace,
Deep meeting deep. No stir can move me,
Nought break the quiet of my release:
  In vain the windy sunlight raves
  At the hush and gloom of polar caves.

"CONTRARY TO NATURE AND ARISTOTLE."

One head of my soul's amphisbaena
Turns to the daytime's dust and sweat;
But evenings come, when I would forget
The sordid strife of the arena.

And then my other self will creep
Along the scented twilight lanes
To where a little house contains
A hoard of books, a gift of sleep.

Its windows throw a friendly light
Between the narrowing shutter slats,
And, golden as the eyes of cats,
Shine me a welcome through the night.

ESCAPE.

I seek the quietude of stones
Or of great oxen, dewlap-deep
In meadows of lush grass, where sleep
Drifts, tufted, on the air or drones
On flowery traffic. Sleep atones
For sin, comforting eyes that weep.
O'er me, Lethean darkness, creep
Unfelt as tides through dead men's bones!

In that metallic sea of hair,
Fragrance! I come to drown despair
Of wings in dark forgetfulness.
No love ... Love is self-known, aspires
To heights unearthly. I ask less,—
Sleep born of satisfied desires.

THE GARDEN.

There shall be dark trees round me:—I insist
On cypresses: I'm terribly romantic—
And glimpsed between shall move the whole Atlantic,
Now leaden dull, now subtle with grey mist,
Now many jewelled, when the waves are kissed
By revelling sunlight and the corybantic
South-Western wind: so, troubled, passion-frantic,
The poet's mind boils gold and amethyst.

There shall be seen the infinite endeavour
Of a sad fountain, white against the sky
And poised as it strains up, but doomed to break
In weeping music; ever fair and ever
Young ... and the bright-eyed wood-gods as they slake
Their thirst in it, are silent, reverently ...

THE CANAL.

No dip and dart of swallows wakes the black
Slumber of the canal:—a mirror dead
For lack of loveliness remembered
From ancient azures and green trees, for lack
Of some white beauty given and flung back,
Secret, to her that gave: no sun has bled
To wake an echo here of answering red;
The surface stirs to no leaf's wind-blown track.

Between unseeing walls the waters rest,
Lifeless and hushed, till suddenly a swan
Glides from some broader river blue as day,
And with the mirrored magic of his breast
Creates within that barren water-way
New life, new loveliness, and passes on.

THE IDEAL FOUND WANTING.

I'm sick of clownery and Owlglass tricks;
Damn the whole crowd of you I I hate you all.
The same, night after night, from powdered stall
To sweating gallery, your faces fix
In flux an idiot mean. The Apteryx
You worship is no victory; you call
On old stupidity, God made to crawl
For tempting with world-wisdom's narcotics.

I'll break a window through my prison! See,
The sunset bleeds among the roofs; comes night,
Dark blue and calm as music dying out.
Is it escape? No, the laugh's turned on me!
I kicked at cardboard, gaped at red limelight;
You laughed and cheered my latest knockabout.

MISPLACED LOVE.

Red wine that slowly leaned and brimmed the shell
Of pearl, where lips had touched, as light and swift
As naked petals of the rose adrift
Upon the lazy-luted ritournelle
Of summer bee-song: laughing as they fell,
Gold memories: dream incense, childhood's gift,
Blue as the smoke that far horizons lift,
Tenuous as the wings of Ariel:—

These treasured things I laid upon the pyre;
And the flame kindled, and I fanned it high,
And, strong in hope, could watch the crumbling past.
Eager I knelt before the waning fire,
Phoenix, to greet thine immortality ...
But there was naught but ashes at the last.

SONNET.

Were I to die, you'd break your heart, you say.
Well, if it do but bend, I'm satisfied—
Bend and rebound—for hearts are temper-tried,
Mild steel, not hardened, with the spring and play
Of excellent tough swords. It's not that way
That you'll be perishing. But when I've died,
When snap! my light goes out, what will betide
You, if the heart-breaks give you leave to stay?

What will be left, I wonder, if you lose
All that you gave me? "All? A year or so
Out of a life," you say. But worlds, say I,
Of kisses timeless given in ecstasy
That gave me Real You. I die: you go
With me. What's left? Limbs, clothes, a pair of shoes?...

SENTIMENTAL SUMMER.

The West has plucked its flowers and has thrown
Them fading on the night. Out of the sky's
Black depths there smiles a greeting from those eyes,
Where all the Real, all I have ever known
Of the divine is held. And not alone
Do I stand here now ... a presence seems to rise:
Your voice sounds near across my memories,
And answering fingers brush against my own.
Yes, it is you: for evening holds those strands
Of fire and darkness twined in one to make
Your loveliness a web of magic mesh,
Whose cross-weft harmony of soul and flesh
Shadows a thought or glows, when smiles awake,
Like sunlight passionate on southern lands.

THE CHOICE.

Comrade, now that you're merry
And therefore true,
Say—where would you like to die
And have your friend to bury
What once was you?
"On the top of a hill
With a peaceful view
Of country where all is still?"...
Great God, not I!
I'd lie in the street
Where two streams meet
And there's noise enough to fill
The outer ear,
While within the brain can beat
Marches of death and life,
Glory and joy and fear,
Peace of the sort that moves
And clash of strife
And routs of armies fleeing.
There would I shake myself clear
Out of the deep-set grooves
Of my sluggish being.

THE HIGHER SENSUALISM.

There's a church by a lake in Italy
Stands white on a hill against the sky?
And a path of immemorial cobbles
Leads up and up, where the pilgrim hobbles
Past a score or so of neat reposories,
Where you stop and breathe and tell your rosaries
To the shrined terra-cotta mannikins,
That expound with the liveliest quirks and grins
Known texts of Scripture. But no long stay
Should the pilgrim make upon his way;
But as means to the end these shrines stand here
To guide to something holier,
The church on the hilltop.

Your heaven's so,
With a path leading up to it past a row
Of votary Priapulids;
At each you pause and tell your beads
Along the quintuple strings of sense:
Then on, to face Heaven's eminence,
New stimulated, new inspired.

SONNET.

If that a sparkle of true starshine be
That led my way; if some diviner thing
Than common thought urged me to fashioning
Close-woven links of burnished poetry;
Then all the heaven that one time dwelt in me
Has fled, leaving the body triumphing.
Dead flesh it seems, with not a dream to bring
Visions that better warm immediacy.

Why have my visions left me, what could kill
That feeble spark, which yet had life and heat?
Fulfilment shewed a present rich and fair:
I strive to mount, but catch the nearest still:
Souls have been drowned between heart's beat and beat,
And trapped and tangled in a woman's hair.

FORMAL VERSES.

I.

Mother of all my future memories,
  Mistress of my new life, which but to-day
Began, when I beheld, deep in your eyes,
My own love mirrored and the warm surprise
  Of the first kiss swept both our souls away,

Your love has freed me; for I was oppressed
  By my own devil, whose unwholesome breath
Tarnished my youth, leaving to me at best
Age lacking comfort of a soul at rest
  And weariness beyond the hope of death.

II.

Ah, those were days of silent happiness!
  I never spoke, and had no need to speak,
  While on the windy down-land, cheek by cheek,
The slow-driven sun beheld us. Each caress
Had oratory for its own defence;
And when I kissed or felt her fingers press,
  I envied not Demosthenes his Greek,
Nor Tully for his Latin eloquence.

PERILS OF THE SMALL HOURS.

When life burns low as the fire in the grate
And all the evening's books are read,
I sit alone, save for the dead
And the lovers I have grown to hate.

But all at once the narrow gloom
Of hatred and despair expands
In tenderness: thought stretches hands
To welcome to the midnight room

Another presence:—a memory
Of how last year in the sunlit field,
Laughing, you suddenly revealed
Beauty in immortality.

For so it is; a gesture strips
Life bare of all its make-believe.
All unprepared we may receive
Our casual apocalypse.

Sheer beauty, then you seemed to stir
Unbodied soul; soul sleeps to-night,
And love comes, dimming spirit's sight,
When body plays interpreter.

COMPLAINT.

I have tried to remember the familiar places,—
  The pillared gloom of the beechwoods, the towns
by the sea,—
I have tried to people the past with dear known faces,
  But you were haunting me.

Like a remorse, insistent, pitiless,
  You have filled my spirit, you were ever at hand;
You have mocked my gods with your new loveliness:
  Broken the old shrines stand.

RETURN TO AN OLD HOME.

In this wood—how the hazels have grown!—
I left a treasure all my own
Of childish kisses and laughter and pain;
Left, till I might come back again
To take from the familiar earth
My hoarded secret and count its worth.
And all the spider-work of the years,
All the time-spun gossamers,
Dewed with each succeeding spring;
And the piled up leaves the Autumns fling
To the sweet corruption of death on death....
At the sudden stir of my spirit's breath
All scattered. New and fair and bright
As ever it was, before my sight
The treasure lay, and nothing missed.
So having handled all and kissed,
I put them back, adding one new
And precious memory of you.

FRAGMENT.

We're German scholars poring over life,
As over a Greek manuscript that's torn
And stained beyond repair. Our eyes of horn
Read one or two poor letters; and what strife,
What books on books begotten for their sake!
But we enjoy it; and meanwhile neglect
The line that's left us perfect from the wrecked
Rich argosy, clear beyond doubts to make
Conjectures of. So in my universe
Of scribbled half-hid meanings you appear,
Sole perfect symbol of the highest sphere;
And life's great matrix crystal, whose depths nurse
Soul's infinite reflections, glows in you
With now uncertain radiance...

THE WALK.

I. THROUGH THE SUBURBS.

Provincial Sunday broods above the town:
The street's asleep; through a dim window drifts
A small romance that hiccoughs up and down
An air all trills and runs and sudden lifts
To yearning sevenths poised ... not Chopin quite,
But, oh, romantic; a tinsel world made bright
With rose and honeysuckle's paper blooms,
And where the moon's blue limelight and the glooms
Of last-act scenes of passion are discreet.
And when the tinkling stops and leaves the street
Blank in the sunlight of the afternoon
You feel a curtain dropped. Poor little tune!
Perhaps our grandmother's dull girlhood days
Were fired by you with radiances of pink,
Heavenly, brighter far than she could think
Anything might be ... till a greater blaze
Tinged life's horizon, when he kissed her first,
Our grandpapa. But a thin ghost still plays
In music down the street, echoing the plaint
Of far romance with its own sadder song
Of Everyday; and as they walk along,...
The young man and the woman, deep immersed
In all the suburb-comedy around ...
They seem to catch coherence in the sound
Of that ghost-music, and the words come faint:—
        Oh the months and the days,
        Oh sleeps and dinners,
        Oh the planning of ways
        And quotidian means!
    Oh endless vistas of mutton and greens,

THE WALK.

Oh weekly mimblings of prayer and praise,
  Oh Evenings with All the Winners!
 Monday sends the clothes to the wash
 And Saturday brings them home again:
 Mon Dieu, la vie est par trop moche
 And Destiny is a sale caboche;
  But I'll give you heaven
  In a dominant seven,
 And you shall not have lived in vain.

"In vain," the girl repeats, "in vain, in vain ..."
Your suburb's whole philosophy leads there.
The ox-stall for our happiness, for pain,
Poignant and sweet, the dull narcotic ache
Of wretchedness, and in resigned despair
A grim contentment ... ashen fruits to slake
A nameless, quenchless thirst. The tinkling rain
Of that small sentimental music wets
Your parching suburb: it may sprout ... who knows?...
In something red and silken like a rose,
In sheaves of almost genuine violets.

Faint chords, your sadness, secular, immense,
Brims to the bursting this poor Actual heart.
For surging through the floodgates that the sense
On sudden lightly opens sweeps the Whole
Into the narrow compass of its part.

He.

Inedited sensation of the soul!
You'd have us bless the Hire-Purchase System,
Which now allows the poorest vampers
To feel, as they abuse their piano's dampers,
That angels have stooped down and kissed 'em
With Ave-Maries from the infinite.
But poor old Infinite's dead. Long live his heir,
Lord Here-and-Now ... for all the rest
Is windy nothingness, or at the best
Home-made Chimera, bodied with despair,
Headed with formless, foolish hope.

She.

No, no!
We live in verse, for all things rhyme
With something out of space and time.

He.

But in the suburb here life needs must flow
In journalistic prose ...

She.

But we have set
Our faces towards the further hills, where yet
The wind untainted and unbound may blow.

II. FROM THE CREST.

So through the squalor, till the sky unfolds
To right and left its fringes, penned no more,
A thin canal, 'twixt shore and ugly shore
Of hovels, poured contiguous from the moulds
Of Gothic horror. Town is left at last,
Save for the tentacles that probe,... a squat
Dun house or two, allotments, plot on plot
Of cabbage, jejune, ripe or passed,
Chequering with sick yellow or verdigris
The necropolitan ground; and neat paved ways
That edge the road ... the town's last nerves ... and cease,
As if in sudden shame, where hedges raise
Their dusty greenery on either hand.
Their path mounts slowly up the hill;
And, as they walk, to right and left expand
The plain and the golden uplands and the blue
Faint smoke of distances that fade from view;
And at their feet, remote and still?
The city spreads itself.

THE WALK.

He.

That glabrous dome that lifts itself so grand,
There in the marish, is the omphalos,
The navel, umbo, middle, central boss
Of the unique, sole, true Cloud-Cuckoo Land.
Drowsy with Sunday bells and Sunday beer
Afoam in silver rumkins, there it basks,
Thinking of labours past and future tasks
And pondering on the end, forever near,
Yet ever distant as the rainbow's spring.
For still in Cuckoo-Land they're labouring,
With hopes undamped and undiscouraged hearts:
A little musty, but superb, they sit,
Piecing a god together bit by bit
Out of the chaos of his sundered parts.
Unmoved, nay pitying, they view the grins
And lewd grimaces of the folk that jeer ...
The vulgar herd, gross monster at the best,
Obscenum Mobile, the uttermost sphere,
Alas, too much the mover of the rest,
Though they turn sungates to its widdershins ...

And in some half a million years perhaps
God may at last be made ... a new, true Pan,
An Isis templed in the soul of man,
An Aphrodite with her thousand paps
Streaming eternal wisdom.
Yes, and man's vessel, all pavilioned out
With silk and flags in the fair wind astream,
Shall make the port at last, with a great shout
Ringing from all her decks, and rocking there shall dream
For ever, and dream true ... calm in those roads
As lovers' souls at evening, when they swim
Between the despairing sunset and the dim
Blue memories of mountains lost to sight
But, like half fancied, half remembered episodes
Of childhood, guessed at through the veils of night.
And the worn sailors at the mast who heard
The first far bells and knew the sound for home,
Who marked the land-weeds and the sand-stained foam
And through the storm-blast saw a wildered bird
Seek refuge at the mast-head ... these at last
Shall earn due praise when all the hubbub's past;

And Cuckoo-Landers not a few shall prove.

She.

You have fast closed the temple gates;
  You stand without in the noon-tides glow,
But the innermost darkness, where God waits,
  You do not know, you cannot know.

THE DEFEAT OF YOUTH AND OTHER POEMS

THE DEFEAT OF YOUTH

I. UNDER THE TREES.

THERE had been phantoms, pale-remembered shapes
Of this and this occasion, sisterly
In their resemblances, each effigy
Crowned with the same bright hair above the nape's
White rounded firmness, and each body alert
With such swift loveliness, that very rest
Seemed a poised movement: ... phantoms that impressed
But a faint influence and could bless or hurt
No more than dreams. And these ghost things were she;
For formless still, without identity,
Not one she seemed, not clear, but many and dim.
One face among the legions of the street,
Indifferent mystery, she was for him
Something still uncreated, incomplete.

II.

Bright windy sunshine and the shadow of cloud
Quicken the heavy summer to new birth
Of life and motion on the drowsing earth;
The huge elms stir, till all the air is loud
With their awakening from the muffled sleep
Of long hot days. And on the wavering line
That marks the alternate ebb of shade and shine,
Under the trees, a little group is deep
In laughing talk. The shadow as it flows
Across them dims the lustre of a rose,
Quenches the bright clear gold of hair, the green
Of a girl's dress, and life seems faint. The light
Swings back, and in the rose a fire is seen,
Gold hair's aflame and green grows emerald bright.

III.

She leans, and there is laughter in the face
She turns towards him; and it seems a door
Suddenly opened on some desolate place
With a burst of light and music. What before
Was hidden shines in loveliness revealed.
Now first he sees her beautiful, and knows
That he must love her; and the doom is sealed
Of all his happiness and all the woes
That shall be born of pregnant years hereafter.
The swift poise of a head, a flutter of laughter—
And love flows in on him, its vastness pent
Within his narrow life: the pain it brings,
Boundless; for love is infinite discontent
With the poor lonely life of transient things.

IV.

Men see their god, an immanence divine,
Smile through the curve of flesh or moulded clay,
In bare ploughed lands that go sloping away
To meet the sky in one clean exquisite line.
Out of the short-seen dawns of ecstasy
They draw new beauty, whence new thoughts are born
And in their turn conceive, as grains of corn
Germ and create new life and endlessly
Shall live creating. Out of earthly seeds
Springs the aerial flower. One spirit proceeds
Through change, the same in body and in soul—
The spirit of life and love that triumphs still
In its slow struggle towards some far-off goal
Through lust and death and the bitterness of will.

V.

One spirit it is that stirs the fathomless deep
Of human minds, that shakes the elms in storm,
That sings in passionate music, or on warm
Still evenings bosoms forth the tufted sleep
Of thistle-seeds that wait a travelling wind.
One spirit shapes the subtle rhythms of thought
And the long thundering seas; the soul is wrought
Of one stuff with the body—matter and mind
Woven together in so close a mesh
That flowers may blossom into a song, that flesh
May strangely teach the loveliest holiest things
To watching spirits. Truth is brought to birth
Not in some vacant heaven: its beauty springs
From the dear bosom of material earth.

VI. IN THE HAY-LOFT.

The darkness in the loft is sweet and warm
With the stored hay ... darkness intensified
By one bright shaft that enters through the wide
Tall doors from under fringes of a storm
Which makes the doomed sun brighter. On the hay,
Perched mountain-high they sit, and silently
Watch the motes dance and look at the dark sky
And mark how heartbreakingly far away
And yet how close and clear the distance seems,
While all at hand is cloud—brightness of dreams
Unrealisable, yet seen so clear,
So only just beyond the dark. They wait,
Scarce knowing what they wait for, half in fear;
Expectance draws the curtain from their fate.

VII.

The silence of the storm weighs heavily
On their strained spirits: sometimes one will say
Some trivial thing as though to ward away
Mysterious powers, that imminently lie
In wait, with the strong exorcising grace
Of everyday's futility. Desire
Becomes upon a sudden a crystal fire,
Defined and hard:—If he could kiss her face,
Could kiss her hair! As if by chance, her hand
Brushes on his ... Ah, can she understand?
Or is she pedestalled above the touch
Of his desire? He wonders: dare he seek
From her that little, that infinitely much?
And suddenly she kissed him on the cheek.

VIII. MOUNTAINS.

A stronger gust catches the cloud and twists
A spindle of rifted darkness through its heart,
A gash in the damp grey, which, thrust apart,
Reveals black depths a moment. Then the mists
Shut down again; a white uneasy sea
Heaves round the climbers and beneath their feet.
He strains on upwards through the wind and sleet,
Poised, or swift moving, or laboriously
Lifting his weight. And if he should let go,
What would he find down there, down there below
The curtain of the mist? What would he find
Beyond the dim and stifling now and here,
Beneath the unsettled turmoil of his mind?
Oh, there were nameless depths: he shrank with fear.

IX.

The hills more glorious in their coat of snow
Rise all around him, in the valleys run
Bright streams, and there are lakes that catch the sun,
And sunlit fields of emerald far below
That seem alive with inward light. In smoke
The far horizons fade; and there is peace
On everything, a sense of blessed release
From wilful strife. Like some prophetic cloak
The spirit of the mountains has descended
On all the world, and its unrest is ended.
Even the sea, glimpsed far away, seems still,
Hushed to a silver peace its storm and strife.
Mountains of vision, calm above fate and will,
You hold the promise of the freer life.

X. IN THE LITTLE ROOM.

London unfurls its incense-coloured dusk
Before the panes, rich but a while ago
With the charred gold and the red ember-glow
Of dying sunset. Houses quit the husk
Of secrecy, which, through the day, returns
A blank to all enquiry: but at nights
The cheerfulness of fire and lamp invites
The darkness inward, curious of what burns
With such a coloured life when all is dead—
The daylight world outside, with overhead
White clouds, and where we walk, the blaze
Of wet and sunlit streets, shops and the stream
Of glittering traffic—all that the nights erase,
Colour and speed, surviving but in dream.

XI.

Outside the dusk, but in the little room
All is alive with light, which brightly glints
On curving cup or the stiff folds of chintz,
Evoking its own whiteness. Shadows loom,
Bulging and black, upon the walls, where hang
Rich coloured plates of beauties that appeal
Less to the sense of sight than to the feel,
So moistly satin are their breasts. A pang,
Almost of pain, runs through him when he sees
Hanging, a homeless marvel, next to these,
The silken breastplate of a mandarin,
Centuries dead, which he had given her.
Exquisite miracle, when men could spin
Jay's wing and belly of the kingfisher!

XII.

In silence and as though expectantly
She crouches at his feet, while he caresses
His light-drawn fingers with the touch of tresses
Sleeked round her head, close-banded lustrously,
Save where at nape and temple the smooth brown
Sleaves out into a pale transparent mist
Of hair and tangled light. So to exist,
Poised 'twixt the deep of thought where spirits drown
Life in a void impalpable nothingness,
And, on the other side, the pain and stress
Of clamorous action and the gnawing fire
Of will, focal upon a point of earth—even thus
To sit, eternally without desire
And yet self-known, were happiness for us.

XIII.

She turns her head and in a flash of laughter
Looks up at him: and helplessly he feels
That life has circled with returning wheels
Back to a starting-point. Before and after
Merge in this instant, momently the same:
For it was thus she leaned and laughing turned
When, manifest, the spirit of beauty burned
In her young body with an inward flame,
And first he knew and loved her. In full tide
Life halts within him, suddenly stupefied.
Sight blackness, lightning-struck; but blindly tender
He draws her up to meet him, and she lies
Close folded by his arms in glad surrender,
Smiling, and with drooped head and half closed eyes.

XIV.

"I give you all; would that I might give more."
He sees the colour dawn across her cheeks
And die again to white; marks as she speaks
The trembling of her lips, as though she bore
Some sudden pain and hardly mastered it.
Within his arms he feels her shuddering,
Piteously trembling like some wild wood-thing
Caught unawares. Compassion infinite
Mounts up within him. Thus to hold and keep
And comfort her distressed, lull her to sleep
And gently kiss her brow and hair and eyes
Seems love perfected—templed high and white
Against the calm of golden autumn skies,
And shining quenchlessly with vestal light.

XV.

But passion ambushed by the aerial shrine
Comes forth to dance, a hoofed obscenity,
His satyr's dance, with laughter in his eye,
And cruelty along the scarlet line
Of his bright smiling mouth. All uncontrolled,
Love's rebel servant, he delights to beat
The maddening quick dry rhythm of goatish feet
Even in the sanctuary, and makes bold
To mime himself the godhead of the place.
He turns in terror from her trance-calmed face,
From the white-lidded languor of her eyes,
From lips that passion never shook before,
But glad in the promise of her sacrifice:
"I give you all; would that I might give more."

XVI.

He is afraid, seeing her lie so still,
So utterly his own; afraid lest she
Should open wide her eyes and let him see
The passionate conquest of her virgin will
Shine there in triumph, starry-bright with tears.
He thrusts her from him: face and hair and breast,
Hands he had touched, lips that his lips had pressed,
Seem things deadly to be desired. He fears
Lest she should body forth in palpable shame
Those dreams and longings that his blood, aflame
Through the hot dark of summer nights, had dreamed
And longed. Must all his love, then, turn to this?
Was lust the end of what so pure had seemed?
He must escape, ah God! her touch, her kiss.

XVII. IN THE PARK.

Laughing, "To-night," I said to him, "the Park
Has turned the garden of a symbolist.
Those old great trees that rise above the mist,
Gold with the light of evening, and the dark
Still water, where the dying sun evokes
An echoed glory—here I recognize
Those ancient gardens mirrored by the eyes
Of poets that hate the world of common folks,
Like you and me and that thin pious crowd,
Which yonder sings its hymns, so humbly proud
Of holiness. The garden of escape
Lies here; a small green world, and still the bride
Of quietness, although an imminent rape
Roars ceaselessly about on every side."

XVIII.

I had forgotten what I had lightly said,
And without speech, without a thought I went,
Steeped in that golden quiet, all content
To drink the transient beauty as it sped
Out of eternal darkness into time
To light and burn and know itself a fire;
Yet doomed—ah, fate of the fulfilled desire!—
To fade, a meteor, paying for the crime
Of living glorious in the denser air
Of our material earth. A strange despair,
An agony, yet strangely, subtly sweet
And tender as an unpassionate caress,
Filled me ... Oh laughter! youth's conceit
Grown almost conscious of youth's feebleness!

XIX.

He spoke abrupt across my dream: "Dear Garden,
A stranger to your magic peace, I stand
Beyond your walls, lost in a fevered land
Of stones and fire. Would that the gods would harden
My soul against its torment, or would blind
Those yearning glimpses of a life at rest
In perfect beauty—glimpses at the best
Through unpassed bars. And here, without, the wind
Of scattering passion blows: and women pass
Glitter-eyed down putrid alleys where the glass
Of some grimed window suddenly parades—
Ah, sickening heart-beat of desire!—the grace
Of bare and milk-warm flesh: the vision fades,
And at the pane shows a blind tortured face."

XX. SELF-TORMENT.

The days pass by, empty of thought and will:
His thought grows stagnant at its very springs,
With every channel on the world of things
Dammed up, and thus, by its long standing still,
Poisons itself and sickens to decay.
All his high love for her, his fair desire,
Loses its light; and a dull rancorous fire,
Burning darkness and bitterness that prey
Upon his heart are left. His spirit burns
Sometimes with hatred, or the hatred turns
To a fierce lust for her, more cruel than hate,
Till he is weary wrestling with its force:
And evermore she haunts him, early and late,
As pitilessly as an old remorse.

XXI.

Streets and the solitude of country places
Were once his friends. But as a man born blind,
Opening his eyes from lovely dreams, might find
The world a desert and men's larval faces
So hateful, he would wish to seek again
The darkness and his old chimeric sight
Of beauties inward—so, that fresh delight,
Vision of bright fields and angelic men,
That love which made him all the world, is gone.
Hating and hated now, he stands alone,
An island-point, measureless gulfs apart
From other lives, from the old happiness
Of being more than self, when heart to heart
Gave all, yet grew the greater, not the less.

XXII. THE QUARRY IN THE WOOD.

Swiftly deliberate, he seeks the place.
A small wind stirs, the copse is bright in the sun:
Like quicksilver the shine and shadow run
Across the leaves. A bramble whips his face,
The tears spring fast, and through the rainbow mist
He sees a world that wavers like the flame
Of a blown candle. Tears of pain and shame,
And lips that once had laughed and sung and kissed
Trembling in the passion of his sobbing breath!
The world a candle shuddering to its death,
And life a darkness, blind and utterly void
Of any love or goodness: all deceit,
This friendship and this God: all shams destroyed,
And truth seen now.
Earth fails beneath his feet.

SONG OF POPLARS

SHEPHERD, to yon tall poplars tune your flute:
Let them pierce, keenly, subtly shrill,
The slow blue rumour of the hill;
Let the grass cry with an anguish of evening gold,
And the great sky be mute.

Then hearken how the poplar trees unfold
Their buds, yet close and gummed and blind,
In airy leafage of the mind,
Rustling in silvery whispers the twin-hued scales
That fade not nor grow old.

"Poplars and fountains and you cypress spires
Springing in dark and rusty flame,
Seek you aught that hath a name?
Or say, say: Are you all an upward agony
Of undefined desires?

"Say, are you happy in the golden march
Of sunlight all across the day?
Or do you watch the uncertain way
That leads the withering moon on cloudy stairs
Over the heaven's wide arch?

"Is it towards sorrow or towards joy you lift
The sharpness of your trembling spears?
Or do you seek, through the grey tears
That blur the sky, in the heart of the triumphing blue,
A deeper, calmer rift?"

So; I have tuned my music to the trees,
And there were voices, dim below
Their shrillness, voices swelling slow
In the blue murmur of hills, and a golden cry
And then vast silences.

MY green aquarium of phantom fish,
Goggling in on me through the misty panes;
My rotting leaves and fields spongy with rains;
My few clear quiet autumn days—I wish

I could leave all, clearness and mistiness;
Sodden or goldenly crystal, all too still.
Yes, and I too rot with the leaves that fill
The hollows in the woods; I am grown less

Than human, listless, aimless as the green
Idiot fishes of my aquarium,
Who loiter down their dim tunnels and come
And look at me and drift away, nought seen

Or understood, but only glazedly
Reflected. Upwards, upwards through the shadows,
Through the lush sponginess of deep-sea meadows
Where hare-lipped monsters batten, let me ply

Winged fins, bursting this matrix dark to find
Jewels and movement, mintage of sunlight
Scattered largely by the profuse wind,
And gulfs of blue brightness, too deep for sight.

Free, newly born, on roads of music and air
Speeding and singing, I shall seek the place
Where all the shining threads of water race,
Drawn in green ropes and foamy meshes. There,

On the red fretted ramparts of a tower
Of coral rooted in the depths, shall break
An endless sequence of joy and speed and power:
Green shall shatter to foam; flake with white flake

Shall create an instant's shining constellation
Upon the blue; and all the air shall be
Full of a million wings that swift and free
Laugh in the sun, all power and strong elation.

Yes, I shall seek that reef, which is beyond
All isles however magically sleeping
In tideless seas, uncharted and unconned
Save by blind eyes; beyond the laughter and weeping

That brood like a cloud over the lands of men.
Movement, passion of colour and pure wings,
Curving to cut like knives—these are the things
I search for:—passion beyond the ken

Of our foiled violences, and, more swift
Than any blow which man aims against time,
The invulnerable, motion that shall rift
All dimness with the lightning of a rhyme,

Or note, or colour. And the body shall be
Quick as the mind; and will shall find release
From bondage to brute things; and joyously
Soul, will and body, in the strength of triune peace,

Shall live the perfect grace of power unwasted.
And love consummate, marvellously blending
Passion and reverence in a single spring
Of quickening force, till now never yet tasted,

But ever ceaselessly thirsted for, shall crown
The new life with its ageless starry fire.
I go to seek that reef, far down, far down
Below the edge of everyday's desire,

Beyond the magical islands, where of old
I was content, dreaming, to give the lie
To misery. They were all strong and bold
That thither came; and shall I dare to try?

WINTER DREAM

OH wind-swept towers,
Oh endlessly blossoming trees,
White clouds and lucid eyes,
And pools in the rocks whose unplumbed blue is pregnant
With who knows what of subtlety
And magical curves and limbs—
White Anadyomene and her shallow breasts
Mother-of-pearled with light.

And oh the April, April of straight soft hair,
Falling smooth as the mountain water and brown;
The April of little leaves unblinded,
Of rosy nipples and innocence
And the blue languor of weary eyelids.

Across a huge gulf I fling my voice
And my desires together:
Across a huge gulf ... on the other bank
Crouches April with her hair as smooth and straight and brown
As falling waters.
Oh brave curve upwards and outwards.
Oh despair of the downward tilting—
Despair still beautiful
As a great star one has watched all night
Wheeling down under the hills.
Silence widens and darkens;
Voice and desires have dropped out of sight.
I am all alone, dreaming she would come and kiss me.

THE FLOWERS

DAY after day,
At spring's return,
I watch my flowers, how they burn
Their lives away.

The candle crocus
And daffodil gold
Drink fire of the sunshine—
Quickly cold.

And the proud tulip—
How red he glows!—
Is quenched ere summer
Can kindle the rose.

Purple as the innermost
Core of a sinking flame,
Deep in the leaves the violets smoulder
To the dust whence they came.

Day after day
At spring's return,
I watch my flowers, how they burn
Their lives away,
Day after day ...

THE ELMS

FINE as the dust of plumy fountains blowing
Across the lanterns of a revelling night,
The tiny leaves of April's earliest growing
Powder the trees—so vaporously light,
They seem to float, billows of emerald foam
Blown by the South on its bright airy tide,
Seeming less trees than things beatified,
Come from the world of thought which was their home.

For a while only. Rooted strong and fast,
Soon will they lift towards the summer sky
Their mountain-mass of clotted greenery.
Their immaterial season quickly past,
They grow opaque, and therefore needs must die,
Since every earth to earth returns at last.

OUT OF THE WINDOW

IN the middle of countries, far from hills and sea,
Are the little places one passes by in trains
And never stops at; where the skies extend
Uninterrupted, and the level plains
Stretch green and yellow and green without an end.
And behind the glass of their Grand Express
Folk yawn away a province through,
With nothing to think of, nothing to do,
Nothing even to look at—never a "view"
In this damned wilderness.
But I look out of the window and find
Much to satisfy the mind.
Mark how the furrows, formed and wheeled
In a motion orderly and staid,
Sweep, as we pass, across the field
Like a drilled army on parade.
And here's a market-garden, barred
With stripe on stripe of varied greens ...
Bright potatoes, flower starred,
And the opacous colour of beans.
Each line deliberately swings
Towards me, till I see a straight
Green avenue to the heart of things,
The glimpse of a sudden opened gate
Piercing the adverse walls of fate ...
A moment only, and then, fast, fast,
The gate swings to, the avenue closes;
Fate laughs, and once more interposes
Its barriers.

The train has passed.

INSPIRATION

NOONDAY upon the Alpine meadows
Pours its avalanche of Light
And blazing flowers: the very shadows
Translucent are and bright.
It seems a glory that nought surpasses—
Passion of angels in form and hue—
When, lo! from the jewelled heaven of the grasses
Leaps a lightning of sudden blue.
Dimming the sun-drunk petals,
Bright even unto pain,
The grasshopper flashes, settles,
And then is quenched again.

SUMMER STILLNESS

THE stars are golden instants in the deep
Flawless expanse of night: the moon is set:
The river sleeps, entranced, a smooth cool sleep
Seeming so motionless that I forget
The hollow booming bridges, where it slides,
Dark with the sad looks that it bears along,
Towards a sea whose unreturning tides
Ravish the sighted ships and the sailors' song.

ANNIVERSARIES

ONCE more the windless days are here,
Quiet of autumn, when the year
Halts and looks backward and draws breath
Before it plunges into death.
Silver of mist and gossamers,
Through-shine of noonday's glassy gold,
Pale blue of skies, where nothing stirs
Save one blanched leaf, weary and old,
That over and over slowly falls
From the mute elm-trees, hanging on air
Like tattered flags along the walls
Of chapels deep in sunlit prayer.
Once more ... Within its flawless glass
To-day reflects that other day,
When, under the bracken, on the grass,
We who were lovers happily lay
And hardly spoke, or framed a thought
That was not one with the calm hills
And crystal sky. Ourselves were nought,
Our gusty passions, our burning wills
Dissolved in boundlessness, and we
Were almost bodiless, almost free.

The wind has shattered silver and gold.
Night after night of sparkling cold,
Orion lifts his tangled feet
From where the tossing branches beat
In a fine surf against the sky.
So the trance ended, and we grew
Restless, we knew not how or why;
And there were sudden gusts that blew
Our dreaming banners into storm;
We wore the uncertain crumbling form
Of a brown swirl of windy leaves,
A phantom shape that stirs and heaves
Shuddering from earth, to fall again
With a dry whisper of withered rain.

Last, from the dead and shrunken days
We conjured spring, lighting the blaze
Of burnished tulips in the dark;
And from black frost we struck a spark
Of blue delight and fragrance new,
A little world of flowers and dew.
Winter for us was over and done:
The drought of fluttering leaves had grown
Emerald shining in the sun,
As light as glass, as firm as stone.
Real once more: for we had passed
Through passion into thought again;
Shaped our desires and made that fast
Which was before a cloudy pain;
Moulded the dimness, fixed, defined
In a fair statue, strong and free,
Twin bodies flaming into mind,
Poised on the brink of ecstasy.

ITALY

THERE is a country in my mind,
Lovelier than a poet blind
Could dream of, who had never known
This world of drought and dust and stone
In all its ugliness: a place
Full of an all but human grace;
Whose dells retain the printed form
Of heavenly sleep, and seem yet warm
From some pure body newly risen;
Where matter is no more a prison,
But freedom for the soul to know
Its native beauty. For things glow
There with an inward truth and are
All fire and colour like a star.
And in that land are domes and towers
That hang as light and bright as flowers
Upon the sky, and seem a birth
Rather of air than solid earth.

ITALY

Sometimes I dream that walking there
In the green shade, all unaware
At a new turn of the golden glade,
I shall see her, and as though afraid
Shall halt a moment and almost fall
For passing faintness, like a man
Who feels the sudden spirit of Pan
Brimming his narrow soul with all
The illimitable world. And she,
Turning her head, will let me see
The first sharp dawn of her surprise
Turning to welcome in her eyes.
And I shall come and take my lover
And looking on her re-discover
All her beauty:—her dark hair
And the little ears beneath it, where
Roses of lucid shadow sleep;
Her brooding mouth, and in the deep
Wells of her eyes reflected stars ...

Oh, the imperishable things
That hands and lips as well as words
Shall speak! Oh movement of white wings,
Oh wheeling galaxies of birds ...!

THE ALIEN

A PETAL drifted loose
From a great magnolia bloom,
Your face hung in the gloom,
Floating, white and close.

We seemed alone: but another
Bent o'er you with lips of flame,
Unknown, without a name,
Hated, and yet my brother.

Your one short moan of pain
Was an exorcising spell:
The devil flew back to hell;
We were alone again.

A LITTLE MEMORY

WHITE in the moonlight,
Wet with dew,
We have known the languor
Of being two.

We have been weary
As children are,
When over them, radiant,
A stooping star,

Bends their Good-Night,
Kissed and smiled:—
Each was mother,
Each was child.

Child, from your forehead
I kissed the hair,
Gently, ah, gently:
And you were

Mistress and mother
When on your breast
I lay so safely
And could rest.

WAKING

DARKNESS had stretched its colour,
Deep blue across the pane:
No cloud to make night duller,
No moon with its tarnish stain;
But only here and there a star,
One sharp point of frosty fire,
Hanging infinitely far
In mockery of our life and death
And all our small desire.

Now in this hour of waking
From under brows of stone,
A new pale day is breaking
And the deep night is gone.
Sordid now, and mean and small
The daylight world is seen again,
With only the veils of mist that fall
Deaf and muffling over all
To hide its ugliness and pain.

But to-day this dawn of meanness
Shines in my eyes, as when
The new world's brightness and cleanness
Broke on the first of men.
For the light that shows the huddled things
Of this close-pressing earth,
Shines also on your face and brings
All its dear beauty back to me
In a new miracle of birth.

WAKING

I see you asleep and unpassioned,
White-faced in the dusk of your hair—
Your beauty so fleetingly fashioned
That it filled me once with despair
To look on its exquisite transience
And think that our love and thought and laughter
Puff out with the death of our flickering sense,
While we pass ever on and away
Towards some blank hereafter.

But now I am happy, knowing
That swift time is our friend,
And that our love's passionate glowing,
Though it turn ash in the end,
Is a rose of fire that must blossom its way
Through temporal stuff, nor else could be
More than a nothing. Into day
The boundless spaces of night contract
And in your opening eyes I see
Night born in day, in time eternity.

BY THE FIRE

WE who are lovers sit by the fire,
Cradled warm 'twixt thought and will,
Sit and drowse like sleeping dogs
In the equipoise of all desire,
Sit and listen to the still
Small hiss and whisper of green logs
That burn away, that burn away
With the sound of a far-off falling stream
Of threaded water blown to steam,
Grey ghost in the mountain world of grey.
Vapours blue as distance rise
Between the hissing logs that show
A glimpse of rosy heat below;
And candles watch with tireless eyes
While we sit drowsing here. I know,
Dimly, that there exists a world,
That there is time perhaps, and space
Other and wider than this place,
Where at the fireside drowsily curled
We hear the whisper and watch the flame
Burn blinkless and inscrutable.
And then I know those other names
That through my brain from cell to cell
Echo—reverberated shout
Of waiters mournful along corridors:
But nobody carries the orders out,
And the names (dear friends, your name and yours)
Evoke no sign. But here I sit
On the wide hearth, and there are you:
That is enough and only true.
The world and the friends that lived in it
Are shadows: you alone remain
Real in this drowsing room,

BY THE FIRE

Full of the whispers of distant rain
And candles staring into the gloom.

VALEDICTORY

I HAD remarked—how sharply one observes
When life is disappearing round the curves
Of yet another corner, out of sight!—
I had remarked when it was "good luck" and "good night"
And "a good journey to you," on her face
Certain enigmas penned in the hieroglyphs
Of that half frown and queer fixed smile and trace
Of clouded thought in those brown eyes,
Always so happily clear of hows and ifs—
My poor bleared mind!—and haunting whys.

VALEDICTORY

There I stood, holding her farewell hand,
(Pressing my life and soul and all
The world to one good-bye, till, small
And smaller pressed, why there I'd stand
Dead when they vanished with the sight of her).
And I saw that she had grown aware,
Queer puzzled face! of other things
Beyond the present and her own young speed,
Of yesterday and what new days might breed
Monstrously when the future brings
A charger with your late-lamented head:
Aware of other people's lives and will,
Aware, perhaps, aware even of me ...
The joyous hope of it! But still
I pitied her; for it was sad to see
A goddess shorn of her divinity.
In the midst of her speed she had made pause,
And doubts with all their threat of claws,
Outstripped till now by her unconsciousness,
Had seized on her; she was proved mortal now.
"Live, only live! For you were meant
Never to know a thought's distress,
But a long glad astonishment
At the world's beauty and your own.
The pity of you, goddess, grown
Perplexed and mortal."

Yet ... yet ... can it be

That she is aware, perhaps, even of me?

And life recedes, recedes; the curve is bare,
My handkerchief flutters blankly in the air;
And the question rumbles in the void:
Was she aware, was she after all aware?

LOVE SONG

DEAR absurd child—too dear to my cost I've found—
God made your soul for pleasure, not for use:
It cleaves no way, but angled broad obtuse,
Impinges with a slabby-bellied sound
Full upon life, and on the rind of things
Rubs its sleek self and utters purr and snore
And all the gamut of satisfied murmurings,
Content with that, nor wishes anything more.

A happy infant, daubed to the eyes in juice
Of peaches that flush bloody at the core,
Naked you bask upon a south-sea shore,
While o'er your tumbling bosom the hair floats loose.

The wild flowers bloom and die; the heavens go round
With the song of wheeling planetary rings:
You wriggle in the sun; each moment brings
Its freight for you; in all things pleasures abound.

You taste and smile, then this for the next pass over;
And there's no future for you and no past,
And when, absurdly, death arrives at last,
'Twill please you awhile to kiss your latest lover.

PRIVATE PROPERTY

ALL fly—yet who is misanthrope?—
The actual men and things that pass
Jostling, to wither as the grass
So soon: and (be it heaven's hope,
Or poetry's kaleidoscope,
Or love or wine, at feast, at mass)
Each owns a paradise of glass
Where never a yearning heliotrope
Pursues the sun's ascent or slope;
For the sun dreams there, and no time is or was.

Like fauns embossed in our domain,
We look abroad, and our calm eyes
Mark how the goatish gods of pain
Revel; and if by grim surprise
They break into our paradise,
Patient we build its beauty up again.

REVELATION

AT your mouth, white and milk-warm sphinx,
I taste a strange apocalypse:
Your subtle taper finger-tips
Weave me new heavens, yet, methinks,
I know the wiles and each iynx
That brought me passionate to your lips:
I know you bare as laughter strips
Your charnel beauty; yet my spirit drinks

Pure knowledge from this tainted well,
And now hears voices yet unheard
Within it, and without it sees
That world of which the poets tell
Their vision in the stammered word
Of those that wake from piercing ecstasies.

MINOAN PORCELAIN

HER eyes of bright unwinking glaze
All imperturbable do not
Even make pretences to regard
The justing absence of her stays,
Where many a Tyrian gallipot
Excites desire with spilth of nard.
The bistred rims above the fard
Of cheeks as red as bergamot
Attest that no shamefaced delays
Will clog fulfilment, nor retard
Full payment of the Cyprian's praise
Down to the last remorseful jot.
Hail priestess of we know not what
Strange cult of Mycenean days!

THE DECAMERON

NOON with a depth of shadow beneath the trees
Shakes in the heat, quivers to the sound of lutes:
Half shaded, half sunlit, a great bowl of fruits
Glistens purple and golden: the flasks of wine
Cool in their panniers of snow: silks muffle and shine:
Dim velvet, where through the leaves a sunbeam shoots,
Rifts in a pane of scarlet: fingers tapping the roots
Keep languid time to the music's soft slow decline.

Suddenly from the gate rises up a cry,
Hideous broken laughter, scarce human in sound;
Gaunt clawed hands, thrust through the bars despairingly,
Clutch fast at the scented air, while on the ground
Lie the poor plague-stricken carrions, who have found
Strength to crawl forth and curse the sunshine and die.

IN UNCERTAINTY TO A LADY

I AM not one of those who sip,
Like a quotidian bock,
Cheap idylls from a languid lip
Prepared to yawn or mock.

I wait the indubitable word,
The great Unconscious Cue.
Has it been spoken and unheard?
Spoken, perhaps, by you ...?

CRAPULOUS IMPRESSION

(To J.S.)

STILL life, still life ... the high-lights shine
Hard and sharp on the bottles: the wine
Stands firmly solid in the glasses,
Smooth yellow ice, through which there passes
The lamp's bright pencil of down-struck light.
The fruits metallically gleam,
Globey in their heaped-up bowl,
And there are faces against the night
Of the outer room—faces that seem
Part of this still, still life ... they've lost their soul.

And amongst these frozen faces you smiled,
Surprised, surprisingly, like a child:
And out of the frozen welter of sound
Your voice came quietly, quietly.
"What about God?" you said. "I have found
Much to be said for Totality.
All, I take it, is God: God's all—
This bottle, for instance ..." I recall,
Dimly, that you took God by the neck—
God-in-the-bottle—and pushed Him across:
But I, without a moment's loss
Moved God-in-the-salt in front and shouted: "Check!"

THE LIFE THEORETIC

WHILE I have been fumbling over books
And thinking about God and the Devil and all,
Other young men have been battling with the days
And others have been kissing the beautiful women.
They have brazen faces like battering-rams.
But I who think about books and such—
I crumble to impotent dust before the struggling,
And the women palsy me with fear.
But when it comes to fumbling over books
And thinking about God and the Devil and all,
Why, there I am.
But perhaps the battering-rams are in the right of it,
Perhaps, perhaps ... God knows.

COMPLAINT OF A POET MANQUÉ

WE judge by appearance merely:
If I can't think strangely, I can at least look queerly.
So I grew the hair so long on my head
That my mother wouldn't know me,
Till a woman in a night-club said,
As I was passing by,
"Hullo, here comes Salome ..."

I looked in the dirty gilt-edged glass,
And, oh Salome; there I was—
Positively jewelled, half a vampire,
With the soul in my eyes hanging dizzily
Like the gatherer of proverbial samphire
Over the brink of the crag of sense,
Looking down from perilous eminence
Into a gulf of windy night.
And there's straw in my tempestuous hair,
And I'm not a poet: but never despair!
I'll madly live the poems I shall never write.

SOCIAL AMENITIES

I AM getting on well with this anecdote,
When suddenly I recall
The many times I have told it of old,
And all the worked-up phrases, and the dying fall
Of voice, well timed in the crisis, the note
Of mock-heroic ingeniously struck—
The whole thing sticks in my throat,
And my face all tingles and pricks with shame
For myself and my hearers.
These are the social pleasures, my God!
But I finish the story triumphantly all the same.

TOPIARY

FAILING sometimes to understand
Why there are folk whose flesh should seem
Like carrion puffed with noisome steam,
Fly-blown to the eye that looks on it,
Fly-blown to the touch of a hand;
Why there are men without any legs,
Whizzing along on little trollies
With long long arms like apes':
Failing to see why God the Topiarist
Should train and carve and twist
Men's bodies into such fantastic shapes:
Yes, failing to see the point of it all, I sometimes wish
That I were a fabulous thing in a fool's mind,
Or, at the ocean bottom, in a world that is deaf and blind,
Very remote and happy, a great goggling fish.

ON THE BUS

SITTING on the top of the 'bus,
I bite my pipe and look at the sky.
Over my shoulder the smoke streams out
And my life with it.
"Conservation of energy," you say.
But I burn, I tell you, I burn;
And the smoke of me streams out
In a vanishing skein of grey.
Crash and bump ... my poor bruised body!
I am a harp of twittering strings,
An elegant instrument, but infinitely second-hand,
And if I have not got phthisis it is only an accident.
Droll phenomena!

POINTS AND LINES

INSTANTS in the quiet, small sharp stars,
Pierce my spirit with a thrust whose speed
Baffles even the grasp of time.
Oh that I might reflect them
As swiftly, as keenly as they shine.
But I am a pool of waters, summer-still,
And the stars are mirrored across me;
Those stabbing points of the sky
Turned to a thread of shaken silver,
A long fine thread.

PANIC

THE eyes of the portraits on the wall
Look at me, follow me,
Stare incessantly:
I take it their glance means nothing at all?
—Clearly, oh clearly! Nothing at all ...

Out in the gardens by the lake
The sleeping peacocks suddenly wake;
Out in the gardens, moonlit and forlorn,
Each of them sounds his mournful horn:
Shrill peals that waver and crack and break.
What can have made the peacocks wake?

RETURN FROM BUSINESS

EVENINGS in trains,
When the little black twittering ghosts
Along the brims of cuttings,
Against the luminous sky,
Interrupt with their hurrying rumour every thought
Save that one is young and setting,
Headlong westering,
And there is no recapture.

STANZAS

THOUGHT is an unseen net wherein our mind
Is taken and vainly struggles to be free:
Words, that should loose our spirit, do but bind
New fetters on our hoped-for liberty:
And action bears us onward like a stream
Past fabulous shores, scarce seen in our swift course;
Glorious—and yet its headlong currents seem
Backwaters of some nobler purer force.

There are slow curves, more subtle far than thought,
That stoop to carry the grace of a girl's breast;
And hanging flowers, so exquisitely wrought
In airy metal, that they seem possessed
Of souls; and there are distant hills that lift
The shoulder of a goddess towards the light;
And arrowy trees, sudden and sharp and swift,
Piercing the spirit deeply with delight.

Would I might make these miracles my own!
Like a pure angel, thinking colour and form,
Hardening to rage in a flame of chiselled stone,
Spilling my love like sunlight, golden and warm
On noonday flowers, speaking the song of birds
Among the branches, whispering the fall of rain,
Beyond all thought, past action and past words,
I would live in beauty, free from self and pain.

POEM

BOOKS and a coloured skein of thoughts were mine;
And magic words lay ripening in my soul
Till their much-whispered music turned a wine
Whose subtlest power was all in my control.

These things were mine, and they were real for me
As lips and darling eyes and a warm breast:
For I could love a phrase, a melody,
Like a fair woman, worshipped and possessed.

I scorned all fire that outward of the eyes
Could kindle passion; scorned, yet was afraid;
Feared, and yet envied those more deeply wise
Who saw the bright earth beckon and obeyed.

But a time came when, turning full of hate
And weariness from my remembered themes,
I wished my poet's pipe could modulate
Beauty more palpable than words and dreams.

All loveliness with which an act informs
The dim uncertain chaos of desire
Is mine to-day; it touches me, it warms
Body and spirit with its outward fire.

I am mine no more: I have become a part
Of that great earth that draws a breath and stirs
To meet the spring. But I could wish my heart
Were still a winter of frosty gossamers.

SCENES OF THE MIND

I HAVE run where festival was loud
With drum and brass among the crowd
Of panic revellers, whose cries
Affront the quiet of the skies;
Whose dancing lights contract the deep
Infinity of night and sleep
To a narrow turmoil of troubled fire.
And I have found my heart's desire
In beechen caverns that autumn fills
With the blue shadowiness of distant hills;
Whose luminous grey pillars bear
The stooping sky: calm is the air,
Nor any sound is heard to mar
That crystal silence—as from far,
Far off a man may see
The busy world all utterly
Hushed as an old memorial scene.
Long evenings I have sat and been
Strangely content, while in my hands
I held a wealth of coloured strands,
Shimmering plaits of silk and skeins
Of soft bright wool. Each colour drains
New life at the lamp's round pool of gold;
Each sinks again when I withhold
The quickening radiance, to a wan
And shadowy oblivion
Of what it was. And in my mind
Beauty or sudden love has shined
And wakened colour in what was dead
And turned to gold the sullen lead
Of mean desires and everyday's
Poor thoughts and customary ways.
Sometimes in lands where mountains throw

Their silent spell on all below,
Drawing a magic circle wide
About their feet on every side,
Robbed of all speech and thought and act,
I have seen God in the cataract.
In falling water and in flame,
Never at rest, yet still the same,
God shows himself. And I have known
The swift fire frozen into stone,
And water frozen changelessly
Into the death of gems. And I
Long sitting by the thunderous mill
Have seen the headlong wheel made still,
And in the silence that ensued
Have known the endless solitude
Of being dead and utterly nought.
Inhabitant of mine own thought,
I look abroad, and all I see
Is my creation, made for me:
Along my thread of life are pearled
The moments that make up the world.

L'APRÈS-MIDI D'UN FAUNE

(From the French of Stéphane Mallarmé.)

I WOULD immortalize these nymphs: so bright
Their sunlit colouring, so airy light,
It floats like drowsing down. Loved I a dream?
My doubts, born of oblivious darkness, seem
A subtle tracery of branches grown
The tree's true self—proving that I have known
No triumph, but the shadow of a rose.
But think. These nymphs, their loveliness ... suppose
They bodied forth your senses' fabulous thirst?
Illusion! which the blue eyes of the first,
As cold and chaste as is the weeping spring,
Beget: the other, sighing, passioning,
Is she the wind, warm in your fleece at noon?
No, through this quiet, when a weary swoon
Crushes and chokes the latest faint essay
Of morning, cool against the encroaching day,
There is no murmuring water, save the gush
Of my clear fluted notes; and in the hush
Blows never a wind, save that which through my reed
Puffs out before the rain of notes can speed
Upon the air, with that calm breath of art
That mounts the unwrinkled zenith visibly,
Where inspiration seeks its native sky.
You fringes of a calm Sicilian lake,
The sun's own mirror which I love to take,
Silent beneath your starry flowers, tell
How here I cut the hollow rushes, well
Tamed by my skill, when on the glaucous gold
Of distant lawns about their fountain cold
A living whiteness stirs like a lazy wave;

And at the first slow notes my panpipes gave
These flocking swans, these naiads, rather, fly
Or dive. Noon burns inert and tawny dry,
Nor marks how clean that Hymen slipped away
From me who seek in song the real A.
Wake, then, to the first ardour and the sight,
O lonely faun, of the old fierce white light,
With, lilies, one of you for innocence.
Other than their lips' delicate pretence,
The light caress that quiets treacherous lovers,
My breast, I know not how to tell, discovers
The bitten print of some immortal's kiss.
But hush! a mystery so great as this
I dare not tell, save to my double reed,
Which, sharer of my every joy and need,
Dreams down its cadenced monologues that we
Falsely confuse the beauties that we see
With the bright palpable shapes our song creates:
My flute, as loud as passion modulates,
Purges the common dream of flank and breast,
Seen through closed eyes and inwardly caressed,
Of every empty and monotonous line.

Bloom then, O Syrinx, in thy flight malign,
A reed once more beside our trysting-lake.
Proud of my music, let me often make
A song of goddesses and see their rape
Profanely done on many a painted shape.
So when the grape's transparent juice I drain,
I quell regret for pleasures past and feign
A new real grape. For holding towards the sky
The empty skin, I blow it tight and lie
Dream-drunk till evening, eyeing it.

Tell o'er

Remembered joys and plump the grape once more.
Between the reeds I saw their bodies gleam
Who cool no mortal fever in the stream
Crying to the woods the rage of their desire:
And their bright hair went down in jewelled fire
Where crystal broke and dazzled shudderingly.
I check my swift pursuit: for see where lie,
Bruised, being twins in love, by languor sweet,
Two sleeping girls, clasped at my very feet.
I seize and run with them, nor part the pair,

Breaking this covert of frail petals, where
Roses drink scent of the sun and our light play
'Mid tumbled flowers shall match the death of day.
I love that virginal fury—ah, the wild
Thrill when a maiden body shrinks, defiled,
Shuddering like arctic light, from lips that sear
Its nakedness ... the flesh in secret fear!
Contagiously through my linked pair it flies
Where innocence in either, struggling, dies,
Wet with fond tears or some less piteous dew.
Gay in the conquest of these fears, I grew
So rash that I must needs the sheaf divide
Of ruffled kisses heaven itself had tied.
For as I leaned to stifle in the hair
Of one my passionate laughter (taking care
With a stretched finger, that her innocence
Might stain with her companion's kindling sense
To touch the younger little one, who lay
Child-like unblushing) my ungrateful prey
Slips from me, freed by passion's sudden death,
Nor heeds the frenzy of my sobbing breath.

Let it pass! others of their hair shall twist
A rope to drag me to those joys I missed.
See how the ripe pomegranates bursting red
To quench the thirst of the mumbling bees have bled;
So too our blood, kindled by some chance fire,
Flows for the swarming legions of desire.
At evening, when the woodland green turns gold
And ashen grey, 'mid the quenched leaves, behold!
Red Etna glows, by Venus visited,
Walking the lava with her snowy tread
Whene'er the flames in thunderous slumber die.
I hold the goddess!

Ah, sure penalty!

But the unthinking soul and body swoon
At last beneath the heavy hush of noon.
Forgetful let me lie where summer's drouth
Sifts fine the sand and then with gaping mouth
Dream planet-struck by the grape's round wine-red star.

Nymphs, I shall see the shade that now you are.

THE LOUSE-HUNTERS

(From the French of Rimbaud).

WHEN the child's forehead, full of torments red,
Cries out for sleep and its pale host of dreams,
His two big sisters come unto his bed,
Having long fingers, tipped with silvery gleams.

They set him at a casement, open wide
On seas of flowers that stir in the blue airs,
And through his curls, all wet with dew, they slide
Those terrible searching finger-tips of theirs.

He hears them breathing, softly, fearfully,
Honey-sweet ruminations, slow respired:
Then a sharp hiss breaks time and melody—
Spittle indrawn, old kisses new-desired.

Down through the perfumed silences he hears
Their eyelids fluttering: long fingers thrill,
Probing a lassitude bedimmed with tears,
While the nails crunch at every louse they kill.

He is drunk with Languor—soft accordion-sigh,
Delirious wine of Love in Idleness;
Longings for tears come welling up and die,
As slow or swift he feels their magical caress.

MORTAL COILS

I: THE GIOCONDA SMILE

I

"Miss Spence will be down directly, sir."

"Thank you," said Mr. Hutton, without turning round. Janet Spence's parlourmaid was so ugly—ugly on purpose, it always seemed to him, malignantly, criminally ugly—that he could not bear to look at her more than was necessary. The door closed. Left to himself, Mr. Hutton got up and began to wander round the room, looking with meditative eyes at the familiar objects it contained.

Photographs of Greek statuary, photographs of the Roman Forum, coloured prints of Italian masterpieces, all very safe and well known. Poor, dear Janet, what a prig—what an intellectual snob! Her real taste was illustrated in that water-colour by the pavement artist, the one she had paid half a crown for (and thirty-five shillings for the frame). How often his had heard her tell the story, how often expatiate on the beauties of that skilful imitation of an oleograph! "A real Artist in the streets," and you could hear the capital A in Artist as she spoke the words. She made you feel that part of his glory had entered into Janet Spence when she tendered him that half-crown for the copy of the oleograph. She was implying a compliment to her own taste and penetration. A genuine Old Master for half a crown. Poor, dear Janet!

Mr. Hutton came to a pause in front of a small oblong mirror. Stooping a little to get a full view of his face, he passed a white, well-manicured finger over his moustache. It was as curly, as freshly auburn as it had been twenty years ago. His hair still retained its colour, and there was no sign of baldness yet—only a certain elevation of the brow. "Shakespearean," thought Mr. Hutton, with a smile, as he surveyed the smooth and polished expanse of his forehead.

Others abide our question, thou art free.... Footsteps in the sea ... Majesty ... Shakespeare, thou shouldst be living at this hour. No, that was Milton, wasn't it? Milton, the Lady of Christ's. There was no lady about him. He was what the women, would call a manly man. That was why they liked him—for the curly auburn moustache and the discreet redolence of tobacco. Mr. Hutton smiled again; he enjoyed making fun of himself. Lady of Christ's? No, no. He was the Christ of Ladies. Very pretty, very pretty. The Christ of Ladies. Mr. Hutton wished there were somebody he could tell the joke to. Poor, dear Janet wouldn't appreciate it, alas?

He straightened himself up, patted his hair, and resumed his peregrination. Damn the Roman Forum; he hated those dreary photographs.

Suddenly he became aware that Janet Spence was in the room, standing near the door. Mr. Hutton started, as though he had been taken in some felonious act. To make these silent and spectral appearances was one of Janet Spence's peculiar talents. Perhaps she had been there all the time, had seen him looking at himself in the mirror. Impossible! But, still, it was disquieting.

"Oh, you gave me such a surprise," said Mr. Hutton, recovering his smile and advancing with outstretched hand to meet her.

Miss Spence was smiling too: her Gioconda smile, he had once called it, in a moment of half-ironical flattery. Miss Spence had taken the compliment seriously, and had always tried to live up to the Leonardo standard. She smiled on his silence while Mr. Hutton shook hands; that was part of the Gioconda business.

"I hope you're well," said Mr. Hutton. "You look it."

What a queer face she had! That small mouth pursed forward by the Gioconda expression into a little snout with a round hole in the middle as though for whistling—it was like a penholder seen from the front. Above the mouth a well-shaped nose, finely aquiline. Eyes large, lustrous, and dark, with the largeness, lustre, and darkness that seems to invite sties and an occasional blood-shot suffusion. They were fine eyes, but unchangingly grave. The penholder might do its Gioconda trick, but the eyes never altered in their earnestness. Above them, a pair of boldly arched, heavily pencilled black eyebrows lent a surprising air of power, as of a Roman matron, to the upper portion of the face. Her hair was dark and equally Roman; Agrippina from the brows upward.

"I thought I'd just look in on my way home," Mr. Hutton went on. "Ah, it's good to be back here"—he indicated with a wave of his hand the flowers in the vases, the sunshine and greenery beyond the windows —"it's good to be back in the country after a stuffy day of business in town."

Miss Spence, who had sat down, pointed to a chair at her side.

"No, really, I can't sit down," Mr. Hutton protested. "I must get back to see how poor Emily is. She was rather seedy this morning." He sat down, nevertheless. "It's these wretched liver chills. She's always getting them. Women—" He broke off and coughed, so as to hide the fact that he had uttered. He was about to say that women with weak digestions ought not to marry; but the remark was too cruel, and he didn't really believe it. Janet Spence, moreover, was a believer in eternal flames and spiritual attachments. "She hopes to be well enough," he added, "to see you at luncheon to-morrow. Can you come? Do!" He smiled persuasively. "It's my invitation too, you know."

She dropped her eyes, and Mr. Hutton almost thought that he detected a certain reddening of the cheek. It was a tribute; he stroked his moustache.

"I should like to come if you think Emily's really well enough to have a visitor."

"Of course. You'll do her good. You'll do us both good. In married life three is often better company than two."

"Oh, you're cynical."

Mr. Hutton always had a desire to say "Bow-wow-wow" whenever that last word was spoken. It irritated him more than any other word in the language. But instead of barking he made haste to protest.

"No, no. I'm only speaking a melancholy truth. Reality doesn't always come up to the ideal, you know. But that doesn't make me believe any the less in the ideal. Indeed, I believe in it passionately the ideal of a matrimony between two people in perfect accord. I think it's realisable. I'm sure it is."

He paused significantly and looked at her with an arch expression. A virgin of thirty-six, but still unwithered; she had her charms. And there was something really rather enigmatic about her. Miss Spence made no reply but continued to smile. There were times when Mr. Hutton got rather bored with the Gioconda. He stood up.

"I must really be going now. Farewell, mysterious Gioconda." The smile grew intenser, focused itself, as it were, in a narrower snout. Mr. Hutton made a Cinquecento gesture, and kissed her extended hand. It was the first time he had done such a thing; the action seemed not to be resented. "I look forward to to-morrow."

"Do you?"

For answer Mr. Hutton once more kissed her hand, then turned to go. Miss Spence accompanied him to the porch.

"Where's your car?" she asked.

"I left it at the gate of the drive."

"I'll come and see you off."

"No, no." Mr. Hutton was playful, but determined. "You must do no such thing. I simply forbid you."

"But I should like to come," Miss Spence protested, throwing a rapid Gioconda at him.

Mr. Hutton held up his hand. "No," he repeated, and then, with a gesture that was almost the blowing of a kiss, he started to run down the drive, lightly on his toes, with long, bounding strides like a boy's. He was proud of that run; it was quite marvellously youthful. Still, he was glad the drive was no longer. At the last bend, before passing out of sight of the house, he halted and turned round. Miss Spence was still standing on the steps, smiling her smile. He waved his hand, and this time quite definitely and overtly wafted a kiss in her direction. Then, breaking once more into his magnificent canter, he rounded the last dark promontory of trees. Once out of sight of the house he let his high paces decline to a trot, and finally to a walk. He took out his handkerchief and began wiping his neck inside his collar. What fools, what fools! Had there ever been such an ass as poor, dear Janet Spence? Never, unless it was himself. Decidedly he was the more malignant fool, since he, at least, was aware of his folly and still persisted in it. Why did he persist? Ah, the problem that was himself, the problem that was other people.

He had reached the gate. A large, prosperous-looking motor was standing at the side of the road.

"Home, M'Nab." The chauffeur touched his cap. "And stop at the cross-roads on the way, as usual," Mr. Hutton added, as he opened the door of the car. "Well?" he said, speaking into the obscurity that lurked within.

"Oh, Teddy Bear, what an age you've been!" It was a fresh and childish voice that spoke the words. There was the faintest hint of Cockney impurity about the vowel sounds.

Mr. Hutton bent his large form and darted into the car with the agility of an animal regaining its burrow.

"Have I?" he said, as he shut the door. The machine began to move. "You must have missed me a lot if you found the time so long." He sat back in the low seat; a cherishing warmth enveloped him.

"Teddy Bear...." and with a sigh of contentment a charming little head declined on to Mr. Hutton's shoulder. Ravished, he looked down sideways at the round, babyish face.

"Do you know, Doris, you look like the pictures of Louise de Kerouaille." He passed his fingers through a mass of curly hair.

"Who's Louise de Kera-whatever-it-is?" Doris spoke from remote distances.

"She was, alas! *Fuit.* We shall all be 'was' one of these days. Meanwhile...."

Mr. Hutton covered the babyish face with kisses. The car rushed smoothly along. McNab's back, through the front window was stonily impassive, the back of a statue.

"Your hands," Doris whispered. "Oh, you mustn't touch me. They give me electric shocks."

Mr. Hutton adored her for the virgin imbecility of the words. How late in one's existence one makes the discovery of one's body!

"The electricity isn't in me, it's in you." He kissed her again, whispering her name several times: Doris, Doris, Doris. The scientific appellation of the sea-mouse, he was thinking as he kissed the throat, she offered him, white and extended like the throat of a victim awaiting the sacrificial knife. The sea-mouse was a sausage with iridescent fur: very peculiar. Or was Doris the sea cucumber, which turns itself inside out in moments of alarm? He would really have to go to Naples again, just to see the aquarium. These sea creatures were fabulous, unbelievably fantastic.

"Oh, Teddy Bear!" (More zoology; but he was only a land animal. His poor little jokes!) "Teddy Bear, I'm so happy."

"So am I," said Mr. Hutton. Was it true?

"But I wish I knew if it were right. Tell me, Teddy Bear, is it right or wrong?"

"Ah, my dear, that's just what I've been wondering for the last thirty years."

"Be serious, Teddy Bear. I want to know if this is right; if it's right that I should be here with you and that we should love one another, and that it should give me electric shocks when you touch me."

"Right? Well, it's certainly good that you should have electric shocks rather than sexual repressions. Read Freud; repressions are the devil."

"Oh, you don't help me. Why aren't you ever serious? If only you knew how miserable I am sometimes, thinking it's not right. Perhaps, you know, there is a hell, and all that. I don t know what to do. Sometimes I think I ought to stop loving you."

"But could you?" asked Mr. Hutton, confident in the powers of his seduction and his moustache.

"No, Teddy Bear, you know I couldn't. But I could run away, I could hide from you, I could lock myself up and force myself not to come to you."

"Silly little thing!" He tightened his embrace.

"Oh, dear, I hope it isn't wrong. And there are times when I don't care if it is."

Mr. Hutton was touched. He had a certain protective affection for this little creature. He laid his cheek against her hair and so, interlaced, they sat in silence, while the car, swaying and pitching a little as it hastened along, seemed to draw in the white road and the dusty hedges towards it devouringly.

"Good-bye, good-bye."

The car moved on, gathered speed, vanished round a curve, and Doris was left standing by the sign-post at the cross-roads, still dizzy and weak with the languor born of those kisses and the electrical touch of those gentle hands. She had to take a deep breath, to draw herself up deliberately, before she was strong enough to start her homeward walk. She had half a mile in which to invent the necessary lies.

Alone, Mr. Hutton suddenly found himself the prey of an appalling boredom.

II

Mrs. Hutton was lying on the sofa in her boudoir, playing Patience. In spite of the warmth of the July evening a wood fire was burning on the hearth. A black Pomeranian, extenuated by the heat and the fatigues of digestion, slept before the blaze.

"Phew! Isn't it rather hot in here?" Mr. Hutton asked as he entered the room.

"You know I have to keep warm, dear." The voice seemed breaking on the verge of tears. "I get so shivery."

"I hope you're better this evening."

"Not much, I'm afraid."

The conversation stagnated. Mr. Hutton stood leaning his back against the mantelpiece. He looked down at the Pomeranian lying at his feet, and with the toe of his right boot he rolled the little dog over and rubbed its white-flecked chest and belly. The creature lay in an inert ecstasy. Mrs. Hutton continued to play Patience. Arrived at an *impasse*, she altered the position of one card, took back another, and went on playing. Her Patiences always came out.

"Dr. Libbard thinks I ought to go to Llandrindod Wells this summer."

"Well—go, my dear—go, most certainly."

Mr. Hutton was thinking of the events of the afternoon: how they had driven, Doris and he, up to the hanging wood, had left the car to wait for them under the shade of the trees, and walked together out into the windless sunshine of the chalk down.

"I'm to drink the waters for my liver, and he thinks I ought to have massage and electric treatment, too."

Hat in hand, Doris had stalked four blue butterflies that were dancing together round a scabious flower with a motion that was like the flickering of blue fire. The blue fire burst and scattered into whirling sparks; she had given chase, laughing and shouting like a child.

"I'm sure it will do you good, my dear."

"I was wondering if you'd come with me, dear."

"But you know I'm going to Scotland at the end of the month."

Mrs. Hutton looked up at him entreatingly. "It's the journey," she said. "The thought of it is such a nightmare. I don't know if I can manage it. And you know I can't sleep in hotels. And then there's the luggage and all the worries. I can't go alone.

"But you won't be alone. You'll have your maid with you." He spoke impatiently. The sick woman was usurping the place of the healthy one. He was being dragged back from the memory of the sunlit down and the quick, laughing girl, back to this unhealthy, overheated room and its complaining occupant.

"I don't think I shall be able to go."

"But you must, my dear, if the doctor tells you to. And, besides, a change will do you good."

"I don't think so."

"But Libbard thinks so, and he knows what he's talking about."

"No, I can't face it. I'm too weak. I can't go alone." Mrs. Hutton pulled a handkerchief out of her black silk bag, and put it to her eyes.

"Nonsense, my dear, you must make the effort."

"I had rather be left in peace to die here." She was crying in earnest now.

"O Lord! Now do be reasonable. Listen now, please." Mrs. Hutton only sobbed more violently. "Oh, what is one to do?" He shrugged his shoulders and walked out of the room.

Mr. Hutton was aware that he had not behaved with proper patience; but he could not help it. Very early in his manhood he had discovered that not only did he not feel sympathy for the poor, the weak, the diseased, and deformed; he actually hated them. Once, as an undergraduate, he spent three days at a mission in the East End. He had returned, filled with a profound and ineradicable disgust. Instead of pitying, he loathed the unfortunate. It was not, he knew, a very comely emotion; and he had been ashamed of it at first. In the end he had decided that it was temperamental, inevitable, and had felt no further qualms. Emily had been healthy and beautiful when he married her. He had loved her then. But now—was it his fault that she was like this?

Mr. Hutton dined alone. Food and drink left him more benevolent than he had been before dinner. To make amends for his show of exasperation he went up to his wife's room and offered to read to her. She was touched, gratefully accepted the offer, and Mr. Hutton, who was particularly proud of his accent, suggested a little light reading in French.

"French? I am so fond of French." Mrs. Hutton spoke of the language of Racine as though it were a dish of green peas.

Mr. Hutton ran down to the library and returned with a yellow volume. He began reading. The effort of pronouncing perfectly absorbed his whole attention. But how good his accent was! The fact of its goodness seemed to improve the quality of the novel he was reading.

At the end of fifteen pages an unmistakable sound aroused him. He looked up; Mrs. Hutton had gone to sleep. He sat still for a little while, looking with a dispassionate curiosity at the sleeping face. Once it had been beautiful; once, long ago, the sight of it, the recollection of it, had moved him with an emotion profounder, perhaps, than any he had felt before or since. Now it was lined and cadaverous. The skin was stretched tightly over the cheekbones, across the bridge of the sharp, bird-like nose. The closed eyes were set in profound bone-rimmed sockets. The lamplight striking on the face from the side emphasised with light and shade its cavities and projections. It was the face of a dead Christ by Morales.

Le squelette était invisible
Au temps heureux de l'art païen.

He shivered a little, and tiptoed out of the room.

On the following day Mrs. Hutton came down to luncheon. She had had some unpleasant palpitations during the night, but she was feeling better now. Besides, she wanted to do honour to her guest. Miss Spence listened to her complaints about Llandrindod Wells, and was loud in sympathy, lavish with advice. Whatever she said was always said with intensity. She leaned forward, aimed, so to speak, like a gun, and fired her words. Bang! the charge in her soul was ignited, the words whizzed forth at the narrow barrel of her mouth. She was a machine-gun riddling her hostess with sympathy. Mr. Hutton had undergone similar bombardments, mostly of a literary or philosophic character—bombardments of Maeterlinck, of Mrs. Besant, of Bergson, of William James. To-day the missiles were medical. She talked about insomnia, she expatiated on the virtues of harmless drugs and beneficent specialists. Under the bombardment Mrs. Hutton opened out, like a flower in the sun.

Mr. Hutton looked on in silence. The spectacle of Janet Spence evoked in him an unfailing curiosity. He was not romantic enough to imagine that every face masked an interior physiognomy of beauty or strangeness, that every woman's small talk was like a vapour hanging over mysterious gulfs. His wife, for example, and Doris; they were nothing more than what they seemed to be. But with Janet Spence it was somehow different. Here one could be sure that there was some kind of a queer face behind the Gioconda smile and the Roman eyebrows.

The only question was: What exactly was there? Mr. Hutton could never quite make out.

"But perhaps you won't have to go to Llandrindod after all," Miss Spence was saying. "If you get well quickly Dr. Libbard will let you off."

"I only hope so. Indeed, I do really feel rather better to-day."

Mr. Hutton felt ashamed. How much was it his own lack of sympathy that prevented her from feeling well every day? But he comforted himself by reflecting that it was only a case of feeling, not of being better. Sympathy does not mend a diseased liver or a weak heart.

"My dear, I wouldn't eat those red currants if I were you," he said, suddenly solicitous. "You know that Libbard has banned everything with skins and pips."

"But I am so fond of them," Mrs. Hutton protested, "and I feel so well to-day."

"Don't be a tyrant," said Miss Spence, looking first at him and then at his wife. "Let the poor invalid have what she fancies; it will do her good." She laid her hand on Mrs. Hutton's arm and patted it affectionately two or three times.

"Thank you, my dear." Mrs. Hutton helped herself to the stewed currants.

"Well, don't blame me if they make you ill again."

"Do I ever blame you, dear?"

"You have nothing to blame me for," Mr. Hutton answered playfully. "I am the perfect husband."

They sat in the garden after luncheon. From the island of shade under the old cypress tree they looked out across a flat expanse of lawn, in which the parterres of flowers shone with a metallic brilliance.

Mr. Hutton took a deep breath of the warm and fragrant air. "It's good to be alive," he said.

"Just to be alive," his wife echoed, stretching one pale, knot-jointed hand into the sunlight.

A maid brought the coffee; the silver pots and the little blue cups were set on a folding table near the group of chairs.

"Oh, my medicine!" exclaimed Mrs. Hutton. "Run in and fetch it, Clara, will you? The white bottle on the sideboard."

"I'll go," said Mr. Hutton. "I've got to go and fetch a cigar in any case."

He ran in towards the house. On the threshold he turned round for an instant. The maid was walking back across the lawn. His wife was sitting up in her deck-chair, engaged in opening her white parasol. Miss Spence was bending over the table, pouring out the coffee. He passed into the cool obscurity of the house.

"Do you like sugar in your coffee?" Miss Spence inquired.

"Yes, please. Give me rather a lot. I'll drink it after my medicine to take the taste away."

Mrs. Hutton leaned back in her chair, lowering the sunshade over her eyes, so as to shut out from her vision the burning sky.

Behind her, Miss Spence was making a delicate clinking among the coffee-cups.

"I've given you three large spoonfuls. That ought to take the taste away. And here comes the medicine."

Mr. Hutton had reappeared, carrying a wineglass, half full of a pale liquid.

"It smells delicious," he said, as he handed it to his wife.

"That's only the flavouring." She drank it off at a gulp, shuddered, and made a grimace. "Ugh, it's so nasty. Give me my coffee."

Miss Spence gave her the cup; she sipped at it. "You've made it like syrup. But it's very nice, after that atrocious medicine."

At half-past three Mrs. Hutton complained that she did not feel as well as she had done, and went indoors to lie down. Her husband would have said something about the red currants, but checked himself; the triumph of an "I told you so" was too cheaply won. Instead, he was sympathetic, and gave her his arm to the house.

"A rest will do you good," he said. "By the way, I shan't be back till after dinner."

"But why? Where are you going?"

"I promised to go to Johnson's this evening. We have to discuss the war memorial, you know."

"Oh, I wish you weren't going." Mrs. Hutton was almost in tears. "Can't you stay? I don't like being alone in the house."

"But, my dear, I promised weeks ago." It was a bother having to lie like this. "And now I must get back and look after Miss Spence."

He kissed her on the forehead and went out again into the garden. Miss Spence received him aimed and intense.

"Your wife is dreadfully ill," she fired off at him.

"I thought she cheered up so much when you came."

"That was purely nervous, purely nervous. I was watching her closely. With a heart in that condition and her digestion wrecked—yes, wrecked—anything might happen."

"Libbard doesn't take so gloomy a view of poor Emily's health." Mr. Hutton held open the gate that led from the garden into the drive; Miss Spence's car was standing by the front door.

"Libbard is only a country doctor. You ought to see a specialist."

He could not refrain from laughing. "You have a macabre passion for specialists."

Miss Spence held up her hand in protest. "I am serious. I think poor Emily is in a very bad state. Anything might happen at any moment."

He handed her into the car and shut the door. The chauffeur started the engine and climbed into his place, ready to drive off.

"Shall I tell him to start?" He had no desire to continue the conversation.

Miss Spence leaned forward and shot a Gioconda in his direction. "Remember, I expect you to come and see me again soon."

Mechanically he grinned, made a polite noise, and, as the car moved forward, waved his hand. He was happy to be alone.

A few minutes afterwards Mr. Hutton himself drove away. Doris was waiting at the cross-roads. They dined together twenty miles from home, at a roadside hotel. It was one of those bad, expensive meals which are only cooked in country hotels frequented by motorists. It revolted Mr. Hutton, but Doris enjoyed it. She always enjoyed things. Mr. Hutton ordered a not very good brand of champagne. He was wishing he had spent the evening in his library.

When they started homewards Doris was a little tipsy and extremely affectionate. It was very dark inside the car, but looking forward, past the motionless form of M'Nab, they could see a bright and narrow universe of forms and colours scooped out of the night by the electric head-lamps.

It was after eleven when Mr. Hutton reached home. Dr. Libbard met him in the hall. He was a small man with delicate hands and well-formed features that were almost feminine. His brown eyes were large and melancholy. He used to waste a great deal of time sitting at the bedside of his patients, looking sadness through those eyes and talking in a sad, low voice about nothing in particular. His person exhaled a pleasing odour, decidedly antiseptic but at the same time suave and discreetly delicious.

"Libbard?" said Mr. Hutton in surprise. "You here? Is my wife ill?"

"We tried to fetch you earlier," the soft, melancholy voice replied. "It was thought you were at Mr. Johnson's, but they had no news of you there."

"No, I was detained. I had a breakdown," Mr. Hutton answered irritably. It was tiresome to be caught out in a lie.

"Your wife wanted to see you urgently."

"Well, I can go now." Mr. Hutton moved towards the stairs.

Dr. Libbard laid a hand on his arm. "I am afraid it's too late."

"Too late?" He began fumbling with his watch; it wouldn't come out of the pocket.

"Mrs. Hutton passed away half an hour ago."

The voice remained even in its softness, the melancholy of the eyes did not deepen. Dr. Libbard spoke of death as he would speak of a local cricket match. All things were equally vain and equally deplorable.

Mr. Hutton found himself thinking of Janet Spence's words. At any moment—at any moment. She had been extraordinarily right.

"What happened?" he asked. "What was the cause?"

Dr. Libbard explained. It was heart failure brought on by a violent attack of nausea, caused in its turn by the eating of something of an irritant nature. Red currants? Mr. Hutton suggested. Very likely. It had been too much for the heart. There was chronic valvular disease: something had collapsed under the strain. It was all over; she could not have suffered much.

III

"It's a pity they should have chosen the day of the Eton and Harrow match for the funeral," old General Grego was saying as he stood, his top hat in his hand, under the shadow of the lych gate, wiping his face with his handkerchief.

Mr. Hutton overheard the remark and with difficulty restrained a desire to inflict grievous bodily pain on the General. He would have liked to hit the old brute in the middle of his big red face. Monstrous great mulberry, spotted with meal! Was there no respect for the dead? Did nobody care? In theory he didn't much care; let the dead bury their dead. But here, at the graveside, he had found himself actually sobbing. Poor Emily, they had been pretty happy once. Now she was lying at the bottom of a seven-foot hole. And here was Grego complaining that he couldn't go to the Eton and Harrow match.

Mr. Hutton looked round at the groups of black figures that were drifting slowly out of the churchyard towards the fleet of cabs and motors assembled in the road outside. Against the brilliant background of the July grass and flowers and foliage, they had a horribly alien and unnatural appearance. It pleased him to think that all these people would soon be dead, too.

That evening Mr. Hutton sat up late in his library reading the life of Milton. There was no particular reason why he should have chosen Milton; it was the book that first came to hand, that was all. It was after midnight when he had finished. He got up from his armchair, unbolted the French windows, and stepped out on to the little paved terrace. The night was quiet and clear. Mr. Hutton looked at the stars and at the holes between them, dropped his eyes to the dim lawns and hueless flowers of the garden, and let them wander over the farther landscape, black and grey under the moon.

He began to think with a kind of confused violence. There were the stars, there was Milton. A man can be somehow the peer of stars and night. Greatness, nobility. But is there seriously a difference between the noble and the ignoble? Milton, the stars, death, and himself—himself. The soul, the body; the higher and the lower nature. Perhaps there was something in it, after all. Milton had a god on his side and righteousness. What had he? Nothing, nothing whatever. There were only Doris's little breasts. What was the point of it all? Milton, the stars, death, and Emily in her grave, Doris and himself—always himself....

Oh, he was a futile and disgusting being. Everything convinced him of it. It was a solemn moment. He spoke aloud: "I will, I will." The sound of his own voice in the darkness was appalling; it seemed to him that he had sworn that infernal oath which binds even the gods: "I will, I will." There had been New Year's days and solemn anniversaries in the past, when he had felt the same contritions and recorded similar resolutions. They had all thinned away, these resolutions, like smoke, into nothingness. But this was a greater moment and he had pronounced a more fearful oath. In the future it was to be different. Yes, he would live by reason, he would be industrious, he would curb his appetites, he would devote his life to some good purpose. It was resolved and it would be so.

In practice he saw himself spending his mornings in agricultural pursuits, riding round with the bailiff, seeing that his land was farmed in the best modern way—silos and artificial manures and continuous cropping, and all that. The remainder of the day should be devoted to serious study. There was that book he had been intending to write for so long—*The Effect of Diseases on Civilisation.*

Mr. Hutton went to bed humble and contrite, but with a sense that grace had entered into him. He slept for seven and a half hours, and woke to find the sun brilliantly shining. The emotions of the evening before had been transformed by a good night's rest into his customary cheerfulness. It was not until a good many seconds after his return to conscious life that he remembered his resolution, his Stygian oath. Milton and death seemed somehow different in the sunlight. As for the stars, they were not there. But the resolutions were good; even in the daytime he could see that. He had his horse saddled after breakfast, and rode round the farm with the bailiff. After luncheon he read Thucydides on the plague at Athens. In the evening he made a few notes on malaria in Southern Italy. While he was undressing he remembered that there was a good anecdote in Skelton's jest-book about the Sweating Sickness. He would have made a note of it if only he could have found a pencil.

On the sixth morning of his new life Mr. Hutton found among his correspondence an envelope addressed in that peculiarly vulgar handwriting which he knew to be Doris's. He opened it, and began to read. She didn't know what to say; words were so inadequate. His wife dying like that, and so suddenly—it was too terrible. Mr. Hutton sighed, but his interest revived somewhat as he read on:

> "Death is so frightening, I never think of it when I can help it. But when something like this happens, or when I am feeling ill or depressed, then I can't help remembering it is there so close, and I think about all the wicked things I have done and about you and me, and I wonder what will happen, and I am so frightened. I am so lonely, Teddy Bear, and so unhappy, and I don't know what to do. I can't get rid of the idea of dying, I am so wretched and helpless without you. I didn't mean to write to you; I meant to wait till you were out of mourning and could come and see me again, but I was so lonely and miserable, Teddy Bear, I had to write. I couldn't help it. Forgive me, I want you so much; I have nobody in the world but you. You are so good and gentle and understanding; there is nobody like you. I shall never forget how good and kind you have been to me, and you are so clever and know so much, I can't understand how you ever came to pay any attention to me, I am so dull and stupid, much less like me and love me, because you do love me a little, don't you, Teddy Bear?"

Mr. Hutton was touched with shame and remorse. To be thanked like this, worshipped for having seduced the girl—it was too much. It had just been a piece of imbecile wantonness. Imbecile, idiotic: there was no other way to describe it. For, when all was said, he had derived very little pleasure from it. Taking all things together, he had probably been more bored than amused. Once upon a time he had believed himself to be a hedonist. But to be a hedonist implies a certain process of reasoning, a deliberate choice of known pleasures, a rejection of known pains. This had been done without reason, against it. For he knew beforehand—so well, so well—that there was no interest or pleasure to be derived from these wretched affairs. And yet each time the vague itch came upon him he succumbed, involving himself once more in the old stupidity. There had been Maggie, his wife's maid, and Edith, the girl on the farm, and Mrs. Pringle, and the waitress in London, and others—there seemed to be dozens of them. It had all been so stale and boring. He knew it would be; he always knew. And yet, and yet.... Experience doesn't teach.

Poor little Doris! He would write to her kindly, comfortingly, but he wouldn't see her again. A servant came to tell him that his horse was saddled and waiting. He mounted and rode off. That morning the old bailiff was more irritating than usual.

Five days later Doris and Mr. Hutton ware sitting together on the pier at Southend; Doris, in white muslin with pink garnishings, radiated happiness; Mr. Hutton, legs outstretched and chair tilted, had pushed the panama back from his forehead, and was trying to feel like a tripper. That night, when Doris was asleep, breathing and warm by his side, he recaptured, in this moment of darkness and physical fatigue, the rather cosmic emotion which had possessed him that evening, not a fortnight ago, when he had made his great resolution. And so his solemn oath had already gone the way of so many other resolutions. Unreason had triumphed; at the first itch of desire he had given way. He was hopeless, hopeless.

For a long time he lay with closed eyes, ruminating his humiliation. The girl stirred in her sleep, Mr. Hutton turned over and looked in her direction. Enough faint light crept in between the half-drawn curtains to show her bare arm and shoulder, her neck, and the dark tangle of hair on the pillow. She was beautiful, desirable. Why did he lie there moaning over his sins? What did it matter? If he were hopeless, then so be it; he would make the best of his hopelessness. A glorious sense of irresponsibility suddenly filled him. He was free, magnificently free. In a kind of exaltation he drew the girl towards him. She woke, bewildered, almost frightened under his rough kisses.

The storm of his desire subsided into a kind of serene merriment. The whole atmosphere seemed to be quivering with enormous silent laughter.

"Could anyone love you as much as I do, Teddy Bear?" The question came faintly from distant worlds of love.

"I think I know somebody who does," Mr. Hutton replied. The submarine laughter was swelling, rising, ready to break the surface of silence and resound.

"Who? Tell me. What do you mean?" The voice had come very close; charged with suspicion, anguish, indignation, it belonged to this immediate world.

"A—ah!"

"Who?"

"You'll never guess." Mr. Hutton kept up the joke until it began to grow tedious, and then pronounced the name "Janet Spence."

Doris was incredulous. "Miss Spence of the Manor? That old woman?" It was too ridiculous. Mr. Hutton laughed too.

"But it's quite true," he said. "She adores me." Oh, the vast joke. He would go and see her as soon as he returned—see and conquer. "I believe she wants to marry me," he added.

"But you wouldn't ... you don't intend...."

The air was fairly crepitating with humour. Mr. Hutton laughed aloud. "I intend to marry you," he said. It seemed to him the best joke he had ever made in his life.

When Mr. Hutton left Southend he was once more a married man. It was agreed that, for the time being, the fact should be kept secret. In the autumn they would go abroad together, and the world should be informed. Meanwhile he was to go back to his own house and Doris to hers.

The day after his return he walked over in the afternoon to see Miss Spence. She received him with the old Gioconda.

"I was expecting you to come."

"I couldn't keep away," Mr. Hutton gallantly replied.

They sat in the summer-house. It was a pleasant place—a little old stucco temple bowered among dense bushes of evergreen. Miss Spence had left her mark on it by hanging up over the seat a blue-and-white Della Robbia plaque.

"I am thinking of going to Italy this autumn," said Mr. Hutton. He felt like a ginger-beer bottle, ready to pop with bubbling humorous excitement.

"Italy...." Miss Spence closed her eyes ecstatically. "I feel drawn there too."

"Why not let yourself be drawn?"

"I don't know. One somehow hasn't the energy and initiative to set out alone."

"Alone...." Ah, sound of guitars and throaty singing. "Yes, travelling alone isn't much fun."

Miss Spence lay back in her chair without speaking. Her eyes were still closed. Mr. Hutton stroked his moustache. The silence prolonged itself for what seemed a very long time.

Pressed to stay to dinner, Mr. Hutton did not refuse. The fun had hardly started. The table was laid in the loggia. Through its arches they looked out on to the sloping garden, to the valley below and the farther hills. Light ebbed away; the heat and silence were oppressive. A huge cloud was mounting up the sky, and there were distant breathings of thunder. The thunder drew nearer, a wind began to blow, and the first drops of rain fell. The table was cleared. Miss Spence and Mr. Hutton sat on in the growing darkness.

Miss Spence broke a long silence by saying meditatively.

"I think everyone has a right to a certain amount of happiness, don't you?"

"Most certainly." But what was she leading up to? Nobody makes generalisations about life unless they mean to talk about themselves. Happiness: he looked back on his own life, and saw a cheerful, placid existence disturbed by no great griefs or discomforts or alarms. He had always had money and freedom; he had been able to do very much as he wanted. Yes, he supposed he had been happy—happier than most men. And now he was not merely happy; he had discovered in irresponsibility the secret of gaiety. He was about to say something about his happiness when Miss Spence went on speaking.

"People like you and me have a right to be happy some time in our lives."

"Me?" said Mr. Hutton surprised.

"Poor Henry! Fate hasn't treated either of us very well."

"Oh, well, it might have treated me worse."

"You're being cheerful. That's brave of you. But don't think I can't see behind the mask."

Miss Spence spoke louder and louder as the rain came down more and more heavily. Periodically the thunder cut across her utterances. She talked on, shouting against the noise.

"I have understood you so well and for so long."

A flash revealed her, aimed and intent, leaning towards him. Her eyes were two profound and menacing gun-barrels. The darkness re-engulfed her.

"You were a lonely soul seeking a companion soul. I could sympathise with you in your solitude. Your marriage ..."

The thunder cut short the sentence. Miss Spence's voice became audible once more with the words:

"... could offer no companionship to a man of your stamp. You needed a soul mate."

A soul mate—he! a soul mate. It was incredibly fantastic. Georgette Leblanc, the ex-soul mate of Maurice Maeterlinck. He had seen that in the paper a few days ago. So it was thus that Janet Spence had painted him in her imagination—a soul-mater. And for Doris he was a picture of goodness and the cleverest man in the world. And actually, really, he was what?—Who knows?

"My heart went out to you. I could understand; I was lonely, too." Miss Spence laid her hand on his knee. "You were so patient." Another flash. She was still aimed, dangerously. "You never complained. But I could guess—I could guess."

"How wonderful of you!" So he was an *âme incomprise*.

"Only a woman's intuition...."

The thunder crashed and rumbled, died away, and only the sound of the ram was left. The thunder was his laughter, magnified, externalised. Flash and crash, there it was again, right on top of them.

"Don't you feel that you have within you something that is akin to this storm?" He could imagine her leaning forward as she uttered the words. "Passion makes one the equal of the elements."

What was his gambit now? Why, obviously, he should have said "Yes," and ventured on some unequivocal gesture. But Mr. Hutton suddenly took fright. The ginger beer in him had gone flat. The woman was serious—terribly serious. He was appalled.

Passion? "No," he desperately answered. "I am without passion."

But his remark was either unheard or unheeded, for Miss Spence went on with a growing exaltation, speaking so rapidly, however, and in such a burningly intimate whisper that Mr. Hutton found it very difficult to distinguish what she was saying. She was telling him, as far as he could make out, the story of her life. The lightning was less frequent now, and there were long intervals of darkness. But at each flash he saw her still aiming towards him, still yearning forward with a terrifying intensity. Darkness, the rain, and then flash! her face was there, close at hand. A pale mask, greenish white; the large eyes, the narrow barrel of the mouth, the heavy eyebrows. Agrippina, or wasn't it rather—yes, wasn't it rather George Robey?

He began devising absurd plans for escaping. He might suddenly jump up, Pretending he had seen a burglar—Stop thief, stop thief!—and dash off into the night in pursuit. Or should he say that he felt faint, a heart attack? or that he had seen, a ghost—Emily's ghost—in the garden? Absorbed in his childish plotting, he had ceased to pay any attention to Miss Spence's words. The spasmodic clutching of her hand recalled his thoughts.

"I honoured you for that, Henry," she was saying.

Honoured him for what?

"Marriage is a sacred tie, and your respect for it, even when the marriage was, as it was in your case, an unhappy one, made me respect you and admire you, and—shall I dare say the word?—"

Oh, the burglar, the ghost in the garden! But it was too late.

"... yes, love you, Henry, all the more. But we're free now, Henry."

Free? There was a movement in the dark, and she was kneeling on the floor by his chair.

"Oh, Henry, Henry, I have been unhappy too."

Her arms embraced him, and by the shaking of her body he could feel that she was sobbing. She might have been a suppliant crying for mercy.

"You mustn't, Janet," he protested. Those tears were terrible, terrible. "Not now, not now! You must be calm; you must go to bed." He patted her shoulder, then got up, disengaging himself from her embrace. He left her still crouching on the floor beside the chair on which he had been sitting.

Groping his way into the hall, and without waiting to look for his hat, he went out of the house, taking infinite pains to close the front door noiselessly behind him. The clouds had blown over, and the moon was shining from a clear sky. There were puddles all along the road, and a noise of running water rose from the gutters and ditches. Mr. Hutton splashed along, not caring if he got wet.

How heartrendingly she had sobbed! With the emotions of pity and remorse that the recollection evoked in him there was a certain resentment: why couldn't she have played the game that he was playing the heartless, amusing game? Yes, but he had known all the time that she wouldn't, she couldn't play that game; he had known and persisted.

What had she said about passion and the elements? Something absurdly stale, but true, true. There she was, a cloud black bosomed and charged with thunder, and he, like some absurd little Benjamin Franklin, had sent up a kite into the heart of the menace. Now he was complaining that his toy had drawn the lightning.

She was probably still kneeling by that chair in the loggia, crying.

But why hadn't he been able to keep up the game? Why had his irresponsibility deserted him, leaving him suddenly sober in a cold world? There were no answers to any of his questions. One idea burned steady and luminous in his mind—the idea of flight. He must get away at once.

IV

"What are you thinking about, Teddy Bear?"

"Nothing."

There was a silence. Mr. Hutton remained motionless, his elbows on the parapet of the terrace, his chin in his hands, looking down over Florence. He had taken a villa on one of the hilltops to the south of the city. From a little raised terrace at the end of the garden one looked down a long fertile valley on to the town and beyond it to the bleak mass of Monte Morello and, eastward of it, to the peopled hill of Fiesole, dotted with white houses. Everything was clear and luminous in the September sunshine.

"Are you worried about anything?"

"No, thank you."

"Tell me, Teddy Bear."

"But, my dear, there's nothing to tell." Mr. Hutton turned round, smiled, and patted the girl's hand. "I think you'd better go in and have your siesta. It's too hot for you here."

"Very well, Teddy Bear. Are you coming too?"

"When I've finished my cigar."

"All right. But do hurry up and finish it, Teddy Bear." Slowly, reluctantly, she descended the steps of the terrace and walked towards the house.

Mr. Hutton continued his contemplation of Florence. He had need to be alone. It was good sometimes to escape from Doris and the restless solicitude of her passion. He had never known the pains of loving hopelessly, but he was experiencing now the pains of being loved. These last weeks had been a period of growing discomfort. Doris was always with him, like an obsession, like a guilty conscience. Yes, it was good to be alone.

He pulled an envelope out of his pocket and opened it; not without reluctance. He hated letters; they always contained something unpleasant—nowadays, since his second marriage. This was from his sister. He began skimming through the insulting home-truths of which it was composed. The words "indecent haste," "social suicide," "scarcely cold in her grave," "person of the lower classes," all occurred. They were inevitable now in any communication from a well-meaning and right-thinking relative. Impatient, he was about to tear the stupid letter to pieces when his eye fell on a sentence at the bottom of the third page. His heart beat with uncomfortable violence as he read it. It was too monstrous! Janet

Spence was going about telling everyone that he had poisoned his wife in order to marry Doris. What damnable malice! Ordinarily a man of the suavest temper, Mr. Hutton found himself trembling with rage. He took the childish satisfaction of calling names—he cursed the woman.

Then suddenly he saw the ridiculous side of the situation. The notion that he should have murdered anyone in order to marry Doris! If they only knew how miserably bored he was. Poor, dear Janet! She had tried to be malicious; she had only succeeded in being stupid.

A sound of footsteps aroused him; he looked round. In the garden below the little terrace the servant girl of the house was picking fruit. A Neapolitan, strayed somehow as far north as Florence, she was a specimen of the classical type—a little debased. Her profile might have been taken from a Sicilian coin of a bad period. Her features, carved floridly in the grand tradition, expressed an almost perfect stupidity. Her mouth was the most beautiful thing about her; the calligraphic hand of nature had richly curved it into an expression of mulish bad temper.... Under her hideous black clothes, Mr. Hutton divined a powerful body, firm and massive. He had looked at her before with a vague interest and curiosity. To-day the curiosity defined and focused itself into a desire. An idyll of Theocritus. Here was the woman; he, alas, was not precisely like a goatherd on the volcanic hills. He called to her.

"Armida!"

The smile with which she answered him was so provocative, attested so easy a virtue, that Mr. Hutton took fright. He was on the brink once more—on the brink. He must draw back, oh! quickly, quickly, before it was too late. The girl continued to look up at him.

"*Ha chiamito*?" she asked at last.

Stupidity or reason? Oh, there was no choice now. It was imbecility every time.

"*Scendo*" he called back to her. Twelve steps led from the garden to the terrace. Mr. Hutton counted them. Down, down, down, down.... He saw a vision of himself descending from one circle of the inferno to the next—from a darkness full of wind and hail to an abyss of stinking mud.

V

For a good many days the Hutton case had a place on the front page of every newspaper. There had been no more popular murder trial since George Smith had temporarily eclipsed the European War by drowning in a warm bath his seventh bride. The public imagination was stirred by this tale of a murder brought to light months after the date of the crime. Here, it was felt, was one of those incidents in human life, so notable because they are so rare, which do definitely justify the ways of God to man. A wicked man had been moved by an illicit passion to kill his wife. For months he had lived in sin and fancied security——only to be dashed at last more horribly into the pit he had prepared for himself. Murder will out, and here was a case of it. The readers of the newspapers were in a position to follow every movement of the hand of God. There had been vague, but persistent, rumours in the neighbourhood; the police had taken action at last. Then came the exhumation order, the post-mortem examination, the inquest, the evidence of the experts, the verdict of the coroner's jury, the trial, the condemnation. For once Providence had done its duty, obviously, grossly, didactically, as in a melodrama. The newspapers were right in making of the case the staple intellectual food of a whole season.

Mr. Hutton's first emotion when he was summoned from Italy to give evidence at the inquest was one of indignation. It was a monstrous, a scandalous thing that the police should take such idle, malicious gossip seriously. When the inquest was over he would bring an action for malicious prosecution against the Chief Constable; he would sue the Spence woman for slander.

The inquest was opened; the astonishing evidence unrolled itself. The experts had examined the body, and had found traces of arsenic; they were of opinion that the late Mrs. Hutton had died of arsenic poisoning.

Arsenic poisoning.... Emily had died of arsenic poisoning? After that, Mr. Hutton learned with surprise that there was enough arsenicated insecticide in his green-houses to poison an army.

It was now, quite suddenly, that he saw it: there was a case against him. Fascinated, he watched it growing, growing, like some monstrous tropical plant. It was enveloping him, surrounding him; he was lost in a tangled forest.

When was the poison administered? The experts agreed that it must have been swallowed eight or nine hours before death. About lunch-time? Yes, about lunch-time. Clara, the parlour-maid, was called. Mrs. Hutton, she remembered, had asked her to go and fetch her medicine. Mr. Hutton had volunteered to go instead; he had gone alone. Miss Spence—ah, the memory of the storm, the white aimed face! the horror of it all!—Miss Spence confirmed Clara's statement, and added that Mr. Hutton had come back with the medicine already poured out in a wine-glass, not in the bottle.

Mr. Hutton's indignation evaporated. He was dismayed, frightened. It was all too fantastic to be taken seriously, and yet this nightmare was a fact it was actually happening.

M'Nab had seen them kissing, often. He had taken them for a drive on the day of Mrs. Hutton's death. He could see them reflected in the wind-screen, sometimes out of the tail of his eye.

The inquest was adjourned. That evening Doris went to bed with a headache. When he went to her room after dinner, Mr. Hutton found her crying.

"What's the matter?" He sat down on the edge of her bed and began to stroke her hair. For a long time she did not answer, and he went on stroking her hair mechanically, almost unconsciously; sometimes, even he bent down and kissed her bare shoulder. He had his own affairs, however, to think about. What had happened? How was it that the stupid gossip had actually come true? Emily had died of arsenic poisoning. It was absurd, impossible. The order of things had been broken, and he was at the mercy of an irresponsibility. What had happened, what was going to happen? He was interrupted in the midst of his thoughts.

"It's my fault—it's my fault!" Doris suddenly sobbed out. "I shouldn't have loved you; I oughtn't to have let you love me. Why was I ever born?"

Mr. Hutton didn't say anything but looked down in silence at the abject figure of misery lying on the bed.

"If they do anything to you I shall kill myself."

She sat up, held him for a moment at arm's length, and looked at him with a kind of violence, as though she were never to see him again.

"I love you, I love you, I love you." She drew him, inert and passive, towards her, clasped him, pressed herself against him. "I didn't know you loved me as much as that, Teddy Bear. But why did you do it—why did you do it?"

Mr. Hutton undid her clasping arms and got up. His face became very red. "You seem to take it for granted that I murdered my wife," he said. "It's really too grotesque. What do you all take me for? A cinema hero?" He had begun to lose his temper. All the exasperation, all the fear and bewilderment of the day, was transformed into a violent anger against her. "It's all such damned stupidity. Haven't you any conception of a civilised man's mentality? Do I look the sort of man who'd go about slaughtering people? I suppose you imagined I was so insanely in love with you that I could commit any folly. When will you women understand that one isn't insanely in love? All one asks for is a quiet life, which you won't allow one to have. I don't know what the devil ever induced me to marry you. It was all a damned stupid, practical joke. And now you go about saying I'm a murderer. I won't stand it."

Mr. Hutton stamped towards the door. He had said horrible things, he knew—odious things that he ought speedily to unsay. But he wouldn't. He closed the door behind him.

"Teddy Bear!" He turned the handle; the latch clicked into place. Teddy Bear! The voice that came to him through the closed door was agonised. Should he go back? He ought to go back. He touched the handle, then withdrew his fingers and quickly walked away. When he was half-way down the stairs he halted. She might try to do something silly—throw herself out of the window or God knows what! He listened attentively; there was no sound. But he pictured her very clearly, tiptoeing across the room, lifting the sash as high as it would go, leaning out into the cold night air. It was raining a little. Under the window lay the paved terrace. How far below? Twenty-five or thirty feet? Once, when he was walking along Piccadilly, a dog had jumped out of a third-storey window of the Ritz. He had seen it fall; he had heard it strike the pavement. Should he go back? He was damned if he would; he hated her.

He sat for a long time in the library. What had happened? What was happening? He turned the question over and over in his mind and could find no answer. Suppose the nightmare dreamed itself out to its horrible conclusion. Death was waiting for him. His eyes filled with tears; he wanted so passionately to live. "Just to be alive." Poor Emily had wished it too, he remembered: "Just to be alive."

There were still so many places in this astonishing world unvisited, so many queer delightful people still unknown, so many lovely women never so much as seen. The huge white oxen would still be dragging their wains along the Tuscan roads, the cypresses would still go up, straight as pillars, to the blue heaven; but he would not be there to see them. And the sweet southern wines—Tear of Christ and Blood of Judas—others would drink them, not he. Others would walk down the obscure and narrow lanes between the bookshelves in the London Library, sniffing the dusty perfume of good literature, peering at strange titles, discovering unknown names, exploring the fringes of vast domains of knowledge. He would be lying in a hole in the ground. And why, why? Confusedly he felt that some extraordinary kind of justice was being done. In the past he had been wanton and imbecile and irresponsible. Now Fate was playing as wantonly, as irresponsibly, with him. It was tit for tat, and God existed after all.

He felt that he would like to pray. Forty years ago he used to kneel by his bed every evening. The nightly formula of his childhood came to him almost unsought from some long unopened chamber of the memory. "God bless Father and Mother, Tom and Cissie and the Baby, Mademoiselle and Nurse, and everyone that I love, and make me a good boy. Amen." They were all dead now all except Cissie.

His mind seemed to soften and dissolve; a great calm descended upon his spirit. He went upstairs to ask Doris's forgiveness. He found her lying on the couch at the foot of the bed. On the floor beside her stood a blue bottle of liniment, marked "Not to be taken"; she seemed to have drunk about half of it.

"You didn't love me," was all she said when she opened her eyes to find him bending over her.

Dr. Libbard arrived in time to prevent any very serious consequences. "You mustn't do this again," he said while Mr. Hutton was out of the room.

"What's to prevent me?" she asked defiantly.

Dr. Libbard looked at her with his large, sad eyes. "There's nothing to prevent you," he said. "Only yourself and your baby. Isn't it rather bad luck on your baby, not allowing it to come into the world because you want to go out of it?"

Doris was silent for a time. "All right," she whispered. "I won't."

Mr. Hutton sat by her bedside for the rest of the night. He felt himself now to be indeed a murderer. For a time he persuaded himself that he loved this pitiable child. Dozing in his chair, he woke up, stiff and cold, to find himself drained dry, as it were, of every emotion. He had become nothing but a tired and suffering carcase. At six o'clock he undressed and went to bed for a couple of hours' sleep. In the course of the same afternoon the coroner's jury brought in a verdict of "Wilful Murder," and Mr. Hutton was committed for trial.

VI

Miss Spence was not at all well. She had found her public appearances in the witness-box very trying, and when it was all over she had something that was very nearly a breakdown. She slept badly, and suffered from nervous indigestion.

Dr. Libbard used to call every other day. She talked to him a great deal—mostly about the Hutton case.... Her moral indignation was always on the boil. Wasn't it appalling to think that one had had a murderer in one's house. Wasn't it extraordinary that one could have been for so long mistaken about the man's character? (But she had had an inkling from the first.) And then the girl he had gone off with—so low class, so little better than a prostitute. The news that the second Mrs. Hutton was expecting a baby the posthumous child of a condemned and executed criminal—revolted her; the thing was shocking an obscenity. Dr. Libbard answered her gently and vaguely, and prescribed bromide.

One morning he interrupted her in the midst of her customary tirade. "By the way," he said in his soft, melancholy voice, "I suppose it was really you who poisoned Mrs. Hutton."

Miss Spence stared at him for two or three seconds with enormous eyes, and then quietly said, "Yes." After that she started to cry.

"In the coffee, I suppose."

She seemed to nod assent. Dr. Libbard took out his fountain-pen, and in his neat, meticulous calligraphy wrote out a prescription for a sleeping draught.

II: PERMUTATIONS AMONG THE NIGHTINGALES

It is night on the terrace outside the Hotel Cimarosa. Part of the garden façade of the hotel is seen at the back of the stage—a bare white wall, with three French windows giving on to balconies about ten feet from the ground, and below them, leading from the terrace to the lounge, a double door of glass, open now, through which a yellow radiance streams out into the night. On the paved terrace stand two or three green iron tables and chairs. To the left a mass of dark foliage, ilex and cypress, in the shadow of which more tables and chairs are set. At the back to the left a strip of sky is visible between the corner of the hotel and the dark trees, blue and starry, for it is a marvellous June evening. Behind the trees the ground slopes steeply down and down to an old city in the valley below, of whose invisible presence you are made aware by the sound of many bells wafted up from a score of slender towers in a sweet and melancholy discord that seems to mourn the passing of each successive hour. When the curtain rises the terrace is almost deserted; the hotel dinner is not yet over. A single guest, COUNT ALBERTO TIRETTA, *is discovered, sitting in a position of histrionic despair at one of the little green tables. A waiter stands respectfully sympathetic at his side,* ALBERTO *is a little man with large lustrous eyes and a black moustache, about twenty-five years of age. He has the pathetic charm of an Italian street-boy with an organ—almost as pretty and sentimental as Murillo's little beggars.*

ALBERTO (*making a florid gesture with his right hand and with his left covering his eyes*). Whereupon, Waiter (*he is reciting a tale of woes*), she slammed the door in my face. (*He brings down his gesticulating right hand with a crash on to the table.*)

WAITER. In your face, Signore? Impossible!

ALBERTO. Impossible, but a fact. Some more brandy, please; I am a little weary. (The waiter uncorks the bottle he has been holding under his arm and fills Alberto's glass.)

WAITER. That will be one lira twenty-five, Signore.

ALBERTO (throwing down a note). Keep the change.

WAITER (bowing). Thank you, Signore. But if I were the Signore I should beat her. (He holds up the Cognac bottle and by way of illustration slaps its black polished flanks.)

ALBERTO. Beat her? But I tell you I am in love with her.

WAITER. All the more reason, then, Signore. It will be not only a stern disciplinary duty, but a pleasure as well; oh, I assure you, Signore, a pleasure.

ALBERTO. Enough, enough. You sully the melancholy beauty of my thoughts. My feelings at this moment are of an unheard-of delicacy and purity. Respect them, I beg you. Some more brandy, please.

WAITER (pouring out the brandy). Delicacy, purity.... Ah, believe me, Signore ... That will be one lira twenty-five.

ALBERTO (throwing down another note with the same superbly aristocratic gesture). Keep the change.

WAITER. Thank you, Signore. But as I was saying, Signore, delicacy, purity.... You think I do not understand such sentiments. Alas, Signore, beneath the humblest shirt-front there beats a heart. And if the Signore's sentiments are too much for him, I have a niece. Eighteen years old, and what eyes, what forms!

ALBERTO. Stop, stop. Respect my feelings, Waiter, as well as the ears of the young lady (he points towards the glass doors). Remember she is an American. (The Waiter, bows and goes into the hotel.)

SIDNEY DOLPHIN *and* MISS AMY TOOMIS

come out together on to the terrace. MISS AMY *supports a well-shaped head on one of the most graceful necks that ever issued from Minneapolis. The eyes are dark, limpid, ingenuous; the mouth expresses sensibility. She is twenty-two and the heiress of those ill-gotten Toomis millions.* SIDNEY DOLPHIN *has a romantic aristocratic appearance. The tailoring of* 1830 *would suit him. Balzac would have described his face as* plein de poésie. *In effect he does happen to be a poet. His two volumes of verse, "Zeotrope and 'Trembling Ears," have been recognised by intelligent critics as remarkable. How far they are poetry nobody, least of all Dolphin himself, is certain. They may be merely the ingenious products of a very cultured and elaborate brain. Mere curiosities; who knows? His age is twenty-seven. They sit down at one of the little iron tables,* ALBERTO *they do not see; the shadow of the trees conceals him. For his part, he is too much absorbed in savouring his own despair to pay any attention to the newcomers. There is a long, uncomfortable silence.* DOLPHIN *assumes the Thinker's mask—the bent brow, the frown, the finger to the forehead,* AMY *regards this romantic gargoyle with some astonishment. Pleased with her interest in him,* DOLPHIN *racks his brains to think of some way of exploiting this curiosity to his own advantage; but he is too shy to play any of the gambits which his ingenuity suggests.* AMY *makes a social effort and speaks, in chanting Middle Western tones.*

AMY. It's been a wonderful day, hasn't it?

DOLPHIN (*starting, as though roused from profoundest thought*). Yes, yes, it has.

AMY. You don't often get it as fine as this in England, I guess.

DOLPHIN. Not often.

AMY. Nor do we over at home.

DOLPHIN. So I should suppose. (*Silence. A spasm of anguish crosses* DOLPHIN'S *face; then he reassumes the old Thinker's mask.* AMY *looks at him for a little longer, then, unable to suppress her growing curiosity, she says with a sudden burst of childish confidence:*)

AMY. It must be wonderful to be able to think as hard as you do, Mr. Dolphin. Or are you sad about something?

DOLPHIN (*looks up, smiles, and blushes; a spell has been broken*). The finger at the temple, Miss Toomis, is not the barrel of a revolver.

AMY. That means you're not specially sad about anything. Just thinking.

DOLPHIN. Just thinking.

AMY. What about?

DOLPHIN. Oh, just life, you know—life and letters.

AMY. Letters? Do you mean love letters.

DOLPHIN. No, no. Letters in the sense of literature; letters as opposed to life.

AMY. (*disappointed*). Oh, literature. They used to teach us literature at school. But I could never understand Emerson. What do you think about literature for?

DOLPHIN. It interests me, you know. I read it; I even try to write it.

AMY (*very much excited*). What, are you a writer, a poet, Mr. Dolphin?

DOLPHIN. Alas, it is only too true; I am.

AMY. But what do you write?

DOLPHIN. Verse and prose, Miss Toomis. Just verse and prose.

AMY (*with enthusiasm*). Isn't that interesting. I've never met a poet before, you know.

DOLPHIN. Fortunate being. Why, before I left England I attended a luncheon of the Poetry Union at which no less than a hundred and eighty-nine poets were present. The sight of them made me decide to go to Italy.

AMY. Will you show me your books?

DOLPHIN. Certainly not, Miss Toomis. That would ruin our friendship. I am insufferable in my writings. In them I give vent to all the horrible thoughts and impulses which I am too timid to express or put into practice in real life. Take me as you find me here, a decent specimen of a man, shy but able to talk intelligently when the layers of ice are broken, aimless, ineffective, but on the whole quite a good sort.

AMY. But I know that man already, Mr. Dolphin. I want to know the poet. Tell me what the poet is like.

DOLPHIN. He is older, Miss Toomis, than the rocks on which he sits. He is villainous. He is ... but there, I really must stop. It was you who set me going, though. Did you do it on purpose.

AMY. Do what on purpose?

DOLPHIN. Make me talk about myself. If you want to get people to like you, you must always lead the conversation on to the subject of their characters. Nothing pleases them so much. They'll talk with enthusiasm for hours and go away saying that you're the most charming, cleverest person they've ever met. But of course you knew that already. You re Machiavellian.

AMY. Machiavellian? You're the first person that's ever said that. I always thought I was very simple and straight-forward. People say about me that.... Ah, now I'*m* talking about myself. That was unscrupulous of you. But you shouldn't have told me about the trick if you wanted it to succeed.

DOLPHIN. Yes. It was silly of me. If I hadn't, you'd have gone on talking about yourself and thought me the nicest man in the world.

AMY. I want to hear about your poetry. Are you writing any now?

DOLPHIN. I have composed the first line of a magnificent epic. But I can't get any further.

AMY. How does it go?

DOLPHIN. Like this (*he clears his throat*). "Casbeen has been, and Moghreb is no more." Ah, the transience of all sublunary things! But inspiration has stopped short there.

AMY. What exactly does it mean?

DOLPHIN. Ah, there you're asking too much, Miss Toomis. Waiter, some coffee for two.

WAITER (*who is standing in the door of the lounge*). Si, Signore. Will the lady and gentleman take it here, or in the gardens, perhaps?

DOLPHIN. A good suggestion. Why shouldn't the lady and gentleman take it in the garden?

AMY. Why not?

DOLPHIN. By the fountain, then, Waiter. We can talk about ourselves there to the tune of falling waters.

AMY. And you shall recite your poetry, Mr. Dolphin. I just love poetry. Do you know Mrs. Wilcox's *Poems of Passion*? (*They go out to the left. A nightingale utters two or three phrases of song and from far down the bells of the city jangle the three-quarters and die slowly away into the silence out of which they rose and came together.*)

(LUCREZIA GRATTAROL *has come out of the hotel just in time to overhear Miss Toomis's last remark, just in time to see her walk slowly away with a hand on* SIDNEY DOLPHIN's *arm.* LUCREZIA *has a fine thoroughbred appearance, an aquiline nose, a finely curved sensual mouth, a superb white brow, a quivering nostril. She is the last of a family whose name is as illustrious in Venetian annals as that of Foscarini, Tiepolo, or Tron. She stamps a preposterously high-heeled foot and tosses her head.*)

LUCREZIA. Passion! Passion, indeed. An American! (She starts to run after the retreating couple, when ALBERTO, who has been sitting with his head between his hands, looks up and catches sight of the newcomer.)

ALBERTO. Lucrezia!

LUCREZIA (starts, for in the shade beneath the trees she had not seen him). Oh! You gave me such a fright, Alberto. I'm in a hurry now. Later on, if you....

ALBERTO (in a desperate voice that breaks into a sob). Lucrezia! You must come and talk to me. You must.

LUCREZIA. But I tell you I can't now, Alberto. Later on.

ALBERTO (the tears streaming down his cheeks). Now, now, now! You must come now. I am lost if you don't.

LUCREZIA (looking indecisively first at ALBERTO and then along the path down which AMY and SIDNEY DOLPHIN have disappeared). But supposing I am lost if I do come?

ALBERTO. But you couldn't be as much lost as I am. Ah, you don't know what it is to suffer. Nur wer die Sehnsucht kennt weiss wass ich leide. Oh, Lucrezia.... (He sobs unrestrainedly.)

LUCREZIA (goes over to where ALBERTO is sitting. She pats his shoulder and his bowed head of black curly hair). There, there, my little Bertino. Tell me what it is. You mustn't cry. There, there.

ALBERTO (drying his eyes and rubbing his head, like a cat, avid of caresses, against her hand). How can I thank you enough, Lucrezia? You are like a mother to me.

LUCREZIA. I know. That's just what's so dangerous.

ALBERTO (lets his head fall upon her bosom). I come to you for comfort, like a tired child, Lucrezia.

LUCREZIA. Poor darling! (She strokes his hair, twines its thick black tendrils round her fingers, ALBERTO is abjectly pathetic.)

ALBERTO (with closed eyes and a seraphic smile). Ah, the suavity, the beauty of this maternal instinct!

LUCREZIA (with a sudden access of energy and passion). The disgustingness of it, you mean. (She pushes him from her. His head wobbles once, as though it were inanimate, before he straightens into life.) The maternal instinct. Ugh. It's been the undoing of too many women. You men come with your sentimental babyishness and exploit it for your own lusts. Be a man, Bertino. Be a woman, I mean, if you can.

ALBERTO (looking up at her with eyes full of doglike, dumb reproach). Lucrezia! You, too? Is there nobody who cares for me? This is the unkindest cut of all. I may as well die. (He relapses into tears.)

LUCREZIA (who has started to go, turns back, irresolute). Now, don't cry, Bertino. Can't you behave like a reasonable being? (She makes as though to go again.)

ALBERTO (through his sobs). You too, Lucrezia! Oh, I can't bear it, I can't bear it.

LUCREZIA (turning back desperately). But what do you want me to do? Why should you expect me to hold your hand?

ALBERTO. I thought better of you, Lucrezia. Let me go. There is nothing left for me now but death. (He rises to his feet, takes a step or two, and then collapses into another chair, unable to move.)

LUCREZIA (torn between anger and remorse). Now do behave yourself sensibly, Bertino. There, there ... you mustn't cry. I'm sorry if I've hurt you. (Looking towards the left along the path taken by AMY and

DOLPHIN.) Oh, damnation! (She stamps her foot.) Here, Bertino, do pull yourself together. (She raises him up.) There, now you must stop crying. (But as soon as she lets go of him his head falls back on to the iron table with an unpleasant, meaty bump. That bump is too much for LUCREZIA. She bends over him, strokes his head, even kisses the lustrous curls.) Oh, forgive me, forgive me! I have been a beast. But, tell me first, what's the matter, Bertino? What is it, my poor darling? Tell me.

ALBERTO. Nobody loves me.

LUCREZIA. But we're all devoted to you, Bertino mio.

ALBERTO. She isn't. To-day she shut the door in my face.

LUCREZIA. She? You mean the French-woman, the one you told me about? Louise, wasn't she?

ALBERTO. Yes, the one with the golden hair.

LUCREZIA. And the white legs. I remember: you saw her bathing.

ALBERTO (lays his hand on his heart). Ah, don't remind me of it. (His face twitches convulsively.)

LUCREZIA. And now she's gone and shut the door in your face.

ALBERTO. In my face, Lucrezia.

LUCREZIA. Poor darling!

ALBERTO. For me there is nothing now but the outer darkness.

LUCREZIA. Is the door shut forever, then?

ALBERTO. Definitively, for ever.

LUCREZIA. But have you tried knocking? Perhaps, after all, it might be opened again, if only a crack.

ALBERTO. What, bruise my hands against the granite of her heart?

LUCREZIA. Don't be too poetical, Bertino mio. Why not try again, in any case?

ALBERTO. You give me courage.

LUCREZIA. There's no harm in trying, you know.

ALBERTO. Courage to live, to conquer. (He beats his breast.) I am a man again, thanks to you, Lucrezia, my inspirer, my Muse, my Egeria. How can I be sufficiently grateful. (He kisses her.) I am the child of your spirit. (He kisses her again.)

LUCREZIA. Enough, enough. I am not ambitious to be a mother, yet awhile. Quickly now, Bertino, I know you will succeed.

ALBERTO (cramming his hat down on his head and knocking with his walking-stick on the ground). Succeed or die, Lucrezia. (He goes out with a loud martial stamp.)

LUCREZIA (to the waiter who is passing across the stage with a coffee-pot and cups on a tray). Have you seen the Signorina Toomis, Giuseppe?

WAITER. The Signorina is down in the garden. So is the Signore Dolphin. By the fountain, Signorina. This is the Signore's coffee.

LUCREZIA. Have you a mother, Giuseppe?

WAITER. Unfortunately, Signorina.

LUCREZIA. Unfortunately? Does she treat you badly, then?

WAITER. Like a dog, Signorina.

LUCREZIA. Ah, I should like to see your mother. I should like to ask her to give me some hints on how to bring up children.

WAITER. But surely, Signorina, you are not expecting, you—ah....

LUCREZIA. Only figuratively, Giuseppe. My children are spiritual children.

WAITER. Precisely, precisely. My mother, alas! is not a spiritual relation. Nor is my fiançée.

LUCREZIA. I didn't know you were engaged.

WAITER. To an angel of perdition. Believe me, Signorina, I go to my destruction in that woman—go with open eyes. There is no escape. She is what is called in the Holy Bible (crosses himself) a Fisher of Men.

LUCREZIA. You have remarkable connections, Giuseppe.

WAITER. I am honoured by your words, Signorina. But the coffee becomes cold. (He hurries out to the left.)

LUCREZIA. In the garden! By the fountain! And there's the nightingale beginning to sing in earnest! Good heavens! what may not already have happened? (She runs out after the waiter.)

(*Two persons emerge from the hotel*, the VICOMTE DE BARBAZANGE *and the* BARONESS KOCH DE WORMS. PAUL DE BARBAZANGE *is a young man—twenty-six perhaps of exquisite grace. Five foot ten, well built, dark hair, sleek as marble, the most refined aristocratic features, and a monocle*, SIMONE DE WORMS *is forty, a ripe Semitic beauty. Five years more and the bursting point of overripeness will have been reached. But now, thanks to massage, powerful corsets, skin foods, and powder, she is still a beauty—a beauty of the type Italians admire, cushioned, steatopygous.* PAUL, *who has a faultless taste in bric-à-brac and women, and is by instinct and upbringing an ardent anti-Semite, finds her infinitely repulsive. The Baronne enters with a loud shrill giggle. She gives* PAUL *a slap with her green feather fan.*)

SIMONE. Oh, you naughty boy! Quelle histoire. Mon Dieu! How dare you tell me such a story!

PAUL. For you, Baronne, I would risk anything even your displeasure.

SIMONE. Charming boy. But stories of that kind.... And you look so innocent, too! Do you know any more like it?

PAUL (*suddenly grave*). Not of that description. But I will tell you a story of another kind, a true story, a tragic story.

SIMONE. Did I ever tell you how I saw a woman run over by a train? Cut to pieces, literally, to pieces. So disagreeable. I'll tell you later. But now, what about your story?

PAUL. Oh, it's nothing, nothing.

SIMONE. But you promised to tell it me.

PAUL. It's only a commonplace anecdote. A young man, poor but noble, with a name and a position to keep up. A few youthful follies, a mountain of debts, and no way out except the revolver. This is all dull and obvious enough. But now follows the interesting part of the story. He is about to take that way out, when he meets the woman of his dreams, the goddess, the angel, the ideal. He loves, and he must die without a word. (*He turns his face away from the Baronne, as though his emotion were too much for him, which indeed it is.*)

SIMONE. Vicomte—Paul—this young man is you?

PAUL (*solemnly*). He is.

SIMONE. And the woman?

PAUL. Oh, I can't, I mayn't tell you.

SIMONE. The woman! Tell me, Paul.

PAUL (*turning towards her and falling on his knees*). The woman, Simone, is you. Ah, but I had no right to say it.

SIMONE (*quivering with emotion*). My Paul. (*She clasps his head to her bosom. A grimace of disgust contorts Paul's classical features. He endures Simone's caresses with a stoical patience.*) But what is this about a revolver? That is only a joke, Paul, isn't it? Say it isn't true.

PAUL. Alas, Simone, too true. (*He taps his coat pocket.*) There it lies. To-morrow I have a hundred and seventy thousand francs to pay, or be dishonoured. I cannot pay the sum. A Barbazange does not survive dishonour. My ancestors were Crusaders, preux chevaliers to a man. Their code is mine. Dishonour for me is worse than death.

SIMONE. Mon Dieu, Paul, how noble you are! (*She lays her hands on his shoulder, leans back, and surveys him at arm's length, a look of pride and anxious happiness on her face.*)

PAUL (*dropping his eyes modestly*). Not at all. I was born noble, and noblesse oblige, as we say in our family. Farewell, Simone, I love you—and I must die. My last thought will be of you. (*He kisses her hand, rises to his feet, and makes as though to go.*)

SIMONE (*clutching him by the arm*). No, Paul, no. You must not, shall not, do anything rash. A hundred and seventy thousand francs, did you say? It is paltry. Is there no one who could lend or give you the money?

PAUL. Not a soul. Farewell, Simone.

SIMONE. Stay, Paul. I hardly dare to ask it of you—you with such lofty ideas of honour—but would you ... from me?

PAUL. Take money from a woman? Ah, Simone, tempt me no more. I might do an ignoble act.

SIMONE. But from me, Paul, from me. I am not in your eyes a woman like any other woman, am I?

PAUL. It is true that my ancestors, the Crusaders, the preux chevaliers, might in all honour receive gifts from the ladies of their choice—chargers, swords, armour, or tenderer mementoes, such as gloves or garters. But money—no; who ever heard of their taking money?

SIMONE. But what would be the use of my giving you swords and horses? You could never use them. Consider, my knight, my noble Sir Paul, in these days the contests of chivalry have assumed a different form; the weapons and the armour have changed. Your sword must be of gold and paper; your breastplate of hard cash; your charger of gilt-edged securities. I offer you the shining panoply of the modern crusader. Will you accept it?

PAUL. You are eloquent, Simone. You could win over the devil himself with that angelic voice of yours. But it cannot be. Money is always money. The code is clear. I cannot accept your offer. Here is the way out. (*He takes an automatic pistol out of his pocket.*) Thank you, Simone, and good-bye. How wonderful is the love of a pure woman.

SIMONE. Paul, Paul, give that to me! (*She snatches the pistol from his hand.*) If anything were to happen to you, Paul, I should kill myself with this. You must live, you must consent to accept the money. You mustn't let your honour make a martyr of you.

PAUL (*brushing a tear from his eyes*). No, I can't.... Give me that pistol, I beg you.

SIMONE. For my sake, Paul.

PAUL. Oh, you make it impossible for me to act as the voices of dead ancestors tell me I should.... For your sake, then, Simone, I consent to live. For your sake I dare to accept the gift you offer.

SIMONE (*kissing his hand in an outburst of gratitude*). Thank you, thank you, Paul. How happy I am!

PAUL. I, too, light of my life.

SIMONE. My month's allowance arrived to-day. I have the cheque here. (*She takes it out of her corsage*.) Two hundred thousand francs. It's signed already. You can get it cashed as soon as the hanks open to-morrow.

PAUL (*moved by an outburst of genuine emotion kisses indiscriminately the cheque, the Baronne, his own hands*). My angel, you have saved me. How can I thank you? How can I love you enough? Ah, mon petit bouton de rose.

SIMONE. Oh, naughty, naughty! Not now, my Paul; you must wait till some other time.

PAUL. I burn with impatience.

SIMONE. Quelle fougue! Listen, then. In an hour's time, Paul chéri, in my boudoir; I shall be alone.

PAUL. An hour? It is an eternity.

SIMONE (*playfully*). An hour. I won't relent. Till then, my Paul. (*She blows a kiss and runs out: the scenery trembles at her passage.*)

(PAUL *looks at the cheque, then pulls out a large silk handkerchief and wipes his neck inside his collar.*) (DOLPHIN *drifts in from the left. He is smoking a cigarette, but he does not seem to be enjoying it.*)

PAUL. Alone?

DOLPHIN. Alas!

PAUL. Brooding on the universe as usual? I envy you your philosophic detachment. Personally, I find that the world is very much too much with us, and the devil too; (*he looks at the cheque in his hand*) and above all the flesh. My god, the flesh.... (*He wipes his neck again.*)

DOLPHIN. My philosophic detachment? But it's only a mask to hide the ineffectual longings I have to achieve contact with the world.

PAUL. But surely nothing is easier. One just makes a movement and impinges on one's fellow-beings.

DOLPHIN. Not with a temperament like mine. Imagine a shyness more powerful than curiosity or desire, a paralysis of all the faculties. You are a man of the world. You were born with a forehead of brass to affront every social emergency. Ah, if you knew what a torture it is to find yourself in the presence of someone a woman, perhaps—someone in whom you take an interest that is not merely philosophic; to find oneself in the presence of such a person and to be incapable, yes, physically incapable, of saying a word to express your interest in her or your desire to possess her intimacy. Ah, I notice I have slipped into the feminine. Inevitably, for of course the person is always a she.

PAUL. Of course, of course. That goes without saying. But what's the trouble? Women are so simple to deal with.

DOLPHIN. I know. Perfectly simply if one's in the right state of mind. I have found that out myself, for moments come alas, how rarely!—when I am filled with a spirit of confidence, possessed by some angel or devil of power. Ah, then I feel myself to be superb. I carry all before me. In those brief moments the whole secret of the world is revealed to me. I perceive that the supreme quality in the human soul is effrontery. Genius in the man of action is simply the apotheosis of charlatanism. Alexander the Great, Napoleon, Mr. Gladstone, Lloyd George—what are they? Just ordinary human beings projected through the magic lantern of a prodigious effrontery and so magnified to a thousand times larger than life. Look at me. I am far more intelligent than any of these fabulous figures; my sensibility is more refined than theirs, I am morally superior to any of them. And yet, by my lack of charlatanism, I am made less than nothing. My qualities are projected through the wrong end of a telescope and the world perceives me far smaller than I really am. But the world—who cares about the world? The only people who matter are the women.

PAUL. Very true, my dear Dolphin. The women.... (*He looks at the cheque and mops himself once more with his mauve silk handkerchief.*)

DOLPHIN. To-night was one of my moments of triumph. I felt myself suddenly free of all my inhibitions.

PAUL. I hope you profited by the auspicious occasion.

DOLPHIN. I did. I was making headway. I had—but I don't know why I should bore you with my confidences. Curious that one should be dumb before intimates and open one's mind to an all but stranger. I must apologise.

PAUL. But I am all attention and sympathy, my dear Dolphin. And I take it a little hardly that you should regard me as a stranger. (*He lays a hand on Dolphin's shoulder.*)

DOLPHIN. Thank you, Barbazange, thank you. Well, if you consent to be the receptacle of my woes, I shall go on pouring them out.... Miss Toomis.... But tell me frankly what you think of her.

PAUL. Well....

DOLPHIN. A little too ingenuous, a little silly even, eh?

PAUL. Now you say so, she certainly isn't very intellectually stimulating.

DOLPHIN. Precisely. But ... oh, those china-blue eyes, that ingenuousness, that pathetic and enchanting silliness! She touches lost chords in one's heart. I love the Chromatic Fantasia of Bach, I am transported by Beethoven's hundred-and-eleventh Sonata; but the fact doesn't prevent my being moved to tears by the last luscious waltz played by the hotel orchestra. In the best constructed brains there are always spongy surfaces that are sensitive to picture postcards and Little Nelly and the End of a Perfect Day. Miss Toomis has found out my Achilles's heel. She is boring, ridiculous, absurd to a degree, but oh! how moving, how adorable.

PAUL. You're done for, my poor Dolphin, sunk—spurlos.

DOLPHIN. And I was getting on so well, was revelling in my new-found confidence, and, knowing its transience, was exploiting it for all I was worth. I had covered an enormous amount of ground and then, hey presto! at a blow all my labour was undone. Actuated by what malice I don't know, la Lucrezia swoops down like a vulture, and without a by-your-leave or excuse of any kind carries off Miss Toomis from under my very eyes. What a woman! She terrifies me. I am always running away from her.

PAUL. Which means, I suppose, that she is always pursuing you.

DOLPHIN. She has ruined my evening and, it may me, all my chances of success. My precious hour of self-confidence will be wasted (though I hope you'll not take offence at the word)—wasted on you.

PAUL. It will return.

DOLPHIN. But when—but when? Till it does I shall be impotent and in agony.

PAUL. I know the agony of waiting. I myself was engaged to a Rumanian princess in 1916. But owing to the sad collapse in the Rumanian rate of exchange I have had to postpone our union indefinitely. It is painful, but, believe me, it can be borne. (*He looks at the cheque and then at his watch.*) There are other things which are much worse. Believe me, Dolphin, it can be borne.

DOLPHIN. I suppose it can. For, when all is said, there are damned few of us who really take things much to heart. Julie de Lespinasses are happily not common. I am even subnormal. At twenty I believed myself passionate: one does at that age. But now, when I come to consider myself candidly, I find that I am really one of those who never deeply felt nor strongly willed. Everything is profoundly indifferent to me. I sometimes try to depress myself with the thought that the world is a cess-pool, that men are pathetic degenerates from the ape whose laboriously manufactured ideals are pure nonsense and find no rhyme in reality, that the whole of life is a bad joke which takes a long time coming to an end. But it really doesn't upset me. I don't care a curse. It's deplorable; one ought to care. The best people do care. Still, I must say I should like to get possession of Miss Toomis. Confound that Grattarol woman. What on earth did she want to rush me like that for, do you suppose?

PAUL. I expect we shall find out now. (PAUL *jerks his head towards the left.* LUCREZIA *and* AMY *are seen entering from the garden,* LUCREZIA *holds her companion's arm and marches with a firm step towards the two men.* AMY *suffers herself to be drugged along.*)

LUCREZIA. Vicomte, Miss Toomis wants you to tell her all about Correggio.

AMY (*rather scared*). Oh, really—I....

LUCREZIA. And (*sternly*)—and Michelangelo. She is so much interested in art.

AMY. But please—don't trouble....

PAUL (*bowing gracefully*). I shall be delighted. And in return I hope Miss Toomis will tell me all about Longfellow.

AMY (*brightening*). Oh yes, don't you just love Evangeline?

PAUL. I do; and with your help, Miss Toomis, I hope I shall learn to love her better.

LUCREZIA (*to* DOLPHIN, *who has been looking from* AMY *to the* VICOMTE *and back again at* AMY *with eyes that betray a certain disquietude*). You really must come and look at the moon rising over the hills, Mr. Dolphin. One sees it best from the lower terrace. Shall we go?

DOLPHIN (*starts and shrinks*). But it's rather cold, isn't it? I mean—I think I ought to go and write a letter.

LUCREZIA. Oh, you can do that to-morrow.

DOLPHIN. But really.

LUCREZIA. You've no idea how lovely the moon looks.

DOLPHIN. But I must....

LUCREZIA (*lays her hand on his sleeve and tows hint after her, crying as she goes*). The moon, the moon.... (PAUL *and* AMY *regard their exit in silence.*)

PAUL. He doesn't look as though he much wanted to go and see the moon.

AMY. Perhaps he guesses what's in store for him.

PAUL (*surprised*). What, you don't mean to say you realised all the time?

AMY. Realised what?

PAUL. About la belle Lucrezia.

AMY. I don't know what you mean. All I know is that she means to give Mr. Dolphin a good talking to. He's so mercenary. It made me quite indignant when she told me about him. Such a schemer, too. You know in America we have very definite ideas about honour.

PAUL. Here too, Miss Toomis.

AMY. Not Mr. Dolphin. Oh dear, it made me so sad; more sad than angry. I can never be grateful enough to Signorina Grattarol.

PAUL. But I'm still at a loss to know exactly what you're talking about.

AMY. And I am quite bewildered myself. Would you have believed it of him? I thought him such a nice man.

PAUL. What has he done?

AMY. It's all for my money, Miss Grattarol told me. She knows. He was just asking me to marry him, and I believe I would have said Yes. But she came in just in the nick of time. It seems he only wanted to marry me because I'm so rich. He doesn't care for me at all. Miss Grattarol knows what he's like. It's awful, isn't it? Oh dear, I wouldn't have thought it of him.

PAUL. But you must forgive him, Miss Toomis. Money is a great temptation. Perhaps if you gave him another chance....

AMY. Impossible.

PAUL. Poor Dolphin! He's such a nice young fellow.

AMY. I thought so too. But he's false.

PAUL. Don't be too hard on him. Money probably means too much to him. It's the fault of his upbringing. No one who has not lived among the traditions of our ancient aristocracy can be expected to have that contempt, almost that hatred of wealth, which is the sign of true nobility. If he had been brought up, as I was, in an old machicolated castle on the Loire, surrounded by ancestral ghosts, imbued with the spirit of the Crusaders and preux chevaliers who had inhabited the place in the past, if he had learnt to know what noblesse oblige really means, believe me, Miss Toomis, he could never have done such a thing.

AMY. I should just think he couldn't, Monsieur de Barbazange.

PAUL. You have no idea, Miss Toomis, how difficult it is for a man of truly noble feelings to get over the fact of your great wealth. When I heard that you were the possessor of a hundred million dollars....

AMY. Oh, I'm afraid it's more than that. It's two hundred million.

PAUL. ... of two hundred million dollars, then ... it only makes it worse; I was very melancholy, Miss Toomis. For those two hundred million dollars were a barrier, which a descendant of Crusaders and preux chevaliers could not overleap. Honour, Miss Toomis, honour forbade. Ah, if only that accursed money had not stood in the way.... When I first saw you oh, how I was moved by that vision of beauty and innocence—I wanted nothing better than to stand gazing on you for ever. But then I heard about those millions. Dolphin was lucky to have felt no restraints. But enough, enough. (*He checks a rising tide of emotion.*) Give poor Dolphin another chance, Miss Toomis. At bottom he is a good fellow, and he may learn in time to esteem you for your own sake and to forget the dazzling millions.

AMY. Never. I can only marry a man who is entirely disinterested.

PAUL. But, can't you see, no disinterested man could ever bring himself to ask you? How could he prove his disinterestedness? No one would believe the purity of his intentions.

AMY (*much moved*). It is for me to judge. I know a disinterested man when I see him. Even in America we can understand honour.

PAUL (*with a sob in his voice*). Good-bye Miss Toomis.

AMY. But no, I don't want it to be good-bye.

PAUL. It must be. Never shall it be said of a Barbazange that he hunted a woman for her money.

AMY. But what does it matter what the world says, if I say the opposite?

PAUL. You say the opposite? Thank you, thank you. But no, good-bye.

AMY. Stop. Oh! you're forcing me to do a most unwomanly thing. You're making me ask you to marry me. You're the only disinterested man I've ever met or, to judge from what I've seen of the world, I'm ever likely to meet. Haven't you kept away from me in spite of your feelings? Haven't you even tried to make me listen to another man—a man not worthy to black your boots? Oh, it's so wonderful, so noble! It's like something in a picture play. Paul, I offer myself to you. Will you take me in spite of my millions?

PAUL (*falling on his knees and kissing the hem of* AMY'S *skirt*). My angel, you're right; what does it matter what the world says as long as you believe in me? Amy, amie, bien-aimée.... Ah, it's too good too, too good to be true! (*He rises to his feet and embraces her with an unfeigned enthusiasm.*)

AMY. Paul, Paul.... And so this is love. Isn't it wonderful?

PAUL (*looking round anxiously*). You mustn't tell anyone about our engagement, my Amy. They might say unpleasant things in the hotel, you know.

AMY. Of course I won't talk about it. We'll keep our happiness to ourselves, won't we?

PAUL. Entirely to ourselves; and to-morrow we'll go to Paris and arrange about being married.

AMY. Yes, yes; we'll take the eight o'clock train.

PAUL. Not the eight o clock, my darling. I have to go to the bank to-morrow to do a little business. We must wait till the twelve thirty.

AMY. Very well, then. The twelve-thirty. Oh, how happy I am!

PAUL. So am I, my sweetheart. More than I can tell you. (*The sound of a window being opened is heard. They look up and see the* BARONESS *dressed in a peignoir of the tenderest blue, emerging on to the right hand of the three balconies.*)

AMY. Oh, my soul! I think I'd better go in. Good-night, my Paul. (*She runs in.*)

SIMONE. Has that horrid little American girl gone? (*She peers down, then, reassured, she blows a kiss to* PAUL.) My Romeo!

PAUL. I come, Juliet.

SIMONE. There's a kiss for you.

PAUL (*throwing kisses with both hands*). And there's one for you. And another, and another. Two hundred million kisses, my angel.

SIMONE (*giggling*). What a lot!

PAUL. It is; you re quite right. Two hundred million.... I come, my Juliet. (*He darts into the hotel, pausing when just inside the door and out of sight of the* BARONESS, *to mop himself once again with his enor-*

mous handkerchief. The operation over, he advances with a resolute step, The BARONESS *stands for a moment on the balcony. Then, seeing* DOLPHIN *and* LUCREZIA *coming in from the left, she retires, closing the window and drawing the curtains behind her.* DOLPHIN *comes striding in*; LUCREZIA *follows a little behind, looking anxiously up at him.*)

LUCREZIA. Please, please....

DOLPHIN. NO, I won't listen to anything more. (*He walks with an agitated step up and down the stage.* LUCREZIA *stands with one hand resting on the back of a chair and the other pressed on her heart.)* Do you mean to say you deliberately went and told her that I was only after her money? Oh, it's too bad, too bad. It's infamous. And I hadn't the faintest notion that she had any money. Besides, I don't want money; I have quite enough of my own. It's infamous, infamous!

LUCREZIA. I know it was a horrible thing to do. But I couldn't help it. How could I stand by and see you being carried off by that silly little creature?

DOLPHIN. But I cared for her.

LUCREZIA. But not as I cared for you. I've got red blood in my veins; she's got nothing but milk and water. You couldn't have been happy with her. I can give you love of a kind she could never dream of. What does she know of passion?

DOLPHIN. Nothing, I am thankful to say. I don't want passion; can't you understand that? I don't possess it myself and don't like it in others. I am a man of sentimental affections, with a touch of quiet sensuality. I don't want passion, I tell you. It's too violent; it frightens me. I couldn't possibly live with you. You'd utterly shatter my peace of mind in a day. Oh, how I wish you'd go away.

LUCREZIA. But Sidney, Sidney, can't you understand what it is to be madly in love with somebody? You can't be so cruel.

DOLPHIN. You didn't think much of my well-being when you interfered between Miss Toomis and me, did you? You've probably ruined my whole life, that's all. I really don't see why you should expect me to have any pity for you.

LUCREZIA. Very well, then, I shall kill myself. (*She bursts into tears.*)

DOLPHIN. Oh, but I assure you, one doesn't kill oneself for things like that. (*He approaches her and pats her on the shoulder.*) Come, come, don't worry about it.

LUCREZIA (*throws her arms round his neck*). Oh, Sidney, Sidney....

DOLPHIN (*freeing himself with surprising energy and promptitude from her embrace*). No, no, none of that, I beg. Another moment and we shall be losing our heads. Personally I think I shall go to bed now. I should advise you to do the same, Miss Grattarol. You're overwrought. We might all be better for a small dose of bromide. (*He goes in.*)

LUCREZIA (*looking up and stretching forth her hands*). Sidney.... (DOLPHIN *does not look round, and disappears through the glass door into the hotel*, LUCREZIA *covers her face with her hands and sits for a little sobbing silently. The nightingale sings on. Midnight sounds with an infinite melancholy from all the twenty campaniles of the city in the valley. From far away comes the spasmodic throbbing of a guitar and the singing of an Italian voice, high-pitched, passionate, throaty. The seconds pass*, LUCREZIA *rises to her feet and walks slowly into the hotel. On the threshold she encounters the* VICOMTE *coming out.*)

PAUL. You, Signorina Lucrezia? I've escaped for a breath of fresh, cool air. Mightn't we take a turn together? (LUCREZIA *shakes her head.*) Ah, well, then, good-night. You'll be glad to hear that Miss Toomis knows all about Correggio now.

(*He inhales a deep breath of air. Then looking at his dinner-jacket he begins brushing at it with his hand. A lamentable figure creeps in from the left. It is* ALBERTO. *If he had a tail, it would be trailing on the ground between his legs.*)

PAUL. Hullo, Alberto. What is it? Been losing at cards?

ALBERTO. Worse than that.

PAUL. Creditors foreclosing?

ALBERTO. Much worse.

PAUL. Father ruined by imprudent speculations?

ALBERTO. No, no, no. It's nothing to do with money.

PAUL. Oh, well, then. It can't be anything very serious. It's women, I suppose.

ALBERTO. My mistress refuses to see me. I have been beating on her door for hours in vain.

PAUL. I wish we all had your luck, Bertino. Mine opens her door only too promptly. The difficulty is to get out again. Does yours use such an awful lot of this evil-smelling powder? I'm simply covered with it. Ugh! (*He brushes his coat again.*)

ALBERTO. Can't you be serious, Paul?

PAUL. Of course I can ... about a serious matter. But you can't expect me to pull a long face about your mistress, can you, now? Do look at things in their right proportions.

ALBERTO. It's no use talking to you. You're heartless, soulless.

PAUL. What you mean, my dear Alberto, is that I'm relatively speaking bodiless. Physical passion never goes to my head. I'm always *compos mentis*. You aren't, that's all.

ALBERTO. Oh, you disgust me. I think I shall hang myself to-night.

PAUL. Do. It will give us something to talk about at lunch to-morrow.

ALBERTO. Monster! (*He goes into the hotel*, PAUL *strolls out towards the garden, whistling an air from Mozart as he goes. The window on the left opens and* LUCREZIA *steps on to her balcony. Uncoiled, her red hair falls almost to her waist. Her nightdress is always half slipping off one shoulder or the other, like those loose-bodied Restoration gowns that reveal the tight-blown charms of Kneller's Beauties. Her feet are bare. She is a marvellously romantic figure, as she stands there, leaning on the balustrade, and with eyes more sombre than night, gazing into the darkness. The nightingales, the bells, the guitar, and passionate voice strike up. Great stars palpitate in the sky. The moon has swum imperceptibly to the height of heaven. In the garden below flowers are yielding their souls into the air, censers invisible. It is too much, too much.... Large tears roll down* LUCREZIA's *cheeks and fall with a splash to the ground. Suddenly, but with the noiselessness of a cat,* ALBERTO *appears, childish-looking in pink pajamas, on the middle of the three balconies. He sees* LUCREZIA, *but she is much too deeply absorbed in thought to have noticed his coming,* ALBERTO *plants his elbows on the rail of the balcony, covers his face, and begins to sob, at first inaudibly, then in a gradual quickening crescendo. At the seventh sob* LUCREZIA *starts and becomes aware of his presence*.)

LUCREZIA. Alberto. I didn't know.... Have you been there long? (ALBERTO *makes no articulate reply, but his sobs keep on growing louder*.) Alberto, are you unhappy? Answer me.

ALBERTO (*with difficulty, after a pause*). Yes.

LUCREZIA. Didn't she let you in?

ALBERTO. No. (*His sobs become convulsive*.)

LUCREZIA. Poor boy.

ALBERTO (*lifting up a blubbered face to the moonlight*). I am so unhappy.

LUCREZIA. You can't be more unhappy than I am.

ALBERTO. Oh yes, I am. It's impossible to be unhappier than me.

LUCREZIA. But I *am* more unhappy.

ALBERTO. You're not. Oh, how can you be so cruel Lucrezia? (*He covers his face once more.*)

LUCREZIA. But I only said I was unhappy Alberto.

ALBERTO. Yes, I know. That showed you weren't thinking of me. Nobody loves me. I shall hang myself to-night with the cord of my dressing-gown.

LUCREZIA. NO, no, Alberto. You mustn't do anything rash.

ALBERTO. I shall. Your cruelty has been the last straw.

LUCREZIA. I'm sorry, Bertino mio. But if you only knew how miserable I was feeling. I didn't mean to be unsympathetic. Poor boy. I'm so sorry. There, don't cry, poor darling.

ALBERTO. Oh, I knew you wouldn't desert me, Lucrezia. You've always been a mother to me. (*He stretches out his hand and seizes hers, which has gone half-way to meet him; but the balconies are too far apart to allow him to kiss it. He makes an effort and fails. He is too short in the body,*) Will you let me come onto your balcony, Lucrezia? I want to tell you how grateful I am.

LUCREZIA. But you can do that from your own balcony.

ALBERTO. Please, please, Lucrezia. You mustn't be cruel to me again. I can't bear it.

LUCREZIA. Well, then.... Just for a moment, but for no more, (BERTINO *climbs from one balcony to the other. One is a little reminded of the trousered monkeys on the barrel organs. Arrived, he kneels down and kisses* LUCREZIA'S *hand.*)

ALBERTO. You've saved me. You've given me a fresh desire to live and a fresh faith in life. How can I thank you enough, Lucrezia, darling?

LUCREZIA (*patting his head*). There, there. *We* are just two unhappy creatures. We must try and comfort one another.

ALBERTO. What a brute I am! I never thought of your unhappiness. I am so selfish. What is it, Lucrezia?

LUCREZIA. I can't tell you, Bertino; but it's very painful.

ALBERTO. Poor child, poor child. (*His kisses, which started at the hand, have mounted, by this time, some way up the arm, changing perceptibly in character as they rise. At the shoulder they have a warmth which could not have been inferred from the respectful salutes which barely touched the fingers.*) Poor darling! You've given me consolation. Now you must let me comfort your unhappiness.

LUCREZIA (*with an effort*). I think you ought to go back now, Bertino.

ALBERTO. In a minute, my darling. There, there, poor Lucrezia. (*He puts an arm round her, kisses her hair and neck.* LUCREZIA *leans her bowed head against his chest. The sound of footsteps is heard. They both look up with scared, wide-open eyes.*)

LUCREZIA. We mustn't be seen here, Bertino. What would people think?

ALBERTO. I'll go back.

LUCREZIA. There's no time. You must come into my room. Quickly.

(*They slip through the French window, but not quickly enough to have escaped the notice of* PAUL, *returning from his midnight stroll. The* VICOMTE *stands for a moment looking up at the empty balcony. He laughs softly to himself, and, throwing his cigarette away, passes through the glass door into the house. All is now silent, save for the nightingales and the distant bells. The curtain comes down for a moment to indicate the passage of several hours. It rises again with the sun.* LUCREZIA's *window opens and she appears on the balcony. She stands a moment with one foot over the threshold of the long window in a listening pose. Then her eyes fall on the better half of a pair of pink pyjamas lying crumpled on the floor, like a body bereft of its soul; with her bare foot she turns it over. A little shudder plucks at her nerves, and she shakes her head as though, by this symbolic act, to shake off something clinging and contaminating. Then she steps out into the full glory of the early sun, stretching out her arms to the radiance. She bows her face into her hands, crying out loud to herself.*) LUCREZIA. Oh, why, why, why? (*The last of these Why's is caught by the* WAITER, *who has crept forth in shirt-sleeves and list-slippers, duster in hand, to clean the tables. He looks up at her admiringly, passes his tongue over his lips. Then, with a sigh, turns to dust the tables.*)

CURTAIN.

III: THE TILLOTSON BANQUET

I

Young Spode was not a snob; he was too intelligent for that, too fundamentally decent. Not a snob; but all the same he could not help feeling very well pleased at the thought that he was dining, alone and intimately, with Lord Badgery. It was a definite event in his life, a step forward, he felt, towards that final success, social, material, and literary, which he had come to London with the fixed intention of making. The conquest and capture of Badgery was an almost essential strategical move in the campaign.

Edmund, forty-seventh Baron Badgery, was a lineal descendant of that Edmund, surnamed Le Blayreau, who landed on English soil in the train of William the Conqueror. Ennobled by William Rufus, the Badgerys had been one of the very few baronial families to survive the Wars of the Roses and all the other changes and chances of English history. They were a sensible and philoprogenitive race. No Badgery had ever fought in any war, no Badgery had ever engaged in any kind of politics. They had been content to live and quietly to propagate their species in a huge machicolated Norman castle, surrounded by a triple moat, only sallying forth to cultivate their property and to collect their rents. In the eighteenth century, when life had become relatively secure, the Badgerys began to venture forth into civilised society. From boorish squires they blossomed into *grands seigneurs*, patrons of the arts, virtuosi. Their property was large, they were rich; and with the growth of industrialism their riches also grew. Villages on their estate turned into manufacturing towns, unsuspected coal was discovered beneath the surface of their barren moorlands. By the middle of the nineteenth century the Badgerys were among the richest of English noble families. The forty-seventh baron disposed of an income of at least two hundred thousand pounds a year. Following the great Badgery tradition, he had refused to have anything to do with politics or war. He occupied himself by collecting pictures; he took an interest in theatrical productions; he was the friend and patron of men of letters, of painters, and musician. A personage, in a word, of considerable consequence in that particular world in which young Spode had elected to make his success.

Spode had only recently left the university. Simon Gollamy, the editor of the *World's Review* (the "Best of all possible Worlds"), had got to know him—he was always on the look out for youthful talent—had seen possibilities in the young man, and appointed him art critic of his paper. Gollamy liked to have young and teachable people about him. The possession of disciples flattered his vanity, and he found it easier, moreover, to run his paper with docile collaborators than with men grown obstinate and case-hardened with age. Spode had not done badly at his new job. At any rate, his articles had been intelligent enough to arouse the interest of Lord Badgery. It was, ultimately, to them that he owed the honour of sitting to night in the dining-room of Badgery House.

Fortified by several varieties of wine and a glass of aged brandy, Spode felt more confident and at ease than he had done the whole evening. Badgery was rather a disquieting host. He had an alarming habit of changing the subject of any conversation that had lasted for more than two minutes. Spode had found it, for example, horribly mortifying when his host, cutting across what was, he prided himself, a particularly subtle and illuminating disquisition on baroque art, had turned a wandering eye about the room and asked him abruptly whether he liked parrots. He had flushed and glanced suspiciously towards him, fancying that the man was trying to be offensive. But no; Badgery's white, fleshy, Hanoverian face wore an expression of perfect good faith. There was no malice in his small greenish eyes. He evidently did genuinely want to know if Spode liked parrots. The young man swallowed his irritation and replied that he did. Badgery then told a good story about parrots. Spode was on the point of capping it with a better story, when his host began to talk about Beethoven. And so the game went on. Spode cut his conversation to suit his host's requirements. In the course of ten minutes he had made a more or less witty epigram on Benvenuto Cellini, Queen Victoria, sport, God, Stephen Phillips, and Moorish architecture. Lord Badgery thought him the most charming young man, and so intelligent.

"If you've quite finished your coffee," he said, rising to his feet as he spoke, "we'll go and look at the pictures."

Spode jumped up with alacrity, and only then realised that he had drunk just ever so little too much. He would have to be careful, talk deliberately, plant his feet consciously, one after the other.

"This house is quite cluttered up with pictures," Lord Badgery complained. "I had a whole wagon-load taken away to the country last week; but there are still far too many. My ancestors would have their portraits painted by Romney. Such a shocking artist, don't you think? Why couldn't they have chosen Gainsborough, or even Reynolds? I've had all the Romneys hung in the servants' hall now. It's such a comfort to know that one can never possibly see them again. I suppose you know all about the ancient Hittites?"

"Well...." the young man replied, with befitting modesty.

"Look at that, then." He indicated a large stone head which stood in a case near the dining-room door. "It's not Greek, or Egyptian, or Persian, or anything else; so if it isn't ancient Hittite, I don't know what it is. And that reminds me of that story about Lord George Sanger, the Circus King...." and, without giving Spode time to examine the Hittite relic, he led the way up the huge staircase, pausing every now and then in his anecdote to point out some new object of curiosity or beauty.

"I suppose you know Deburau's pantomimes?" Spode rapped out as soon as the story was over. He was in an itch to let out his information about Deburau. Badgery had given him a perfect opening with his ridiculous Sanger. "What a perfect man, isn't he? He used to...."

"This is my main gallery," said Lord Badgery, throwing open one leaf of a tall folding door. "I must apologise for it. It looks like a roller-skating rink." He fumbled with the electric switches and there was suddenly light—light that revealed an enormous gallery, duly receding into distance according to all the laws of perspective. "I dare say you've heard of my poor father," Lord Badgery continued. "A little insane, you know; sort of mechanical genius with a screw loose. He used to have a toy railway in this room. No end of fun he had, crawling about the floor after his trains. And all the pictures were stacked in the cellars. I can't tell you what they were like when I found them: mushrooms growing out of the Botticellis. Now I'm rather proud of this Poussin; he painted it for Scarron."

"Exquisite!" Spode exclaimed, making with his hand a gesture as though he were modelling a pure form in the air. "How splendid the onrush of those trees and leaning figures is! And the way they're caught up, as it were, and stemmed by that single godlike form opposing them with his contrary movement! And the draperies...."

But Lord Badgery had moved on, and was standing in front of a little fifteenth-century Virgin of carved wood.

"School of Rheims," he explained.

They "did" the gallery at high speed. Badgery never permitted his guest to halt for more than forty seconds before any work of art. Spode would have liked to spend a few moments of recollection and tranquillity in front of some of these lovely things. But it was not permitted.

The gallery done, they passed into a little room leading out of it. At the sight of what the lights revealed, Spode gasped.

"It's like something out of Balzac," he exclaimed. "Un de ces salons dorés où se déploie un luxe insolent. You know."

"My nineteenth-century chamber," Badgery explained. "The best thing of its kind, I flatter myself, outside the State Apartments at Windsor."

Spode tiptoed round the room, peering with astonishment at all the objects in glass, in gilded bronze, in china, in leathers, in embroidered and painted silk, in beads, in wax, objects of the most fantastic shapes and colours, all the queer products of a decadent tradition, with which the room was crowded. There were paintings on the walls—a Martin, a Wilkie, an early Landseer, several Ettys, a big Haydon, a slight pretty water-colour of a girl by Wainewright, the pupil of Blake and arsenic poisoner, a score of others. But the picture which arrested Spode's attention was a medium sized canvas representing Troilus riding into Troy among the flowers and plaudits of an admiring crowd, and oblivious (you could see from his expression) of everything but the eyes of Cressida, who looked down at him from a window, with Pandarus smiling over her shoulder.

"What an absurd and enchanting picture!" Spode exclaimed.

"Ah, you've spotted my Troilus." Lord Badgery was pleased.

"What bright harmonious colours! Like Etty's, only stronger, not so obviously pretty. And there's an energy about it that reminds one of Haydon. Only Haydon could never have done anything so impeccable in taste. Who is it by?" Spode turned to his host inquiringly.

"You were right in detecting Haydon," Lord Badgery answered, "It's by his pupil, Tillotson. I wish I could get hold of more of his work. But nobody seems to know anything about him. And he seems to have done so little."

This time it was the younger man who interrupted.

"Tillotson, Tillotson...." He put his hand to his forehead. A frown incongruously distorted his round, floridly curved face. No ... yes, I have it. He looked up triumphantly with serene and childish brows. "Tillotson, Walter Tillotson—the man's still alive."

Badgery smiled. "This picture was painted in 1846, you know."

"Well, that's all right. Say he was born in 1820, painted his masterpiece when he was twenty-six, and it's 1913 now; that's to say he's only ninety-three. Not as old as Titian yet."

"But he's not been heard of since 1860," Lord Badgery protested.

"Precisely. Your mention of his name reminded me of the discovery I made the other day when I was looking through the obituary notices in the archives of the *World's Review*.(One has to bring them up to date every year or so for fear of being caught napping if one of these t old birds chooses to shuffle off suddenly.) Well, there, among them—I remember my astonishment at the time—there I found Walter Tillotson's biography. Pretty full to 1860, and then a blank, except for a pencil note in the early nineteen hundreds to the effect that he had returned from the East. The obituary has never been used or added to. I draw the obvious conclusion: the old chap isn't dead yet. He's just been overlooked somehow."

"But this is extraordinary," Lord Badgery exclaimed. "You must find him, Spode—you must find him. I'll commission him to paint frescoes round this room. It's just what I've always vainly longed for a real nineteenth-century artist to decorate this place for me. Oh, we must find him at once—at once."

Lord Badgery strode up and down in a state of great excitement.

"I can see how this room could be made quite perfect," he went on. "We'd clear away all these cases and have the whole of that wall filled by a heroic fresco of Hector and Andromache, or 'Distraining for Rent', or Fanny Kemble as Belvidera in 'Venice Preserved' anything like that, provided it's in the grand manner of the 'thirties and 'forties. And here I'd have a landscape with lovely receding perspectives, or else something architectural and grand in the style of Belshazzar's feast. Then we'll have this Adam fireplace taken down and replaced by something Mauro-Gothic. And on these walls I'll have mirrors, or no! let me see...."

He sank into meditative silence, from which he finally roused himself to shout:

"The old man, the old man! Spode, we must find this astonishing old creature. And don't breathe a word to anybody. Tillotson shall be our secret. Oh, it's too perfect, it's incredible! Think of the frescoes."

Lord Badgery's face had become positively animated. He had talked of a single subject for nearly a quarter of an hour.

II

Three weeks later Lord Badgery was aroused from his usual after-luncheon somnolence by the arrival of a telegram. The message was a short one. "Found.—SPODE." A look of pleasure and intelligence made human Lord Badgery's clayey face of surfeit. "No answer," he said. The footman padded away on noiseless feet.

Lord Badgery closed his eyes and began to contemplate. Found! What a room he would have! There would be nothing like it in the world. The frescoes, the fireplace, the mirrors, the ceiling.... And a small, shrivelled old man clambering about the scaffolding, agile and quick like one of those whiskered little monkeys at the Zoo, painting away, painting away.... Fanny Kemble as Belvidera, Hector and Andromache, or why not the Duke of Clarence in the Butt, the Duke of Malmsey, the Butt of Clarence. ... Lord Badgery was asleep.

Spode did not lag long behind his telegram. He was at Badgery House by six o'clock. His lordship was in the nineteenth-century chamber, engaged in clearing away with his own hands the bric-à-brac. Spode found him looking hot and out of breath.

"Ah, there you are," said Lord Badgery. You see me already preparing for the great man's coming. Now you must tell me all about him.

"He's older even than I thought," said Spode. "He's ninety-seven this year. Born in 1816. Incredible, isn't it! There, I'm beginning at the wrong end."

"Begin where you like," said Badgery genially.

"I won't tell you all the incidents of the hunt. You've no idea what a job I had to run him to earth. It was like a Sherlock Holmes story, immensely elaborate, too elaborate. I shall write a book about it some day. At any rate, I found him at last."

"Where?"

"In a sort of respectable slum in Holloway, older and poorer and lonelier than you could have believed possible. I found out how it was he came to be forgotten, how he came to drop out of life in the way he did. He took it into his head, somewhere about the 'sixties, to go to Palestine to get local colour for his religious pictures—scapegoats and things, you know. Well, he went to Jerusalem and then on to Mount Lebanon and on and on, and then, somewhere in the middle of Asia Minor, he got stuck. He got stuck for about forty years."

"But what did he do all that time?"

"Oh, he painted, and started a mission, and converted three Turks, and taught the local Pashas the rudiments of English, Latin, and perspective, and God knows what else. Then, in about 1904, it seems to have occurred to him that he was getting rather old and had been away from home for rather a long time. So he made his way back to England, only to find that everyone he had known was dead, that the dealers had never heard of him and wouldn't buy his pictures, that he was simply a ridiculous old figure of fun. So he got a job as a drawing-master in a girl's school in Holloway, and there he's been ever since, growing older and older, and feebler and feebler, and blinder and deafer, and generally more gaga, until finally the school has given him the sack. He had about ten pounds in the world when I found him. He lives in a kind of black hole in a basement full of beetles. When his ten pounds are spent, I suppose he'll just quietly die there."

Badgery held up a white hand. "No more, no more. I find literature quite depressing enough. I insist that life at least shall be a little gayer. Did you tell him I wanted him to paint my room?"

"But he can't paint. He's too blind and palsied."

"Can't paint?" Badgery exclaimed in horror. "Then what's the good of the old creature?"

"Well, if you put it like that...." Spode began.

"I shall never have my frescoes. Ring the bell, will you?"

Spode rang.

"What right has Tillotson to go on existing if he can't paint?" went on Lord Badgery petulantly. "After all, that was his only justification for occupying a place in the sun."

"He doesn't have much sun in his basement."

The footman appeared at the door.

"Get someone to put all these things back in their places," Lord Badgery commanded, indicating with a wave of the hand the ravaged cases, the confusion of glass and china with which he had littered the floor, the pictures unhooked. "We'll go to the library, Spode; it's more comfortable there."

He led the way through the long gallery and down the stairs.

"I'm sorry old Tillotson has been such a disappointment," said Spode sympathetically.

"Let us talk about something else; he ceases to interest me.

"But don't you think we ought to do something about him? He's only got ten pounds between him and the workhouse. And if you'd seen the black-beetles in his basement!"

"Enough enough. I'll do everything you think fitting."

"I thought we might get up a subscription amongst lovers of the arts."

"There aren't any," said Badgery.

"No; but there are plenty of people who will subscribe out of snobbism."

"Not unless you give them something for their money."

"That's true. I hadn't thought of that." Spode was silent for a moment. "We might have a dinner in his honour. The Great Tillotson Banquet. Doyen of the British Art. A Link with the Past. Can't you see it in the papers? I'd make a stunt of it in the *World's Review*. That ought to bring in the snobs."

"And we'll invite a lot of artists and critics—all the ones who can't stand one another. It will be fun to see them squabbling." Badgery laughed. Then his face darkened once again. "Still," he added, "it'll be a very poor second best to my frescoes. You'll stay to dinner, of course."

"Well, since you suggest it. Thanks very much."

III

The Tillotson Banquet was fixed to take place about three weeks later. Spode, who had charge of the arrangements, proved himself an excellent organiser. He secured the big banqueting-room at the Café Bomba, and was successful in bullying and cajoling the manager into giving fifty persons dinner at twelve shillings a head, including wine. He sent out invitations and collected subscriptions. He wrote an article on Tillotson in the *World's Review*—one of those charming, witty articles couched in the tone of amused patronage and contempt with which one speaks of the great men of 1840. Nor did he neglect Tillotson himself. He used to go to Holloway almost every day to listen to the old man's endless stories about Asia Minor and the Great Exhibition of '51 and Benjamin Robert Haydon. He was sincerely sorry for this relic of another age.

Mr. Tillotson's room was about ten feet below the level of the soil of South Holloway. A little grey light percolated through the area bars, forced a difficult passage through panes opaque with dirt, and spent itself, like a drop of milk that falls into an inkpot, among the inveterate shadows of the dungeon. The place was haunted by the spur smell of damp plaster and of woodwork that has begun to moulder secretly at the heart. A little miscellaneous furniture, including a bed, a washstand and chest of drawers, a table and one or two chairs, lurked in the obscure corners of the den or ventured furtively out into the open. Hither Spode now came almost every day, bringing the old man news of the progress of the banquet scheme. Every day he found Mr. Tillotson sitting in the same place under the window, bathing, as it were, in his tiny puddle of light. "The oldest man that ever wore grey hairs," Spode reflected as he looked at him. Only there were very few hairs left on that bald, unpolished head. At the sound of the visitor's knock Mr. Tillotson would turn in his chair, stare in the direction of the door with blinking, uncertain eyes. He was always full of apologies for being so slow in recognising who was there.

"No discourtesy meant," he would say, after asking. "It's not as if I had forgotten who you were. Only it's so dark and my sight isn't what it was."

After that he never failed to give a little laugh, and, pointing out of the window at the area railings, would say:

"Ah, this is the plate for somebody with good sight. It's the place for looking at ankles. It's the grand stand."

It was the day before the great event. Spode came as usual, and Mr. Tillotson punctually made his little joke about the ankles, and Spode, as punctually laughed.

"Well, Mr. Tillotson," he said, after the reverberation of the joke had died away, "to-morrow you make your re-entry into the world of art and fashion. You'll find some changes."

"I've always had such extraordinary luck," said Mr. Tillotson, and Spode could see by his expression that he genuinely believed it, that he had forgotten the black hole and the black-beetles and the almost exhausted ten pounds that stood between him and the workhouse. "What an amazing piece of good fortune, for instance, that you should have found me just when you did. Now, this dinner will bring me back to my place in the world. I shall have money, and in a little while—who knows?—I shall be able to see well enough to paint again. I believe my eyes are getting better, you know. Ah, the future is very rosy."

Mr. Tillotson looked up, his face puckered into a smile, and nodded his head in affirmation of his words.

"You believe in the life to come?" said Spode, and immediately flushed for shame at the cruelty of the words.

But Mr. Tillotson was in far too cheerful a mood to have caught their significance.

"Life to come," he repeated. "No, I don't believe in any of that stuff not since 1859. The 'Origin of Species' changed my views, you know. No life to come for me, thank you! You don't remember the excitement of course. You re very young Mr. Spode."

"Well, I'm not so old as I was," Spode replied. "You know how middle-aged one is as a schoolboy and undergraduate. Now I'm old enough to know I'm young."

Spode was about to develop this little paradox further, but he noticed that Mr. Tillotson had not been listening. He made a note of the gambit for use in companies that were more appreciative of the subtleties.

"You were talking about the 'Origin of Species,'" he said.

"Was I?" said Mr. Tillotson, waking from reverie.

"About its effect on your faith, Mr. Tillotson."

"To be sure, yes. It shattered my faith. But I remember a fine thing by the Poet Laureate, something about there being more faith in honest doubt, believe me, than in all the ... all the ...: I forget exactly what; but you see the train of thought. Oh, it was a bad time for religion. I am glad my master Haydon never lived to see it. He was a man of fervour. I remember him pacing up and down his studio in Lisson Grove, singing and shouting and praying all at once. It used almost to frighten me. Oh, but he was a wonderful man, a great man. Take him for all in all, we shall not look upon his like again. As usual, the Bard is right. But it was all very long ago, before your time, Mr. Spode."

"Well, I'm not as old as I was," said Spode, in the hope of having his paradox appreciated this time. But Mr. Tillotson went on without noticing the interruption.

"It's a very, very long time. And yet, when I look back on it, it all seems but a day or two ago. Strange that each day should seem so long and that many days added together should be less than an hour. How clearly I can see old Haydon pacing up and down! Much more clearly, indeed, than I see you, Mr. Spode. The eyes of memory don t grow dim. But my sight is improving, I assure you; it's improving daily. I shall soon be able to see those ankles." He laughed like a cracked bell—one of those little old bells, Spode fancied, that ring, with much rattling of wires, in the far-off servants quarters of ancient houses. "And very soon," Mr. Tillotson went on, "I shall be painting again. Ah, Mr. Spode, my luck is extraordinary. I believe in it, I trust in it. And after all, what is luck? Simply another name for Providence, in spite of the Origin of Species and the rest of it. How right the Laureate was when he said that there was more faith in honest doubt, believe me, than in all the ... er, the ... er ... well, you know. I regard you, Mr. Spode, as the emissary of Providence. Your coming marked a turning-point in my life, and the beginning, for me, of happier days. Do you know, one of the first things I shall do when my fortunes are restored will be to buy a hedgehog."

"A hedgehog, Mr. Tillotson?"

"For the blackbeetles. There's nothing like a hedgehog for beetles. It will eat blackbeetles till it's sick, till it dies of surfeit. That reminds me of the time when I told my poor great master Haydon—in joke, of course—that he ought to send in a cartoon of King John dying of a surfeit of lampreys for the frescoes in the new Houses of Parliament. As I told him, it's a most notable event in the annals of British liberty—the providential and exemplary removal of a tyrant."

Mr. Tillotson laughed again—the little bell in the deserted house; a ghostly hand pulling the cord in the drawing-room, and phantom footmen responding to the thin, flawed note.

"I remember he laughed, laughed like a bull in his old grand manner. But oh, it was a terrible blow when they rejected his design, a terrible blow. It was the first and fundamental cause of his suicide."

Mr. Tillotson paused. There was a long silence. Spode felt strangely moved, he hardly knew why, in the presence of this man, so frail, so ancient, in body three parts dead, in the spirit so full of life and hopeful patience. He felt ashamed. What was the use of his own youth and cleverness? He saw himself suddenly as a boy with a rattle scaring birds rattling his noisy cleverness, waving his arms in ceaseless and futile activity, never resting in his efforts to scare away the birds that were always trying to settle in his mind. And what birds! widewinged and beautiful, all those serene thoughts and faiths and emotions that only visit minds that have humbled themselves to quiet. Those gracious visitants he was for ever using all his energies to drive away. But this old man, with his hedgehogs and his honest doubts and all the rest of it—his mind was like a field made beautiful by the free coming and going, the unafraid alightings of a multitude of white, bright-winged creatures. He felt ashamed. But then, was it possible to alter one's life? Wasn't it a little absurd to risk a conversion? Spode shrugged his shoulders.

"I'll get you a hedgehog at once," he said. "They're sure to have some at Whiteley's."

Before he left that evening Spode made an alarming discovery. Mr. Tillotson did not possess a dress-suit. It was hopeless to think of getting one made at this short notice, and, besides, what an unnecessary expense!

"We shall have to borrow a suit, Mr. Tillotson. I ought to have thought of that before."

"Dear me, dear me." Mr. Tillotson was a little chagrined by this unlucky discovery. "Borrow a suit?"

Spode hurried away for counsel to Badgery House. Lord Badgery surprisingly rose to the occasion. "Ask Boreham to come and see me," he told the footman, who answered his ring.

Boreham was one of those immemorial butlers who linger on, generation after generation, in the houses of the great. He was over eighty now, bent, dried up, shrivelled with age.

"All old men are about the same size," said Lord Badgery. It was a comforting theory. "Ah, here he is. Have you got a spare suit of evening clothes, Boreham?"

"I have an old suit, my lord, that I stopped wearing in let me see was it nineteen seven or eight?"

"That's the very thing. I should be most grateful, Boreham, if you could lend it to me for Mr. Spode here for a day."

The old man went out, and soon reappeared carrying over his arm a very old black suit. He held up the coat and trousers for inspection. In the light of day they were deplorable.

"You've no idea, sir," said Boreham deprecatingly to Spode you've no idea how easy things get stained with grease and gravy and what not. However careful you are, sir—however careful.

"I should imagine so." Spode was sympathetic.

"However careful, sir."

"But in artificial light they'll look all right."

"Perfectly all right," Lord Badgery repeated. "Thank you, Boreham; you shall have them back on Thursday."

"You're welcome, my lord, I'm sure." And the old man bowed and disappeared.

On the afternoon of the great day Spode carried up to Holloway a parcel containing Boreham's retired evening-suit and all the necessary appurtenances in the way of shirts and collars. Owing to the darkness and his own feeble sight Mr. Tillotson was happily unaware of the defects in the suit. He was in a state of extreme nervous agitation. It was with some difficulty that Spode could prevent him, although it was only three o'clock, from starting his toilet on the spot.

"Take it easy, Mr. Tillotson, take it easy. We needn't start till half-past seven, you know."

Spode left an hour later, and as soon as he was safely out of the room Mr. Tillotson began to prepare himself for the banquet. He lighted the gas and a couple of candles, and, blinking myopically at the image that fronted him in the tiny looking-glass that stood on his chest of drawers, he set to work, with all the ardour of a young girl preparing for her first ball. At six o'clock, when the last touches had been given, he was not unsatisfied.

He marched up and down his cellar, humming to himself the gay song which had been so popular in his middle years:

"*Oh, oh, Anna, Maria Jones!*

Queen of the tambourine, the cymbals, and the bones!"

Spode arrived an hour later in Lord Badgery's second Rolls-Royce. Opening the door of the old man's dungeon, he stood for a moment, wide-eyed with astonishment, on the threshold. Mr. Tillotson was standing by the empty grate, one elbow resting on the mantelpiece, one leg crossed over the other in a jaunty and gentlemanly attitude. The effect of the candlelight shining on his face was to deepen every line and wrinkle with intense black shadow; he looked immeasurably old. It was a noble and pathetic head. On the other hand, Boreham's out-worn evening-suit was simply buffoonish. The coat was too long in the sleeves and the tail; the trousers bagged in elephantine creases about his ankles. Some of the grease-spots were visible even in candlelight. The white tie, over which Mr. Tillotson had taken infinite pains and which he believed in his purblindness to be perfect, was fantastically lop-sided. He had buttoned up his waistcoat in such a fashion that one button was widowed of its hole and one hole of its button. Across his shirt front lay the broad green ribbon of some unknown Order.

"Queen of the tambourine, the cymbals, and the bones," Mr. Tillotson concluded in a gnat-like voice before welcoming his visitor.

"Well, Spode, here you are. I'm dressed already, you see. The suit, I flatter myself, fits very well, almost as though it had been made for me. I am all gratitude to the gentleman who was kind enough to lend it to me; I shall take the greatest care of it. It's a dangerous thing to lend clothes. For loan oft loseth both itself and friend. The Bard is always right."

"Just one thing," said Spode. "A touch to your waistcoat." He unbuttoned the dissipated garment and did it up again more symmetrically.

Mr. Tillotson was a little piqued at being found so absurdly in the wrong.

"Thanks, thanks," he said, protestingly, trying to edge away from his valet. "It's all right, you know; I can do it myself. Foolish oversight. I flatter myself the suit fits very well."

"And perhaps the tie might...." Spode began tentatively. But the old man would not hear of it.

"No, no. The tie's all right. I can tie a tie, Mr. Spode. The tie's all right. Leave it as it is, I beg."

"I like your Order."

Mr. Tillotson looked down complacently at his shirt front. "Ah, you've noticed my Order. It's a long time since I wore that. It was given me by the Grand Porte, you know, for services rendered in the Russo-Turkish War. It's the Order of Chastity, the second class. They only give the first class to crowned heads, you know—browned heads and ambassadors. And only Pashas of the highest rank get the second. Mine's the second. They only give the first class to crowned heads...."

"Of course, of course," said Spode.

"Do you think I look all right, Mr. Spode?" Mr. Tillotson asked, a little anxiously.

"Splendid, Mr. Tillotson—splendid. The Order's, magnificent."

The old man's face brightened once more. "I flatter myself," he said, "that this borrowed suit fits me very well. But I don't like borrowing clothes. For loan oft loseth both itself and friend, you know. And the Bard is always right."

"Ugh, there's one of those horrible beetles!" Spode exclaimed.

Mr. Tillotson bent down and stared at the floor. "I see it," he said, and stamped on a small piece of coal, which crunched to powder under his foot. "I shall certainly buy a hedgehog."

It was time for them to start. A crowd of little boys and girls had collected round Lord Badgery's enormous car. The chauffeur, who felt that honour and dignity were at stake, pretended not to notice the children, but sat gazing, like a statue, into eternity. At the sight of Spode and Mr. Tillotson emerging from the house a yell of mingled awe and derision went up. It subsided to an astonished silence as they climbed into the car. "Bomba's," Spode directed. The Rolls-Royce gave a faintly stertorous sigh and began to move. The children yelled again, and ran along beside the car, waving their arms in a frenzy of excitement. It was then that Mr. Tillotson, with an incomparably noble gesture, leaned forward and tossed among the seething crowd of urchins his three last coppers.

IV

In Bomba's big room the company was assembling. The long gilt-edged mirrors reflected a singular collection of people. Middle-aged Academicians shot suspicious glances at youths whom they suspected, only too correctly, of being iconoclasts, organisers of Post-Impressionist Exhibitions. Rival art critics, brought suddenly face to face, quivered with restrained hatred. Mrs. Nobes, Mrs. Cayman, and Mrs. Mandragore, those indefatigable hunters of artistic big game, came on one another all unawares in this well-stored menagerie, where each had expected to hunt alone, and were filled with rage. Through this crowd of mutually repellent vanities Lord Badgery moved with a suavity that seemed unconscious of all the feuds and hatreds. He was enjoying himself immensely. Behind the heavy waxen mask of his face, ambushed behind the Hanoverian nose, the little lustreless pig's eyes, the pale thick lips, there lurked a small devil of happy malice that rocked with laughter.

"So nice of you to have come, Mrs. Mandragore, to do honour to England's artistic past. And I'm so glad to see you've brought dear Mrs. Cayman. And is that Mrs. Nobes, too? So it is! I hadn't noticed her before. How delightful! I knew we could depend on your love of art."

And he hurried away to seize the opportunity of introducing that eminent sculptor, Sir Herbert Herne, to the bright young critic who had called him, in the public prints, a monumental mason.

A moment later the Maître d'Hôtel came to the door of the gilded saloon and announced, loudly and impressively, "Mr. Walter Tillotson." Guided from behind by young Spode, Mr. Tillotson came into the room slowly and hesitatingly. In the glare of the lights his eyelids beat heavily, painfully, like the wings of an imprisoned moth, over his filmy eyes. Once inside the door he halted and drew himself up with a conscious assumption of dignity. Lord Badgery hurried forward and seized his hand.

"Welcome, Mr. Tillotson—welcome in the name of English art!"

Mr. Tillotson inclined his head in silence. He was too full of emotion to be able to reply.

"I should like to introduce you to a few of your younger colleagues, who have assembled here to do you honour."

Lord Badgery presented everyone in the room to the old painter, who bowed, shook hands, made little noises in his throat, but still found himself unable to speak. Mrs. Nobes, Mrs. Cayman, and Mrs. Mandragore all said charming things.

Dinner was served; the party took their places. Lord Badgery sat at the head of the table, with Mr. Tillotson on his right hand and Sir Herbert Herne on his left. Confronted with Bomba's succulent cooking and Bomba's wines, Mr. Tillotson ate and drank a good deal. He had the appetite of one who has lived on greens and potatoes for ten years among the blackbeetles. After the second glass of wine he began to talk, suddenly and in a flood, as though a sluice had been pulled up.

"In Asia Minor," he began, "it is the custom when one goes to dinner, to hiccough as a sign of appreciative fullness. *Eructavit cor meum*, as the Psalmist has it; he was an Oriental himself."

Spode had arranged to sit next to Mrs. Cayman; he had designs upon her. She was an impossible woman, of course, but rich and useful; he wanted to bamboozle her into buying some of his young friends' pictures.

"In a cellar?" Mrs. Cayman was saying, "with, blackbeetles? Oh, how dreadful! Poor old man! And he's ninety-seven, didn't you say? Isn't that shocking! I only hope the subscription will be a large one. Of course, one wishes one could have given more oneself. But then, you know, one has so many expenses, and things are so difficult now."

"I know, I know," said Spode, with feeling.

"It's all because of Labour," Mrs. Cayman explained. "Of course, I should simply love to have him in to dinner sometimes. But, then, I feel he's really too old, too *farouche* and *gâteux*; it would not be doing a kindness to him, would it? And so you are working with Mr. Gollamy now? What a charming man, so talented, such conversation...."

"*Eructavit cor meum*," said Mr. Tillotson for the third time. Lord Badgery tried to head him off the subject of Turkish etiquette, but in vain.

By half-past nine a kinder vinolent atmosphere had put to sleep the hatreds and suspicions of before dinner. Sir Herbert Herne had discovered that the young Cubist sitting next him was not insane and actually knew a surprising amount about the Old Masters. For their part these young men had realised that their elders were not at all malignant; they were just very stupid and pathetic. It was only in the bosoms of Mrs. Nobes, Mrs. Cayman, and Mrs. Mandragore that hatred still reigned undiminished. Being ladies and old-fashioned, they had drunk almost no wine.

The moment for speech-making arrived. Lord Badgery rose to his feet, said what was expected of him, and called upon Sir Herbert to propose the toast of the evening. Sir Herbert coughed, smiled and began. In the course of a speech that lasted twenty minutes he told anecdotes of Mr. Gladstone, Lord Leighton, Sir Almo Tadema, and the late Bishop, of Bombay; he made three puns, he quoted Shakespeare and Whittier, he was playful, he was eloquent, he was grave.... At the end of his harangue Sir Herbert handed to Mr. Tillotson a silk purse containing fifty-eight pounds ten shillings, the total amount of the subscription. The old man's health was drunk with acclamation.

Mr. Tillotson rose with difficulty to his feet. The dry, snakelike skin of his face was flushed; his tie was more crooked than ever; the green ribbon of the Order of Chastity of the second class had somehow climbed tip his crumpled and maculate shirt front.

"My lords, ladies, and gentlemen," he began in a choking voice, and then broke down completely. It was a very painful and pathetic spectacle. A feeling of intense discomfort afflicted the minds of all who looked upon that trembling relic of a man, as he stood there weeping and stammering. It was as though a breath of the wind of death had blown suddenly through the room, lifting the vapours of wine and tobacco-smoke, quenching the laughter and the candle flames. Eyes floated uneasily, not knowing where to look. Lord Badgery, with great presence of mind, offered the old man a glass of wine. Mr. Tillotson began to recover. The guests heard him murmur a few disconnected words.

"This great honour ... overwhelmed with kindness ... this magnificent banquet ... not used to it ... in Asia Minor ... *eructuvit cor meum.*"

At this point Lord Badgery plucked sharply at one of his long coat tails. Mr. Tillotson paused, took another sip of wine, and then went on with a newly won coherence and energy.

"The life of the artist is a hard one. His work is unlike other men's work, which may be done mechanically, by rote and almost, as it were, in sleep. It demands from him a constant expense of spirit. He gives continually of his best life, and in return he receives much joy, it is true much fame, it may be—but of material blessings, very few. It is eighty years since first I devoted my life to the service of art; eighty years, and almost every one of those years has brought me fresh and painful proof of what I have been saying: the artist's life is a hard one."

This unexpected deviation into sense increased the general feeling of discomfort. It became necessary to take the old man seriously, to regard him as a human being. Up till then he had been no more than an object of curiosity, a mummy in an absurd suit of evening-clothes with a green ribbon across the shirt front. People could not help wishing that they had subscribed a little more. Fifty-eight pounds ten it wasn't enormous. But happily for the peace of mind of the company, Mr.

Tillotson paused again, took another sip of wine, and began to live up to his proper character by talking absurdly.

"When I consider the life of that great man, Benjamin Robert Haydon, one of the greatest men England has ever produced...." The audience heaved a sigh of relief; this was all as it should be. There was a burst of loud bravoing and clapping. Mr. Tillotson turned his dim eyes round the room, and smiled gratefully at the misty figures he beheld. "That great man, Benjamin Robert Haydon," he continued, "whom I am proud to call my master and who, it rejoices my heart to see, still lives in your memory and esteem, that great man, one of the greatest that England has ever produced, led a life so deplorable that I cannot think of it without a tear."

And with infinite repetitions and divagations, Mr. Tillotson related the history of B.R. Haydon, his imprisonments for debt, his battle with the Academy, his triumphs, his failures, his despair, his suicide. Half-past ten struck. Mr. Tillotson was declaiming against the stupid and prejudiced judges who had rejected Haydon's designs for the decoration of the new Houses of Parliament in favour of the paltriest German scribblings.

"That great man, one of the greatest England has ever produced, that great Benjamin Robert Haydon, whom I am proud to call my master and who, it rejoices me to see, still lives on in your memory and esteem—at that affront his great heart burst; it was the unkindest cut of all. He who had worked all his life for the recognition, of the artist by the State, he who had petitioned every Prime Minister, including the Duke of Wellington, for thirty years, begging them to employ artists to decorate public buildings, he to whom the scheme for decorating the Houses of Parliament was undeniably due...." Mr. Tillotson lost a grip on his syntax and began a new sentence. "It was the unkindest cut of all, it was the last straw. The artist's life is a hard one."

At eleven Mr. Tillotson was talking about the pre-Raphaelites. At a quarter past he had begun to tell the story of B.R. Haydon all over again. At twenty-five minutes to twelve he collapsed quite speechless into his chair. Most of the guests had already gone away; the few who remained made haste to depart. Lord Badgery led the old man to the door and packed him into the second Rolls-Royce. The Tillotson Banquet was over; it had been a pleasant evening, but a little too long.

Spode walked back to his rooms in Bloomsbury, whistling as he went. The arc lamps of Oxford Street reflected in the polished surface of the road; canals of dark bronze. He would have to bring that into an article some time. The Cayman woman had been very successfully nobbled. "Voi che sapete," he whistled—somewhat out of tune, but he could not hear that.

When Mr. Tillotson's landlady came in to call him on the following morning, she found the old man lying fully dressed on his bed. He looked very ill and very, very old; Boreham's dress-suit was in a terrible state, and the green ribbon of the Order of Chastity was ruined. Mr. Tillotson lay very still, but he was not asleep. Hearing the sound of footsteps, he opened his eyes a little and faintly groaned. His landlady looked down at him menacingly.

"Disgusting!" she said, "disgusting, I call it. At your age."

Mr. Tillotson groaned again. Making a great effort, he drew out of his trouser pocket a large silk purse, opened it, and extracted a sovereign.

"The artist's life is a hard one, Mrs. Green," he said, handing her the coin. "Would you mind sending for the doctor? I don't feel very well. And oh, what shall I do about these clothes? What shall I say to the gentleman who was kind enough to lend them to me? Loan oft loseth both itself and friend. The Bard is always right."

IV: GREEN TUNNELS

"In the Italian gardens of the thirteenth century...." Mr. Buzzacott interrupted himself to take another helping of the risotto which was being offered him. "Excellent risotto this," he observed. "Nobody who was not born in Milan can make it properly. So they say."

"So they say," Mr. Topes repeated in his sad, apologetic voice, and helped himself in his turn.

"Personally," said Mrs. Topes, with decision, "I find all Italian cooking abominable. I don't like the oil—especially hot. No, thank you." She recoiled from the proffered dish.

After the first mouthful Mr. Buzzacott put down his fork. "In the Italian gardens of the thirteenth century," he began again, making with his long, pale hand a curved and flowery gesture that ended with a clutch at his beard, "a frequent and most felicitous use was made of green tunnels."

"Green tunnels?" Barbara woke up suddenly from her tranced silence. "Green tunnels?"

"Yes, my dear," said her father. "Green tunnels. Arched alleys covered with vines or other creeping plants. Their length was often very considerable."

But Barbara had once more ceased to pay attention to what he was saying. Green tunnels—the word had floated down to her, through profound depths of reverie, across great spaces of abstraction, startling her like the sound of a strange-voiced bell. Green tunnels—what a wonderful idea. She would not listen to her father explaining the phrase into dullness. He made everything dull; an inverted alchemist, turning gold into lead. She pictured caverns in a great aquarium, long vistas between rocks and scarcely swaying weeds and pale, discoloured corals; endless dim green corridors with huge lazy fishes loitering aimlessly along them. Green-faced monsters with goggling eyes and mouths that slowly opened and shut. Green tunnels....

"I have seen them illustrated in illuminated manuscripts of the period," Mr. Buzzacott went on; once more he clutched his pointed brown beard—clutched and combed it with his long fingers.

Mr. Topes looked up. The glasses of his round owlish spectacles flashed as he moved his head. "I know what you mean," he said.

"I have a very good mind to have one, planted in my garden here."

"It will take a long time to grow," said Mr. Topes. "In this sand, so close to the sea, you will only be able to plant vines. And they come up very slowly very slowly indeed." He shook his head and the points of light danced wildly in his spectacles. His voice drooped hopelessly, his grey moustache drooped, his whole person drooped. Then, suddenly, he pulled himself up. A shy, apologetic smile appeared on his face. He wriggled uncomfortably. Then, with a final rapid shake of the head, he gave vent to a quotation:

But at my back I always hear
Time's winged chariot hurrying near."

He spoke deliberately, and his voice trembled a little. He always found it painfully difficult to say something choice and out of the ordinary; and yet what a wealth of remembered phrase, what apt new coinages were always surging through his mind!

"They don't grow so slowly as all that," said Mr. Buzzacott confidently. He was only just over fifty, and looked a handsome thirty-five. He gave himself at least another forty years; indeed, he had not yet begun to contemplate the possibility of ever concluding.

"Miss Barbara will enjoy it, perhaps—your green tunnel." Mr. Topes sighed and looked across the table at his host's daughter.

Barbara was sitting with her elbows on the table, her chin in her hands, staring in front of her. The sound of her own name reached her faintly. She turned her head in Mr. Topes's direction and found herself confronted by the glitter of his round, convex spectacles. At the end of the green tunnel—she stared at the shining circles—hung the eyes of a goggling fish. They approached, floating, closer and closer, along the dim submarine corridor.

Confronted by this fixed regard, Mr. Topes looked away. What thoughtful eyes! He couldn't remember ever to have seen eyes so full of thought. There were certain Madonnas of Montagna, he reflected, very like hen mild little blonde Madonnas with slightly snub noses and very, very young. But he was old; it would be many years, in spite of Buzzacott, before the vines grew up into a green tunnel. He took a sip of wine; then, mechanically, sucked his drooping grey moustache.

"Arthur!"

At the sound of his wife's voice Mr. Topes started, raised his napkin to his mouth. Mrs. Topes did not permit the sucking of moustaches. It was only in moments of absent-mindedness that he ever offended, now.

"The Marchese Prampolini is coming here to take coffee," said Mr. Buzzacott suddenly. "I almost forgot to tell you."

"One of these Italian marquises, I suppose," said Mrs. Topes, who was no snob, except in England. She raised her chin with a little jerk.

Mr. Buzzacott executed an upward curve of the hand in her direction. "I assure you, Mrs. Topes, he belongs to a very old and distinguished family. They are Genoese in origin. You remember their palace, Barbara? Built by Alessi."

Barbara looked up. "Oh yes," she said vaguely. "Alessi. I know." Alessi: Aleppo—where a malignant and a turbaned Turk. *And* a turbaned; that had always seemed to her very funny.

"Several of his ancestors," Mr. Buzzacott went on, "distinguished themselves as vice-roys of Corsica. They did good work in the suppression of rebellion. Strange, isn't it"—he turned parenthetically to Mr. Topes—"the way in which sympathy is always on the side of rebels? What a fuss people made of Corsica! That ridiculous book of Gregorovius, for example. And the Irish, and the Poles, and all the rest of them. It always seems to me very superfluous and absurd."

"Isn't it, perhaps, a little natural?" Mr. Topes began timorously and tentatively, but his host went on without listening.

"The present marquis," he said, "is the head of the local Fascisti. They have done no end of good work in this district in the way of preserving law and order and keeping the lower classes in their place."

"Ah, the Fascisti," Mrs. Topes repeated approvingly. "One would like to see something of the kind in England. What with all these strikes...."

"He has asked me for a subscription to the funds of the organisation. I shall give him one, of course."

"Of course." Mrs. Topes nodded. "My nephew, the one who was a major during the war, volunteered in the last coal strike. He was sorry, I know, that it didn't come to a fight. 'Aunt Annie,' he said to me, when I saw him last, 'if there had been a fight we should have knocked them out completely—completely.'"

In Aleppo, the Fascisti, malignant *and* turbaned, were fighting, under the palm trees. Weren't they palm trees, those tufted green plumes?

"What, no ice to-day? *Niente gelato?*" inquired Mr. Buzzacott as the maid put down the compote of peaches on the table.

Concetta apologised. The ice-making machine in the village had broken down. There would be no ice till to-morrow.

"Too bad," said Mr. Buzzacott. "*Troppo male, Concetta.*"

Under the palm trees, Barbara saw them: they pranced about, fighting. They were mounted on big dogs, and in the trees were enormous many-coloured birds.

"Goodness me, the child's asleep." Mrs. Topes was proffering the dish of peaches. "How much longer am I to hold this in front of your nose, Barbara?"

Barbara felt herself blushing. "I'm so sorry," she mumbled, and took the dish clumsily.

"Day-dreaming. It's a bad habit."

"It's one we all succumb to sometimes," put in Mr. Topes deprecatingly, with a little nervous tremble of the head.

"You may, my dear," said his wife. "I do not."

Mr. Topes lowered his eyes to his plate and went on eating.

"The marchese should be here at any moment now," said Mr. Buzzacott, looking at his watch. "I hope he won't be late. I find I suffer so much from any postponement of my siesta. This Italian heat," he added, with growing plaintiveness, "one can't be too careful."

"Ah, but when I was with my father in India," began Mrs. Topes in a tone of superiority: "he was an Indian civilian, you know...."

Aleppo, India—always the palm trees. Cavalcades of big dogs, and tigers too.

Concetta ushered in the marquis. Delighted. Pleased to meet. Speak English? Yés, yéss. *Pocchino*. Mrs. Topes: and Mr. Topes, the distinguished antiquarian. Ah, of course; know his name very well. My daughter. Charmed. Often seen the signorina bathing. Admired the way she dives. Beautiful—the hand made a long, caressing gesture. These athletic English signorine. The teeth flashed astonishingly white in the brown face, the dark eyes glittered. She felt herself blushing again, looked away, smiled foolishly. The marquis had already turned back to Mr. Buzzacott.

"So you have decided to settle in our Carrarese."

Well, not settled exactly; Mr. Buzzacott wouldn't go so far as to say settled. A villine for the summer months. The winter in Rome. One was forced to live abroad. Taxation in England.... Soon they were all talking. Barbara looked at them. Beside the marquis they all seemed half dead. His face flashed as he talked; he seemed to be boiling with life. Her father was limp and pale, like something long buried from the light; and Mr. Topes was all dry and shrivelled; and Mrs. Topes looked more than ever like something worked by clockwork. They were talking about Socialism and Fascisti, and all that. Barbara did not listen to what they were saying; but she looked at them, absorbed.

Good-bye, good-bye. The animated face with its flash of a smile was turned like a lamp from one to another. Now it was turned on her. Perhaps one evening she would come, with her father, and the Signora Topes. He and his sister gave little dances sometimes. Only the gramophone, of course. But that was better than nothing, and the signorina must dance divinely—another flash—he could see that. He pressed her hand again. Good-bye.

It was time for the siesta.

"Don't forget to pull down the mosquito netting, my dear," Mr. Buzzacott exhorted. "There is always a danger of anophylines."

"All right, father." She moved towards the door without turning round to answer him. He was always terribly tiresome about mosquito nets. Once they had driven through the Campagna in a hired cab, completely enclosed in an improvised tent of netting. The monuments along the Appian Way had loomed up mistily as through bridal veils. And how everyone had laughed. But her father, of course, hadn't so much as noticed it. He never noticed anything.

"Is it at Berlin, that charming little Madonna of Montagna's?" Mr. Topes abruptly asked. "The one with the Donor kneeling in the left-hand corner as if about to kiss the foot of the Child." His spectacles flashed in Mr. Buzzacott's direction.

"Why do you ask?"

"I don't know. I was just thinking of it."

"I think you must mean the one in the Mond Collection."

"Ah yes; very probably. In the Mond...."

IV: GREEN TUNNELS

Barbara opened the door and walked into the twilight of her shuttered room. It was hot even here; for another three hours it would hardly be possible to stir. And that old idiot, Mrs. Topes, always made a fuss if one came in to lunch with bare legs and one's after-bathing tunic. "In India we always made a point of being properly and adequately dressed. An Englishwoman must keep up her position with natives, and to all intents and purposes Italians *are* natives." And so she always had to put on shoes and stockings and a regular frock just at the hottest hour of the day. What an old ass that woman was! She slipped off her clothes as fast as she could. That was a little better.

Standing in front of the long mirror in the wardrobe door she came to the humiliating conclusion that she looked like a piece of badly toasted bread. Brown face, brown neck and shoulders, brown arms, brown legs from the knee downwards; but all the rest of her was white, silly, effeminate, townish white. If only one could run about with no clothes on till one was like those little coppery children who rolled and tumbled in the burning sand! Now she was just underdone, half-baked, and wholly ridiculous. For a long time she looked at her pale image. She saw herself running, bronzed all over, along the sand; or through a field of flowers, narcissus and wild tulips; or in soft grass under grey olive trees. She turned round with a sudden start. There, in the shadows behind her.... No, of course there was nothing.

It was that awful picture in a magazine she had looked at, so many years ago, when she was a child. There was a lady sitting at her dressing-table, doing her hair in front of the glass; and a huge, hairy black monkey creeping up behind her. She always got the creeps when she looked at herself in a mirror. It was very silly. But still. She turned away from the mirror, crossed the room, and, without lowering the mosquito curtains, lay down on her bed. The flies buzzed about her, settled incessantly on her face. She shook her head, flapped at them angrily with her hands. There would be peace if she let down the netting. But she thought of the Appian Way seen mistily through the bridal veil and preferred to suffer the flies. In the end she had to surrender; the brutes were too much for her. But, at any rate, it wasn't the fear of anophylines that made her lower the netting.

Undisturbed now and motionless, she lay stretched stiffly out under the transparent bell of gauze. A specimen under a glass case. The fancy possessed her mind. She saw a huge museum with thousands of glass cases, full of fossils and butterflies and stuffed birds and mediæval spoons and armour and Florentine jewellery and mummies and carved ivory and illuminated manuscripts. But in one of the cases was a human being, shut up there alive.

All of a sudden she became horribly miserable. "Boring, boring, boring," she whispered, formulating the words aloud. Would it never stop being boring? The tears came into her eyes. How awful everything was! And perhaps it would go on being as bad as this all her life. Seventeen from seventy was fifty three. Fifty three years of it. And if she lived to a hundred there would be more than eighty.

The thought depressed her all the evening. Even her bath after tea did her no good. Swimming far out, far out, she lay there, floating on the warm water. Sometimes she looked at the sky, sometimes she turned her head towards the shore. Framed in their pinewoods, the villas looked as small and smug as the advertisement of a seaside resort. But behind them, across the level plain, were the mountains. Sharp, bare peaks of limestone, green woodland slopes and grey-green expanses of terraced olive trees—they seemed marvellously close and clear in this evening light. And beautiful, beautiful beyond words. But that, somehow, only made things worse. And Shelley had lived a few miles farther up the coast, there, behind the headland guarding the Gulf of Spezia. Shelley had been drowned in this milk-warm sea. That made it worse too.

The sun was getting very low and red over the sea. She swam slowly in. On the beach Mrs. Topes waited, disapprovingly. She had known somebody, a strong man, who had caught cramp from staying in too long. He sank like a stone. Like a stone. The queer people Mrs. Topes had known! And the funny things they did, the odd things that happened to them.

Dinner that evening was duller than ever. Barbara went early to bed. All night long the same old irritating cicada scraped and scraped among the pine trees, monotonous and regular as clockwork. Zip zip, zip zip zip. Boring, boring. Was the animal never bored by its own noise? It seemed odd that it shouldn't be. But, when she came to think of it, nobody ever did get bored with their own noise. Mrs. Topes, for example; she never seemed to get bored. Zip zip, zip zip zip. The cicada went on without pause.

Concetta knocked at the door at half-past seven. The morning was as bright and cloudless as all the mornings were. Barbara jumped up, looked from one window at the mountains, from the other at the sea; all seemed to be well with them. All was well with her, too, this morning. Seated at the mirror, she did not so much as think of the big monkey in the far obscure corner of the room. A bathing dress and a bath-gown, sandals, a handkerchief round her head, and she was ready. Sleep had left no recollection of last night's mortal boredom. She ran downstairs.

"Good morning, Mr. Topes."

Mr. Topes was walking in the garden among the vines. He turned round, took off his hat, smiled a greeting.

"Good morning, Miss Barbara." He paused. Then, with an embarrassed wriggle of introduction he went on; a queer little falter came into his voice. "A real Chaucerian morning, Miss Barbara. A May-day morning—only it happens to be September. Nature is fresh and bright, and there is at least one specimen in this dream garden"—he wriggled more uncomfortably than ever, and there was a tremulous glitter in his round spectacle lenses of the poet's 'yonge fresshe folkes.' He bowed in her direction, smiled deprecatingly, and was silent. The remark, it seemed to him, now that he had finished speaking, was somehow not as good as he had thought it would be.

Barbara laughed. "Chaucer! They used to make us read the *Canterbury Tales* at school. But they always bored me. Are you going to bathe?"

"Not before breakfast." Mr. Topes shook his head. "One is getting a little too old for that."

"Is one?" Why did the silly old man always say 'one' when he meant 'I'? She couldn't help laughing at him. "Well, I must hurry, or else I shall be late for breakfast again, and you know how I catch it."

She ran out, through the gate in the garden wall, across the beach, to the striped red-and-white bathing cabin that stood before the house. Fifty yards away she saw the Marchese Prampolini, still dripping from the sea, running up towards his bathing hut. Catching sight of her, he flashed a smile in her direction, gave a military salute. Barbara waved her hand, then thought that the gesture had been too familiar—but at this hour of the morning it was difficult not to have bad jolly manners—and added the corrective of a stiff bow. After all, she had only met him yesterday. Soon she was swimming out to sea, and, ugh! what a lot of horrible huge jelly-fish there were.

Mr. Topes had followed her slowly through the gate and across the sand. He watched her running down from the cabin, slender as a boy, with long, bounding strides. He watched her go jumping with great splashes through the deepening water, then throw herself forward and begin to swim. He watched her till she was no more than a small dark dot far out.

Emerging from his cabin, the marquis met him walking slowly along the beach, his head bent down and his lips slightly moving as though he were repeating something, a prayer or a poem, to himself.

"Good morning, signore." The marquis shook him by the hand with a more than English cordiality.

"Good morning," replied Mr. Topes, allowing his hand to be shaken. He resented this interruption of his thoughts.

"She swims very well, Miss Buzzacott."

"Very," assented Mr. Topes, and smiled to himself to think what beautiful, poetical things he might have said, if he had chosen.

"Well, so, so," said the marquis, too colloquial by half. He shook hands again, and the two men went their respective ways.

Barbara was still a hundred yards from the shore when she heard the crescendo and dying boom of the gong floating out from the villa. Damn! she'd be late again. She quickened her stroke and came splashing out through the shallows, flushed and breathless.

She'd be ten minutes late, she calculated; it would take her at least that to do her hair and dress. Mrs. Topes would be on the war-path again; though what business that old woman had to lecture her as she did, goodness only knew. She always succeeded in making herself horribly offensive and unpleasant.

The beach was quite deserted as she trotted, panting, across it, empty to right and left as far as she could see. If only she had a horse to go galloping at the water's edge, miles and miles. Right away down to Bocca d'Arno she'd go, swim the river—she saw herself crouching on the horse's back, as he swam, with legs tucked up on the saddle, trying not to get her feet wet—and gallop on again, goodness only knew where.

In front of the cabin she suddenly halted. There in the ruffled sand she had seen a writing. Big letters, faintly legible, sprawled across her path.

O CLARA D'ELLÉBEUSE.

She pieced the dim letters together. They hadn't been there when she started out to bathe. Who?... She looked round. The beach was quite empty. And what was the meaning? "O Clara d'Ellébeuse." She took her bath-gown from the cabin, slipped on her sandals, and ran back towards the house as fast as she could. She felt most horribly frightened.

It was a sultry, headachey sort of morning, with a hot sirocco that stirred the bunting on the flagstaffs. By midday the thunderclouds had covered half the sky. The sun still blazed on the sea, but over the mountains all was black and indigo. The storm broke noisily overhead just as they were drinking their after-luncheon coffee.

"Arthur," said Mrs. Topes, painfully calm, "shut the shutters, please."

She was not frightened, no. But she preferred not to see the lightning. When the room was darkened, she began to talk, suavely and incessantly.

Lying back in her deep arm-chair, Barbara was thinking of Clara d'Ellébeuse. What did it mean and who was Clara d'Ellébeuse? And why had he written it there for her to see? He—for there could be no doubt who had written it. The flash of teeth and eyes, the military salute; she knew she oughtn't to have waved to him. He had written it there while she was swimming out. Written it and then run away. She rather liked that—just an extraordinary word on the sand, like the footprint in *Robinson Crusoe.*

"Personally," Mrs. Topes was saying, "I prefer Harrod's."

The thunder crashed and rattled. It was rather exhilarating, Barbara thought; one felt, at any rate, that something was happening for a change. She remembered the little room half-way up the stairs at Lady Thingumy's house, with the book-shelves and the green curtains and the orange shade on the light; and that awful young man like a white slug who had tried to kiss her there, at the dance last year. But that was different—not at all serious; and the young man had been so horribly ugly. She saw the marquis running up the beach, quick and alert. Copper coloured all over, with black hair. He was certainly very handsome. But as for being in love, well ... what did that exactly mean? Perhaps when she knew him better. Even now she fancied she detected something. O Clara d'Ellébeuse. What an extraordinary thing it was.

With his long fingers Mr. Buzzacott combed his beard. This winter, he was thinking, he would put another thousand into Italian money when the exchange was favourable. In the spring it always seemed to drop back again. One could clear three hundred pounds on one's capital if the exchange went down to seventy. The income on three hundred was fifteen pounds a year, and fifteen pounds was now fifteen hundred lire. And fifteen hundred lire, when you came to think of it, was really sixty pounds. That was to say that one would make an addition of more than one pound a week to one's income by this simple little speculation. He became aware that Mrs. Topes had asked him a question.

"Yes, yes, perfectly," he said.

Mrs. Topes talked on; she was keeping up her morale. Was she right in believing that the thunder sounded a little less alarmingly loud and near?

Mr. Topes sat, polishing his spectacles with a white silk handkerchief. Vague and myopic between their puckered lids, his eyes seemed lost, homeless, unhappy. He was thinking about beauty. There were certain relations between the eyelids and the temples, between the breast and the shoulder; there were certain successions of sounds. But what about them? Ah, that was the problem—that was the problem. And there was youth, there was innocence. But it was all very obscure, and there were so many phrases, so many remembered pictures and melodies; he seemed to get himself entangled among them. And he was after all so old and so ineffective. He put on his spectacles again, and definition came into the foggy world beyond his eyes. The shuttered room was very dark. He could distinguish the Renaissance profile of Mr. Buzzacott, bearded and delicately featured. In her deep arm-chair Barbara appeared, faintly white, in an attitude relaxed and brooding. And Mrs. Topes was nothing more than a voice in the darkness. She had got on to the marriage of the Prince of Wales. Who would they eventually find for him?

Clara d'Ellébeuse, Clara d'Ellébeuse. She saw herself so clearly as the *marchesa*. They would have a house in Rome, a palace. She saw herself in the Palazzo Spada—it had such a lovely vaulted passage leading from the courtyard to the gardens at the back. "MARCHESA PRAMPOLINI, PALAZZO SPADA, ROMA"—a great big visiting-card beautifully engraved. And she would go riding every day in the Pincio. "*Mi porta il mio cavallo*" she would say to the footman, who answered the bell. *Porta*? Would that be quite correct? Hardly. She'd have to take some proper Italian lessons to talk to the servants. One must never be ridiculous before servants. "*Voglio il mio cavallo.* Haughtily one would say it sitting at one's writing-table in a riding-habit, without turning round. It would be a green riding-habit, with a black tricorne hat, braided with silver.

"*Prendero la mia collazzione al letto.*" Was that right for breakfast in bed? Because she would have breakfast in bed, always. And when she got up there would be lovely looking glasses with three panels where one could see oneself sideface. She saw herself leaning forward, powdering her nose, carefully, scientifically. With the monkey creeping up behind? Ooh. Horrible! *Ho paura di questa scimmia, questo scimmione.*

She would come back to lunch after her ride. Perhaps Prampolini would be there; she had rather left him out of the picture so far. "*Dov' è il Marchese?*" "*Nella sala di pranza, signora.*" I began without you, I was so hungry. *Pasta asciutta.* Where have you been, my love? Riding, my dove. She supposed they'd get into the habit of saying that sort of thing. Everyone seemed to. And you? I have been out with the Fascisti.

Oh, these Fascisti! Would life be worth living when he was always going out with pistols and bombs and things? They would bring him back one day on a stretcher. She saw it. Pale, pale, with blood on him. *Il signore è ferito. Nel petto. Gruvamente. E morto.*

How could she bear it? It was too awful; too, too terrible. Her breath came in a kind of sob; she shuddered as though she had been hurt. *E morto, E morto.* The tears came into her eyes.

She was roused suddenly by a dazzling light. The storm had receded far enough into the distance to permit of Mrs. Topes's opening the shutters.

"It's quite stopped raining."

To be disturbed in one's intimate sorrow and self-abandonment at a death-bed by a stranger's intrusion, an alien voice.... Barbara turned her face away from the light and surreptitiously wiped her eyes. They might see and ask her why she had been crying. She hated Mrs. Topes for opening the shutters; at the inrush of the light something beautiful had flown, an emotion had vanished, irrecoverably. It was a sacrilege.

Mr. Buzzacott looked at his watch. "Too late, I fear, for a siesta now," he said. "Suppose we ring for an early tea."

"An endless succession of meals," said Mr. Topes, with a tremolo and a sigh. "That's what life seems to be—real life."

"I have been calculating"—Mr. Buzzacott turned his pale green eyes towards his guest—"that I may be able to afford that pretty little *cinque* cassone, after all. It would be a bit of a squeeze." He played with his beard. "But still...."

After tea, Barbara and Mr. Topes went for a walk along the beach. She didn't much want to go, but Mrs. Topes thought it would be good for her; so she had to. The storm had passed and the sky over the sea was clear. But the waves were still breaking with an incessant clamour on the outer shallows, driving wide sheets of water high up the beach, twenty or thirty yards above the line where, on a day of calm, the ripples ordinarily expired. Smooth, shining expanses of water advanced and receded like steel surfaces moved out and back by a huge machine. Through the rain-washed air the mountains appeared with an incredible clarity. Above them hung huge masses of cloud.

"Clouds over Carrara," said Mr. Topes, deprecating his remark with a little shake of the head and a movement of the shoulders. "I like to fancy sometimes that the spirits of the great sculptors lodge among these marble hills, and that it is their unseen hands that carve the clouds into these enormous splendid shapes. I imagine their ghosts"—his voice trembled—"feeling about among superhuman conceptions, planning huge groups and friezes and monumental figures with blowing draperies; planning, conceiving, but never quite achieving. Look, there's something of Michelangelo in that white cloud with the dark shadows underneath it." Mr. Topes pointed, and Barbara, nodded and said, "Yes, yes," though she wasn't quite sure which cloud he meant. "It's like Night on the Medici tomb; all the power and passion are brooding inside it, pent up. And there, in that sweeping, gesticulating piece of vapour—you see the one I mean—there's a Bernini. All the passion's on the surface, expressed; the gesture's caught at its most violent. And that sleek, smug white fellow over there, that's a delicious absurd Canova." Mr. Topes chuckled.

"Why do you always talk about art?" said Barbara. "You bring these dead people into everything. What do I know about Canova or whoever it is?" They were none of them alive. She thought of that dark face, bright as a lamp with life. He at least wasn't dead. She wondered whether the letters were still there in the sand before the cabin. No, of course not; the rain and the wind would have blotted them out.

Mr. Topes was silent; he walked with slightly bent knees and his eyes were fixed on the ground; he wore a speckled black-and-white straw hat. He always thought of art; that was what was wrong with him. Like an old tree he was; built up of dead wood, with only a few fibres of life to keep him from rotting away. They walked on for a long time in silence.

"Here's the river," said Mr. Topes at last.

A few steps more and they were on the bank of a wide stream that came down slowly through the plain to the sea. Just inland from the beach it was fringed with pine trees; beyond the trees one could see the plain, and beyond the plain were the mountains. In this calm light after the storm everything looked strange. The colours seemed deeper and more intense than at ordinary times. And though all was so clear, there was a mysterious air of remoteness about the whole scene. There was no sound except the continuous breathing of the sea. They stood for a little while, looking; then turned back.

Far away along the beach two figures were slowly approaching. White flannel trousers, a pink skirt.

"Nature," Mr. Topes enunciated, with a shake of the head. "One always comes back to nature. At a moment such as this, in surroundings like these, one realises it. One lives now—more quietly, perhaps, but more profoundly. Deep watery. Deep waters...."

The figures drew closer. Wasn't it the marquis? And who was with him? Barbara strained her eyes to see.

"Most of one's life," Mr. Topes went on, "is one prolonged effort to prevent oneself thinking. Your father and I, we collect pictures and read about the dead. Other people achieve the same results by drinking, or breeding rabbits, or doing amateur carpentry. Anything rather than think calmly about the important things."

Mr. Topes was silent. He looked about him, at the sea, at the mountains, at the great clouds, at his companion. A frail Montagna madonna, with the sea and the westering sun, the mountains and the storm, all eternity as a background. And he was sixty, with all a life, immensely long and yet timelessly short, behind him, an empty life. He thought of death and the miracles of beauty; behind his round, glittering spectacles he felt inclined to weep.

The approaching couple were quite near now.

"What a funny old walrus," said the lady.

"Walrus? Your natural history is quite wrong." The marquis laughed. "He's much too dry to be a walrus. I should suggest some sort of an old cat."

"Well, whatever he is, I'm sorry for that poor little girl. Think of having nobody better to go about with!"

"Pretty, isn't she?"

"Yes, but too young, of course."

"I like the innocence."

"Innocence? Cher ami! These English girls. Oh, la la! They may look innocent But, believe me...."

"Sh, sh. They'll hear you."

"Pooh, they don't understand Italian."

The marquis raised his hand. "The old walrus...." he whispered; then addressed himself loudly and jovially to the newcomers.

"Good evening, signorina. Good evening, Mr. Topes. After a storm the air is always the purest, don't you find, eh?"

Barbara nodded, leaving Mr. Topes to answer. It wasn't his sister. It was the Russian woman, the one of whom Mrs. Topes used to say that it was a disgrace she should be allowed to stay at the hotel. She had turned away, dissociating herself from the conversation; Barbara looked at the line of her averted face. Mr. Topes was saying something about the Pastoral Symphony. Purple face powder in the daylight; it looked hideous.

"Well, au revoir."

The flash of the marquis's smile was directed at them. The Russian woman turned back from the sea, slightly bowed, smiled languidly. Her heavy white eyelids were almost closed; she seemed the prey of an enormous ennui.

"They jar a little," said Mr. Topes when they were out of earshot—"they jar on the time, on the place, on the emotion. They haven't the innocence for this ... this...."—he wriggled and tremoloed out the just, the all too precious word—"this prelapsarian landscape."

He looked sideways at Barbara and wondered what she was so thoughtfully frowning over. Oh, lovely and delicate young creature! What could he adequately say of death and beauty and tenderness? Tenderness....

"All this," he went on desperately, and waved his hand to indicate the sky, the sea, the mountains, "this scene is like something remembered, clear and utterly calm; remembered across great gulfs of intervening time."

But that was not really what he wanted to say.

"You see what I mean?" he asked dubiously. She made no reply. How could she see? "This scene is so clear and pure and remote; you need the corresponding emotion. Those people were out of harmony. They weren't clear and pure enough." He seemed to be getting more muddled than ever. "It's an emotion of the young and of the old. You could feel it, I could feel it. Those people couldn't." He was feeling his way through obscurities. Where would he finally arrive? "Certain poems express it. You know Francis Jammes? I have thought so much of his work lately. Art instead of life, as usual; but then I'm made that way. I can't help thinking of Jammes. Those delicate, exquisite things he wrote about Clara d'Ellébeuse."

"Clara d'Ellébeuse?" She stopped and stared at him.

"You know the lines?" Mr. Topes smiled delightedly. "This makes me think, you make me think of them. '*F'aime dans les temps Clara d'Ellébeuse....*' But, my dear Barbara, what is the matter?"

She had started crying, for no reason whatever.

V: NUNS AT LUNCHEON

"What have I been doing since you saw me last?" Miss Penny repeated my question in her loud, emphatic voice. "Well, when did you see me last?"

"It must have been June," I computed.

"Was that after I'd been proposed to by the Russian General?

"Yes; I remember hearing about the Russian General."

Miss Penny threw back her head and laughed. Her long ear-rings swung and rattled corpses hanging in chains: an agreeably literary simile. And her laughter was like brass, but that had been said before.

"That was an uproarous incident. It's sad you should have heard of it. I love my Russian General story. '*Vos yeux me rendent fou.*'" She laughed again.

Vos yeux—she had eyes like a hare's, flush with her head and very bright with a superficial and expressionless brightness. What a formidable woman. I felt sorry for the Russian General.

"'*Sans coeur et sans entrallies*,'" she went on, quoting the poor devil's words. "Such a delightful motto, don't you think? Like '*Sans peur et sans reproche*.' But let me think; what have I been doing since then?" Thoughtfully she bit into the crust of her bread with long, sharp, white teeth.

"Two mixed grills," I said parenthetically to the waiter.

"But of course," exclaimed Miss Penny suddenly. "I haven't seen you since my German trip. All sorts of adventures. My appendicitis; my nun."

"Your nun?"

"My marvellous nun. I must tell you all about her."

"Do." Miss Penny's anecdotes were always curious. I looked forward to an entertaining luncheon.

"You knew I'd been in Germany this autumn?"

"Well, I didn't, as a matter of fact. But still—"

"I was just wandering round." Miss Penny described a circle in the air with her gaudily jewelled hand. She always twinkled with massive and improbable jewellery.

"Wandering round, living on three pounds a week, partly amusing myself, partly collecting material for a few little articles. 'What it Feels Like to be a Conquered Nation'—sob-stuff for the Liberal press, you know—and 'How the Hun is Trying to Wriggle out of the Indemnity,' for the other fellows. One has to make the best of all possible worlds, don't you find? But we mustn't talk shop. Well, I was wandering round, and very pleasant I found it. Berlin, Dresden, Leipzig. Then down to Munich and all over the place. One fine day I got to Grauburg. You know Grauburg? It's one of those picture-book German towns with a castle on a hill, hanging beer-gardens, a Gothic church, an old university, a river, a pretty bridge, and forests all round. Charming. But I hadn't much opportunity to appreciate the beauties of the place. The day after I arrived there—bang!—I went down with appendicitis—screaming, I may add."

"But how appalling!"

"They whisked me off to hospital, and cut me open before you could say knife. Excellent surgeon, highly efficient Sisters of Charity to nurse me—I couldn't have been in better hands. But it was a bore being tied there by the leg for four weeks—a great bore. Still, the thing had its compensations. There was my nun, for example. Ah, here's the food, thank Heaven!"

The mixed grill proved to be excellent. Miss Penny's description of the pun came to me in scraps and snatches. A round, pink, pretty face in a winged coif; blue eyes and regular features; teeth altogether too perfect—false, in fact; but the general effect extremely pleasing. A youthful Teutonic twenty eight.

"She wasn't my nurse," Miss Penny explained. "But I used to see her quite often when she came in to have a look at the *tolle Engländerin*. Her name was Sister Agatha. During the war, they told me, she had converted any number of wounded soldiers to the true faith—which wasn't surprising, considering how pretty she was."

"Did she try and convert you?" I asked.

"She wasn't such a fool." Miss Penny laughed, and rattled the miniature gallows of her ears.

I amused myself for a moment with the thought of Miss Penny's conversion—Miss Penny confronting a vast assembly of Fathers of the Church, rattling her earrings at their discourses on the Trinity, laughing her appalling laugh at the doctrine of the Immaculate Conception, meeting the stern look of the Grand Inquisitor with a flash of her bright, emotionless hare's eyes. What was the secret of the woman's formidableness?

But I was missing the story. What had happened? Ah yes, the gist of it was that Sister Agatha had appeared one morning, after two or three days absence, dressed, not as a nun, but in the overalls of a hospital charwoman, with a handkerchief instead of a winged coif on her shaven head.

"Dead," said Miss Penny; "she looked as though she were dead. A walking corpse, that's what she was. It was a shocking sight. I shouldn't have thought it possible for anyone to change so much in so short a time. She walked painfully, as though she had been ill for months, and she had great burnt rings round her eyes and deep lines in her face. And the general expression of unhappiness—that was something quite appalling."

She leaned out into the gangway between the two rows of tables, and caught the passing waiter by the end of one his coat-tails. The little Italian looked round with an expression of surprise that deepened into terror on his face.

"Half a pint of Guinness," ordered Miss Penny. "And, after this, bring me some jam roll."

"No jam roll to-day, madam."

"Damn!" said Miss Penny. "Bring me what you like, then."

She let go of the waiter's tail and resumed her narrative.

"Where was I? Yes, I remember. She came into my room, I was telling you, with a bucket of water and a brush, dressed like a charwoman. Naturally I was rather surprised. 'What on earth are you doing, Sister Agatha?' I asked. No answer. She just shook her head, and began to scrub the floor. When she'd finished, she left the room without so much as looking at me again. 'What's happened to Sister Agatha?' I asked my nurse when she next came in. 'Can't say.'—'Won't say,' I said. No answer. It took nearly a week to find out what really had happened. Nobody dared tell me; it was *strengst verboten*, as they used to say in the good old days. But I wormed it out in the long run. My nurse, the doctor, the charwomen—I got something out of all of them. I always get what I want in the end." Miss Penny laughed like a horse.

"I'm sure you do," I said politely.

"Much obliged," acknowledged Miss Penny. "But to proceed. My information came to me in fragmentary whispers. 'Sister Agatha ran away with a man.'—Dear me.—'One of the patients.'—You don't say so.—'A criminal out of the jail.'—The plot thickens.—'He ran away from her.'—It seems to grow thinner again.—'They brought her back here; she's been disgraced. There's been a funeral service for her in the chapel—coffin and all. She had to be present at it—her own funeral. She isn't a nun any more. She has to do charwoman's work now, the roughest in the hospital. She's not allowed to speak to anybody, and nobody's allowed to speak to her. She's regarded as dead.'" Miss Penny paused to signal to the harassed little Italian. "My small 'Guinness,'" she called out.

"Coming, coming," and the foreign voice cried "Guinness" down the lift, and from below another voice echoed, "Guinness."

"I filled in the details bit by bit. There was our hero, to begin with; I had to bring him into the picture, which was rather difficult, as I had never seen him. But I got a photograph of him. The police circulated one when he got away; I don't suppose they ever caught him." Miss Penny opened her bag. "Here it is," she said. "I always carry it about with me; it's become a superstition. For years, I remember, I used to carry a little bit of heather tied up with string. Beautiful, isn't it? There's a sort of Renaissance look about it, don't you think? He was half-Italian, you know."

Italian. Ah, that explained it. I had been wondering how Bavaria could have produced this thin-faced creature with the big dark eyes, the finely modelled nose and chin, and the fleshy lips so royally and sensually curved.

"He's certainly very superb," I said, handing back the picture.

Miss Penny put it carefully away in her bag. "Isn't he?" she said. "Quite marvellous. But his character and his mind were even better. I see him as one of those innocent, childlike monsters of iniquity who are simply unaware of the existence of right and wrong. And he had genius—the real Italian genius for engineering, for dominating and exploiting nature. A true son of the Roman aqueduct builders he was, and a brother of the electrical engineers. Only Kuno—that was his name—didn't work in water; he worked in women. He knew how to harness the natural energy of passion; he made devotion drive his mills. The commercial exploitation of love-power, that was his specialty. I sometimes wonder," Miss Penny added in a different tone, "whether I shall ever be exploited, when I get a little more middle-aged and celibate, by one of these young engineers of the passions. It would be humiliating, particularly as I've done so little exploiting from my side."

She frowned and was silent for a moment. No, decidedly, Miss Penny was not beautiful; you could not even honestly say that she had charm or was attractive. That high Scotch colouring, those hare's eyes, the voice, the terrifying laugh, and the size of her, the general formidableness of the woman. No, no, no.

"You said he had been in prison," I said. The silence, with all its implications, was becoming embarrassing.

Miss Penny sighed, looked up, and nodded. "He was fool enough," she said, "to leave the straight and certain road of female exploitation for the dangerous courses of burglary. We all have our occasional accesses of folly. They gave him a heavy sentence, but he succeeded in getting pneumonia, I think it was, a week after entering jail. He was transferred to the hospital. Sister Agatha, with her known talent for saving souls, was given him as his particular attendant. But it was he, I'm afraid, who did the converting."

Miss Penny finished off the last mouthful of the ginger pudding which the waiter had brought in lieu of jam roll.

"I suppose you don't smoke cheroots," I said, as I opened my cigar-case.

"Well, as a matter of fact, I do," Miss Penny replied. She looked sharply round the restaurant. "I must just see if there are any of those horrible little gossip paragraphers here to-day. One doesn't want to figure in the social and personal column to-morrow morning: 'A fact which is not so generally known as it ought to be is, that Miss Penny, the well-known woman journalist, always ends her luncheon with a six-inch Burma cheroot. I saw her yesterday in a restaurant—not a hundred miles from Carmelite Street—smoking like a house on fire.' You know the touch. But the coast seems to be clear, thank goodness."

She took a cheroot from the case, lit it at my proffered match, and went on talking.

"Yes, it was young Kuno who did the converting. Sister Agatha was converted back into the worldly Melpomene Fugger she had been before she became the bride of holiness."

"Melpomene Fugger?"

"That was her name. I had her history from my old doctor. He had seen all Grauburg, living and dying and propagating for generations. Melpomene Fugger why, he had brought little Melpel into the world, little Melpchen. Her father was Professor Fugger, the great Professor Fugger, the *berümter Geolog*. Oh, yes, of course, I know the name. So well.... He was the man who wrote the standard work on Lemuria—you know, the hypothetical continent where the lemurs come from. I showed due respect. Liberal-minded he was, a disciple of Herder, a world-burgher, as they beautifully call it over there. Anglophile, too, and always ate porridge for breakfast—up till August 1914. Then, the radiant morning of the fifth, he renounced it for ever, solemnly and with tears in his eyes. The national food of a people who had betrayed culture and civilisation—how could he go on eating it? It would stick in his throat. In future he would have a lightly boiled egg. He sounded, I thought, altogether charming. And his daughter, Melpomene—she sounded charming, too; and such thick, yellow pig-tails when she was young! Her mother was dead, and a sister of the great Professor's ruled the house with an iron rod. Aunt Bertha was her name. Well, Melpomene grew up, very plump and appetising. When she was seventeen, something very odious and disagreeable happened to her. Even the doctor didn't know exactly what it was; but he wouldn't have been surprised if it had had something to do with the then Professor of Latin, an old friend of the family's, who combined, it seems, great erudition with a horrid fondness for very young ladies."

Miss Penny knocked half an inch of cigar ash into her empty glass.

"If I wrote short stories," she went on reflectively "(but it's too much bother), I should make this anecdote into a sort of potted life history, beginning with a scene immediately after this disagreeable event in Melpomene's life. I see the scene so clearly. Poor little Melpel is leaning over the bastions of Grauburg Castle, weeping into the June night and the mulberry trees in the garden thirty feet below. She is besieged by the memory of what happened this dreadful afternoon. Professor Engelmann, her father's old friend, with the magnificent red Assyrian beard.... Too awful—too awful! But then, as I was saying, short stones are really too much bother; or perhaps I'm too stupid to write them. I bequeath it to you. You know how to tick these things off."

"You're generous."

"Not at all," said Miss Penny. "My terms are ten per cent commission on the American sale. Incidentally there won't be an American sale. Poor Melpchen's history is not for the chaste public of Those States. But let me hear what you propose to do with Melpomene now you've got her on the castle bastions."

"That's simple," I said. "I know all about German university towns and castles on hills. I shall make her look into the June night, as you suggest; into the violet night with its points of golden flame. There will be the black silhouette of the castle, with its sharp roofs and hooded turrets, behind her. From the hanging beer-gardens in the town below the voices of the students, singing in perfect four-part harmony, will float up through the dark-blue spaces. '*Röslein, Röslein, Röslein rot*' and '*Das Ringlein sprang in zwei*'—the heart-rendingly sweet old songs will make her cry all the more. Her tears will patter like rain among the leaves of the mulberry trees in the garden below. Does that seem to you adequate?"

"Very nice," said Miss Penny. "But how are you going to bring the sex problem and all of its horrors into the landscape?"

"Well, let me think." I called to memory those distant foreign summers when I was completing my education. "I know. I shall suddenly bring a swarm of moving candles and Chinese lanterns under the mulberry trees. You imagine the rich lights and shadows, the jewel-bright leafage, the faces and moving limbs of men and women, seen for an instant and gone again. They are students and girls of the town come out to dance, this windless, blue June night, under the mulberry trees. And now they begin, thumping round and round in a ring, to the music of their own singing.

"*Wir können spielen*
Vio-vio-vio-lin
Wir können spielen
Vi-o-lin

"Now the rhythm changes, quickens.

"*Und wir können tanzen Bumstarara,*
Bumstarara, Bumstarara,
Und wir können tanzen Bumstarara,
Bumstarara-rara.

"The dance becomes a rush, an elephantine prancing on the dry lawn under the mulberry trees. And from the bastion Melpomene looks down and perceives, suddenly and apocalyptically, that everything in the world is sex, sex, sex. Men and women, male and female—always the same, and all, in the light of the horror of the afternoon, disgusting. That's how I should do it, Miss Penny."

"And very nice, too. But I wish you could find a place to bring in my conversation with the doctor. I shall never forget the way he cleared his throat, and coughed before embarking on the delicate subject. 'You may know, ahem, gracious Miss,' he began—'you may know that religious phenomena are often, ahem, closely connected with sexual causes.' I replied that I had heard rumours which might justify me in believing this to be true among Roman Catholics, but that in the Church of England —and I for one was a practitioner of Anglicanismus—it was very different. 'That might be,' said the doctor; he had had no opportunity in the course of his long medical career of personally studying Anglicanismus. But he could vouch for the fact that among his patients, here in Grauburg, mysticismus was very often mixed up with the *Geschlechtsleben.* Melpomene was a case in point. After that hateful afternoon she had become extremely religious; the Professor of Latin had diverted her emotions out of their normal channels. She rebelled against the placid Agnosticismus of her father, and at night, in secret, when Aunt Bertha's dragon eyes were closed, she would read such forbidden books as *The Life of St. Theresa, The Little Flowers of St. Francis, The Imitation of Christ*, and the horribly enthralling *Book of Martyrs*. Aunt Bertha confiscated, these works whenever she came upon them; she considered them more pernicious than the novels of Marcel Prévost. The character of a good potential housewife might be completely undermined by reading of this kind. It was rather a relief for Melpomene when Aunt Bertha shuffled off, in the summer of 1911, this mortal coil. She was one of those indispensables of whom one makes the discovery, when they are gone, that one can get on quite as well without them. Poor Aunt Bertha!"

"One can imagine Melpomene trying to believe she was sorry, and horribly ashamed to find that she was really, in secret, almost glad." The suggestion seemed to me ingenious, but Miss Penny accepted it as obvious.

"Precisely," she said; "and the emotion would only further confirm and give new force to the tendencies which her aunt's death left her free to indulge as much as she liked. Remorse, contrition—they would lead to the idea of doing penance. And for one who was now wallowing in the martyrology, penance was the mortification of the flesh. She used to kneel for hours, at night, in the cold; she ate too little, and when her teeth ached, which they often did,—for she had a set, the doctor told me, which had given trouble from the very first,—she would not go and see the dentist, but lay awake at night, savouring to the full her excruciations, and feeling triumphantly that they must, in some strange way, be pleasing to the Mysterious Powers. She went on like that for two or three years, till she was poisoned through and through. In the end she went down with gastric ulcer. It was three months before she came out of hospital, well for the first time in a long space of years, and with a brand new set of imperishable teeth, all gold and ivory. And in mind, too, she was changed—for the better, I suppose. The nuns who nursed her had made her see that in mortifying herself she had acted supererogatively and through spiritual pride; instead of doing right, she had sinned. The only road to salvation, they told her, lay in discipline, in the orderliness of established religion, in obedience to authority. Secretly, so as not to distress her poor father, whose Agnosticismus was extremely dogmatic, for all its unobtrusiveness, Melpomene became a Roman Catholic. She was twenty-two. Only a few months later came the war and Professor Fugger's eternal renunciation of porridge. He did not long survive the making of that patriotic gesture. In the autumn of 1914 he caught a fatal influenza. Melpomene was alone in the world. In the spring of 1915 there was a new and very conscientious Sister of Charity at work among the wounded, in the hospital of Grauburg. Here," explained Miss Penny, jabbing the air with her forefinger, "you put a line of asterisks or dots to signify a six years' gulf in the narrative. And you begin again right in the middle of a dialogue between Sister Agatha and the newly convalescent Kuno."

"What's their dialogue to be about?" I asked.

"Oh, that's easy enough," said Miss Penny. "Almost anything would do. What about this, for example? You explain that the fever has just abated; for the first time for days the young man is fully conscious. He feels himself to be well, reborn, as it were, in a new world—a world so bright and novel and jolly that he can't help laughing at the sight of it. He looks about him; the flies on the ceiling strike him as being extremely comic. How do they manage to walk upside down?

They have suckers on their feet, says Sister Agatha, and wonders if her natural history is quite sound. Suckers on their feet—ha, ha! What an uproarious notion! Suckers on their feet—that's good, that's damned good! You can say charming, pathetic, positively tender things about the irrelevant mirth of convalescents the more so in this particular case, where the mirth is expressed by a young man who is to be taken back to jail as soon as he can stand firmly on his legs. Ha, ha! Laugh on, unhappy boy. It is the quacking of the Fates, the Parcæ, the Norns!"

Miss Penny gave an exaggerated imitation of her own brassy laughter. At the sound of it the few lunchers who still lingered at the other tables looked up, startled.

"You can write pages about Destiny and its ironic quacking. It's tremendously impressive, and there's money in every line."

"You may be sure I shall."

"Good! Then I can get on with my story. The days pass and the first hilarity of convalescence fades away. The young man remembers and grows sullen; his strength comes back to him, and with it a sense of despair. His mind broods incessantly on the hateful future. As for the consolations of religion, he won't listen to them. Sister Agatha perseveres—oh, with what anxious solicitude!—in the attempt to make him understand and believe and be comforted. It is all so tremendously important, and in this case, somehow, more important than in any other. And now you see the *Geschlechtsleben* working yeastily and obscurely, and once again the quacking of the Norns is audible. By the way," said Miss Penny, changing her tone and leaning confidentially across the table, "I wish you'd tell me something. Tell me, do you really—honestly, I mean—do you seriously believe in literature?"

"Believe in literature?"

"I was thinking?" Miss Penny explained, "of Ironic Fate and the quacking of the Norns and all that."

"'M yes."

"And then there's this psychology and introspection business; and construction and good narrative and word pictures and *le mot juste* and verbal magic and striking metaphors."

I remembered that I had compared Miss Penny's tinkling ear-rings to skeletons hanging in chains.

"And then, finally, and to begin with—Alpha and Omega—there's ourselves, two professionals gloating, with an absolute lack of sympathy, over a seduced nun, and speculating on the best method of turning her misfortunes into cash. It's all very curious, isn't it?—when one begins to think about it dispassionately."

"Very curious," I agreed. "But, then, so is everything else if you look at it like that."

"No, no," said Miss Penny. "Nothing's so curious as our business. But I shall never get to the end of my story if I get started on first principles."

Miss Penny continued her narrative. I was still thinking of literature. Do you believe in it? Seriously? Ah! Luckily the question was quite meaningless. The story came to me rather vaguely, but it seemed that the young man was getting better; in a few more days, the doctor had said, he would be well—well enough to go back to jail. No, no. The question was meaningless. I would think about it no more. I concentrated my attention again.

"Sister Agatha," I heard Miss Penny saying, "prayed, exhorted, indoctrinated. Whenever she had half a minute to spare from her other duties she would come running into the young man's room. 'I wonder if you fully realise the importance of prayer?' she would ask, and, before he had time to answer, she would give him a breathless account of the uses and virtues of regular and patient supplication. Or else, it was: 'May I tell you about St. Theresa?' or 'St. Stephen, the first martyr—you know about him, don't you?' Kuno simply wouldn't listen at first. It seemed so fantastically irrelevant, such an absurd interruption to his thoughts, his serious, despairing thoughts about the future. Prison was real, imminent and this woman buzzed about him with her ridiculous fairy-tales. Then, suddenly, one day he began to listen, he showed signs of contrition and conversion. Sister Agatha announced her triumph to the other nuns, and there was rejoicing over the one lost sheep. Melpomene had never felt so happy in her life, and Kuno, looking at her radiant face, must have wondered how he could have been such a fool as not to see from the first what was now so obvious. The woman had lost her head about him. And he had only four days now—four days in which to tap the tumultuous love power, to canalise it, to set it working for his escape. Why hadn't he started a week ago? He could have made certain of it then. But now? There was no knowing. Four days was a horribly short time."

"How did he do it?" I asked, for Miss Penny had paused.

"That's for you to say," she replied, and shook her ear-rings at me. "I don't know. Nobody knows, I imagine, except the two parties concerned and perhaps Sister Agatha's confessor. But one can reconstruct the crime, as they say. How would you have done it? You're a man, you ought to be familiar with the processes of amorous engineering."

"You flatter me," I answered. "Do you seriously suppose—" I extended my arms. Miss Penny laughed like a horse. "No. But, seriously, it's a problem. The case is a very special one. The person, a nun, the place, a hospital, the opportunities, few. There could be no favourable circumstances—no moonlight, no distant music; and any form of direct attack would be sure to fail. That audacious confidence which is your amorist's best weapon would be useless here."

"Obviously," said Miss Penny. "But there are surely other methods. There is the approach through pity and the maternal instincts. And there's the approach through Higher Things, through the soul. Kuno must have worked on those lines, don't you think? One can imagine him letting himself be converted, praying with her, and at the same time appealing for her sympathy and even threatening—with a great air of seriousness—to kill himself rather than go back to jail. You can write that up easily and convincingly enough. But it's the sort of thing that bores me so frightfully to do. That's why I can never bring myself to write fiction. What is the point of it all? And the way you literary men think yourselves so important—particularly if you write tragedies. It's all very queer, very queer indeed."

I made no comment. Miss Penny changed her tone and went on with the narrative.

"Well," she said, "whatever the means employed, the engineering process was perfectly successful. Love was made to find out a way. On the afternoon before Kuno was to go back to prison, two Sisters of Charity walked out of the hospital gates, crossed the square in front of it, glided down the narrow streets towards the river, boarded a tram at the bridge, and did not descend till the car had reached its terminus in the farther suburbs. They began to walk briskly along the high road out into the country. 'Look!' said one of them, when they were clear of the houses; and with the gesture of a conjurer produced from nowhere a red leather purse. 'Where did it come from?' asked the other, opening her eyes. Memories of Elisha and the ravens, of the widow's cruse, of the loaves and fishes, must have floated through the radiant fog in poor Melpomene's mind. 'The old lady I was sitting next to in the tram left her bag open. Nothing could have been simpler.' 'Kuno! You don't mean to say you stole it?' Kuno swore horribly. He had opened the purse. 'Only sixty marks. Who'd have thought that an old camel, all dressed up in silk and furs, would only have sixty marks in her purse. And I must have a thousand at least to get away. It's easy to reconstruct the rest of the conversation down to the inevitable, 'For God's sake, shut up,' with which Kuno put an end to Melpomene's dismayed moralising. They trudge on in silence. Kuno thinks desperately. Only sixty marks; he can do nothing with that. If only he had something to sell, a piece of jewellery, some gold or silver anything, anything. He knows such a good place for selling things. Is he to be caught again for lack of a few marks? Melpomene is also thinking. Evil must often be done that good may follow. After all, had not she herself stolen Sister Mary of the Purification's clothes when she was asleep after night duty? Had not she run away from the convent, broken her vows? And yet how convinced she was that she was doing rightly! The mysterious Powers emphatically approved; she felt sure of it. And now there was the red purse. But what was a red purse in comparison with a saved soul—and, after all, what was she doing hut saving Kuno's soul?" Miss Penny, who had adapted the voice and gestures of a debater asking rhetorical questions, brought her hand with a slap on to the table. "Lord, what a bore this sort of stuff is!" she exclaimed. "Let's get to the end of this dingy anecdote as quickly as possible. By this time, you must imagine, the shades of night were falling fast—the chill November twilight, and so on; but I leave the natural descriptions to you. Kuno gets into the ditch at the roadside and takes off his robes. One imagines that he would feel himself safer in trousers, more capable of acting with decision in a crisis. They tramp on for miles. Late in the evening they leave the high road and strike up through the fields towards the forest. At the fringe of the wood they find one of those wheeled huts where the shepherds sleep in the lambing season.

"The real 'Maison du Berger.'"

"Precisely," said Miss Penny, and she began to recite:

"Si ton coeur gémissant du poids de notre vie
Se traine et se débat comme un aigle blessé....

"How does it go on? I used to adore it all so much when I was a girl.

"Le seuil est perfumé, l'alcôve est large et sombre,
Et là parmi les fleurs, nous trouverons dans l'ombre,
Pour nos cheveux unis un lit silencieux.

"I could go on like this indefinitely."

"Do," I said.

"No, no. No, no. I'm determined to finish this wretched story. Kuno broke the padlock of the door. They entered. What happened in that little hut?" Miss Penny leaned forward at me. Her large hare's eyes glittered, the long ear-rings swung and faintly tinkled. "Imagine the emotions of a virgin of thirty, and a nun at that, in the terrifying presence of desire. Imagine the easy, familiar brutalities of the young man. Oh, there's pages to be made out of this—the absolutely impenetrable darkness, the smell of straw, the voices, the strangled crying, the movements! And one likes to fancy that the emotions pulsing about in that confined space made palpable vibrations like a deep sound that shakes the air. Why, it's ready-made literature, this scene. In the morning," Miss Penny went on, after a pause, "two woodcutters on their way to work noticed that the door of the hut was ajar. They approached the hut cautiously, their axes raised and ready for a blow if there should be need of it. Peeping in, they saw a woman in a black dress lying face downward in the straw. Dead? No; she moved, she moaned. 'What's the matter?' A blubbered face, smeared with streaks of tear-clotted grey dust, is lifted towards them. 'What's the matter?'—'He's gone!' What a queer, indistinct utterance. The woodcutters regard one another. What does she say? She's a foreigner, perhaps. 'What's the matter?' they repeat once more. The woman bursts out violently crying. 'Gone, gone! He's gone,' she sobs out in her vague, inarticulate way. 'Oh, gone. That's what she says. Who's gone?'—'He's left me.'—'What?'—'Left me....'—'What the devil...? Speak a little more distinctly.'—'I can't,' she wails; 'he's taken my teeth.'—'Your what?—'My teeth!'—and the shrill voice breaks into a scream, and she falls back sobbing into the straw. The woodcutters look significantly at one another. They nod. One of them applies a thick yellow-nailed forefinger to his forehead."

Miss Penny looked at her watch. "Good heavens!" she said, "it's nearly half-past three. I must fly. Don't forget about the funeral service," she added, as she put on her coat. "The tapers, the black coffin, in the middle of the aisle, the nuns in their white-winged coifs, the gloomy chanting, and the poor cowering creature without any teeth, her face all caved in like an old woman's, wondering whether she wasn't really and in fact dead—wondering whether she wasn't already in hell. Good-bye."

The Poetical Works of Elizabeth Barrett Browning - Volume IV
Elizabeth Barrett Browning
Benediction Classics, 2011
212 pages
ISBN: 978-1-78139-027-6

Available from www.amazon.com, www.amazon.co.uk

Elizabeth Barrett Browning (6 March 1806 - 29 June 1861) was an English poet and one of the most prominent poets of her time. During her lifetime her poetry gained great applaud both in England and in the United States.. This Volume contains the following poems, including "How do I love thee? Let me count the ways": Poems A Child's Grave At Florence. Catarina To Camoens Life And Love. A Denial. Proof And Disproof. Question And Answer. Inclusions. Insufficiency. Sonnets From The Portuguese Casa Guidi Windows. Poems Before Congress Napoleon Iii. In Italy. The Dance. A Tale Of Villafranca. Told In Tuscany. A Court Lady. An August Voice. Christmas Gifts. Italy And The World. A Curse For A Nation. Prologue. The Curse. Last Poems Little Mattie. A False Step. Void In Law. Lord Walter's Wife. Bianca Among The Nightingales. My Kate. A Song For The Ragged School Of London. Written In Rome. May's Love. Amy's Cruelty. My Heart And I. The Best Thing In The World. Where's Agnes?

Paradise Lost, Paradise Regained, and other poems.
The Poetical Works Of John Milton
John Milton
Benediction Classics, 2012
576 pages
ISBN: 978-1-78139-173-0

Available from www.amazon.com, www.amazon.co.uk

This book contains John Milton's poetical works, with line numbers and footnotes. This includes Paradise lost, Paradise Regain'd and Sampson Agonistes as well as forty-nine other works.

The Divine Comedy / La Divina Commedia - Parallel Italian / English Translation
Dante Alighieri
Benediction Classics, 2012
488 pages
ISBN: 978-1-78139-319-2

Available from www.amazon.com, www.amazon.co.uk

This edition gives a side-by-side parallel translation of Dante's Divine Comedy using Longfellow's translation. The Divine Comedy is an epic poem written by Dante Alighieri between 1308 and his death in 1321. It is generally considered to be the preeminent work of Italian literature and one of the greatest works of world literature. The poem is written in the Tuscan dialect, and the poem helped establish this dialect as the standardized Italian language. The poem is divided into three parts: Inferno, Purgatorio, and Paradiso. At the superficial level, the poem describes Dante's travels through Hell, Purgatory, and Heaven; but at a deeper level, it is an allegory of the soul's journey towards God. In order to articulate this journey towards God, Dante uses on medieval Christian theology and philosophy, especially Thomistic philosophy and the Summa Theologica of Thomas Aquinas. Longfellow's translation is considered to be the best translation, overall. Longfellow, being a poet himself, was able to create a flowing translation that has not been surpassed.

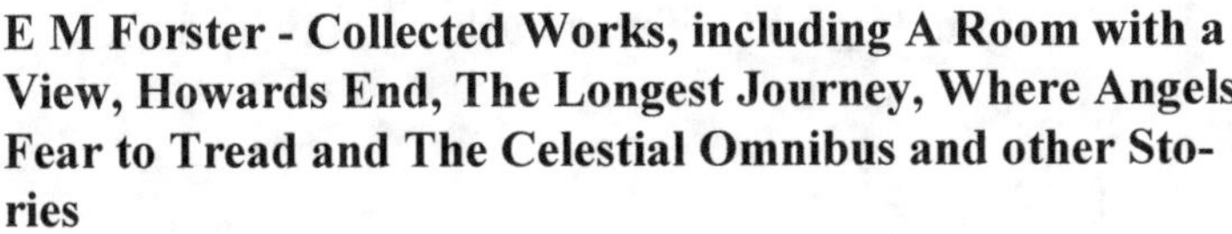
E M Forster - Collected Works, including A Room with a View, Howards End, The Longest Journey, Where Angels Fear to Tread and The Celestial Omnibus and other Stories
E M Forster
Oxford City Press, 2013
808 pages
ISBN: 978-1-78139-373-4

Available from www.amazon.com, www.amazon.co.uk

Edward Morgan Forster (1879 - 1970) is best known for his beautiful novels - ironic with delicious plots, highlighting the hypocrisy and discrimination in early 20th-century British society.

Also from Benediction Books ...

Wandering Between Two Worlds: Essays on Faith and Art
Anita Mathias
Benediction Books, 2007
152 pages
ISBN: 0955373700

Available from www.amazon.com, www.amazon.co.uk

In these wide-ranging lyrical essays, Anita Mathias writes, in lush, lovely prose, of her naughty Catholic childhood in Jamshedpur, India; her large, eccentric family in Mangalore, a sea-coast town converted by the Portuguese in the sixteenth century; her rebellion and atheism as a teenager in her Himalayan boarding school, run by German missionary nuns, St. Mary's Convent, Nainital; and her abrupt religious conversion after which she entered Mother Teresa's convent in Calcutta as a novice. Later rich, elegant essays explore the dualities of her life as a writer, mother, and Christian in the United States-- Domesticity and Art, Writing and Prayer, and the experience of being "an alien and stranger" as an immigrant in America, sensing the need for roots.

About the Author

Anita Mathias is the author of *Wandering Between Two Worlds: Essays on Faith and Art*. She has a B.A. and M.A. in English from Somerville College, Oxford University, and an M.A. in Creative Writing from the Ohio State University, USA. Anita won a National Endowment of the Arts fellowship in Creative Non-fiction in 1997. She lives in Oxford, England with her husband, Roy, and her daughters, Zoe and Irene.

Anita's website:
http://www.anitamathias.com, and
Anita's blog Dreaming Beneath the Spires:
http://dreamingbeneaththespires.blogspot.com

The Church That Had Too Much
Anita Mathias
Benediction Books, 2010
52 pages
ISBN: 9781849026567

Available from www.amazon.com, www.amazon.co.uk

The Church That Had Too Much was very well-intentioned. She wanted to love God, she wanted to love people, but she was both hampered by her muchness and the abundance of her possessions, and beset by ambition, power struggles and snobbery. Read about the surprising way The Church That Had Too Much began to resolve her problems in this deceptively simple and enchanting fable.

About the Author

Anita Mathias is the author of *Wandering Between Two Worlds: Essays on Faith and Art*. She has a B.A. and M.A. in English from Somerville College, Oxford University, and an M.A. in Creative Writing from the Ohio State University, USA. Anita won a National Endowment of the Arts fellowship in Creative Non-fiction in 1997. She lives in Oxford, England with her husband, Roy, and her daughters, Zoe and Irene.

Anita's website:
http://www.anitamathias.com, and
Anita's blog Dreaming Beneath the Spires:
http://dreamingbeneaththespires.blogspot.com

www.ingramcontent.com/pod-product-compliance
Lightning Source LLC
Chambersburg PA
CBHW081128300726
48982CB00005B/882

* 9 7 8 1 7 8 1 3 9 4 8 6 1 *